CRANE POND

Richard Francis

CRANE POND

A NOVEL OF SALEM

Europa
editions

Europa Editions
214 West 29th Street
New York, N.Y. 10001
www.europaeditions.com
info@europaeditions.com

Library of Congress Cataloging in Publication Data is available
ISBN 978-1-60945-351-0

Francis, Richard
Crane Pond. A Novel of Salem

Book design by Emanuele Ragnisco
www.mekkanografici.com

Prepress by Grafica Punto Print – Rome

Printed in the USA

For Jo

First, We have the Peoples *Enjoyment*, That was, An **Hedge**. The Hebrew word here notes, A *Wall*, made either of *Stone* or *Wood*. The Metaphor Signifies, The *Protection* of God, about our Comforts; with a *Defence* and *Shelter* from Innumerable Mischiefs . . .
Next, We have the Peoples *Misery*. That was, A **Gap**. The Hebrew word here notes, A *Breach*, at which Destroying *Enemies* may make their Entrance . . .
Lastly, We have the *Expectation* of our God concerning such a People. He says, *I Sought for a Man, that should make up the Hedge, and stand in the Gap*. . . .
So then, there is a most Solemn and Weighty CASE; indeed, the *more* Solemn and Weighty, because it is, OUR OWN, *Case*: where-with I am now to Entertain you.

—Cotton Mather, *Memorable Passages, relating to New-England* (Boston, 1694)

CONTENTS

CRANE POND

List of Principal Characters

Sewall Household:
Samuel Sewall, merchant and part-time judge; Hannah, his wife
Their children: Hannah Jr; Samuel Jr; Elizabeth (Betty); Joseph;
    Mary; Sarah
Their dead children: John; Hull; Stephen; Judith
Their servants: Sarah; Bastian; Susan

Pirates:
Thomas Hawkins, captain of a Salem fishing boat
Thomas Pound, pilot of HM *Rose*
Thomas Johnson, who glared at Sewall
Four common pirates

Stephen Sewall household:
Stephen Sewall, brother of Samuel; Margaret Sewall, his wife
Betty Parris, 9, daughter of Samuel Parris, the minister at Salem
    Village, temporarily fostered in this household

Samuel Sewall's fellow judges:
Jonathan Corwin, one of the justices involved in the prelimi-
    nary examinations
Thomas Danforth, who became a critic of the trials
John Hathorne, chief interrogator during the preliminary
    examinations
Nathaniel Saltonstall, who also became a critic of the trials
Wait Still Winthrop, advocate of the pirates' cause

William Stoughton, chief judge of the Court of Oyer and Terminer; also acting deputy governor, later acting governor, Massachusetts Bay

Ministers:
James Bayley, former minister at Salem Village
Cotton Mather, perhaps the most learned man in New England; his father Increase Mather, who negotiated the new Massachusetts Bay charter; both of the North Church, Boston
Nicholas Noyes, minister at Salem Town, hater of wigs and witchcraft
Samuel Parris, minister at Salem Village, in whose manse the witchcraft began
Samuel Willard, South Church, Boston, Samuel Sewall's minister

Those accused of witchcraft:
John Alden, friend of Samuel Sewall, sailor and Indian fighter
Bridget Bishop, first witch to be tried
George Burroughs, former minister at Salem Village
Martha Carrier, designated consort of George Burroughs in American Hell
Giles Corey, who refused to plead; Martha Corey, his wife
Sarah Good, a muttering woman
Tituba Indian, slave of Samuel Parris, also an accuser
George Jacobs, an old man on crutches; Margaret Jacobs, his granddaughter (briefly an accuser)
Susannah Martin, who was beaten by John Pressy in 1668
Rebecca Nurse, whose sisters Mary Easty and Sarah Cloyse were also accused
Sarah Osborne, who was visited by a *thing*
John Proctor, innkeeper, and his wife Elizabeth
John Willard, no relation of the minister Samuel Willard

Accusers:

George Barker, auditor of witches

Sarah Churchill, servant of George Jacobs

John Pressy, who described an encounter with Susannah Martin in 1668

Ann Putnam, aged 11, the most prolific accuser

Mary Warren, the serving girl in the Proctors' inn

Mary Walcott, aged 17

Abigail Williams, aged 11

Susan Wilson, who witnessed Mr. Burroughs' Satanic sacrament

Captain Wormwood, who accused George Burroughs of supernatural feats of strength

Other characters:

Anne, housekeeper to the Salem Town minister Nicholas Noyes

Jeremiah Belcher, Samuel Sewall's tenant on Hogg Island; Mrs. Belcher, his wife; the young Belcher

Simon Bradstreet, acting governor of Massachusetts Bay colony

Thomas Brattle, critic of the witchcraft trials

Mr. Checkley, general store owner, employer of Sam Sewall Jr

William and Abigail Dummer, kinfolk of Hannah Sewall, farmers

John Eliot, translator of the Bible into Algonquian

Thomas Fiske, greengrocer, foreman of the witchcraft jury

Samuel Gaskill, who fell into Boston harbour, friend of Sam Sewall Jr

Jacob Goodale, the victim of Giles Corey in 1675

Mr. Hobart, Sam Sewall Jr's tutor

John Hurd, tailor and neighbour of Samuel Sewall; Nurse Hurd, his wife

Jane, a slave, the sweetheart, then wife, of Bastian, the Sewall household servant

Jacob Melyen, a critic of the trials

Michael Perry, bookshop owner, employer of Sam Sewall Jr

Sir William Phips, governor of Massachusetts Bay

Thomas Putnam, father of Ann Putnam, accuser

Robert Walker, elderly member of South Church congregation, sufferer from sleeping sickness

Josiah Willard, son of the minister, friend of Sam Sewall Jr

Captain Wing, landlord of the Castle Tavern, maker of fine pies

Madam Winthrop, defender of the pirates; wife of Wait Still Winthrop, judge

PART 1
PIRATES

The **Unsettlements** that we have had since the *Revolution*, have they not rendred us like the *Sea,* which cannot rest, whose Waters cast up Mire and Mud?

—COTTON MATHER, *Memorable Passages, relating to New-England* (Boston, 1694)

CHAPTER 1

Here comes Samuel Sewall, making his way to break-fast on a cold January morning in 1690, the windows filled with snow-light.

'My dear,' wife Hannah says. 'You've brought the bed with you.'

He pats the coverlet that is spread over his ample nightshirt like a shawl and smiles. The fire is burning brightly in the grate but their hall is large, and Boston is cold in the winter. 'First prayer,' he says, 'then pie.'

'Pie?' Hannah asks.

'Ha, pie,' says young Sam.

'Pie!' Betty exclaims, as if it's a war cry.

Daughter Hannah gives her shy smile, not sure whether to be for pie or against.

Two-year-old Joseph, sitting on a heap of cushions to raise him up in his chair, waves his spoon.

Sewall's own smile has faded. 'The venison pie, from yesterday,' he explains.

'I know the pie,' Hannah tells him. 'I made the pie. Well, Sarah made it while I talked to her. But I just wondered if it elbowed out the prayer a little. You put the two so close together.'

'Father is full of pie-ety,' cries Sam suddenly.

Sam is eleven, unable to do the simplest sum. He'll bend over his book for hours, trying to figure out, if one apple costs such and such, then how much for seven? Or rather look out of the window or scribble drawings on the page while he should be doing the calculation. But then he will fire off some quip as if being young is itself a trigger of wit.

'It's Hannah's turn to read the lesson,' Sewall says, taking his chair at the head of the table. Hannah blushes and squirms. She's ten, but youth doesn't spark *her*. In fact her long and bony awkwardness already has a spinsterish quality to it. Her spectacles look anxiously across at him, two pale discs. Her mother looks anxiously across at him too, hand grasping young Hannah's forearm. Sewall, abashed, suddenly chilled, raises his arms to pull the coverlet tighter.

'Father,' Betty tells him, 'you look just like an angel flapping his wings.'

She is nine, but hardly needs her youth to generate wit, having plenty of that on her own account. Sewall knows too well how daughter Hannah will read the lesson, bumping into word after word like obstacles in a fog. 'Perhaps Betty needs to read the lesson instead, to stop her being so foolish,' he says.

'Oh yes, father,' whispers Hannah. She looks nervously at Betty to see her reaction but Betty is pleased. She loves to read.

Both his daughters are happy at this outcome. Is that a good thing? Perhaps it would be better for Hannah if she were forced. She might learn to improve. And perhaps Betty wants to read for the wrong reason or in the wrong way, to show off. Every action is weighed, each and every one, however small, and sometimes you can't tell which way the scales have moved.

'Pay attention to the meaning,' he tells Betty. She nods vigorously. 'You, too,' he tells Hannah, who also nods. Their mother, head bowed towards the table top, gives one nod, grown-up currency being more valuable. Her nod is one of agreement, of parental alliance, to encourage the children. He turns to Sam. 'We must all pay attention to the meaning.' Sam doesn't nod. He has put a horrible grimace on his face, picked up the knife from beside his plate, and is trying to see himself reflected in the blade. Sewall gives him a long look but Sam is impervious to looks.

The reading is Isaiah, Chapter 24, one of the most dismal passages in the whole Bible. Betty makes the most of its gloom, so much so that Sewall's uneasiness increases. It's one thing being expressive, quite another to sound like an actress. Play-acting is banned in New England for good reason, because it's a sort of lying.

'"Behold",' Betty says. She looks up from the Bible and screws up her eyes as if the breakfast table is a vast wilderness. '"The Lord maketh the earth empty, and turneth it upside down"'—her voice sinks to a whisper—'and scattereth abroad the inhabitants thereof."'

Suddenly she stops dead. For a moment Sewall thinks it's a pause for effect and this time he decides he must intervene. These are not her words, they belong to God. Then he looks up and sees her raspberry face, eyes brimming with tears. Before he can speak she has left the room.

Suddenly all is quiet. The three remaining children, Sam, Hannah, and little Joseph, stare at her empty chair as if in amazement that she has suddenly become invisible. Wife Hannah looks at the door through which Betty has passed. The unspoken words of today's text hang in the air. *God's people have broken the everlasting covenant.*

'I'll go to her,' wife Hannah says. As she leaves the room she almost collides with Sarah coming in with the remains of the pie on a large platter. Pieces of venison have tumbled out of the pastry following yesterday's dissection at dinnertime and the gravy has jellied a little so it gleams pleasantly. Sarah poises her body as one might hold a finger to the wind to gauge its direction. Then she puts the pie down on the table, gives everyone a long-suffering look as if whatever difficulty that has arisen has been aimed at her personally, and leaves without a word.

'Hannah,' Sewall tells his daughter, '*you* may serve the pie.'

Hannah gives a sigh of pleasure. This she can do. But his pie is compromised. He can't enjoy it with Betty so full of woe. He remembers, fourteen months before, standing on the deck of the ship *America* on his way to England and eating the pasty his wife had prepared—without assistance on that occasion from Sarah, talking to no one as she baked except (silently) to him, as if composing an intimate message out of pastry and mutton. Pie is meant to be a happy dish. He sighs.

Wife Hannah comes back in. 'She's in the cupboard again,' she tells Sewall. He nods, dabs his mouth, and rises to his feet. The cupboard is in fact a little cloakroom off the vestibule. Betty has turned it into an occasional chapel for her most despairing devotions. Sewall knocks on the door. 'Can I come in?' he asks, and is answered by a little snuffle. He enters anyway. He's still wearing his coverlet and is almost too wide for the doorway.

Betty is crouched in the corner, sobbing. Sewall closes the door on the two of them. 'Is it as before?' he whispers. The room is now completely dark. Perhaps Betty hopes God can't find her here. He gropes for her himself, locates her thin shoulder, lowers himself beside her. 'Dearest child,' he says, 'tell me.'

As she tries to speak, her sobs turn into hiccups like a baby's do. 'I'm so frightened—,' she says.

'What are you frightened of?'

'You know.'

'It's good to say it aloud.'

'That I am not saved,' Betty says.

'The passage concerned the people of God. It wasn't about you in particular.'

'But we *are* the people of God. Perhaps we have broken the cov—covenant.'

These words send a chill down Sewall's spine. Everywhere you look, in Boston, in Massachusetts Bay, you can find examples of backsliding, of loss of faith. Of course you can find examples of piety and virtue too, but who knows how good and evil balance out? And Indians allied with the French attack the settlements at regular intervals, as if they wish to reclaim the land for their pagan deities, turning the earth upside down and scattering the inhabitants thereof. 'What I mean is, we each have a separate soul,' Sewall says. 'You can only be responsible for your own.'

'But that's what frightens me, my own. I'm so afraid.' She hiccups again then suddenly she is crying loudly, and Sewall feels a sympathetic sob rise up in his own chest. 'I am afraid that you, and mother,' she finally manages to gasp out, 'and my brothers and sister will go to heaven, and I will go to hell all alone. I will never see any of you again, and the torments will torment so much I won't be able to bear them.'

'If that should happen, do you know what I would do? I would ask God if very kindly He would let me go to hell myself, so that I could be with you again.'

'That's silly, father.'

'In heaven you can have what you wish. And that would be what I would wish, so that you would never be alone. For all eternity.' His voice wobbles at the solemnity of the thought.

Her hand, like a small animal, seeks his out. 'Shall we pray together?' he asks. Her knees thud softly on to the planks as she kneels, and he manoeuvres himself into prayer beside her.

On go his breeches, his shirt, his waistcoat, his cravat. Then his coat and finally a special bonnet of his own design.

He's not yet forty but his hair is thinning (even though he frequently washes it with rum). He fears a cold in the head but abominates wigs, which nowadays are everywhere.

Sewall's bonnet is black, with flaps to go over his ears, and it fastens under his chin to prevent it from being blown off in a high wind. He cut out the cloth and stitched it himself, peering at the work by candlelight through a succession of winter evenings. Hannah asked him why he didn't commission their neighbour John Hurd, who is a tailor, to make him one and Sewall told her that the man's eyesight had deteriorated with age and his expertise could no longer be relied on, which was true enough but not the complete reason. He felt strangely obstinate about completing his own design but at the same time was nervous that a craftsman would laugh at it.

He first wore his home-made bonnet two weeks before to the meeting house. He was uneasy about his reception not simply because of possible imperfections but also because he was well-known amongst the congregation of the South Church for his stance on the topic of wigs. Perhaps the wig-wearers would have their revenge?

In fact no one said a word (though he did hear some muttering behind his back as he went to his pew). And the bonnet has been a boon in the severe cold of this winter. Sewall tried to write an aide-mémoire to himself in his bedchamber this morning but despite a good fire in the room the ink was frozen in his inkwell. It was because of this that he decided to wear his coverlet (on top of his nightshirt) to breakfast.

The note was to have been about this morning's proceedings at the Court of Assistants, the body charged with administering governance and justice to the colony of Massachusetts Bay. He is one of the Assistants and therefore, ex officio, a part-time judge.

Pirates.

His wife comes to the door with him to bid farewell.

'Betty is calmer now,' she tells him. She wants him not to worry.

'See if you can persuade her to eat something,' he suggests. 'She could have my pie. Or a portion of it.'

Hannah smiles up at him. He can read her smile. Or rather he knows that her smile means she can read *him*: he thinks (she thinks) that appetite is an index of spiritual recovery. Well, so it is, so he does. The body will be resurrected so it makes sense to build it up, like a squirrel preparing for winter. Also he thinks (she thinks) that though he wants Betty to be fed, he would nevertheless like some small piece of his pie, some insignificant morsel that would not deprive his daughter, to be reserved until he comes back. Well, so he does.

Hannah fastens his cloak for him then raises her hand and slides her finger and thumb under one of the flaps of his hat, clasps the lobe of his ear and gently tugs it, rather as you might tug the tongue of your shoe to straighten it. Since he started wearing his bonnet this has become a habit of hers. She smiles, then gives him a serious look. 'Be careful,' she tells him

'The pirates will be in shackles,' he points out. 'They are no threat now.'

She nods. 'Be careful anyhow,' she says.

CHAPTER 2

The court chamber is in the Town House, down near the harbour. Sewall plods along a cart track through the snow, one foot placed exactly in front of the other to keep within the groove. The sky is low and dirty and a cold wind blows; from time to time a snowflake stings his cheek, hard like grit.

A good fire has been lit in the chamber, and he warms his backside at it while waiting for his fellow judges (selected for their experience from the roster of Assistants) to assemble. Jackson, the serving man, brings him a tankard of ale which has had a red-hot poker applied. Finally, he is one of seven judges to take their places on the bench and to be faced by an equal number of pirates, who shuffle into the room with shackles on their arms and legs. The court clerk reads out the names.

Thomas Pound, a dark-haired fellow, small but with an air of authority even now, even here. He inspects the judges one by one, not with impertinence but as to the manner born, as if *he* is the judge.

Next, Thomas Hawkins, bigger, almost shambling, with long pale hair in a pigtail, nautical fashion. These two Thomases are the ringleaders. Then yet another Thomas, one Johnson, the only one of the pirates to look the part, with an expression both scowling and hangdog at once. The others are rank and file, ordinary seadogs who will follow a captain wherever he takes them, spitting their tobacco juice on the polished floor of the council chamber.

Thomas Pound is, or was, pilot of the frigate *Rose*, a vessel assigned to Massachusetts Bay three years previously. Since then, his ship has sailed upon strange and uncharted waters, as has the whole of Massachusetts Bay colony, ever since King James ll cancelled the charter which gave its laws and government their legitimacy. Samuel Pepys, his secretary to the navy, commissioned the *Rose* to patrol the Massachusetts coast after the king installed the roundly hated Governor Andros to take charge of the colony's affairs while the constitutional niceties were sorted out.

Sewall tried to play his part. Furnished with Hannah's pasty, a barrel of beer, and many other necessities, though none of them as necessary as that pasty, he took ship to England to assist in negotiating a solution, though was soon elbowed aside by Increase Mather, one of the leading ministers of Massachusetts Bay, who became the colony's official delegate and is in London still, negotiating the new charter. (Thwarted in his hopes of courtly intrigue, Sewall filled his year in England by attending to family affairs and seeing the sights.)

Then King James was ousted in the Glorious Revolution of William and Mary, great news for New England (at least as was at first supposed, since King William was committed to the Puritan cause). The people of Boston rose up and put Governor Andros into prison.

But it was the task of the ship *Rose*, pilot Mr. Pound, to uphold the king's authority. Since Andros was the appointed representative of that authority, the vessel duly entered Boston harbour bent on securing his release. The populace were perplexed as to what to do. It was the king's vessel and they didn't wish to be disloyal; only, of course, there was now a different king. A party from the harbour boarded the ship. Its captain suggested that to avoid the embarrassment (for both sides) of clear-cut capture, they should simply remove the sails.

Now, nine months later, it's clear that King William wishes

to exert a tighter control over his colony's affairs than even his predecessor did. Precisely because he is sympathetic to their Puritanism he wants to ensure they continue to toe the line.

In the interval Thomas Pound, his ship not pilotable for want of sails, joined forces with a friend by the name of Thomas Hawkins, who happened to own a fishing boat. The two decided to go off in search of French vessels and try their luck at a little privateering (King William had gone to war with the French, who were therefore fair game). But instead of the enemy they came across a ketch out of Salem, the *Mary*, and captured that.

Wait Still Winthrop, a fellow judge, leans over to speak into Sewall's ear. 'It could have been a simple mistake,' he suggests. 'And then they were in too deep. In such an eventuality you can hardly say sorry and go on your way.' Mr. Winthrop's breath is a little sour. Sewall recoils as far as he dares. Too deep, yes: that's the whole tendency of the sea.

The pirates, as they now were (having missed the profession of privateering altogether), captured more ships. Soon there was a hue and cry. A Captain Pease was commissioned to go after them. As it happened he set sail in that same ketch *Mary*, by now relinquished by the pirates who had taken over a bigger vessel. There was a desperate battle. Captain Pease was killed, as were many of his men, and many of the pirates too. But seven were captured, the seven here in court today.

'It's a muddle,' whispers Judge Winthrop.

Indeed it is. A king is deposed. His sailing ship becomes another king's sailing ship, and then is made into a sailing ship that doesn't sail. A naval officer and a fisherman are privateers, then pirates. The ship *Mary* is a commercial vessel, a pirate ship, an instrument of the law.

Sewall thinks about his own experience of the sea, just three months ago while returning from his mission to England. His ship the *America* had fallen behind its escort. Strange vessels were seen in the distance, flittering on the horizon. Perhaps French, possibly rogue—which would be even worse since they followed no rules of warfare except a cut throat to ensure tales were never told, that no hearings, like those taking place today in Boston's council chamber, would ever happen. In this emergency Sewall remembered that he had never made a will. At once he retired to his cabin and wrote it.

In the end there was no emergency. The ships proved to be Jerseymen, friendly enough. When he arrived home he showed his will to Hannah who said, But, husband, if the ship had sunk the will would have done too.

Sewall looked at her, amazed at his own stupidity.

Perhaps, suggested young Sam, a seagull could have fetched it in its beak and brought it home.

In the middle of the ocean there are no gulls, Sewall said.

Except you, my dear, Hannah told him.

He thought of that paper bobbing on the waves, slowly surrendering his intentions to the sea.

Anyhow, father, said daughter Hannah, you came home safely, and your will came too. She sighed with satisfaction at this outcome.

Now, in the Court of Assistants, Sewall thinks about the ocean's tendency to swallow up all order and legality, to wash the very words off the page.

The piracy is proved, the men are sentenced to hang. Only Wait Still Winthrop abstains. But in fact the court has no other sanction. Sewall looks at each condemned man in turn, just as Pound looked at the bench of judges at the beginning of the proceedings. Sewall does not believe in averting his gaze when sentence is passed.

Pound and Hawkins remain stoical. Thomas Johnson ignores the rest of the panel of judges to give Sewall a savage stare, as if the verdict is entirely his responsibility. One of the common sailors mutters something. The others follow their captains' example and show little emotion. Their shoulders sag a little in disappointment that their lives have come to this. One runs his finger round his collar as if he wants to do so while he still can, stretches his chin forward.

At supper Hannah passes Sewall his reserved piece of pie. The others are having Indian bread with cheese. Sewall inspects the helping. It looks as if Betty has taken none, or very little. He holds up the plate and offers it to her but she tells him, rather crossly, that she's content with what she has. They eat without conversation though Hannah keeps giving him significant looks. She wants to know about the outcome of the pirates' trial but won't discuss such events in front of the children.

Suddenly a cry, loud and sad as the hoot of an owl. It's Sam. For a moment Sewall thinks he's deliberately imitating the bird but then sees the boy's cheeks are streaming with tears. 'Whatever is the matter?' Hannah cries.

Young Sam is so despairing that for a moment he cannot speak, or perhaps his mouth is full of cheese. Then he manages to blurt out, 'I'm afraid I will die!'

'Do you feel ill?' Sewall asks him.

'No, no, father,' he replies impatiently. 'I'm afraid of *dying*!'

Perhaps he's caught the contagion from Betty, and being a less spiritual child thinks in terms of the physical event rather than of arrangements in the afterlife. If so, he has passed the infection onwards already. Joseph is crying heartily out of sympathy, while buds of tears form in the corners of daughter Hannah's eyes and Betty's lips quiver as she chews.

'Oh death,' Sewall sings, using the York tune (he acts as precentor in the South Meeting House), 'where is thy sting? Oh grave, where is thy victory?'

The words seem to calm Sam down. Hannah stares at her brother as if waiting to know whether she is allowed to feel better too, or whether they should both relapse. Joseph, bored with grief, has scrambled off his chair and is playing on the floor, his little gown tented over his knees.

'What was it, my boy?' Sewall asks.

'I was remembering when little Stephen died, father.'

Ah. Sewall remembers it too, so well. All the family now think of it. Wife Hannah was brought to bed of Stephen three years before. The baby died just after he had cut his first two teeth. Next day the family processed to the vaults for the placement of his little coffin, two by two. Sewall had the arm of his wife, little Sam (then only nine years old) escorted his sister Hannah, and Betty was led by her uncle Stephen, after whom the baby was named. There was no baby Joseph then. As the coffin was lowered into the vault, one of the bearers slipped and it was nearly dropped.

On the way home and after they arrived there for the funeral meats, the children wept bitterly, Sam most of all.

On the Sabbath the weather is too harsh for wife Hannah to go to church since she has a cold. The girls insist on staying behind to dose her with egg yolk and conserve of red roses. Sam goes with Sewall, however. After his outbreak of grief the other day he would benefit from the support of the minister, and Mr. Willard, with his deep measured tones, can be a comforting figure. Also Mr. Willard's son Josiah is Sam's best friend.

It's so cold in the South Meeting House that the communion bread makes a sad rattle when broken into the plates. Afterwards Sewall neighbours a little while Sam and Josiah play about (unfortunately they did the same inside, at least until the tithe-man gave them each a poke with the knob end of his staff). Mr. Usher tells Sewall that the weather is even colder in Muscovy, where your spittle freezes before it hits the ground. He goes on to say that last week he went to Thursday

Lecture at Braintree, where the sermon was on the danger of over-attachment to the things of this world. Afterwards, the minister discovered that while he was delivering it his house was being robbed and upwards of forty shillings stolen. Sewall and his friend exchange a look of enquiry, as if to ask whether it would be appropriate to laugh a little, or not. On the whole, the looks decide, perhaps not, particularly by the door of a meeting house.

When they arrive home Sewall finds Judge Winthrop waiting for him in his study. Sewall is chilled to the marrow and Mr. Winthrop, by contrast, seated by the fire as if it belongs to him, is done to a turn. Sewall is also hungry and Mr. Winthrop's presence is an obstacle to dinner.

They exchange greetings. Then Mr. Winthrop broaches what's on his mind: the pirates.

Sewall takes a deep breath. 'Mr. Winthrop,' he says. 'Today is the Sabbath. It's not a day to discuss these affairs.'

'I must disagree, Mr. Sewall. It is a very good day to talk about mercy. It is the best of days on which to discuss charity.'

'There's nothing to discuss,' Sewall tells him. 'The court considered the evidence. It found the men guilty of piracy. It sentenced them to be hanged. That's the way of it.'

'That is the mere skeleton of justice. I am talking about its flesh, its heart.'

'Justice—,' Sewall begins. He's not sure what he'll say next but has noticed that if you begin with a sufficiently resonant word others will bob along in its wake. But his resonant word sinks beneath the waves.

'The flesh I refer to is Madam Winthrop's,' Winthrop explains.

'I beg your pardon?'

'It is flesh of her flesh.'

Sewall looks at him in astonishment. An inappropriate *pinkness* flashes into his mind.

'My wife is kin to several of them,' Mr. Winthrop explains. 'Her brother is married to Hawkins's sister. Also one of the crew is a cousin of hers. She's from Salem, as you know. They are all seagoing folk over there.'

Indeed they mostly are. Sewall's beloved brother Stephen is one of the leading lights, town clerk, town this and that, not himself a sailor in point of fact but surrounded by those who are, just as the houses of the town are surrounded by the sea. It can be glimpsed down every alleyway, from every garden, between many of the buildings, a silver-tongued ocean bent on insinuating itself into the land. Its presence has made Salem a plump and prosperous place.

'All the more reason for them to need protection from pirates,' Sewall points out.

'Mr. Sewall, my wife is distraught. *I* am distraught.'

Sewall doesn't appreciate being *Mr. Sewalled* in that peremptory fashion. 'Mr. *Win*throp,' he replies, 'you know the expression well enough: Justice is blind. It is the same for an Indian, a negro, or a relation of Madam Winthrop.' He is aware this is not always exactly the case. 'Or should be,' he adds a little lamely.

'You insult my wife, comparing her to such people.'

'I don't mean to,' he says, blushing. 'My point was simply that one can't make exceptions for personal reasons.'

Mr. Winthrop obviously realises he too has been hasty, and adopts a more moderate tone. 'This is still a small colony, Mr. Sewall. We don't know everybody but we usually know *of* them, or we know somebody who does.' Sewall accepts the truth of this. More than that, he *loves* the truth of it, even though it has its darker side (he finds himself going to funerals of people he knows, or nearly knows, almost every week). 'It adds a certain flavour to all our affairs,' Mr. Winthrop continues.

The smell of roasting beef is wafting into the room. Sewall inhales it as discreetly as possible. 'A *sav*our,' he agrees.

'Exactly,' says Mr. Winthrop. 'A savour.' He gives Sewall a significant look, hoping he has driven his point home: justice subtly seasoned with personal knowledge and connections.

'Mr. Winthrop, may I ask you a question? Do you know why we use hanging as the chosen method of execution of felons rather than some other strategy, lopping off of the head, for example?'

Mr. Winthrop is clearly baffled by this turn in the discussion. 'Ah, no,' he replies.

'I think the reason is that hanging involves no direct action by an individual.' This is a matter Sewall has put some thought into. 'It's merely a conspiracy, so to speak, between the fixity of the rope and the weight of the body. In short, it emphasises that justice is impersonal after all. Perhaps we can continue this discussion at dinner, if you would like to stay and take it with us.'

Mr. Winthrop has the aghast look of a man facing the prospect of discussing hanging while eating roast beef, as Sewall expected (and rather hoped) he would. 'Thank you, no,' he replies. 'Madam Winthrop is expecting me. And this afternoon I plan to go and see Governor Bradstreet.'

Simon Bradstreet, very advanced in years, is acting governor pending the implementation of the new charter. He's one of the founding fathers of the colony, having come over on the ship *Arbella* in 1630. Because he recalls the time when the settlement was tiny, the governor may be sympathetic to Mr. Winthrop's 'personal' argument. Mr. Winthrop is making a threat.

'Give Mr. Bradstreet my best respects and duty,' Sewall says with as much aplomb as he can muster. 'And Madam Winthrop too, of course.'

Boston is quiet that night. The streets are muffled by a new fall of snow, and the drifts are too deep for the watchman to watch and the lamplighter to light. Once, around midnight, there's a forlorn moo from the Sewalls' cow, stabled in an outhouse at the back of their property.

Sewall wakes, he doesn't know why. Perhaps the cow has mooed again. She couldn't be blamed for complaining about the intense cold. Then he becomes aware of a form standing at the foot of the bed. His heart pounds so loudly he's afraid that it will wake Hannah. He doesn't want her awakened into the middle of his own fear—another person's terror is more terrifying than one's own. And, by reflex, he will experience Hannah's enhanced terror in turn. He has been on such a fear shuttle before.

As his eyes learn to make use of the dim coals of the fire, he realises that whoever it is is small. 'Betty?' he whispers.

'No, sir,' the small shape whispers back. 'Susan.' Susan is their youngest servant, just fourteen.

'Susan? Whatever is the matter?'

'Susan?' Hannah asks, surfacing. Then, in a different tone, 'Susan?'

'Yes, madam.'

'Is it one of the children?' They have had nine children from their marriage so far, four alive and five dead. It wouldn't be the first time a servant has brought them terrible news in the small hours of the night.

'No, madam.'

'Who then?' asks Sewall.

'Me, sir,' Susan replies.

'Are you ill?' asks Hannah.

'Afraid, madam.'

'Of what?'

'I'm afraid—' her voice cracks, a sob breaking through it like a weed in the pavement—'I'm going to die.' That contagion again!

'We must all die, Susan,' Sewall reminds her.

'Husband!' exclaims Hannah. 'That doesn't help in this case.'

Susan continues to sob. She does so timidly, awkward at being in her employers' chamber while they are sitting up in their bed, each with a starched white night cap.

'Well,' asks Sewall, discomfited, 'what must I do?'

'Stir up the fire, get the poor girl warm. I can hear her teeth chattering.' This is a pretence so Susan won't be embarrassed by her tears.

Sewall puts more logs on the fire. He sits Susan upon a stool right by the hearth to catch the warmth, and Hannah fetches a blanket from the chest and places it around her shoulders. Susan's eyes are fixed on the logs, watching fresh flames spring out from them. 'That is how the spirit is rekindled,' he tells her, 'under God's grace.'

She continues to stare at the fire greedily, and asks: 'Is God's grace like wood, then?'

He is taken aback by her literalness. Sometimes he believes he knows what grace is, when he feels elated or even just contented in his mind. Then wonders if those moods are nothing but elation and contentment after all, and he has fixed the word grace to them as you might hoist a flag up a ship's mast. His deepest fear is that he might never have experienced grace at all.

He took the covenant at the South Church just before his and Hannah's first child was born. He prepared for the moment for weeks. It was necessary to give his reasons for joining the church, and he wrote these out on a piece of paper, taking pride in the neat and comprehensive list. But he intended to supplement it by giving a full and public confession of all his sins, both the big ones and the little, so that he could be admitted to the congregation with a clear conscience, and experience grace with a spirit that was fully prepared for it. But when he had finished reading, his confession went clean out of his head.

It was the most important task he'd ever set himself, and he forgot it as casually as if it had been an errand to a shop. When he was back in his pew and it was too late, he tried to reassure himself that God could take the intent for the execution, that He would be able to hear the confession even though it had not been spoken. But the following week when he went to the meeting house, he encountered the aged Goodman Walker, who had known his family for ever, had been acquainted with his grandfather back in England, and Walker gave him no blessing, no greeting even, and failed to welcome him into the congregation.

This neglect filled him with terror. Perhaps he wasn't a member of the congregation after all, not a member of the congregation of the South Church, not a member of the congregation of the saints. He looked desperately round the meeting house hoping for a sight of Christ, who must after all be here. He would be overjoyed just to get a glimpse of Him going out through the door, but saw nothing. When he got home he told his woes to Hannah.

'Dear husband,' she said, in a calming, almost amused voice. She was only a girl of eighteen at that time but her big belly gave her a comforting authority. 'Goodman Walker is an old, old man. And all his life he has suffered from the sleeping sickness.' This was true. Walker would talk of a far-off, long ago Manchester, where lavender grew in the streets and folk danced around maypoles to the accompaniment of music, sinful practice though that was. Robert Walker had slept away so much of his life that those days existed fresh in his mind. He might have been surrendering to narcolepsy at the very moment Sewall encountered him, sleep sifting down into his eyes like sand in an hourglass.

Sewall took comfort from Hannah's words, but doubt niggled away. In true conversion there is a change of the person as a whole and he did not feel completely changed. To believe yourself saved when you were not, to imagine you were one of the elect when your forgetfulness suggested the opposite, would be as great a sin as could be imagined. It would be a kind of acting. And John, the baby Hannah was then expecting, developed convulsions a few months after he was born and died, as did so many of his siblings to come. The Lord could compose His frowning countenance from the deaths of babies.

'*We* are the logs, I think,' Sewall tells Susan. 'And grace is the tinder that sets us alight.'

Susan sighs, reassured. Sewall wonders if his apparent confidence has some hypocrisy in it. But surely God would want him to calm this child's doubts even if his own must remain?

Susan stares at the fire like a diminutive squaw by her wigwam's hearth. Sewall and Hannah try to stay awake so she will not feel alone in the room but he has the odd experience, lying there, of hearing himself snore, and when he opens his eyes she has gone and only the stool remains before the fire, the blanket neatly folded on top of it. He suddenly remembers that Goodman Walker, now long dead, used to take lavender drops in a vain attempt to combat his sleeping sickness. Perhaps his memories of Manchester lavender sprang from *them*?

CHAPTER 3

E arly in the morning of 27 January, the day arranged for
the pirates' executions, there's a knock on the door.
Sarah comes into the parlour while the family is still at
breakfast. 'Madam Winthrop sends her respects,' she says,
'and—'

'Madam Winthrop?' asks Hannah, amazed.

'That's who she *said* she was,' Sarah says darkly, as if
Madam Winthrop might be an imposter.

'I'll see her in my chamber,' Hannah tells Sewall. She has
a separate bedroom where she sleeps in the later stages of
pregnancy, and otherwise uses as a sort of study, for reading
and writing letters in, and sometimes entertaining women
friends.

Because she hasn't been spoken to directly, Sarah pretends
not to have heard. 'What shall I tell her, then?' she asks.

'Tell her to come to my chamber,' Hannah replies patiently.

'She'll be disappointed.'

'Why should she be?'

'She asked to see the master.'

Hannah rolls her eyes, partly in exasperation at Sarah's
deliberate obtuseness, partly (perhaps) to register surprise that
Sewall has dealings of his own with Madam Winthrop.

Sewall drains off his breakfast beer and rises to his feet. He
shakes his head, partly to show his own impatience at Sarah's
obstinacy, partly (perhaps) as a sort of reply to Hannah. 'Show
Madam Winthrop into my study.' Sarah sighs and leaves the

room. Sewall goes up to his study and gives the fire a quick poke.

'Madam Winthrop,' announces Sarah.

'Good day to you, madam.' He gives her a little bow, poker dangling from his hand. Madam Winthrop makes the merest nod of acknowledgement. 'You may go, Sarah,' Sewall tells his housekeeper, waving the poker with unintentional ferocity. Even so, she leaves reluctantly. 'Madam Sewall sends her regards,' he continues, putting the poker back on the hearth. Madam Winthrop nods again in response to Madam Sewall's regards. She is wearing a cloak and hood in Watchet blue (as an importer, Sewall is familiar with all the colours of cloth), with a fur tippet and a muff suspended by ribbons from her neck. To his amazement she raises her right leg and points it at him.

'Look at what I have waded through.' She waggles her foot to ensure she has snagged his attention. Her stockings and the hem of her gown are stained with water and mud splashes. She looks as if she is dancing in a particularly provocative fashion. Some words of Increase Mather (referring to the third chapter of Isaiah) come back into Sewall's head: *It is spoken of as the great sin of the Daughters of* Sion, *that they did walk with stretched-out necks, and with wanton eyes, walking and mincing as they go, and making a tinkling with their feet.* These are from a pamphlet entitled *An Arrow Against Sacred and Profane Dancing*, which arrow was to be imagined shooting through the air at the retreating back of a man who tried to set up dancing classes in Boston, announcing that they would take place on Thursdays, Lecture Day, when Boston's midweek sermon is given (thus implying that the citizens should abandon God and resort to dancing instead).

'I've walked here from my house,' Madam Winthrop explains, finally lowering her leg. The distance must be upwards of a mile. 'Now the snow is melting, the roads are miry beyond belief. They have spoiled and damnified my gown. I have come concerning the pirates.'

'Surely you could have sent a servant?'

'I wanted to speak to you in person. My husband is at Governor Bradstreet's again to plead for them. All the judges are to assemble there.'

'But they are to die this afternoon.' When Sewall woke this morning and remembered it was execution day he felt relief that matters were finally being resolved, that the tension created by Mr. Winthrop was coming to an end. Now here is Madam Winthrop stirring things up again. And the smaller the interval of time remaining, the denser and more turbulent the agitation within it might be.

'That's why I've been hurrying.'

'Madam,' he says as firmly as possible, 'this is a strictly judicial matter.'

'Some of these so-called pirates are Salem people,' she replies. 'You know Salem well yourself. You know it's a small community. Your brother is a prominent citizen after all. We take care of each other in Salem.' She has not lived in Salem since her marriage but still thinks of herself as a member of the community, which rather proves her point.

Sewall registers the reference to his brother Stephen. Perhaps she's making a subtle threat? She's a woman of influence, after all. 'I'll do what I can,' he says, then immediately wishes he hadn't. It sounds as if he's giving way. Sure enough her face lights up triumphantly. He tries to correct himself. 'I will do what I think is best.'

The other judges are already assembled at Governor Bradstreet's when Sewall arrives. The old man is sitting in a large wooden chair which emphasises how shrivelled and little he has become. It suddenly strikes Sewall that the New World is not so new after all. But he is alert still, and his years have given him a kind of sweetness, like a dried-up prune or raisin.

Mr. Winthrop is holding forth: the confusion of allegiances, the turbid politics of the time, the implicit muddle of the sea itself, the possibility of misunderstanding or mistake, the regard the men are held in in Salem. Everyone waits for the governor to comment. 'Perhaps this is not a matter for a blanket decision,' he says finally. 'Perhaps we need to consider each man separately.'

'But they were a *crew*,' Mr. Winthrop says.

'And a crew is composed of individuals, each with his own . . . ' The governor tails off. With age he's sometimes lost for words. He presses the tips of the fingers of his right hand together then opens them out again to indicate the particular quiddity each man possesses.

'In that case,' Sewall offers cautiously, 'perhaps we should begin with the ringleaders. Pound, I believe, is the senior man here—'

'I think,' says Major Saltonstall, 'we should start at the other end, with the common sailors.'

'Why so?' asks Mr. Winthrop.

'Because they have to obey orders.'

Nathaniel Saltonstall, known in some quarters as 'carrot head' on account of his red hair, knows about orders, being a military man as well as a justice. He is in Boston for the pirate trials but lives in the frontier town of Haverhill under continual threat from hostile Indians, and is responsible for the defence of his fellow townspeople. But he also knows how to *dis*obey orders. When Governor Andros was foisted on the colony by King James, Saltonstall refused to serve on the assembly as a matter of principle, and received a prison sentence for his pains.

They review the cases of Alexander Brown and James Tuthill first. Saltonstall makes the point that these men had no

executive powers but were just simple sailors. Sewall opposes
the suggestion on the grounds that whether you are small or
mighty you have the moral responsibility to do right and not
wrong. The pirates chose whether to put to sea or not. They
chose how to behave when they were bobbing on the ocean.
Captain Pease was murdered, as were many of his men. True,
it's impossible now to determine who killed whom. What happened was murder in a general sort of way, with all the men
participating. For that reason it's appropriate, in his opinion,
for the men to be considered *as* a crew.

He looks nervously at the governor as he makes this point,
but Bradstreet's countenance remains benevolent, absorbed in
the argument. Also, Sewall concludes, the plain fact is that the
men were given a fair trial and were found guilty. There is no
ground for appeal.

He makes no headway against the other judges. They all
shuffle into place behind Saltonstall. 'Well, Mr. Sewall,'
Governor Bradstreet says, 'you're in a minority of one. We
need to be unanimous to overturn the decision of the court.

All the judges look at Sewall, men of affairs, grave men.
What he's being asked to do is err on the side of mercy, if
indeed it be to err at all. He raises his head. 'I concede these
two cases,' he says, 'but I must stand firm on the rest.'

He has not been back at home for long, and is just preparing for his dinner, when there's a knock at the door. The judges
trail in, most of them looking both hostile and uneasy.
'Gentlemen,' says Sewall reproachfully, 'I was about to say my
prayers.'

'There's no time for that,' Winthrop replies, then realising
he's been brusque, even sacrilegious, adds, 'though we would
all, I'm sure, benefit from a prayer in a little while. At the end
of our business.'

Sewall devoutly wishes the pirates in hell, which is just the place the other judges wish to extricate them from, at least for the time being. He points out that Governor Bradstreet is not with them. They explain he has agreed his vote should be cast for him on the grounds that the infirmity of age makes travel difficult. Sewall realises this means he must have signed the relevant reprieve documents in case they were to be enacted. Once again Sewall is left all alone.

This time of course the other judges argue that the men should be considered as a crew after all. If two have been reprieved, why not three? Why not all of them?

Eventually Sewall concedes the argument in relation to two more—common sailors, though not as common as the ones already pardoned. He sticks firm with Thomas Johnson's conviction, however, remembering the man's stare. When their eyes locked, Sewall felt that he could see through Johnson's pair to a lurching deck awash with blood, and the havoc the man was wreaking there.

Winthrop's servant, waiting in the hall, is sent off with the reprieves for the two less common common sailors. At this very moment, the five condemned will be sitting at the back of the North Meeting House in shackles, listening to Cotton Mather, son of Increase and the most learned (and fervent) man in the colony, delivering them a final sermon.

Now Thomas Pound becomes the topic. Sewall has always thought him the ringleader of the whole malevolent enterprise. He was an officer in His Majesty's Navy and surely would therefore have authority over the captain of a tin-pot fishing vessel. Not so, according to Mr. Winthrop. Hawkins was the captain of his boat, and a captain is a captain, no matter what. In other words, the argument goes, Pound should be treated essentially as a common sailor too, albeit an even less common one than either of the last two.

Sewall feels bitter at the way things are turning out. He wanted to treat the pirates as a crew; the other judges, under the influence of the governor, decided to consider them singly. Then when it suited their cause, they decided the pirates *should* be considered as a crew after all. Meanwhile they have become a crew themselves, leaving Sewall to stand all alone.

He looks at the brave countenance of Nathaniel Saltonstall. An honest man, though perhaps inclined to drink too much (Sewall is very fond of a drink himself). He still has a kind smile on his face and shows none of the impatience of the others. 'I concede Pound,' Sewall says sharply.

Winthrop nods, careful to avoid any sign of triumph, and passes round the reprieve document for signature. Then he steps out of the room in search of his man, who should be back by now after delivering the reprieves for the last two. The sermon will be over, even allowing for the fact that Mr. Mather was delivering it. The two newly reprieved men will have been released from their shackles and will be discovering their liberty again, dazed with joy. Despite his doubts, Sewall feels a moment of happiness at their happiness.

The remaining three, Hawkins, Pound and Johnson, will be in the cart trundling along on their way to the place of execution. Mr. Winthrop's man, on horseback, should be able to intercept them before it arrives, and pass the order for the release of Pound.

Mr. Winthrop returns to the room. 'There is still Hawkins's case to be considered,' he announces. The other judges have been fastening their cloaks, pulling on their gloves, preparing to go. There's a collective sigh. For once Sewall feels part of this crew: he sighs too. 'If we have let the rest of the men off—,' Winthrop says.

'Except Johnson,' interjects Sewall.

'—Except Johnson, then we need to consider whether Hawkins merits the same treatment. He has always been a decent man, a God-fearing fisherman, married to my—'

'We have established that he is the captain,' Sewall points out, 'and therefore must take responsibility.'

'Let us say,' puts in Nathaniel Saltonstall, 'that Hawkins is, so to speak, the brain or head of this crew.'

'Exactly my point,' Sewall reminds him with returning confidence.

'Why then,' Saltonstall continues, 'the other men, that is to say, the crew, may be considered the body. If the body is guiltless in its acts—'

'Excepting Johnson,' says Sewall.

'Always excepting Johnson,' Saltonstall agrees, 'why then the brain, or head, which is responsible for the acts of the body, must be considered guiltless also.'

Suddenly Sewall feels overwhelmed. He has done all he can. He can feel his shoulders droop. Mr. Winthrop must observe this because he doesn't wait for Sewall to speak but simply says, 'It'll be touch and go whether we can get to him before it's too late.' While the paper is being passed round, he rushes out of the room, but immediately returns. 'My man is not yet back from the last errand,' he says.

The final insult: Sewall has to send his own man, Bastian, on horseback to the execution ground.

The judges file out, one by one. The prayer has been forgotten. Most contrive to avoid Sewall's gaze as they bid him farewell. Nathaniel Saltonstall, however, heartily shakes him by the hand. He still has the kindly smile. Strangely, even though he has conformed to Saltonstall's wish, Sewall feels shame-faced when looking at that open countenance, as if he has in some complex way let him down, so that Saltonstall's sympathy is an acknowledgement of his own weakness.

Boston's place of execution is by the shore south of the harbour, and almost a mile from the Sewalls' house. By some peculiarity of wind or water, the sound of the crowd usually carries over to them on execution days. Today, while they are eating their belated dinner, they hear a sudden distant groan of disappointment. Wife Hannah looks enquiringly at Sewall.

He guesses what it is. Hawkins has been reprieved while on the very ladder itself. There is nothing more dismaying to an eager crowd than the sight of a condemned person climbing back down to the world he has already left.

Only Thomas Johnson will hang today.

CHAPTER 4

It's an April day, with a blue sky and puffy white clouds, though there are still fingers of old snow here and there. Sewall is in his orchard, building a new henhouse with the aid of his black servant, Bastian. Or to be more accurate, Bastian is building a new henhouse with help from Sewall, who is holding the little roof in place and has a mouthful of nails, passing one to his servant when required.

The chickens stand around near their old tumbledown residence, watching all this activity with furrowed brows and grumbling gently. Even the family's little black cow is interested and pokes her head over the fence of her pasture. She was let out of her shed for the first time this morning when Bastian decided there were signs of growth in the grass, and Sewall enjoyed watching her frisk about in the winy air as she celebrated the outside world again. The Daughters of Sion had no business to stretch out their necks and tinkle their feet but the Bible does endorse dancing at the end of mourning—as in Jeremiah, for example, when Jacob is redeemed. *Then shall the virgin rejoice in the dance, both young men and old together: for I will turn their mourning into joy . . .* If the virgins and the young and old men can dance when released from grief, why not the little cow when escaping the long captivity of winter?

Young Joseph is crouched beside Sewall and Bastian, playing farms with wooden animals. These include toy cows and chickens, and looking down at his play is suddenly like viewing this Boston back garden from a great height, or more particularly looking at the fields round Sewall's childhood home of Newbury, Massachusetts, from the top of Old Town Hill, and seeing the tiny sheep and orchards and rows of Indian corn way below: perceiving the homely and diminutive world from the fastness of heaven.

Bastian asks for another nail and Sewall passes him one. But Bastian is supporting the henhouse with one hand so requires Sewall to hold the nail in place while he strikes it with his hammer. Sewall crouches down, grips the shaft of the nail and waits for the blow. At that very moment comes a call of 'Good day!'

Sewall twists his head upwards to see who it is but is stunned by a sudden cry of terror. He cries out himself in response, that fear shuttle again, and nails fly from his mouth. Joseph starts bawling too. Bastian grips Sewall's arm. 'Master, it's only Captain Wing,' he explains.

Sewall stumbles to his feet. Captain Wing is now laughing heartily. He is a big burly good-humoured man, a fellow congregant of the South Church, and runs the Castle Tavern on Marlborough Town just off Dock Square, where Sewall often dines. He used to have a mop of fair hair, though sadly that has now been buried in a wig. 'I'm sorry, Captain Wing,' Sewall says, 'you startled me. I think you startled young Joseph too.' He looks down at his son, who has stopped crying. 'It's only Captain Wing,' he tells him. Joseph glowers briefly at Captain Wing and resumes his play.

'It is my place to apologise,' Captain Wing says. 'When you turned your head towards me, I had the strangest impression. I thought you'd become some sort of monster with iron fangs.' Bastian, still squatting on his haunches, laughs gleefully at this.

'Ah,' says Sewall. 'No, my teeth are passably sound and I don't need false ones.' He wonders whether to lead on to a comment about the unnecessariness of false *hair* but decides against it. 'I was sad to hear of the misfortune that struck Moses Bradford,' he says instead.

A conduit in the tavern's courtyard brings water in for brewing and last week a small boy tumbled into it. Moses leapt in to rescue him. The boy was quickly fished out by other customers of the ordinary but Moses was too bulky and awkward (perhaps too full of beer) to be saved. Captain Wing's face falls. 'He was a brave man,' he says, then adds, 'and a good customer.' His expression becomes more regretful than ever.

'He died doing a good deed. He has gone straight to heaven.'

'Yes.' Captain Wing looks doubtful. Perhaps he's reflecting that not everything in Bradford's past life might have suggested that destination. Still, Sewall is confident that what you are at the moment of death is the key. Not that you can *earn* salvation at that (or any other) moment. But you can show that it is justified—that God elected you to be one of His saints before you were even born—by the manner of your passing. He senses that Captain Wing has come about some other matter, however. He raises an eyebrow inquiringly. He has a suspicion he knows the gist of it.

'Mr. Sewall,' Captain Wing says, 'I've come to ask your advice.'

'I see. Would this business have to do with chairs?'

'Chairs?'

'There was talk at the meeting house that you have a room fitted with seats.'

'You can't expect customers to eat and drink standing up.'

Bang, bang. Bastian has resumed work on the henhouse. He's being tactful, Sewall suspects. 'These are seats in rows, as I understand it, not seats around tables.'

'Ah,' says Captain Wing, looking a little sheepish. 'They are in the back room of the tavern. It's scarcely used. The truth of the matter is that an acquaintance of mine was looking for a room in which . . .' his voice tails off a little, necessitating a clearing of the throat, ' . . .to do magic tricks.'

Sewall saw magic tricks himself when he was in London,

performed in the street. He remembers one in particular, involving a dried pea and three walnut shells. The practitioner was clearly a rogue, with quick fingers and deft hands perfectly suited to picking pockets when they were not whizzing his shells about. To Sewall's astonishment, after his trick the sharper demanded the sum of five shillings, claiming that this was the amount he had wagered. Sewall had no recollection of wagering any amount at all, and it wasn't something he would do in any case, for the simple reason that gambling is a sin. But while he tried to explain that there was no *contractus ludi*, the pea-man's cronies began crowding around. They were a villainous crew, ragged and grimy, some bearing scars and others lacking limbs (one an eye), so Sewall handed over the extortionate amount they demanded to an accompaniment of jeering huzzas, and quickly fled while his own person remained intact. 'When miracles are not performed by God,' he says, 'they are a kind of persecution of the people.'

'I just wanted a little income from letting that room,' Wing replies. 'It's hardly used.'

'Since the man's practice is unlawful, involving deception, then giving him accommodation would be unlawful too.'

'I was just hoping to amuse my customers,' Wing explains, 'but as it is offensive I will remedy it.' He nods his acceptance, though his big honest face looks glum.

Bastian has stopped hammering. There's an awkward pause in the conversation. Sewall casts about in his mind for something to say that will make things easier again between himself and Captain Wing. Before he can come up with anything, little Joseph suddenly cries: 'News from heaven!'

Sewall looks down at him in astonishment. Joseph is absorbed in his farm toys as if he hasn't spoken at all. 'Joseph my love, what did you say?'

Still busy pushing a cow along on the grass, Joseph repeats, 'News from heaven.' Since only the back of his bowed head is visible, the voice seems to be coming from nowhere, from heaven itself.

'What news, Joseph?'

'The bad people are coming.'

Captain Wing and Sewall exchange glances. 'And where are these bad people coming from?' Sewall asks.

'Everywhere,' Joseph replies.

Captain Wing lays a hand on Sewall's arm. 'It's hardly surprising,' he says. 'People talk of nothing else but the French and the Indians, and attacks, and massacres.' That's true, of course. Only two weeks previously there was a horrible massacre at Salmon Falls in Maine, with almost a hundred murdered and even small children of Joseph's age tortured to death. But Sewall and wife Hannah shield the children from news of the war, Joseph most of all.

He asks Bastian if he has said anything to the child; Bastian shakes his head indignantly. Sewall sends him to fetch Hannah and the household servants. Nobody has put words into the infant's mouth or ideas into his head. Hannah picks Joseph up and hugs him, wanting to protect her child from that world of dark snowy forests, lonely settlements, French attacks and Indian savagery. She's pregnant again, and at such times always especially caring of her living children.

But Sewall is much affected too. He remembers how, in the winter, young Betty retired to her cupboard in despair at reading how the people of God had broken the covenant. Perhaps his children have the gift of prophecy and are foretelling the destruction of the colony. He lies awake for hours that night listening for noises of enemies invading his garden and breaking into his house.

A couple of weeks later Sewall accompanies the acting deputy governor, William Stoughton, on a mission to New York. They will attend a congress of the American colonies to coordinate a military response to the French and their Indian allies in the wake of the massacre at Salmon Falls.

Stoughton is a severe unflinching man with a pale face and black rings under his eyes. He doesn't wear a wig but grows his own grey hair long down each side of his head. He tends to hold his mouth a little open as if wishing to have it ready at a moment's notice to rebuke any foolishness you may utter. He's a bachelor of sixty in a fashion that suggests a wife and children would have been an unnecessary frivolity in a life devoted to duty.

They clop south in silence for a time, and then Stoughton says in his dry considering voice, 'A sad business about the pirates, Mr. Sewall.'

'The pirates?' Sewall asks, perplexed.

'I meant to discuss that fiasco with you before, but the opportunity hasn't arisen.'

'Ah, the pirates.' Sewall has buried that memory over the last few months.

'The life of justice was mocked on that occasion, with those helter-skelter reprieves.'

Sewall feels himself blushing. He's glad the two escorts are following at a discreet distance. 'Our governor signed some of those releases before we had even discussed them.'

'Governor Bradstreet is a good man, but that's neither here nor there. Justice isn't negotiable.'

These words give him a pang—they recall his own assertion to Mr. Winthrop that justice is blind. 'Maybe not,' he says, 'but people who knew them well spoke in their favour.'

'Mr. Winthrop, I take it,' says Stoughton grimly. 'And Madam, no doubt. Their arguments were telling, I imagine.'

Sewall tries to remember what their arguments actually were but can't. Something about the vicissitudes of the sea. 'They spoke to the character of some of the men, who are well-known in Salem.'

'Character isn't the point. It's *doings* that concern us as justices, not how a man might pass himself off in society, not a matter of who his friends and relations might be. As for Madam Winthrop, women have their affections, and often they pass them on to their menfolk. And to others.'

He talks, Sewall realises, as if affections mean the same thing as *in*fections. His detachment must be lonely but no doubt it gives his judgement an impartial accuracy more tangled-up mortals cannot achieve. Mr. Stoughton is looking across at him still. Their road is passing though small fields with the occasional patch of woodland, and sometimes a glimpse of the sea to the left. The sky has a muffled gleam like pewter. Stoughton's eyes are the same shade, and since he's silhouetted against the sky there's an odd sense of looking straight through his head, the perfect image of impartiality: suggesting no taint of the personal in judgements made therein.

That's what Sewall himself professed to believe in, in those arguments with his colleagues. He blushes with shame. He is pink and Stoughton is grey, which sums up the difference between them.

Ten days later Sewall arrives home. The congress has agreed to send a pan-colonial force to Albany. As he goes through his own gate a couple of chickens scuttle away from him and he stares at their retreating rear ends in surprise. When he set off on his journey they were ensconced in their new henhouse with a secure run of their own. Someone must have left the little door open.

Before he reaches the front door the family spot him and Betty runs out and into his arms. Next comes his wife, her pregnant stomach preceding her, with Joseph holding her hand and looking up at him shyly as if he has already forgotten who he might be. Then Sam, careful not to hurry in childish enthusiasm, but pleased nevertheless. Stupidly, at this moment when Sewall should feel happy, those renegade chickens are roosting inside his head. 'The hens have got free,' he complains.

Hannah laughs. 'They must have wanted to greet you.'

'The fox might greet *them*.'

'Not with all of us standing here.'

He becomes aware that something is not right. For a second he can't work out what it is. Then it dawns. 'Where's young Hannah?' An uncomfortable silence. His heart lurches. 'What's happened to her?'

Sarah, Susan and Bastian are standing a little behind the family group and with them is a neighbour, Nurse Hurd. Sewall has been assuming that she was making a social visit, but of course she is also regularly summoned to help with sickness in the house.

'Indoors,' Hannah says, looking guilty. 'She's a little droopy, that's all.'

Daughter Hannah is slumped in Sewall's own chair, her rear pushed up against its back so her feet don't reach the floor. She looks even younger than her years. Her head is flopped forward limply over her chest but she raises it when she hears him approach and smiles weakly.

'How are you, my love?' he asks. He knows the answer and hopes his fear doesn't show in his voice.

'I don't feel very well,' she replies, too young to dissemble.

'I think you must go to bed. Then you'll soon feel better.' He turns towards Nurse Hurd, who has followed him in. 'That's right, isn't it, Nurse?'

'Yes, Mr. Sewall, bed rest is the best cure. And I will give her powdered fox lungs, as much as will cover a threepenny bit.'

'All right, father. I'm so glad you are home.' She smiles again, though her smile manages to include a small grimace at the prospect of fox lungs. Something about her reaction upsets him, an acceptance of her fate, a kind of passivity. Here he is, a thirty-eight-year-old man in rude health, and here is his child, struggling and in danger. It seems unjust. Or rather it seems to reflect justice of a deep sort, divine justice. Her illness is the inevitable result of his weakness.

He takes a vow not to heed the opinion of others in the future. 'Save me from the fear of man, that brings a snare,' he prays under his breath. He will do what he thinks is right, or rather, what God wishes him to do. *In return let my daughter Hannah recover from the smallpox.* But there can be no 'return'. That was the merchant in him speaking. You do not make deals with God. You cannot earn a cure for yourself or for one you love, any more than you can earn salvation. All you can do is be the sort of good person whom evil cannot touch, as oil cannot mix with water.

Within days there are fifty or sixty pocks on Hannah's face, and many more on her arms. They sail over the surface of her body like reprieved pirates sailing over the surface of the ocean. But then they begin to fade. Within a couple of weeks Hannah is down from her bedchamber and with Sam and Betty and Joseph once more. She is only lightly marked. Sewall thanks God, and promises to be strong and vigilant from now on.

PART 2
WITCHCRAFT

If our *Walls* had not been broken down, had worse things than *Indians*, even **Devils**, broke in upon us, as they have sadly done, to Confound us with such *Praeternatural Operations as have been the just Astonishment of the World?*

—COTTON MATHER, *Memorable Passages, relating to New-England* (Boston, 1694)

CHAPTER 5

Sewall sits and watches at the window, his habit first thing on Christmas morning. It's snowing heavily as if to blot out the day. He fears it will keep everyone in their houses and prevent the shops from opening, as if Boston is celebrating Christmas papist-fashion even though it isn't. There's no such thing as a holiday, or Holy Day, because all days are holy. Religion is not intermittent.

A week ago, he went to visit young Sam at the home of Mr. Hobart, minister at Newton. Sam is helping with the chores in exchange for receiving tuition from Mr. Hobart, who is well-known as a teacher (Sam is thirteen now, time for him to get experience at living in another household). He asked if he could come home for Christmas and Sewall spoke to him sternly, telling him that Christmas was no different from any other day. Now he wishes he had taken another tack. God would understand the difference between Sam visiting home because it's Christmas and Sam visiting home because he needs to visit home. It's just that Sewall is frightened of confusing himself by making such fine discriminations. Perhaps he fears that Sam coming home would have *felt* like Christmas, whatever Christmas might feel like.

There's a sudden cry and Sewall starts, but it's just a passing carter rebuking his horse, which is finding the going difficult. And the cart is piled high with large sections of dead pig. In fact a head is staring back at him from the top of the mound, its mouth laughing through the jiggling flakes. Sewall rushes out of the house, hails the carter. 'Where are you off to?' he asks.

'None of your business.'

'Do you know what day it is?'

'It's any other day to me.'

'And to me.'

The man tugs his lead-rein. 'I have to go. I'm taking this to Goodhew, the butcher.'

'So Goodhew is open today?'

The carter turns back and gives him a sharp look. The last thing Sewall wants is to make him feel guilty because he's working today. A solution suddenly presents itself. 'Let me buy a piece of pork, my man.'

'These are for the shop.'

Sewall gets out his purse. 'I will save my piece a journey. I'll pay the shop price.'

'I don't know what the shop price is.'

'Well, a good price.' He takes out three shillings. 'This price.'

The carter's eyes brighten. 'It comes from Westfield, this pork does,' he explains, perhaps hoping by giving the pork a pedigree to justify the amount of money he intends to accept.

The pieces are very large, obviously intended to be subdivided in the shop. The tang of raw meat collides strangely with the iron of snowy air. The small eyes of the pig's head resting on top of the mound look down at Sewall while he chooses. A little drift of snow on its scalp gives the effect of a wig. He becomes aware of other heads grinning at him from different places in the heap. He picks out a leg which proves almost too heavy to carry and staggers up his path with it while the carthorse sets off again, its hooves oddly thudless on the snow.

His wife and Sarah are in the kitchen and look up in amazement as he enters bearing meat. 'Husband, what have you done?' asks Hannah.

He looks down at the meat he is carrying like a mighty club.

'I bought it from a passing cart,' he explains. He gives the leg a swing and hoists it with a thump on to the table.

'I was going to boil some eels and serve them on sippets,' grumbles Sarah. 'I had some off an Indian yesterday, for sixpence.' She glares at the meat which is now lying on the table top like a whale washed up by the sea. 'That leg of pork is enough to feed an army.'

'We can have a feast,' he says. Hannah gives him a sudden hopeful glance.

He realises she thinks he must have relented. 'To mark the *absence* of Christmas.'

Hannah and Sarah decide to spit-roast the pork on the big fire in the main room. While this is being done, Sewall retires to his study to pray. He prays for Sam, over in Newton, that he may not feel too lonely or tired. He prays for his timid daughter Hannah, that she might blossom. He prays for his spirited daughter Betty, that she might be free of fear of hell. Or rather, since we must all fear hell, that being the whole purpose of hell's existence, that she won't be overwhelmed by fear of hell. That hell, in short, will simply be useful to her. Then for little Joseph, that he might fulfil his prophetic promise and become a man of God. And for baby Mary, that she might continue to thrive.

He prays for his dead children too, for John, the firstborn, whose death followed Sewall's failure to confess his sins when he was admitted into the South Church, for little Hull, who suffered from fits but lived long enough to say the word *apple*, for Henry, who snored gently until he died on a bleak December morning, for Stephen, whose entombment made the family weep so inconsolably, especially young Sam, and for Judith, his only lost daughter (so far).

When they'd come away from the graveyard after consigning Judith's coffin (bearing the year 1690 made with little nails) into the tomb, a man called out at them: 'Pitiful dogs!'

Sewall recoiled as if shot by an arrow, his hand over his heart. Tears sprang into his eyes. The abusive man looked embarrassed at his bull's-eye and sneaked away. 'Husband,' Hannah said, squeezing Sewall's arm, 'take no notice. He's addled in his wits.'

Obviously that was true, but Sewall took no comfort in it at first. A man with no brains in his head might be the perfect vehicle to articulate God's judgement. It was as if the lunatic had been licensed to tell him that Judith's death was caused by his laxity in the matter of the pirates.

When he'd returned from the trip to New York and discovered Hannah with the smallpox he had vowed to do what was right in future without taking notice of any man's—or woman's—objections. The smallpox had duly abated, but since then Sewall still found himself caring about what the world thought of him and fearing the disapproval of his peers. He wished to rise to a position of importance and influence in the community, and strangely you can only achieve that by allowing yourself to *be* influenced by others, as if influence is a sort of currency, to be given and returned.

'He said *dogs*,' Sewall had told Hannah.

'I know he did, my dear,' she said consolingly. His heart warmed at the thought that she could still wish to cheer him while she was trembling with grief herself.

'I mean, he didn't say *dog*, in the singular. Perhaps it wasn't a remark directed at me.'

'I think it was a remark directed at the world in general.'

'Certainly *you* aren't a pitiful dog, my love,' he assured her. 'Not even a lunatic could think that.'

'I must admit to feeling a little pitiful, just at present,' she'd told him.

But whether the man's barb was directed at him or not, Sewall is the pitiful one after all. Even after making that undertaking on his arrival from New York, he was perfectly aware, day in day out, that he was guilty of a myriad of tiny cowardices, of retreats from decisiveness, of allowing issues to be obfuscated by sensitivity to the opinions of others. God reprieved daughter Hannah in order to give him another chance, and when he failed to take it, confiscated baby Judith instead. Sewall's lack of firmness created a kind of aperture in the tissue of things, through which his poor defenceless baby fell.

Fourteen months after Judith's death, Mary was born. Already she has survived for two months, and still shows no signs of illness or pining away. Sewall named her for Jesus's mother in the hope that by invoking that imperishable womb he can ensure that his daughter has come out of Hannah's without carrying within her some secret malady, and that her own tiny womb will grow to adulthood and nurture babies in its turn.

Now, on Christmas Day 1691, Samuel Sewall kneels on his study floor while snowflakes fall past the window and around his house a pale and silent Boston goes about its daily business, and he prays that God will send him a sign that he has been forgiven for his weaknesses.

Suddenly there's a hubbub downstairs and then the door bursts open. He looks up startled from his devotions. Betty is there, panting and wide-eyed. She gulps with excitement before she manages to speak. 'Father,' she announces, 'the house is on fire!'

Sewall struggles to his feet, conscious of his awkward bulk, while his little girl, neat as a fish, spins round and runs back down the stairs again. He cries out after her, terrified that she might be heading back into an inferno, 'Elizabeth, Elizabeth!' (using her full name in this extremity, since God must be listening) while he descends into the smoke. His whole household seems to be in the main room, crisscrossing like ships in a fog. He blunders through them.

'It's just the chimney on fire,' says his wife's voice. 'Calm yourself, my dear.'

'I thought—,' he says wildly, '—are the children—?'

'Everyone is fine. Baby is with her nurse. I expect she's still sleeping.'

His voice chokes up. He had thought Betty was about to be taken from him, for his continued sins. He had thought that was the sign. But here she is, admiring the blazing hearth. He pretends he has a cough, caused by the smoke.

'Father, must we run outside?' Betty asks him joyously. Hearing her question Joseph lets out a kind of Indian war whoop.

'Will the house burn down?' young Hannah asks. Unlike her brother and sister she is frightened.

The hearth is a sheet of flame, and smoke is curling down from the chimney, but just at this moment along comes Bastian with a pan of water drawn from the hogshead that stands by the kitchen door (as per order of the Court of Assistants) in case of just this sort of emergency. 'No,' Sewall tells her, 'Bastian will save the day.'

'Your pork is the culprit,' his wife points out. 'It dripped fat into the flames.'

Suddenly he feels in control. 'Children,' he announces magisterially, 'when you remove the cause, you eradicate the effect.' He wraps a handkerchief around his hand and lifts the spit from its rest, holding it aloft like a spear. The leg of pork, still skewered, is blackened and now looks as if it came from a smaller pig altogether. As soon as he has accomplished this, Bastian flings his pan of water.

Sewall heads towards the kitchen like a standard-bearer, his family following him, clouds of steam from the hissing hearth following them. He puts the spit down on the table top and uses a poker to push the pork from it. Then he takes a knife and cuts a slice off the end. Within a black circle the meat looks well-cooked but eatable. 'We shall make a good dinner of this after all,' he announces.

They have their feast to celebrate not celebrating Christmas in the kitchen since the hall is so smoky. While he eats Sewall reflects on the sign that has been sent him. The fire was like a picture of hell, though small while hell is limitless, and extinguishable while hell is eternal. Perhaps God is telling him that his sin in reprieving those pirates is not as great as he imagines.

'I bought the pork this morning,' he tells the children, wanting to remind them that purchases can be made on Christmas Day. 'It's from Westfield.'

'Is that a good place for it to be from, father?' young Hannah asks.

'The very best place,' Sewall assures her. He has no idea whether Westfield is indeed known for its pork, though the carter seemed to think so. 'Let's hope that our dear Sam is eating so well, over in Newton.'

Yes, yes, agree the children, let us hope.

'It's excellent pork,' says wife Hannah, 'though it tastes a little of chimneys.'

'Our little black cow is dead,' says Bastian.

'What?' Sewall exclaims. It seems he has only to blink and someone or something dies: a child or an animal, or one of his white-oak trees on Hogg Island, the property he and Hannah own in the middle of Boston harbour. Last night he slept a restless sleep and at one point dreamed of moans and howlings that he thought (in his dream) must be coming from the damned in hell.

He follows Bastian out of the back door and through thick snow to the cow's stable. It's late January and has been snowing since Christmas. In fact he had worried whether the cow was warm enough at night, though as she still produced their milk every morning he'd convinced himself she wasn't coming to harm. That assumption must have been his blink.

But the cow hasn't died of cold. She is lying on her side with her throat torn. Her teeth are bared and the mirthless smile coupled with the smell of blood reminds Sewall of the grinning head on top of that cartload of pork on Christmas Day. 'I had to hit her on the head with my big hammer,' Bastian says. 'She was in such distress.'

'Who did this to her?' Sewall imagines Indians creeping round the house, as he had that time when little Joseph made his prophecy. Only yesterday came news of an attack on York, a few miles north of Sewall's home town of Newbury. The minister there was shot from his horse and killed along with fifty or so others, and about ninety people were captured, often a worse fate than dying outright.

'A dog.'

'A dog?'

'A big dog. Its tracks are still in the snow.'

Those moans and howls of his dream had been despairing moos and the triumphant baying of a hound!

'I seen a big black dog around the place these last few days.'

'It was black? Are you sure?'

Bastian laughed. 'Black as me, Mr. Sewall.'

Many dogs are black; nothing extraordinary in that. But Sewall shivers.

At breakfast, everyone is subdued—indeed tears roll down young Hannah's cheeks, since she is the most softhearted of them all. Wife Hannah gives Sewall a meaningful glance. 'I think, husband, that we need to draw a lesson from this sad event.' For a moment Sewall's heart pounds. Has she guessed his weakness? Perhaps he should confess it here and now, in front of his children, so that they know their father is a compromiser who sent pirates back to plague the seas. He looks at them in turn (though baby Mary is upstairs in her cradle, and Sam is oblivious over in Newton). Joseph would not understand. Betty is pale and tense already, no doubt worrying whether cows go to heaven or hell and which one she will find *her*self in in due course. Hannah clumsily wipes her eyes with the back of her hand—she would be frightened at the thought of bloodthirsty pirates on the loose.

Confession will simply give the children an anxiety which by rights belongs to him. So instead he makes his prayer a general one, but concludes with an image appropriate to the fate of a dairy animal: 'And may we trust in God, who will nourish our spirit and provide the breast of our supplies.'

Hannah raises an eyebrow at the incongruity of God offering us His breast, but of course the deity is beyond, or rather inclusive of, gender difference. That must be so since men and women are both made in His image. This was explained to Sewall once by Cotton Mather, with much clearing of the throat and rolling of the eyes. He is interested in matters scientific as well as theological and is particularly happy when those two spheres come together. The vagina (Mr. Mather muttered) is a kind of penis in reverse; the ovaries are inward testicles. He was less certain about the womb, but there is a gland in the man's body where the fertilising element is stored, perhaps that is a kind of womb. And of course both sexes have breasts, though the male kind is not made use of (but Thomas Bartolinus, in his *Historiarum Anatomicarum Rariorum*, writes of a Danish man whose breasts did contain milk).

Because of this spiritual unity of the sexes Sewall can express the hope of one day being married to Jesus, though he often feels sad at the thought that in heaven he will no longer be married to Hannah, death being a kind of divorce.

A few days later Mr. Cotton Mather comes to call.

He is wearing a large black cloak, the shoulders besprinkled with snowflakes, and big boots. Also a wig but a small one, perhaps as a concession to Sewall's feelings, with a little bow at the back. In fact diminutive wigs annoy Sewall even more than voluminous ones since they mimic more closely the hair the wearer would actually have possessed if he hadn't cut it off to make the wig fit snugly. 'Mr. Sewall, how are you?' he asks.

'Well enough, Mr. Mather. And you, I hope.'

'I am very well indeed, thank you.' He gives a little bow of acknowledgement. Then springs it on Sewall. 'Strange news from Salem.'

Sewall can't stop himself giving out a little groan. 'Not those pirates?'

Mr. Mather is taken aback in turn. 'Which pirates?'

'Those reprieved pirates. Hawkins and the others.'

'No, no, not those—oh, but here's another strange thing. Indeed I have it with me, I think.' He digs into the pockets of his coat. 'Yes, here it is, sent to me from England by my father.' He takes out a sheet of paper and passes it to Sewall. 'Take a look at that.'

Sewall inspects it. 'It's a printed map of Boston harbour,' he says.

'Yes, yes, of course. But look at the bottom to see who *fecit*.'

Sewall screws up his eyes to read the small print at the bottom. 'It was made by Pound,' he says, 'Thomas Pound.' Then, in a whisper: 'Thomas Pound.'

'The very one. He has been made a captain in the Royal Navy. And has drawn this very accurate map of Boston harbour. I had forgotten that you were concerned in that business of the reprieves.'

Sewall looks at the paper again, hoping that Cotton Mather won't notice his hand shaking. Certainly it's a meticulous map of the harbour. His own property, Hogg Island, is shown in exquisite detail, with the bulk of Noddle's Island just below it like a bat that is batting a little ball into the air. The hand that drew this would have been in the grave if Sewall had had his way. And now Pound has been promoted to a captaincy in the Royal Navy. Does that mean that the reprieves were the right decision after all? Or has he, Sewall, helped to turn the world upside down, so that pirates are now naval officers, and mis-rule is gathering momentum?

'But what I meant,' Mather says, 'was the other one.'

'You mean Hawkins?' Sewall asks. Perhaps *he* is a captain in the Royal Navy too. Perhaps Thomas Johnson, if he hadn't been the sole pirate to go to the gallows, would have been an admiral by now.

'No, no, the other *Salem*. Not Salem Town, but Salem Village.'

Salem Village is a tatty little rural community three or four miles inland from its prosperous namesake. Not a place for pirates, or seafarers of any sort. Sewall has passed through it from time to time when going overland to visit his brother Stephen (in good weather it's usually quicker to go by ferry). There are no shops, just a nearby inn and a meeting house that hasn't been up many years but is already the worse for wear. Sewall is acquainted with two of its former ministers, his friend James Bayley, an old man now, and in poor health, and a Harvard classmate, George Burroughs. Neither stayed long because the stipend was paltry. And it was only a year or two ago that the church there was grudgingly given permission to admit its congregation to the full covenant and administer communion.

'What has happened there?' Sewall asks. His head is still awash with the pirates. And Salem Village is exactly the sort of place where nothing *can* ever happen. There are many town-ships and villages and hamlets like it in the remoter corners of New England, little communities that were set up by the early settlers in expectation that they would thrive but which have been passed by as the country has developed, places where America never quite arrived.

'What has happened there,' says Cotton Mather, his voice rising to that sermonical piping note that underpins all his emphases, 'what has happened there, Mr. Sewall, is witchcraft.'

It concerns two children. The whole matter is delicate because it happened in the Salem Village parsonage. In fact one of the girls involved, Betty Parris, is the nine-year-old daughter of the current minister, Samuel Parris, the other being her cousin, Abigail Williams, herself just eleven. They had been using a Venus glass, and then been overtaken by strange fits, paroxysms of the limbs, foaming at the mouth.

'What's a Venus glass?' Sewall asks.

'A piece of paganism, as the name implies,' Mather tells him, his neck reddening with indignation like a cockerel. Then, as the technicalities of the matter take over his attention, his voice becomes enthusiastic, expository. 'You take a tumbler or a wine goblet, and pour in the white of an egg. Then you raise the glass to your eye, peer in, and try to discern in that foggy liquid the features of your future husband. Or wife, should the fortune-teller be male. In this case, husband. Indeed, husbands.'

'And the shock of doing this was enough to prostrate the girls? Perhaps they turned out to be very ugly husbands.'

'I'm sure they used other detestable conjurings,' says Mr. Mather, glaring at his levity. 'I have experience of these matters. They may have performed tricks with nails, and horse-shoes, and peas—'

'I myself once saw a trick performed with a pea.'

Mr. Mather gives him another withering look. 'And sieves and keys, there's no end of household implements that can be used.'

'But these are only children's games. Little Joseph plays with his farm toys for hours at a time. For him they are real. But no one else takes them seriously.'

'To play at farms is to be a farmer in miniature. The order of things is left intact. *These* children were trying to subvert that order.'

'But only in a childish way.'

'The Devil is always waiting to come into our world. And what he wishes for most is a soft entrance.'

That word, Devil, gives Sewall a twinge of fear. He thinks of his own Betty. She too becomes prostrate when her imagination is fevered. She whispers in her dark cupboard of hell and damnation. She cries and rails and sobs. How readily could some outsider add up those clues and decide she is possessed? How terrible, to think of his little girl's soul as the Devil's soft entrance! 'I find it hard to believe that the Devil can possess the soul of a child,' he says.

Just at this moment little Joseph enters the room, carrying his handbook.

'Father—'

'Joseph, you know you should knock before entering my study.' The boy ponders this for a moment then meekly trots back to the open door and knocks on its far side. 'Come in, Joseph.'

He trots back. 'Father—'

'Joseph, I have a visitor, as you can see. Say good morning to Mr. Mather.'

'Good morning, Mr. Mather.'

Mr. Mather, hands clasped behind his back, gravely inclines both head and wig.

'Father,' says Joseph once more, with an infant's patience (and persistence). He holds his little book up towards Sewall, who takes it.

'What is it you want me to see?'

'I've written my name.'

Sewall bought the boy this primer from Michael Perry's bookshop, near the Town House. Just last week he started attending dame school. It gave Sewall and Hannah a pang to see their little fellow, not yet four years old, with his hair brushed, his little frock crisp and clean, clutching his hornbook in one hand and his older sister Hannah's hand with the other as she took him off for his first morning at Mrs. Townsend's house. Both children exhibited a sort of diminutive self-importance, Joseph because of his first foray into the outside world, Hannah because of the responsibility of escorting her little brother.

On the flyleaf Mrs. Townsend has printed out JOSEPH, HIS BOOK, and underneath the child has attempted to copy what she has written. He has only managed two letters, as a matter of fact. The first is J, which is leaning strangely, like a tipsy reveller resting against a wall (Sewall saw enough of these during the time he acted as a constable), and the other is a snakelike S. In fact the letter S is pictured as a snake in the hornbook's alphabet, which suggests Joseph has conned his lesson.

'That is fine work, Joseph. See, Mr. Mather, the excellent J and S.'

'Very good indeed,' says Mr. Mather, passing the book back to Joseph. 'You are a forward towardly scholar and I hope, young man, that this is the first small vanguard of a host and multitude of letters that will sweep down from the high places—' he raises an arm as if to point to a force of alphabetic Canaanites (or possibly Indians) gathered on the slopes, then lowers it in a grand sweeping motion— 'and crowd your page.' Joseph has looked up in bafflement, then down at his book as if hoping to spot a host and multitude already in occupation. Meanwhile Mr. Mather takes a penny from his pocket and gives it to him.

'Thank you, Mr. Mather,' prompts Sewall.

'Thank you, Mr. Mather,' chants Joseph, and scurries away.

Cotton Mather has had time to collect his thoughts. 'Some children have soft and tender souls,' he explains, 'others vigorous and resistant ones. Some can be overcome by the blandishments of Satan, others not, just like the rest of us. But of course, being children, there is more chance their innocence and naivety will succumb to evil wiles and wheedling and empty promises than if they had some knowledge of the ways of the world and the mysteries of the spirit.'

Suddenly there's a scream and a commotion. It sounds as if it's coming from one of the bedrooms. Betty's voice—perhaps she's in despair again. Given their conversation, the very last thing Sewall wants is for Mr. Mather to conclude she is possessed, or even *resisting* possession

But Mr. Mather is pulling on his gloves. He seems not to have noticed the scream. Or perhaps he is pretending not to. 'I must be going,' he says. 'I must be back in my study at two o'clock prompt.' He has a sign on the outside of his study door, *Be Short*. There is always another book to be written.

The two men go down the stairs together as if the sounds of wailing now filling the house are no more significant than dogs barking or birds singing. As soon as he has gone, Sewall turns and races back up to find out what on earth is going on. The bedroom shared by Betty and Hannah seems to be heaving with people. Betty is sitting on the bed weeping, her face in her hands, being tended to by her mother. Joseph is cowering behind a dresser, being harangued by Sarah. Young Hannah is standing lost and wet-eyed in the middle of the room, biting her thumbnail. 'What on earth is the matter?' Sewall asks.

'Joseph threw a coin at Betty, and it cut her forehead,' wife Hannah tells him.

Betty is clutching a bloody cloth to her forehead. Sewall moves her reluctant hands away and inspects the damage.

There's quite a long cut, and he worries that it may leave a scar. Stitching would only make it worse. She'll need a tight bandage to hold the edges together. The coin must have been spinning like a tiny wheel so that the edge sliced through Betty's skin. He looks over at the skulking Joseph. Suddenly the room seems to darken. Perhaps a black cloud has covered the sky and dimmed the window.

The child has his hands flat over his face and is turned towards the wall. His posture puts Sewall in mind of our first parents and their transgression in the Garden of Eden. He recalls Joseph's attempt at an S in his hornbook, how it took the form of a wriggling serpent. After all, the child went on to transform a gift from a minister of God into a weapon to wound his sister. So much for the innocence of children.

Sewall gives little Joseph a smacking, the child crying and Sewall sorrowing too, though whether in anguish at his guilt or at the thought that he is just a little boy, and it was only a penny, he isn't quite sure.

A thaw in early February. For a few days it feels almost springlike. Sam is home for a little break from Mr. Hobart's, and goes off to visit his best friend Josiah Willard, son of the minister. Darkness falls and still he doesn't return. Sewall sends Bastian over to Mr. Willard's house to fetch him but he comes back empty-handed.

He and Sewall go off into the streets to ask if the watchmen have seen the boys but nobody has. They return to the house and Sewall sits by the fire with Hannah to wait. Little Mary sleeps nearby in her cot, and Joseph is upstairs in bed. The two older girls are talking in the kitchen with Susan, quite oblivious—they've grown used to Sam not being at home in any case.

The minutes pass with deadly slowness. The fire grows dim, as if registering their diminishing hopes. Sewall offers up a prayer for their son's safety and Hannah mutters amen as if the word sticks in her throat, as if she resents having to ask for an outcome that ought to be freely given, as if she is bitter already at a loss she doesn't even know she has suffered. Sewall wishes he'd impressed upon Sam the necessity of coming home before dark, then remembers he did do exactly that. Impressing anything on Sam is like trying to mould quicksilver.

Bastian comes in to see if there is anything he can do. 'What time is it, Bastian?' Sewall asks. He can't bear to look up at the clock himself.

'Near eight, Mr. Sewall.'

The darkness is already more than three hours deep.

Ten minutes later there's a hue-and-cry at the front door. Bastian gets there first as if to shield his employers from any blows that may come. On the step are men with lanterns, in wet cloaks and hats, big boots. And in the middle of them is young Sam, swathed in an enormous shawl, his face pale as the moon.

Sewall makes up the fire and he and Hannah stand the boy in front of it and revolve him slowly like a piece of meat on a spit, so as to warm him evenly all the way through. Betty, young Hannah and Susan have come in from the kitchen in response to the clamour. Betty laughs at the sight of her absurd brother while Hannah stares at him wide-eyed and Susan looks to one side, embarrassed.

It turns out that Sam and Josiah had met up with a couple of other boys and the foursome took it into their heads to go fishing in Boston harbour. Sewall is incredulous. Fishing in February! Despite the thaw there are still ice floes in the water. But the boys had got it into their heads that cod and alewives are especially plump and delicious when fished out of very cold waters. Sam is not even fond of fish but in Sewall's experience that has never stopped a fisherman yet, nor an idiotic boy. They had got hold of rods, lines and hooks from one of the boys' parents' outhouses, and then commandeered Sewall's rowing boat, which is used for visits to Hogg Island and is moored at his own wharf (where lighters from merchant vessels he has an interest in sometimes tie up).

Absorbed in their fishing they drifted a long way out. Only when darkness fell did they realise their predicament and then they rowed for an age towards the distant lights of the town, their hands numb with cold. But at a certain point they became aware of a large passenger ship coming in. Immediately, they took it into their heads to turn about and row towards it in order to see if they could recognise any of the people on deck coming all the way from England.

The ship's lanterns caught them when they were almost under the bows. The captain yelled out orders but the boys misunderstood and turned the wrong way, giving the side of the ship a glancing blow. One of them, Samuel Gaskill, fell in the water, but luckily his cap floated up to mark the exact spot and the others were able to pull him out.

The commotion was heard from the shore, and soon a vessel was launched to tow them back. Then the lads were taken to the Sign of the Three Mariners, given blankets or shawls, and questioned. This is a tavern known for strange women (in Solomon's sense) but perhaps the boys were too wet and cold to pay them much attention. Finally they were taken to their homes in turn, Samuel Gaskill being the first and young Sam the last of the four.

'I think we've lost the fish, father,' Sam confesses. 'They were still in the boat. Someone will have taken them by morning. And the boat is a bit broken,' he concludes.

Next day Mr. Willard calls to discuss the escapade. He has confined Josiah to the house with mountains of theology to con as punishment. Sewall is sorry about this because it leaves Sam bereft during his remaining days at home. Sewall had contented himself with pointing out to Sam how frantic he and Hannah felt when their boy went missing and secretly he's rather glad his son showed enough pluck to have an adventure, though the thought of four lads becoming benighted as they drifted out to sea in an open boat sends shivers down his spine.

Mr. Willard is tall with a dark complexion and a brooding countenance. He is learned (though no rival to the Mathers) and a fine minister to the South Church, though prone to hot temper. He and Sewall have fierce arguments from time to time. He's surprised and disappointed at Sewall's leniency. 'If we don't discipline them, they're liable to follow the path of those Salem girls. It's a dangerous time for children.'

'Ah yes,' says Sewall. 'Mr. Mather told me about that pair.'

'There are four of them now.'

Double the number already, as if the affliction is breeding. Mr. Willard explains that a girl called Ann Putnam, eleven or twelve years old, and an older one, Betty Hubbard, are showing the same symptoms as the first two. But now all four have started to attribute blame. They say they're being persecuted by the spectres of three women in their village.

'I can't see,' says Sewall, 'how a night-time fishing spree is going to expose our boys to an approach from the Devil. Or from his accomplices.'

Mr. Willard has not been long gone when Sewall's brother Stephen comes to call. He's smaller than Sewall, thickset, with an honest ruddy face and long hair (all his own). His legs are somewhat bandy but far from detracting from his appearance the effect is to give him a sturdy quality (at least in the opinion of his big brother), as if he would be hard to push over. He's in Boston on some business, so of course the Sewalls insist he must stay the night. Sewall tells him about Sam's adventure, which greatly amuses him. 'I'm glad you don't take it too seriously,' Sewall says. 'Mr. Willard was very glum. He thought it might lead to a case of the sort of possession that's broken out near you.'

'Well, we know how Mr. Willard can be prone to glumness. I'm so happy you didn't become a minister, Sam, despite all your education. The problem with being a minister is you don't just have your own sins to worry about but everyone else's too. Mine are quite enough for me.'

If Sewall talked in similar vein it would be flippant, but this way of putting things suits Stephen's nature, as much him as the way he walks or screws up his eyes to look at you (perhaps into you).

For Sewall himself, the question of whether to become a minister was a fraught one that took several years to resolve. It's true, Harvard pushes you in that direction. Out of the eleven students in his year, seven are clergymen. But after his marriage he became interested in his father-in-law's business affairs, and at last decided being a merchant was the right career for him too. And the other duties he soon began to take on, as a constable, militia captain, colony publisher, councillor, most of all as a justice, served to bridge the gulf between commerce and civic responsibility.

'Yes, there are strange goings on in that poor little namesake of ours,' Stephen continues. 'As you know it's always been a horrible pit, but now it's a horrible pit where people jump at their own shadows. Or each other's shadows, I suppose I should say. Do you know we have little Betty Parris at our house?'

Sewall is taken aback.

'Yes,' says Stephen, 'you may well look startled. You yourself are responsible, as a matter of fact.'

'But I've never even set eyes on her.'

'Ah, but Mr. Mather had a meeting with her father, the parson, who is the jumpiest of the lot. He's terrified that people will think his daughter is in league with the Devil, and that he is too. Mr. Mather told him you and he had discussed the matter and that you seemed to believe the children must be innocent. He suggested the best way to establish this is to take the little girl away from the place for a while. In my own opinion the best solution would be to take *every*one away from that hole, but that's another story. Anyway, Mr. Parris says where to? and Mr. Mather says why not to Mr. Sewall's? but Mr. Parris thinks Boston is too far for a distressed nine-year-old, and then they remember they have another Mr. Sewall closer to hand.'

'They couldn't have made a better choice, Sam.' Indeed, Stephen's sunny disposition might be enough to dispel the shadows cast by Salem Village. He himself would have been too anxious to comfort the little girl, too sympathetic even. In the cupboard with Betty he finds himself weeping as much as she does. 'But what about the other children?'

'Spare me, brother. One's enough to be going on with.'

'And is she recovering?'

'When she arrived she would suddenly spring out of herself, so to say, like a jack-in-the-box. One minute you could be having a sensible conversation with her, insofar as you *can* have a sensible conversation with a child that age, and the next she's running amuck, screaming and crying out that the Black Man has come and is promising to take her to a golden city. Margaret takes her by the hand and says, "Now, dear, what's all the fuss about? There's no need to shout. We're not deaf. Just tell that Black Man he's a liar." You know what Margaret's like. It seemed to have a calming effect. But to tell you the truth I was worried my own children would catch the contagion. I suppose my Sam is too young to know what's going on, but little Margaret is four now.'

'But the contagion isn't passed from child to child. Mr. Willard tells me it comes from the spectres of three women of the village.'

'You know me, Sam. I'm practical. I like to be able to picture what's going on in my mind's eye. I can't quite understand how those spectres do what they do. If the Devil told me to haunt someone I wouldn't know where to start. Satan would soon be disappointed in me.'

'Salem Village is a small place. I believe, Stephen, that you're far enough away from it.' Sewall reminds himself again of Stephen's positive, robust nature. To be far away isn't just a matter of geography. And of Stephen's wife's too. Margaret Sewall is more outgoing than Hannah, a lively dark-haired woman, pretty and plump, who laughs a lot.

'And you're even further,' says Stephen. 'Think yourself lucky, brother, that you're well out of it.'

I t's an uneasy time. The new charter was ratified at the Court of St James in January. The royal power is to be much increased. In particular, the king will personally appoint the governors of the colony. But to sweeten the pill he's allowed Increase Mather, who has negotiated on behalf of Massachusetts for the last four years, to nominate the first holder of the post under the new charter. Mather has chosen Sir William Phips, to Sewall's perplexity. Phips is an adventurer—hardly better than a pirate himself—who located a sunken galleon loaded with treasure on the seabed near Jamaica and after a number of tries and at least one mutiny from his cutthroat crew finally found a way of getting its cargo to the surface. Perhaps he is a man for these times.

Sir William won't arrive until sometime in May. A specific court to handle the witchcraft cases will then be set up. Sewall is to hold himself in readiness for appointment to that court. In the meantime, two of his colleagues from Salem Town, John Hathorne and Jonathan Corwin, are appointed to conduct preliminary examinations of the accused, these to take place in the Salem Village meeting house.

Cotton Mather huffs and puffs around one windy afternoon with the latest news of these examinations, wig askew and cheeks crimson.

'I now have a professional stake in these proceedings,' Sewall points out. 'I don't want to be swayed by the winds of opinion.'

'I am not a conveyor of *opinion*,' Mather protests. 'I attended the opening examinations and simply wished to report their substance to you, as a person with an interest in the matters under scrutiny. There's no virtue in ignorance.'

One of the accused, Goody Good, is well-known as a muttering woman. She wanders round the village with her mouth opening and closing angrily but people can't make out what she is actually saying. Sewall imagines curses coming from another realm as though accidentally overheard, from a malignant world folded into our own as shadows are folded into the brightness of day.

Another, Goody Osborne, is involved in property transactions, strange business for one of her sex. There are rumours of inappropriate transactions of another kind as well. Goody Osborne tried to turn the tables by claiming she was haunted just like the girls accusing her. 'One night she was lying in bed and a *thing* grasped the back of her head.'

'A thing?'

'A thing. It gripped her hair and tried to pull her towards the door of her bedroom. So she says.'

'What kind of a thing?'

'I use the word "thing" to indicate a being which has been given no name in the world we see around us. But she says it was like an Indian, all in black.'

Sewall is startled. He has been expecting a Beelzebub or a Mephistopheles, not a savage. But of course Indians grasp the hair as a prelude to scalping. 'Perhaps it *was* an Indian,' he suggests. 'A *real* Indian.'

'A spectre is as real as any other phenomenon.'

'If it was a spectre, then surely she was being haunted, just like the afflicted girls.'

'Ah,' says Mather, 'but under further examination, she confessed it may all have been a dream.'

Just as Cotton Mather insists that spectres are as real as

flesh and blood phenomena, so Sewall suspects that dreams can be as true as daytime truths. He says as much.

'Are the children dreaming when they writhe in pain while the examinations are going on?' Mr. Mather asks. 'When they choke and struggle with their eyes bulging? When their limbs are forced into unnatural attitudes? The point is, Mr. Sewall, that the adversaries are unseen but the results of their actions are clearly visible.' He's obviously now convinced of the children's innocence. 'It's a matter of evidence, like following footprints in the sand,' he continues. 'You can't sit in a court of law and judge someone by their *dreams* because dreams do *not* leave footprints in the sand.'

'By the same token,' Sewall says, 'I have *not* seen those witches haunting the children with my very eyes. Which is why I wish to keep a distance from any account of the examinations.'

'I'm simply addressing your own claim that Goody Osborne is one of the afflicted rather than a witch. She admitted in the examination not just that this *thing*'s visitation might be merely a dream, but also that she hasn't been to church for many a month. Do you ever think about the towns and villages of our commonwealth in the night-time?'

This is a strategy favoured in sermon-giving, catching the congregation, just as they doze off, with the sharp immediacy of a question that charges towards them from an unexpected quarter. 'Our little candles in that great darkness?' continues Mather, his voice now orotund (albeit with a somewhat fluting timbre), following the cadences of a previously aired idea.

Of course Sewall thinks of such things. Whenever he is out on business or pleasure he is aware of the day inexorably declining through winter afternoons or summer evenings, of the looming danger of being benighted. Many a time he hurries through a meeting or a pudding so he can set off home without further delay, and when he arrives safely by the light of the moon or the stars he always says *Laus Deo*, Praise the Lord, as his front door shuts behind him.

'This was a pagan land before our fathers and grandfathers settled here,' Mather continues, as though Sewall is a roomful of people. 'A land of Devil worship. Outside the scope of our plantations, a pagan land it remains. And when a weak sister like Goody Osborne steps out of the light of our candles and away from the congregation of the saints, she must enter the darkness that still surrounds our settlements. It's been waiting all along for her to stray, and indeed for any or all of us.' He pauses to give Sewall time to understand what he knows already—that no one is exempt from the importunity of darkness. 'That's why she stated that the thing in her bedroom was like an Indian, all in black. In the interests of painting a convincing picture of the so-called apparition, she accidentally let slip the truth of her new allegiance.'

Cotton Mather's face shows the satisfaction of a verdict reached, as if it is he who is the judge. Sewall tries to take him up on the question of paganism. Many Indians have converted to Christianity already, and despite the atrocities that are being committed in the frontier towns by those tribes that have allied themselves to France, he believes Indians hold the key to America's destiny—indeed that they are an indispensable part of God's plan for humankind.

In reply Mather talks of the Indians who went to Mexico to settle there. This journey was strangely like the passage of the Israelites through the wilderness. But whereas the latter were conducted by God to the Promised Land, the Indians were led to Mexico by the Devil in the form of an idol they called Vitzlipulitzli. 'They carried him in an ark of reeds, and housed him at night in a tabernacle. This is proof positive that the Indian is *Simia Dei*, the Ape of God. Indeed it is my belief that they are the Devil's chosen people and were led by him to settle the American continent just as God's people were led to *their* promised land. And I fear they may have forged an alliance with witches to restore the land to heathenish ways once more.'

Sewall earnestly wishes to bring the discussion to an end. 'The matter of guilt has yet to be decided,' he reminds Mather.

'But there is a witness,' Mather informs him. 'Apart from the girls, I mean.'

This, it turns out, is a slave belonging to Samuel Parris, a woman called Tituba Indian. Mather gives a meaningful nod as he gives her married name. Her husband, John Indian, belongs to Parris too. Sewall has no brief for slavery. It appals him that people should buy a man or a woman with no more concern than if they were purchasing a horse, and he is taken aback at the thought of a minister of religion indulging in such a practice. The girls accused Tituba, who confessed immediately (no doubt, Sewall thinks, she's used to doing what she's told). The Devil had come to her accompanied by four women, Goody Good, Goody Osborne, and two others she didn't recognise. Also a tall man from Boston. In short the conspiracy is growing.

These witches hurt the children and make Tituba do the same. A thing (another phenomenon for which there is no earthly name, though it somewhat resembles a hog) tells Tituba to kill the children. Then, as though the thing's resemblance has triggered a rhyme in the very nature of things, it is transformed into a dog, a black dog. There was a red rat and a black rat. And when the witches wanted to torment the girls they flew to them on sticks. And on the subject of flying there was a bird amongst this hubbub of animals, a yellow one, owned by the tall man from Boston. And the yellow bird flew from the tall man's hand and alighted on Goody Good's, then suckled her between her fingers.

'Suckled?' asks Sewall, thinking he might have misheard.

'There must have been a nipple in situ, for that purpose.'

A few months since, a black dog killed the cow that supplied his household with its milk and Sewall uttered a prayer to God, asking him to offer his breast for their supplies. Now he hears tell of a black dog once more, this time in its natural abode, a witches' coven. And news of demonic suckling. Ever since that wretched business of the pirates Sewall has found it difficult to pray, and has gained scant satisfaction or spiritual ease from church worship, even the singing of psalms, which used to be his great delight. His voice holds firm but his spirit fails to rise, as if he has lost his heart's true baritone. Now the possible explanation dawns.

There is the darkness; here is the light.

Here is the rule of the Lord; there is the aping of God.

There are two domains, one a dim reflection, a dismal parody, of the other. When he, Sewall, reprieved those pirates, he unwittingly helped to create an overlap between the two. How else to explain a pirate almost instantly becoming a captain in the royal navy? No wonder Sewall has since found it impossible to gain any satisfaction or comfort in the observances of Christian worship. It may have been that his prayers to God have been redirected to Vitzlipulitzli as the consequence of this unintentional switching of loyalty. In Boston he prayed for God to offer his breast; in Salem Village a nipple appeared between a witch's fingers.

Cotton Mather finally takes his leave. He has a particular talent for feeling put-upon, so contrives to suggest that this conversation has kept him from more important matters, grumbling to himself about a sermon awaiting completion as they proceed through the vestibule to the front door. Sewall leans round him to open the latch and is surprised by a gust of wind that all but shuts the door again, blowing out not just the candle he's carrying but the pair ensconced in the panelling. Mather has to clutch hold of his wig to prevent it flying off, and to sidestep this indignity immediately adverts to his earlier rhetorical flight. 'The big dark,' he announces, then, pleased with this description, repeats it, 'big dark,' raising his arm to point outside before scuttling off into the night.

'Laus Deo,' Sewall mutters in his wake. He tries to justify

this in his mind as an anticipation of Cotton Mather's safe arrival home rather than as what it actually is, a thank-you for his departure at long last. Then he closes the door.

As he feels his way past the cupboard he can make out little sounds from within, groans and whimpers. Betty again, wrestling with her despair. Or perhaps, it suddenly occurs to him, with a witch.

CHAPTER 8

At breakfast next morning Sewall makes an announcement. 'I shall catch the ferry to Salem Town today.'
Wife Hannah is raising a portion of bannock to her mouth. She lowers it on hearing this news. 'The wind is still blowing,' she says. 'The sea will be high.'

'I crossed the Atlantic a little while ago, don't forget. I think I can manage a short trip up the coast. And if the sea is *too* high the ferry won't sail.'

'Father, may I come with you?' Betty asks. Her sister Hannah observes her intently while she says this, then looks anxiously towards her father.

'No!' Sewall exclaims, more firmly than is warranted.

'Can *I* come, father?' pipes up little Joseph. Daughter Hannah peers short-sightedly at him just as she had at Betty. Joseph is waving a piece of bannock in one hand. He pulls a morsel off it with the other and puts it into his mouth, entirely unconcerned about the outcome of his question. Young Hannah turns towards Sewall once again to hear his ruling.

'No, Joseph, not today,' Sewall replies in a more accommodating tone.

Young Hannah settles back in her chair, relieved. If her brother and sister had been able to go, their momentum might have pulled her along too, and set her afloat on that high sea. 'I am going to consult with Mr. Noyes,' Sewall explains. 'Upon a matter in the Book of Revelation.' Nicholas Noyes is the minister at Salem Town, and an old school friend of Sewall's. The two often meet to discuss topics of mutual interest, in particular Biblical prophecy and the scandal of periwigs.

'I thought you were going to visit my Uncle Stephen and Aunt Margaret,' says Betty. 'I like going to see them.'

'Can't Revelation wait till the weather is better?' wife Hannah asks.

'It's a question of prophecy that we need to settle.'

'But these prophecies have waited hundreds of years—surely they can wait a little longer?'

'Some of them may be coming to fulfilment. There may not be time to delay longer,' Sewall explains. A memorable apothegm coined by Mr. Noyes comes into his mind: Prophecy is history antedated; and history is postdated prophecy, words which give Revelation's most dizzying flights the urgency of fact.

'You must call on brother Stephen and sister Margaret while you are there, in any case,' Hannah tells him. 'To see how they are and give them my good wishes.'

'*I* would like to call on them and see how they are,' Betty says.

'I'd love to see Margaret again,' wife Hannah agrees, a little wistfully. 'She always raises my spirits.'

Sewall fears she will imitate her children and ask to come too. 'I will ask them to visit us soon,' he tells her. He feels compelled to add: 'Unless you want to come with me today.' He drops his face so he doesn't look her in the eye, ashamed at the lack of enthusiasm in his voice.

'Oh no,' says Hannah at once. 'Besides, I have a headache.'

He raises his head to give her a sympathetic look, though his sympathy is freighted with relief.

Sewall will be arriving at his destination—at his destinations—uninvited and unexpected, and there's no question of a home-made pasty to take with him on the journey, given the short notice (not to mention Hannah's poorly head), so as he heads for the ferry he calls in at Wing's ordinary to buy one of the meat pies that establishment is well known for.

It's oddly pleasant to step out of the bright breezy morning into the inn's beery dimness. Captain Wing greets him effusively, as he has done ever since Sewall stymied his plan to have a man performing tricks in the building's back room, as if that rebuke was an act of friendship rather than a reprimand—which, indeed, it was. The pie he wraps for Sewall is so raised and golden it's almost spherical, like a melon. Sewall carefully places it in his satchel, making sure the gravy will not leak on to the Bible he is carrying with him, and then steps from the atmosphere of baking and brewing into the exhilarating emptiness of the outside air.

When he arrives at the wharf the sea is brisk and blue, with spray blowing from the wave crests. He rests his gaze on Hogg Island across the harbour, his own property, peering (so to speak) round the shoulder of Noddle's Island that lies in front of it. Even at this distance, in the crystal atmosphere he can make out the tracery of trees he has planted himself, chestnuts and white oaks, and a little line of blue smoke from the chimney of his tenant, Jeremiah Belcher, rising at an angle before the wind.

As he stands on the wharf, projecting his attention across the water to that little knob of land, Sewall recalls his favourite passage in the whole Bible, chapter 10 of Revelation, concerning an angel with a rainbow on his head who set his right foot on the earth and his left foot upon the sea. Sewall has always interpreted this as predicting the discovery of America, with the right foot standing upon Europe, and the left coming to rest on newfound land across the ocean. Mr. Noyes agrees with this interpretation, which of course implies that America has a glorious part to play in the establishment of Christ's kingdom on earth.

There's a handful of passengers waiting for the boat to

depart. Finally the ferryman opens his little gate to let them board. 'Is it safe to sail, with this wind?' Sewall asks him.

The captain twists his gnarled and weather-beaten face into what is presumably a smile. 'We'll whip along so quick we won't have time to sink,' he replies.

As they leave the shelter of the harbour for the wilder water beyond, Sewall is overtaken by remorse at his dishonesty this morning. He had pretended his purpose was to visit Nicholas Noyes when in fact his principal intention was— is—to call upon his brother and family, in order to see how young Betty Parris is coping. Last night the idea struck him that if Mr. Parris's Betty could find sanctuary with brother Stephen and sister Margaret, then perhaps *his* Betty can do the same.

It's important for him to try to ascertain this without having his family with him and turning his reconnoitring into a social visit. So when at breakfast Betty said that she thought he intended to visit her uncle and aunt, he instantly gave her the lie, letting her and the others believe that Mr. Noyes was in fact his Salem destination. It was an untruth on behalf of his daughter's salvation. He once told her that he would go to hell to keep her company, after all.

One of the passengers has a fishing rod with him, and has flung his line over the side to catch what he may. Over comes the captain with a limping stride, club-footed Sewall now sees, and says to the hopeful fisherman, 'You have no chance, with the way we're running before the wind. No fish could swim fast enough to catch up with your hook.' Then he laughs with his shoulders hunched, as he did before. The fisherman is abashed, uncertain whether to be obstinate and leave his rod in position, or acquiescent and put it away. He decides to fish on but aloofly, drumming his fingers on the rail and glancing sidelong at his speeding float as if fishing is of little importance to him, and never has been.

Maybe the lie will be exorcised if Sewall visits Mr. Noyes first, and discusses Revelation with him, as he said he intended to do. On the other hand, maybe acting out his lie will be like acting in general, turning mendacious words into deeds and introducing falsehood into the texture of life itself. He cannot decide which of these alternatives is valid.

He suddenly remembers the pie in his satchel. He can hardly eat it while walking through the streets of Salem. In any case, wrestling with his conscience has given him an appetite— or perhaps it's the motion of the ferry and the sea breeze. The plump roundness of the pie makes it impossible to bite into but he remembers he has a penknife with him so is able to rest the pie on top of his satchel, with the hard surface of his Bible conveniently beneath the leather, and cut off a slice. Once the first inroad is made, the rest yields readily enough. Inside is veal and ham in a white sauce.

At last the speeding ferry swerves into Salem's neat harbour, abruptly losing the wind as it does so. The passengers assemble by the exit gate while the captain and his crew tie the boat up to the wharf. Sewall is standing next to the erstwhile fisherman, who after a moment or two gives a confidential jerk of the head then unbuttons his coat a little, inviting him to peer inside. Sewall makes out a brave codfish snuggled in by the man's chest—presumably secreted there so as not to contradict the captain and cause some awkwardness or bad temper. 'How did you manage to catch it?' he whispers.

'I don't know,' the man whispers back. 'Perhaps it swam at great speed. It was a young spirited fish when on the line. Or maybe it came at us from the opposite direction.'

For some reason this encounter cheers Sewall up as he walks through the Salem streets. It's as though the fish outpaced the hook or (if from the other direction) collided with it, out of sheer impudence and bravado in order to dispel the glumness given off by that ferry captain. He feels he's taking a

leaf out of the exuberant codfish's book: yes, he *will* go to see
Mr. Noyes first off; yes, he *will* discuss Revelation with him.

But now, as luck would have it, he bumps into his brother
Stephen, who is delighted to see him so unexpectedly, claps his
hand on his shoulder and immediately hurries him off to his
house.

This is a foursquare building in a street running parallel to
the shore, with a slice of blue sea visible between two houses
opposite. At the front Stephen and Margaret grow vegetables,
the seedlings neatly planted in rows to await the summer, and
to one side there's a small orchard, complete with pig, now
dozing on its side like a large pink squash. As they enter the little gate, Margaret comes to the door—she must have seen
them through the window. Like her husband she has a cheerful open face. Her complexion is dark (curly black hair shows
as a kind of coronet below her lace cap) and emphasises the
white teeth of her smile. Sewall can't resist admiring her
rounded figure in its mulberry-coloured skirt and bodice. He
switches his attention back to the pig, the apple trees, and the
new vegetables, complimenting her on her garden.

He is led inside. Margaret insists he should stay to dinner.
He explains that he is on his way to see Mr. Noyes, but she
counters by telling him that they will dine early in that case.
She rushes off to arrange matters before Sewall has time to
mention the veal and ham pie, and Stephen takes him into a
small room at the back of the house that he uses as an office.
His desk is covered with papers but he opens a drawer in it
and takes out two pipes, each already loaded with tobacco. He
hands one to his brother, then puts a taper to the log fire that's
burning merrily in the grate.

They puff in silence for a while, Stephen relaxed, Sewall
pretending to be so while waiting for the moment to broach
the business that has brought him here. 'What news of the
witchcraft in Salem Village?' he finally asks.

'It gets bigger,' Stephen tells him. 'The afflicted increase in number, then the witches expand in ratio, then the afflicted increase in turn and so on ad infinitum. What do you think of Mr. Hathorne, the chief examiner?'

Sewall has known John Hathorne, a justice of Salem Town, for some years. 'A person who knows his own mind.'

'A most hectoring man. If he imagines there's a witch hiding beneath a rock he'll quickly haul her out.' Stephen is easygoing and pragmatic, with an instinctive recoil from transcendence.

Still, the ground is now prepared for Sewall to broach the subject he has come here to discuss. 'How's young Betty Parris getting along?'

'Wait,' Stephen says, and leaves the room. He's back a little later with a pleased smile on his face. He goes to his chair and resumes his pipe. A few more minutes pass, then the door opens again and in comes a little girl with a large tray. 'This is a young friend who is staying with us,' Stephen says. 'Her name is Betty Parris.'

Betty tries a curtsey, the tray angling dangerously as she bends her knees. Stephen gets up to help her. They put it on top of the papers on his desk and, as he steadies the jug, the child carefully pours out cider. She brings Sewall his glass, holding it in both hands, her little face staring severely at the ruffled surface. 'Thank you, my dear,' he says, taking it from her just before it sloshes over the edge. She curtseys again, more successfully this time, and hurries back to the tray. Then she returns with almonds and raisins. 'Would you like some?' he asks, offering the bowl back to her.

'We have our own in the kitchen. Me and Margaret and Sammy,' she tells him, and skips off.

'As you can see,' says Stephen, when she is gone. Betty has forgotten his cider, as well as his nuts and raisins, so he helps himself.

'Does she relapse?'

'No longer. She seems like any other child now.' He takes a good pull of his cider and sighs in contentment.

'It's good for children to live away from home for a while,' Sewall says, as if it's a casual observation. 'As you know my Sam is staying with Mr. Hobart. He moans and groans, but I think he's profiting from it. And girls can benefit too, as little Betty Parris proves. I suppose it helps to gain confidence and cope with company, which must stand a woman in good stead when she's running a household of her own. And this is such a good place for a young person to be. With your kind wife— and your kind self' (he adds hurriedly) 'as well as the good sea air.' He takes a deep breath by way of clincher but all he can detect is tobacco smoke with an admixture of cider, delightful scents both but not relevant to his argument.

'You know that if you would like your daughter to stay with us a while, she would be very welcome,' Stephen tells him.

Sewall is elated though he feels a little awkward even in his triumph, aware that his conversational stratagems have been detected—but of course that was the whole intention. Luckily at this point Betty Parris trots in again to announce that dinner is ready. They are to have fried alewife, already in a dish on the table, followed by bacon and eggs. 'I needed dishes that could be prepared quickly,' Margaret explains apologetically, 'since you are on your way to visit Mr. Noyes.'

'Two of my favourites, as it happens,' Sewall tells her quite sincerely. Perhaps the pipe and cider have refreshed his palate because he feels hungry again

'Are you going to discuss periwigs with our minister?' Margaret asks, obviously aware that Mr. Noyes shares Sewall's hatred of the fashion. She looks amused. This whole household is always on the point of precipitating into merriment. Sewall wonders why his own should be so solemn, with his Betty and even young Sam succumbing to despair; with daughter

Hannah so often pent and anxious; with little Joseph uttering portentous prophecy and, perhaps under the influence of that S that lurks in his name, turning Cotton Mather's gift of a penny into a weapon to hurt his sister Betty with (though the wound has healed already and left no scar after all); and with his beloved wife Hannah sometimes tired and headachy.

Yet they are happy with each other, he reminds himself, and laugh when it's called for. They are a pious household in a way his brother's is not, though Sewall suspects (and hopes) that God loves this one just the same (after all, he, Sewall, loves his careless Sam just as much as his intense Elizabeth).

Betty comes up with a bottle of wine. She can't reach high enough to pour it in his glass so Sewall takes it from her and does the honours for himself and Stephen (Margaret shakes her head: she has a glass of beer at hand). Stephen takes a swig then performs a sort of fanfarole with his right arm as prelude to an announcement. 'Brother Sam has done us a great honour, Margaret,' he proclaims.

Margaret looks intently at her husband, then again at Sewall who takes a large mouthful of alewife to keep busy. 'He wishes his daughter Hannah to stay with us for a time!' Stephen concludes.

Sewall emits a noise that might be described as indescribable, something between a gasp and a moan. He can feel his face turn purple and his eyes fling out tears as if there is no longer room in his head to hold them. He points to his mouth by way of blaming the alewife which has indeed gone down the wrong way, so pursuing today's theme of lies turning into truth.

'Water!' cries Margaret. Betty rushes importantly towards the door in order to go and fetch some. Sewall waves his hand to call her back and takes a long draught of his wine, thinking feverishly as he does so. Hannah is the obvious candidate for a stay here. It's a logical enough assumption on Stephen's part. She's thirteen, a normal age for a girl to go away for a time.

Betty Parris is much younger, but of course she's a special case, a child suffering from the witchcraft affliction that's running rampant in Salem Village. He can hardly admit he wants his own Betty, herself only eleven, to come here for a parallel reason: the possibility that the affliction has struck her over in Boston. To say this would be to betray his child.

CHAPTER 9

Nicholas Noyes is in his garden pruning a standard rosebush, his stout body bent as far as it will go (not very far) towards the plant he's addressing, rather as if paying court to a green and spindly maiden.

'Come in, come in,' he says impatiently when he becomes aware of Sewall's arrival, as if he's been waiting for him. He ushers him towards the open front door with his pruning hook. 'You're just in time.' Noyes opens the door to the kitchen. 'Anne,' he calls to his housekeeper (Mr. Noyes is a bachelor), 'lay another place at table, if you will. Mr. Sewall is come to dine with me.'

Sewall's mouth falls open in dismay; for a second he almost tries to object and explain, but Mr. Noyes is rubbing his hands together in anticipation, and he can't bring himself to. They have a fine piece of roast beef with pease pudding. Anne has added a few drops of vinegar to the latter, just as Sewall likes, and the food is so good he almost forgets this is his third dinner in succession. They drink beer with it and while they eat they have the discussion of Revelation that Sewall has promised himself.

Both men agree that the angel who straddles the Atlantic Ocean has his left foot on the New World, prophesying its discovery as the land where the Millennium will be inaugurated. Chapter 17 of Revelation tells of the seven angels who pour out their vials in turn by way of preparation for that event. The sixth pours his into the River Euphrates, which consequently dries up to enable the Kings of the East to make their way across it. Noyes and Sewall suspect that this episode stands for the successful crossing of the ocean and that the Kings of the East are the English settlers.

For Sewall himself, this theory receives support from a claim by the great missionary John Eliot who in 1663 published a translation of the Bible into Algonquian, and who believed that the Indians were descended from the lost tribes of Israel and that when they were all converted to Christianity Jesus would once again walk the earth, the American earth. Mr. Noyes, by contrast, agrees with Cotton Mather that the Indians are in fact the Anti-Christ, and that they represent the final impediment to the Second Coming. 'The Indians are dark and swarthy, like the Black Man himself,' he tells Sewall.

'According to Mr. Thorowgood,' Sewall replies, 'the Indians share a number of customs and rituals with the Jews. They hate pork, and practice circumcision. Also they segregate their women in a little wigwam apart from the rest of the tribe during their feminine seasons.' Just as he says the last phrase, in comes Anne with their pudding, a handsome cake accompanied by glasses of sack-posset. Sewall looks anxiously at her face but she shows no sign of having heard his reference to feminine seasons.

As soon as she has left, Mr. Noyes, in a very loud voice, exclaims: 'Bombardo-gladio-funhat-flami-loquentes!' then stares at Sewall, his eyes angry as those of a charging bull. He takes a spoonful of sack-posset and swallows it in a strangely adversarial fashion while his look remains fixed.

Sewall looks back at him in amazement. To fill in the difficult pause he takes a spoonful of sack-posset also, but consumes his in a tentative, even interrogative manner. 'Do you recognise that word?' Mr. Noyes finally asks him. 'It's Mr. Cotton Mather's coinage. Cod Algonquian. I took the trouble to learn it by heart.' He clearly takes pride in his second-hand ownership of this portmanteau word. 'It's meant as a satire on the long-winded speech and furious warlikeness of the Indians.'

'There are Latin words buried in it,' Sewall says, 'though as I understand the matter, the true Algonquian language may be flecked with elements of *Hebrew*, at least according to some scholars, which fact if proved would confirm the Biblical ancestry of the Indian nation.'

'Some scholars find Hebrew there, some find Phoenician, some Trojan. Do you know what I find? Nothing. Nothing but pagan Indian. That's all *I* can detect. If the Indian language possessed good civilised words the people might be guided by them towards good civilised behaviour, instead of murdering, raping and scalping our poor brothers and sisters.'

'But they *will* have a word to guide them, the word that guides us all. Some of the friend-Indians have it already, and others will gain it when they study Mr. Eliot's Bible.'

'I fear the reverse may be true,' Noyes replies ominously. 'Which is to say that the Indians are guiding the weaker members of our community towards their own pagan wickedness. Do you know what Tituba had to say at her second examination? I attended and heard her with my own ears. She said that she met a man who claimed to be God, can you imagine? It's bad enough when some rogue impersonates an honest man, but to strut around pretending to be God!' He shakes his head in disbelief at the scandal. 'Then this *Mr.* God says he will see her again the Wednesday following, at the minister's house. At Mr. Parris's own house! And at the appointed hour no less than four apparitions troop in with him, his diabolical retinue I suppose you might call it.' He cuts himself another slice of cake, then offers the knife to Sewall somewhat as an afterthought. Sewall has to remind himself that Mr. Noyes is a man used to eating alone. He almost refuses the offer, feeling quite replete by now, but then thinks that might suggest he is offended, so takes the knife and cuts himself another slice. 'These apparitions then had the impudence to enter Mr. Parris's study, where he was praying,' resumes Mr. Noyes.

'Did Mr. Parris see them for himself, in that case?'

'Of course not! If you are in conversation with the true God, the false one is no more than a worm underfoot. So there we have them, side by side: God and *Mr.* God, that is to say, God and the Devil: true religion and wicked impiety. Just as white people and savages have lived side by side in this colony since our fathers settled here.'

He sighs with satisfaction at having brought his argument to a close, then goes on to explain what happened next. Mr. God told Tituba he would return the following Friday. When he came he had a book with him. He wanted Tituba to sign it by way of agreeing to serve him for a period of six years. The man offered her a pin fastened to a stick to write in his book with, a blood quill, telling her to scratch her arm and then put an X. There were other names in the book, nine in all. Tituba couldn't read, of course, but Mr. God said that Goody Good was one of the signatories to this satanic contract, and also Goody Osborne. Somehow Tituba herself avoided signing after all—'So she *claims*, at least,' Noyes says. 'Though you mustn't believe all that a slave like her tells you.'

'I must keep my mind impartial,' says Sewall, 'since I may be trying these cases in due course.'

'You will keep a clear head on the matter,' says Mr. Noyes, 'particularly since yours isn't obscured by a periwig. I am writing an essay on that topic. In it I explain that anyone with any skill at physiognomy will know that that hair—' he points across the table at Sewall's declining hair—'cannot grow on this head—' he points upwards towards his own absence of hair—'any more than saltmarsh hay can grow on the top of a hill.'

Sewall almost protests at the unkindness of this comparison, but instead looks across at the clock. 'Almost time for the ferry,' he says. 'I must hurry. Thank you so much for an excellent meal, and please congratulate Anne for me also.'

As he heads towards the door, Mr. Noyes grasps him by the elbow, puts his face up close, and solemnly says, 'Malleus maleficarum. Hammer of heretics. That is what you must be, Mr. Sewall, when the cases come to trial. The witchcraft is spreading apace. It has already infected some who are close to us, or who seemed to be.'

Sewall recalls that *Malleus Maleficarum* is the title of a book published two centuries ago, to do with hunting down witches. 'That is what we all must be, in this time of threat,' Nicholas Noyes concludes. 'Hammers.'

It's six o'clock when Sewall arrives home. Hannah opens the door to him. 'Ah, my dear,' he says, 'I've something to tell you.'

'I have something to tell you, too,' she replies. She looks a little tired and strained, as she often does after a headache, but is wearing her good gown of sprigged muslin (he imported the material from London especially for her as part of a consignment he was shipping over) and a starched lace cap. 'Mr. Stoughton is here.'

Sewall is too startled to speak. For Mr. Stoughton to turn up at his house in person, without a prior arrangement, and wait for his return until becoming benighted, suggests some emergency has taken place. 'I insisted he must sleep here,' Hannah continues. 'He can't ride all the way back to Dorchester at this time of night. Sarah is busy preparing a late dinner or early supper for the two of you, whichever you wish to call it. I expect you're hungry after your day on the ocean waves.'

'I must go in directly and see what he's come about.'

She smiles a little wanly. 'I'm glad to have you back safely.'

'Laus Deo.'

'What was it you wanted to tell *me*?'

'Oh.' He's been so busy speculating about Mr. Stoughton's motive in coming here that he almost forgot. 'A family matter. I'll speak to you about it when Mr. Stoughton's gone.'

'I know he's an eminent man,' Hannah says, 'but . . .'

'But what?'

Hannah lowers her voice to a whisper. 'He frightens the children. They've scampered off to their holes like mice being chased by a cat.'

'I'll go and beard the lion in his den,' Sewall tells her. 'Or rather in *my* den.' He places his hands on her hips and squeezes gently, then walks past her to his study.

Before Sewall and Mr. Stoughton can settle down to talk, Sarah comes in and summons them to dine. 'You'd better have it at once,' she says, 'before it gets cold.'

Hannah and the children had their dinner before his arrival and stay carefully (or fearfully) out of the way. Sarah has baked a dish of pigeons with parsnips, and Sewall has Bastian bring up some of his Passado from the cellar. Sewall pours them each a glass of wine, and then serves Mr. Stoughton a couple of the birds. He hesitates over whether he can get away with only taking one himself, but Stoughton is watching the platter intently as if to make sure of the symmetry of the meal. Sewall has to encourage yet another lie to blossom into truth: in this case the lie of appetite must justify itself by consumption. The mendacities have come thick and fast today, some deliberate, others accidental, wave upon wave of them, yet never, as far as Sewall (inspecting his own intentions) can see, intended with malice. He sighs at the swarming complexity of it all, and takes a second pigeon.

Stoughton has come on Salem Village business, as Sewall guessed. 'At present we have no proper powers to engage with this outbreak, despite the urgent need to act,' Stoughton tells him. 'New England is in danger of being lost.'

'I suppose that is what our rulers feared when they drew up a new charter for us.'

'I am not talking about the Court of St James. New England is in danger of being lost even here, *in* New England. There is a dark time coming on our colony—on our province, as we must learn to call it when the new charter takes effect.'

A dark time. Sewall recalls little Joseph's prophecy, two years ago: the bad people are coming.

'The number of accused witches is growing very fast,' Stoughton says, 'upwards of twenty already.' Twenty? Mr. Noyes told Sewall only this afternoon that Tituba had counted nine signatories in the Devil's book. Fast indeed. 'Worse still, the outbreak isn't confined to the Goody Goods of this world who never bother to attend divine service.'

Stoughton pauses, as if visualising the Goody Goods of this world (a sorry company indeed) in his mind's eye. 'The flotsam and jetsam.' He cuts himself a morsel of pigeon breast with a deft manoeuvre of his knife that would have done credit to a surgeon, impales a slice of parsnip to accompany it, slips the portion into his mouth, and immediately begins chewing with tiny but very rapid movements, like a squirrel consuming a nut. 'Yesterday a woman called Nurse came up before the examiners. She's a widow of some means and one of the congregation of the saints, a covenanted member of Mr. Noyes's church in Salem Town since the days when the Salem Village congregation couldn't participate in the full covenant itself. But because it's not always possible for her to travel to divine service there, she also goes regularly to Mr. Parris's meetings in the village. At the end of her hearing she was remanded in custody to await trial.'

Unlike Mr. Stoughton, Sewall has been chewing slowly to allow his digestion as much time as possible to reconcile itself to each instalment, but now hurriedly swallows his mouthful. 'How can that be, if she's one of the saints?' he asks. He's assumed all along that the witch congregation (if that's the correct word for it) will be drawn from those outside the Christian community, from those who have not taken the covenant or who have lapsed from it and no longer go to church.

Mr. Parris, Stoughton continues, knowing Mrs. Nurse's examination was just about to take place (he is acting as clerk to the court), preached a remarkable sermon on this difficult issue last Sunday. Mr. Stoughton has received a full report. The text was John, chapter 6, verse 70, when Jesus says to the disciples: 'Have I not chosen you twelve, and one of you is a Devil?' The church is a garden, Mr. Parris had concluded, and contains weeds as well as flowers. 'He admirably prepared the way for what was to follow,' Stoughton affirms. 'The indictment of a member of the congregation. Of two congregations.'

'But should he have done so?' Sewall asks. 'Isn't that a kind of interference in the course of justice.'

'All Mr. Parris has done is define the possibility of a certain kind of wickedness. You might as well say that the Ten Commandments, by telling us that murder is a sin, are being unfair to murderers. Rebecca Nurse is simply awaiting trial. The course of justice will be *our* responsibility, at a later date.'

There's a pause. Mr. Stoughton takes another mouthful of his dinner, disposes of it as before, then resumes. 'However, there was some ill-feeling about this case in the village. Voices have been raised. People who don't know any better are crying foul play. Mrs. Nurse has her friends and allies. She is not a Tituba Indian or a Goody Osborne. Or, as I said before, a Goody Good. And in three days' time there is to be another examination, this time of *two* accused witches. One of them is a woman called Sarah Cloyse. She is Rebecca Nurse's sister.'

'Ah,' says Sewall. Here they are, two men of affairs, dealing with the possibility of social unrest. 'And who is the other one?'

'Elizabeth Proctor, also a woman of some standing. She and her husband have an inn—'

'I think I know it!' Sewall exclaims. It's outside Salem Village on the main highway to Salem Town. When going overland to visit his brother, Sewall has stopped there to have refreshment and bait his horse. The landlord, John Proctor, is a stocky irascible man, very sure of himself. Sewall can remember him haranguing his young maidservant, the jade as he called her, that her servings were too large. As Sewall recalls it, his own plateful was barely adequate. Proctor threatened to whip the girl should she offend again.

'They have a farm, too,' Stoughton says. 'These Proctors are people of property. They have weight in the community. That's why it's important that the examiners have weight of their own, to counterbalance theirs.' He has decided to beef up the proceedings when the court next meets. On this occasion, the examining justices already on duty, Jonathan Corwin and John Hathorne, are to be joined by five more, and Sewall is to be one of them. The examinations will be held in Nicholas Noyes's capacious and smart meeting house in Salem Town rather than in Samuel Parris's decrepit and cramped building in Salem Village. Mr. Noyes himself suggested this.

'Mr. Noyes?' asks Sewall in surprise. 'Is he an officer of the court? I di—I was with him this very afternoon.'

'He was merely acting as a friend to the court, as any citizen might.'

Sewall remembers Noyes's comments about the need to be a *malleus maleficarum*, instructions almost. Perhaps he already knew that Sewall would be coming back to Salem in a day or two. Perhaps he already knew the names of those to be examined, and was keeping the news to himself at dinner today.

Sewall feels slightly resentful, jealous even, of the possibility that Mr. Noyes has gained privileged access.

And yesterday Mr. Mather took it upon himself to puff his way round to impart the latest news. And last Sunday Mr. Parris aimed a sermon at the possibility that a covenanted church-member like Rebecca Nurse might be an interloper in the house of God. It's natural the clergy should take an active interest in the witchcraft since it attacks Christianity itself, but for a moment Sewall feels a judge's resentment at clerical interference in legal matters.

The other judges have all already agreed but since Sewall was not at home, Stoughton has had to wait for him. He gives Sewall a somewhat acidic look as he tells him this. 'There are other justices in Boston you could have sought out,' Sewall replies a little indignantly. 'You could have agreed to attend the examination yourself.'

Stoughton shakes his head. 'I think I will be more useful at a later stage. In any case we particularly wanted *you* to be on the bench. You have a reputation for fairness and impartiality which will be helpful in this instance.' He says the words as if they are hardly a compliment at all, as he might say, we needed a *small* man to fit on the bench, owing to its narrowness. 'Time is short. I have brought you a copy of the court papers. You need to study them tomorrow.'

One thing Samuel Sewall is not is a small man, particularly at present. When the meal is over he feels he can hardly rise from the table.

CHAPTER 10

Sewall spends the following morning in his study, perusing the papers of the examinations so far. Each case dovetails into the next so it's necessary to have some knowledge of all of them. By the same token the two women, Sarah Cloyse and Elizabeth Putnam, are going to be examined jointly when the court convenes the day after tomorrow. The witchcraft is a collective enterprise.

After some hours he goes to the window. He needs to give his eyes a rest, or perhaps his soul. It's a lovely day, and Hannah is pushing baby Mary up and down the path, taking the air. He decides to go down to join them for a few minutes.

'What is it you had to tell me?' Hannah asks when he catches her up. Little Mary, now six months old, gives him a welcoming smile from the cushion on which she is reclining in her little cart. His family news has slipped his mind in the agitation brought on by Mr. Stoughton's visit.

'Ah yes. I was talking with Stephen—' It occurs to him that this introduction sounds a little like a cabal between brothers, so adds—'and with Margaret, of course, about our Hannah.'

Silence is of two sorts. There is the empty kind, like a room into which you can walk, and the solid variety, like a wall with which you collide. His wife's current silence is of the latter type. After enduring it for a few seconds he continues, 'We agreed it would do her good to stay with them for—'

'*You* agreed!'

'Yes, we thought—'

Little Mary, sensing the difficulty of the situation, gives out a couple of tentative sobs, looking worriedly from face to face as if to check whether this is an appropriate reaction. 'Shush,' Hannah tells her, then turns back towards Sewall. 'So,' she says, 'this *we*, this *we* that came to an agreement about *our* daughter—'

'It was simply a conversation.'

'A cosy conversation between you and beautiful Margaret Sewall of Salem Town.'

'It wasn't *cosy*. We were all at dinner—'

'You never told me you had dinner there. I thought you came home hungry. I had Sarah bake you all those pigeons.' It's as if Sewall's mendacity has given the birds wings again, despite having been cooked, and they're flying home to roost.

As if to deflect her adults from this unhappy conversation, Mary tries another smile, which at once turns into a tiny belch. Hannah bends down, lifts her up and pats her on the back. 'Hannah is my child,' she says when this has been done. 'I went to all the trouble of giving birth to her, just as I did to this one. I gave birth to all of them, those who still live and those who have already died. Let Margaret have conversations and agreements about her own children. She already has one extra one who by rights belongs to someone else. She doesn't need any more.'

'You don't mind Sam being at Mr. Hobart's,' Sewall says.

'That was *our* decision. It was necessary for him. He needs to grow up. And it's the usual thing for children of his age. They all need to grow up.'

Sewall is aware of her taking comfort from this truism, which allows Sam's deficiencies to be swallowed up in the general immaturity of his peers. 'Well, Hannah is now the age Sam was when he first went off. Perhaps *she* needs to grow up too.'

'Hannah is different. She's such a gentle child. You can't say Sam is gentle. Not like Hannah. He's a boy. He's—'

'Not gentle, no. But he *is* vulnerable. Nevertheless I think placing him with Mr. Hobart has been a success, on the whole. I tried him again with a multiplication sum during my last visit and he got the answer nearly correct. Only a few apples adrift.' He sighs at the memory. 'He told me he's grown tired of apples and wishes to calculate some other fruit.'

'Hannah is quite good at arithmetic already.'

'I was thinking more—' He waves his arm vaguely in the direction of that 'more', which encompasses society at large, and sighs again. 'Intercourse with the world. I was thinking more of her intercourse with the world.'

'It's because she's short-sighted. She can't always make out who is approaching her. That's why she flees.' Young Hannah has the habit of rushing abruptly to the chamber she shares with Betty, like a startled animal. 'You wouldn't like it if instead of it being Mr. This or Madam That, there was just a vague shape coming towards you, like one of those witches the girls complain of in Salem Village.'

'Those witches come in their habitual form. Apparently the girls see them clearly.'

'Well, they must have better eyes for the supernatural than Hannah has for the natural.' She puts the baby back into her cart. 'I won't have her going to Salem.' She straightens up and looks Sewall in the eye. 'I won't have her being frightened.' She's tearful at the very thought.

Sewall is about to remind her of the difference between Salem Town and Salem Village, but then pauses. The fact that the examination is going to take place the day after tomorrow in Salem *Town* seems to threaten the distinction between the two places. 'Perhaps we need to send her somewhere else,' he finally agrees. 'Where she is in no danger.'

They finish on that note, not exactly in harmony but at least not in open conflict. He tries to tickle little Mary under the chin but she immediately grimaces in an exaggerated childlike way as if being choked. This little failure to please his youngest daughter makes him feel suddenly tired.

As he makes his way back to his study it occurs to him that he has conducted the argument with his wife just as if he's always had it in mind to send Hannah off for the sake of her development, rather than Betty for the sake of her soul. He can't decide whether this means that his lie has now become entrenched or that it has mutated into truth.

Mr. Noyes stands at the doorway of the meeting house to greet the examining justices as they file in. With his black cloak flapping in the sea-breeze he looks like an enormous crow with ruffled feathers. The judges are topped and tailed by clergy, since Mr. Parris brings up the rear in his capacity of clerk to the court. He's been fulfilling that role during the examinations in his own meeting house in Salem Village, and it was decided that for continuity's sake he should do so today in Salem Town. He seems a nervous and watchful man (the jumpiest of the lot, Stephen called him), as well he might be, given that the Devil visited his manse while he was oblivious and deep in prayer.

The Salem meeting house, like Sewall's own South Church in Boston, indeed like all the New England meeting houses, has a raised-up pulpit halfway down one of the long sides of the oblong building, with a bench or fore-seat each side of its steps for elders and wardens to sit on facing the congregation. This is where the judges will sit today, and little tables have been set in front of the fore-seats where they can write their notes. Facing them are pews which run most of the length of the building with an open area between them and the judges (rather like a stage in a theatre, Sewall imagines). Chairs have been placed at the left of this stage for the accused, and to the right for the accusers.

Mr. Parris takes his place at a little table at the end of the left-hand fore-seat, sharpens his quill, opens his inkpot, arranges his papers. The crowds pour in until the meeting house is entirely full, with people standing in the aisles. Mr. Noyes, who would normally be officiating from the pulpit, has reserved a place for himself in the front pew.

Eventually two burly men acting as court officers push the doors shut against the indignant residue, and the Essex County Marshall, a white bearded man with a gold chain of office round his neck, calls the room to order. Mr. Noyes promptly steps forward to the front, stands with his head bowed before the judges, and offers up a prayer for the success of their endeavours (whatever the word success might mean in these circumstances). Then he resumes his place in the front pew and the marshall leads the two accused women in.

Sarah Cloyse is perhaps fifty years old, in a brown gown and apron. Elizabeth Proctor is much younger and wearing a grey cloak with a hood and a matching grey skirt and bodice beneath. They both look tired and timid. They take their places, each with her head lowered, and then the marshall brings in the accusers. These are all young girls, mostly just children, some as young as ten or eleven, and none older than seventeen or so. As they take their places, a man in one of the pews towards the back rises to his feet, and starts shouting, a big, chunky figure with a red face. Sewall recognises the innkeeper, John Proctor, who is furiously proclaiming the innocence of his wife.

'She's only here today because of that little bitch, Mary Warren!' he shouts, pointing at one of the afflicted girls who Sewall recalls serving him in the inn, a thin spotty creature with a pale face and straggly hair. 'She'll get better soon enough after a good thrashing!' Sewall suspects the girl has already had thrashings enough: she has a thrashed look about her. 'All these stupid girls are the same,' Proctor rants on, 'idle wenches who need to be set to work. Give them some *proper* work to do. That will cure these imaginings.'

Presiding Justice Danforth has risen to his feet. 'I take it you are Mr. Proctor,' he says.

'Yes, sir, your honour, I am,' Proctor replies in a more normal tone. 'But this business here is all—' He shakes his head in despair at what this business is.

'Mr. Proctor, you have a right to attend this examination, since your wife is one of the accused. But if you cause any more disturbance I will have you removed.'

Proctor looks at his wife and raises his hand in her direction, as if in greeting. He is considerably older than she is, by twenty years or even more. He resumes his seat but then calls out, though less loudly than before, 'My advice is hang them, hang them!' He seems concerned that he may not have made his meaning clear and adds, 'Those stupid girls, I mean,' nodding his head towards the row of accusers.

Mr. Danforth gives him a long, appraising stare and then, satisfied that this intervention is at an end, indicates that the examinations should begin.

A little girl called Ann Putnam is the first to testify. Danforth nods to Hathorne, who asks: 'Ann, who hurt you?'

Ann is about eleven, dressed up by her parents for this court appearance in her Sunday clothes, a neat green bodice and skirt with a little apron and a white cap. The afflicted girls all around her make encouraging noises and gestures. She points vaguely towards the two accused.

'*Tell* us who hurt you, Ann,' interposes Mr. Danforth.

'Goody Proctor,' she mutters. Elizabeth Proctor gives a small gasp and puts her hand to her heart. 'Then Goody Cloyse,' she adds. Sarah Cloyse gasps in turn and also puts her hand to her heart.

'What did Goody Proctor do to you?' asks Hathorne.

'She choked me and brought me a book.'

'And Goody Cloyse?'

'She came too. She came first. She brought the book to me. She bit me.'

Suddenly Goody Cloyse rises to her feet. 'You are a grievous liar!' she exclaims furiously.

'Liar!' agrees a voice from the spectators—John Proctor again.

Now one of the girls is screaming, a terrible animal cry of pain repeated over and over again. Her cries have that shrillness of pitch only the young can achieve, and they hurt Sewall's ears. 'Whatever is the matter, girl?' he asks her.

'She is Mary Walcott,' Hathorne explains, 'Mary, tell Mr. Sewall who is hurting you at the moment.'

The screams subside. 'Goody Cloyse,' Mary replies in a shuddering voice.

'Come here and touch her then,' Hathorne tells her. She steps gingerly towards Goody Cloyse, and then Hathorne raises her hand until it makes contact with the woman's forearm. Immediately Mary gives out a long sigh and her whole form relaxes. Hathorne points her back to her place while Goody Cloyse looks on in apparent bafflement. 'Has she hurt you before?' Hathorne asks her.

'Many times.'

'Did she bring you the book?'

'Yes, she did.'

'What were you to do with it?'

'Touch it and there would be no more pain.' She suddenly goes limp as wax in a flame and collapses to the floor. The whole meeting house falls silent. Sewall begins to rise to his feet to go and help her but is stayed by Hathorne's hand. One of the court ushers comes from the side door he's guarding, puts his hands under the girl's armpits and lifts her up as easily as if she is a doll, placing her back on her seat. After a few moments she opens her eyes again.

'Did Goody Cloyse come alone?' Hathorne continues.

'Sometimes she comes alone, sometimes with Goody Proctor and Goody Nurse. Sometimes with many others.'

'Which others?'

Mary Walcott looks blank for a moment. Then says, 'I do not know,' and suddenly faints again, lolling to one side on her chair. The court usher tidies her back into a sitting position but this time Hathorne moves on to another of the afflicted, Abigail Williams, the child who was playing with Betty Parris in the Salem Village manse when the witchcraft began.

'Abigail Williams! Did you see a company at Mr. Parris's house eating and drinking?'

Sewall looks across at Mr. Parris to see how he takes this first direct reference to his dwelling, the house of a minister of God now apparently become a rendezvous for evil spirits. Mr. Parris remains bent intently over his papers, scratching away with his quill, eyes screwed up as if he needs spectacles.

'Yes, sir,' the child answers.

'How many were there?'

'About forty.'

Sewall gasps. Every time he hears about this Devil worship the number has doubled.

'And did they tell you what it was they drank?'

'They said it was our blood and that they had drunk it twice that day.'

'Mary Walcott!' Hathorne says suddenly, like a schoolmaster turning his attention to a dreamy child. 'Mary Walcott,' he repeats, now he has her attention, 'have you seen a white man?'

She gathers herself, nods, then speaks in a whisper. 'Yes sir, a great many times.'

'What sort of man was he?'

'A fine grave man.' She nods again, as if agreeing with herself. 'He was a fine grave man, and when he came he made all the witches tremble.' The Devil of course is the Black Man, but Sewall reminds himself that on this occasion he was disguised as God. He can assume any disguise, even this one, for, as Paul says in 2 Corinthians, Chapter 11, verse 14, *Satan himself is transformed into an angel of light.*

'Which witches were these, who saw the grave man and trembled?'

'They were Goody Cloyse, Goody Nurse, Goody Corey and Goody Good.'

There is a commotion to the left. Sarah Cloyse calls for water and Elizabeth Proctor grasps hold of her to stop her falling. Immediately there is an answering commotion from the right. One child is barking like a dog; another bleating like a sheep. One seems to be riding an invisible horse, from which she falls with a scream. Yet another calls out: 'Her spirit has gone to prison, to visit her sister Nurse!' Sewall has forgotten that Cloyse is sister to another of the accused. This infection or infestation spreads through families, and his scalp prickles at the thought.

'Elizabeth Proctor!' cries Hathorne. Elizabeth Proctor nearly drops Goody Cloyse in shock. 'Elizabeth Proctor,' Hathorne says again in quieter tones, 'do you understand the seriousness of the charges laid against you?' She looks at him with large brown eyes filled with tears, and slowly nods. Goody Cloyse's head is resting on her shoulder, her mouth open and eyes closed, breathing roughly, snoring perhaps.

Hathorne turns to the other side of the room. 'And you, the afflicted ones, you must speak the truth or answer for it before God. Ann Putnam, does Goody Proctor hurt you?'

Ann Putnam opens her mouth to reply, but nothing comes out, or rather nothing but a strange mumble. The sound reminds Sewall of noises he has made himself when he has been speaking in a dream and woken up halfway through, and so has been able to listen for a moment to his own dream language in the daylight world.

'Abigail Williams!' says Hathorne. Abigail does not start

like Mary Walcott and Elizabeth Proctor did—even surprise can be unsurprising eventually. 'Does this woman hurt *you*?'

'Yes, often.'

'Does she bring the book for you to sign?'

'Yes, sir, and she tells me that her maid has signed it already.'

Mary Warren, the jade as Proctor described her (as well as 'little bitch'), burbles something incomprehensible just as Ann Putnam did, and collapses into a fit, foaming at the mouth, her eyes rolled up so only the whites are showing.

Elizabeth Proctor stares at Abigail Williams, then holds out her arms towards the little girl. 'Dear child,' she says in a cajoling voice, as a mother might do if her patience has been stretched to the limit and she's making a final effort to keep her temper or her wits. 'Dear child, it is not so. Dear child, remember there is another judgement than the one in this court.'

Immediately both Abigail Williams and Ann Putnam fall into fits. Hathorne turns towards Elizabeth Proctor and glares, making it clear he doesn't like to hear this court slighted, even by comparison with a higher one. But then Ann Putnam, still unconscious and drooling, raises an arm and points towards the ceiling. She speaks in a voice blurred by spittle. 'Look,' she says, even though her own eyes remain closed, 'there's Goody Proctor, up there upon the beam.'

'No!' cries Elizabeth Proctor in despair.

'No!' comes that deep voice from the main body of the hall, her husband. 'No! These girls are lying! This child is lying!'

'Mr. Proctor,' says Justice Danforth, 'the child is not even conscious. How can she be lying?'

'You can lie with your eyes shut as well as open,' says Proctor. '*All* these children are lying.'

Pandemonium. One of the girls cries out; 'He's a wizard!', pointing at Proctor, who rises from his seat and strides towards the front. He is pointing back, at his accuser, then at Ann

Putnam, then at all the other children in turn, shouting, Liar! Liar! as he does. Children shriek and fall to the ground, as if his pointing arm is a gun and *Liar* the detonation. Sewall raises his eyes from this bedlam up towards the roof beam. Did something shift abruptly in the shadows, the way a bird sitting on a branch suddenly moves itself an interval to the right or the left by a mere shrug of its shoulders?

'Ann Putnam!' cries Hathorne. 'Tell us who has just hurt you!'

Ann Putnam rises to her feet. She lifts her arm with a strange authority, lifts it slowly, in a manner that makes Proctor's pointings look suddenly baffled and frenetic. 'It is Goodman Proctor who hurt me,' she says.

There's a gasp from the crowd. Proctor stops in his tracks, clearly stunned. His pointing arm turns back from its targets to his own chest. 'Me?' he mouths.

'Goodman Proctor! Goodman Proctor!' the other children call. 'Goodman Proctor! Goodman Proctor!'

Suddenly a piercing voice cuts through the chorus. 'There he is!' An arm is pointing upwards. 'There he is, up in the roof! There he is, up there on the beam!'

All heads move together to peer upwards—except Sewall's. He stares in fascination as John Proctor's own head moves backwards like all the others, part of that silent chorus of craning faces, in order to inspect *himself* up there in the rooftrees. It must be like peering into the depths of a terrible mirror, one that shows not the blemishes of a complexion but the deepest perversions of the spirit itself. Then Sewall's own gaze follows all the others up to the timbers once more.

There they are, perched side by side. He can't see them, but after all they inhabit the invisible world, so that is how it must be. The children can see them because they have sharper senses, in the same way as they can hear the screaming of bats. And they have the advantage of being more recently in, more proximate to, the invisible realm. He has observed in respect of his own babies and children, both the still living and the now dead, how close is that veil or curtain or door to where children play their games or lie in their cots.

He pictures these Proctors as man and wife birds, with sharp beaks and raptor eyes, peering down at the throng just as the throng, corporeal Proctors included, peer upwards towards *them*.

Now Abigail Williams cries, 'There he goes! There goes Goodman Proctor.'

'Where's he going?' a querulous voice calls out.

'He's going to Mrs. Pope!' cries Abigail Williams.

There's a yapping sound from a small fat woman standing near the front of the audience. She is wearing a large grey shawl and voluminous rusty brown gown that falls all the way to the floor, so that she looks like a little volcano running with lava. At Abigail's words she falls back into her pew, clutching at her bosom.

Another of the afflicted girls—Sewall cannot see which one it is—has taken up the call now. 'There goes Proctor!' she cries. 'He's going to lift up Mrs. Pope's legs!'

Sewall is astounded to see Mrs. Pope slide sideways in her seat as her short legs slowly rise. Her skirts hang down from them, revealing two plump calves in green knitted stockings

'Goodman Proctor, what do you say to these things?' asks Hathorne in a loud triumphant voice, pointing towards Mrs. Pope with the unfortunate effect that the word *things* seems to be referring to her legs.

Proctor's face has gone red as claret, with rage or shame. 'There's nothing I can say. This is all nonsense.' He waves a hand at the strange tableau, a woman leaning back in the pew of a meeting house with her legs sticking up into the air while the crowd stares at her in wonder and the girls at the front of the building cry and moan and fall down. 'I am innocent of this,' he says, shaking his head. 'It's all a . . .' He doesn't say what it is. It's evident he has no word for it.

'That is what *you* say,' says Hathorne, 'but the Devil says otherwise. The children could see you were going to lift Mrs. Pope's legs before you even did it. The Devil is bringing you out.'

Suddenly Mrs. Proctor speaks up. She is no longer supporting Goody Cloyse who is sitting in the chair beside her staring off into the far distance. 'Why would the Devil bring him out,' Mrs. Proctor asks, 'if John is in league with him, as these children claim?' Sewall is taken aback at seeing her come to the defence of her husband even though she has just seen his spectre molesting another woman, further evidence that they are allied in evil, side by side on their perch.

As soon as she has spoken, Abigail Williams and Ann Putnam rush towards her across the front of the meeting house. Seeing them approaching, Elizabeth Proctor rises to her feet, but in any case they stop short just before they reach her, as if colliding with a pane of glass. Mrs. Proctor resumes her chair again. Abigail draws back her arm as though about to throw a ball a great distance. Then she clenches her fist and makes as if to strike Mrs. Proctor. Her fist moves slowly slowly through the thickened air towards Mrs. Proctor's head but then her hand unclenches and her fingers gradually open so that in the end all that happens is that their tips gently touch Mrs. Proctor's hood. 'My fingers are burnt!' she cries, and thrusts her hand into its opposite armpit, squeezing it with her upper arm as if to squeeze out the agony like water from a sponge.

Ann Putnam meanwhile flings her own hands up to the sides of her head as if afflicted with a terrible headache. She sinks to her knees, crying with pain.

Sewall watches the suffering of the two girls in horror. It seems to be his fate to look on helplessly while children suffer.

CHAPTER 11

When the proceedings have come to an end, Danforth turns to his fellow justices. 'I don't think we need to retire to consider our decision,' he states.

'I think we do,' Sewall says.

'But it is simply a matter of yea or nay.'

Sewall takes a deep breath. 'Nevertheless,' he says, pointing at the expectant crowd. The judges' deliberations, even if brief and perfunctory, need to be made independently of the emotions swirling about this building.

Mr. Danforth looks up and down the row of justices, but the others all stare down at the tables in front of them. He sighs. As if this is a cue Mr. Noyes rises from his pew, steps over, and offers them the use of his parsonage just next door. The justices process up his garden path, past his freshly pruned roses. He scurries round them and shows them into the parlour. Having made sure everyone is settled, he exits backwards through the far door, as if wanting to keep them all in his sight until the last possible moment

Mr. Parris sharpens his quill. Mr. Danforth clears his throat. But before the business can begin, here is Mr. Noyes again, accompanied by Anne, the two of them each bearing a tray with bottles and wineglasses on it, and dishes of little biscuits. The refreshments have appeared so quickly they must have been set out in advance in hopes that the judges would adjourn here. Mr. Danforth begins to wave his hosts away but thinks better of it and sighs instead. It will be quicker to let them serve everyone without argument.

'It was dreadful in there, wasn't it?' Noyes whispers to Sewall as he pours him his glass. 'The suffering of those poor children. I shall go and pray now,' he announces to the company, 'that God will guide you in your deliberations.' Once again he backs out of the room, pointing towards the bottles and nodding as an indication that the justices should feel free to recharge their glasses when required.

Mr. Danforth gives him a few seconds to get well clear of the far side of the door, then at last begins the discussion. 'After what we have seen, I believe that the matter is clear-cut,' he says. 'I must remind you of Sir Matthew Hale's remarks, in his printed observations on those witches he condemned in England in, I think, 1681. Though the Devil cannot himself be brought to earthly trial, those covenanted servants by means of whom he performs his mischief are answerable to the full rigour of the law. I suggest we agree on the following mittimus, that Sarah Cloyse, Elizabeth Proctor, and John Proctor, for high suspicion of acts of witchcraft performed on the bodies of . . . and so on and so forth, should be committed to prison by order of the Council and so on and so forth. We can sign the paper and leave the details and correct form for Mr. Parris to insert later on, under Mr. Hathorne's guidance.' Mr. Hathorne nods. Mr. Parris scratches with his quill. 'In the meantime we should return into the examination room and announce that the three accused are to be remanded in custody awaiting trial.'

There's a murmur of agreement. Sewall lifts his glass for another sip (Mr. Noyes's wine is excellent; Sewall himself imported it from France on his behalf, before the outbreak of King William's War) but freezes just as the glass is poised against his lips. *Three* accused? John Proctor?

His heart thumps. Perhaps this is another test.

For a moment he is tempted to let the issue go. Trying to voice an opinion in the teeth of an opposing argument is exhausting, like bellowing into a strong wind, and after the events of today he hardly has the energy for it. Then he lowers his glass. 'Excuse me.'

'Yes, Mr. Sewall,' Mr. Danforth replies, his voice tinged with suspicious weariness.

'How can we remand *three* accused to prison? We have only examined—'

'Mr. Sewall, you are aware of the function of the preliminary examination of accused people in these unusual circumstances. It is a requirement of Massachusetts law that—'

'There *is* no Massachusetts law,' puts in another of the judges, Major Appleton, a tall man with apple cheeks, as though they have been dictated by his name. 'In my opinion that is the cause of this whole sorry affair in the first place. What can anyone expect, what can King William himself expect, God bless him, when laws are in abeyance? The Devil gets a whiff of this state of affairs, he straightaway thinks to himself, now is the time to recruit witches, before the new charter takes effect. He rubs his hands together at the thought of it, down there in hell, and says to himself, now is the time to—'

'Yes, yes, Major Appleton,' says Danforth, 'that may be true in a technical sense, but—'

'That's the very sense the Devil understands. There's nobody more technical than he is. Which is why he's so interested in getting people to sign his book while he can. He follows people around with a pen behind his ear. He—'

'Major Appleton, will you let me proceed?'

'Kah!' exclaims Major Appleton, disappointed at being prevented from exploring the Devil's opportunism any further. He shakes his bewigged head like a spaniel leaving a pond.

'It's a requirement of Massachusetts law that two witnesses are necessary for an accused person to be remanded for trial. In the case of witchcraft allegations this requirement is extremely difficult to fulfil. If you hit somebody on the head, passers-by may testify to your crime. If you invisibly torment someone, who is to say they saw it? That is why, in these cases, the preliminary examination is of particular importance. The crimes the accused were indicted for have been committed again, in full view of the court. The Devil could not resist the opportunity. Or his agents could not.'

'That is not my point,' Sewall complains. 'I perfectly understand the importance of the preliminary examinations in these cases.'

Danforth rests his head in his hands. 'What *is* your point, Mr. Sewall?' he asks.

'It is simply a question of mathematics,' says Sewall. 'We examined two accused, and seem to be proposing to remand three.' This is why, he thinks, it's so important young Sam should become competent at calculating apples.

'This witchcraft develops so fast that we have to run to keep up with it. The examination provided clear evidence of the guilt of three people.'

'There *was* no examination, in Proctor's case.'

'Mr. Sewall, you are talking about when and thereafter, about *now* and about *then*. About how matters are ordered in time. The Devil doesn't listen to the chiming of a clock. He makes his appointments to suit himself. Mr. Parris, perhaps in writing the mittimus you can confront this little difficulty. Then we will meet tomorrow afternoon to view the document and to see if we can agree on it. Is that acceptable to you, Mr. Sewall?'

This is at least a concession, so Sewall assents. If he makes a further protest he will sound as if he is becoming querulous and difficult on purpose, and lose any authority he has gained.

Sewall is staying with Stephen and Margaret. They dine together mid-afternoon, a treat of salmon, neats' tongues, and some lamb. It seems strange to be in a domestic setting again. He feels like a traveller from far away.

Stephen rises to pour him more wine.

'Where is our little maidservant?' Sewall asks in an attempt to seem sociable. 'She brought me my wine the last time I was here.'

'She is sewing her cushion,' Margaret replies. 'She has so far embroidered a tree and a house on it. The tree has two apples and the house has two windows. But it isn't haunted.'

'How can you tell?' Stephen asks her, in the tone of someone encouraging another in the telling of a joke.

'I looked through one of the windows, and saw no Devil inside.' Husband and wife both laugh at this flight of fancy.

Sewall is irritated by their levity. 'So she is cured of her affliction?'

'We believe so,' Stephen says.

'She is just an ordinary little girl,' Margaret puts in. 'Brother Sam, you must never let yourself forget. They are all ordinary little girls.'

'I thought her father might come over to see her this afternoon before going back to Salem Village,' Sewall says.

'He thinks it best to keep away for the time being,' Stephen tells him. 'If she sees him she'll want to return home, and that wouldn't be good for her, given everything that's going on there at the moment.' He shakes his head. 'Not good for anyone. If I had my way everybody in that sorry place would be taken somewhere else and made to sew trees and houses on the covers of cushions.'

'That might leave the door open for the Devil,' Sewall says, feeling this was a good riposte to Margaret's fancy of the window. He is in fact thinking of a sermon Cotton Mather has recently given on the subject of a gap in the hedge through which the Devil can come in.

There's an awkward silence. Stephen and Margaret are

strangely impervious to the threat that has erupted so close by. But now he's broken their mood, Sewall goes on to tell them what Mr. Noyes told him, when he finally left the meeting house.

Mr. Noyes attended Mr. Parris's sermon at Salem Village last week. Just as the Christian settlers used Salem Town as a port of entry into the New World, so the Devil and his cohorts were using that town's *namesake* as their means of entry into New England—but whereas the pilgrims had brought Christianity to a pagan land, these invaders wished to eradicate it and return the country to its wilderness state. Those young girls, Ann Putnam, Abigail Williams, and the rest, were the community's line of defence, Mr. Parris said, despite their youth and frailty, resisting this invasion at the cost of terrible suffering. Sewall nearly adds that this makes them far from 'ordinary little girls' but forbears, for fear of hurting Margaret's feelings.

'I suppose,' says Stephen, 'if you are flying through the air on sticks you might be content to make landfall in a muddy field rather than a nice safe harbour.' He looks through the window at the sea which sparkles in spring sunshine between the two houses opposite, and shakes his head. He still isn't prepared to give full weight to the terrible drama that's unfolding just three or four miles away. 'Let the Devil have that place and be welcome, is what I say.'

Margaret rises and begins to stack their plates. 'We are so looking forward to having dear Hannah here to stay,' she says. 'She's a quiet thoughtful girl, and will be a good example for Margaret to follow, and even more for our Sam, who gets up to all sorts of tricks. Rather like *your* Sam, brother, even though he is so young.'

'Ah,' says Sewall. 'Yes. To tell you the truth, I've been discussing that with Hannah—with wife Hannah, I mean to say.' He can feel himself blushing. Margaret stops in mid-clatter and stares down at him. Stephen looks across the table with

the sort of smile that lingers dimly on a face for a few moments
after the arrival of bad news, like light in the west after the sun
has set.

'And?' asks Stephen.

Before Sewall can answer, in comes Betty to show her finished cushion. For some reason she chooses to trot round to
Sewall first. For a moment he considers peering in through her
house's askew windows in hopes of lightening the atmosphere,
but thinks better of it. Instead, he just congratulates her and
gives her a penny, remembering that unfortunate penny Mr.
Mather gave Joseph as he does so and advising her to spend it
wisely. Then she goes to Margaret and Stephen in their turn.
They both admire her work but she carries her cushion from
the room a little sadly, aware of the distractedness that taints
their praise.

'Hannah and I,' continues Sewall, 'we thought that on
reflection it would be unwise . . . to send our Hannah here.'

'Unwise,' Margaret repeats in a chilly tone. Stephen looks
up at her imploringly, fearful of family estrangement.

Sewall is tempted to blame it all on wife Hannah, to explain
that he himself was enthusiastic about the idea but that she had
vetoed it. But it would be unkind to let her take all the blame.
Then inspiration strikes. 'I realised there would be a problem.'

'Oh yes?' asks Stephen, looking hopefully across the table.

'Look at me. Here I am today, and tomorrow, for this examination. What if my Hannah were here? I can hardly stay away
like Mr. Parris has chosen to, since it's the home of my own
dear brother and sister. I may well have to return to Salem for
further examinations. And the new governor will be here in a
month. The trials themselves will start when he has introduced
the new charter, and they may take place here too. I hope I'll
be able to stay with you when it's necessary. But if my Hannah
were living here too she'd have no opportunity at all to find her
own feet.'

There's an almost audible sigh from Margaret and Stephen, both of them relieved that they don't need to be offended with him and wife Hannah after all. Sewall is equally relieved, more so if anything, since it is even more painful to cause offence than receive it. Strangely, his explanation, though plucked out of the air, has the ring of truth. It would indeed be a hopeless situation for young Hannah if he was incessantly coming back and forth. But this particular difficulty never occurred to him and wife Hannah when they discussed the matter. It's *retrospectively* true.

But, after all, truth must be tenseless.

The following afternoon everyone assembles again in the Salem Town meeting house. Once more the pews are full and a crowd is milling about outside. The judges file in, with Mr. Noyes in his capacity of host taking the head and Mr. Parris the tail. Mr. Noyes then backs towards his place in the front pew with certain flounces and flourishes.

'Are you ready, Mr. Parris?' asks Danforth.

Parris nods. He's a good-looking man, brown-eyed, with an aquiline nose and brown hair which cascades to his shoulders on each side like a wig even though his own, an example of how nature can outdo artifice. There's something aloof about him, however—Cotton Mather informed Sewall he was unpopular with many of his parishioners.

'In that case, Mr. Marshall,' Danforth says, 'call in the accused.'

The marshall and his stewards bring in Goody Cloyse and the two Proctors, John following the women in like the afterthought he is. The afflicted children are not in position today but nevertheless as the prisoners enter there's a threatening rumble from the audience, though one or two voices cry out in support of the Proctors.

'Please read the indictments,' Danforth asks Parris.

Parris begins with Sarah Cloyse. 'On the 11th day of April 1692, by the Grace of God, and divers other days and times, both before as after, certain detestable arts called witch-craft and sorceries, hath used and practised in upon and against Mary Walcott of Salem Village, single woman, by which wicked arts the said Mary Walcott, the 11th day of April and divers other days and times as well before as after is and was tortured, afflicted, pined, consumed, wasted and tor-mented. Sworn witnesses, Mary Walcott, Ann Putnam, Mercy Lewis.'

Mr. Danforth reminds the court that the precedent for tak-ing pining and wasting as proof of witchcraft is to be found in Keble in respect of the Lancashire witch trials in England, and also in Bernard's *Guide to Jurymen*. The judges give their assent and remand her to Boston jail, pending trial. Immediately the marshall brings out a set of shackles and fastens them to Cloyse's arms and legs, while she struggles and weeps. 'There's no need for all this,' she cries out to the judges when she has been chained up, 'I'm a defenceless woman. What harm can I do?'

Mr. Hathorne answers for the justices. 'Not much in your bodily form, perhaps. But these chains are to hamper your spectral flights.'

With that, two of the stewards escort her from the meeting house to a waiting cart outside, each taking an elbow. She walks stiff-legged, clanking as she goes.

The same indictment is read out against Elizabeth Proctor, with the same consequence, except that there are murmurs of discontent from some of the onlookers, and a few cries of 'Shame!' She makes no appeal but stands head bowed and sobbing while the shackles are put on. Then she turns and raises her manacled arms towards her husband. The heaviness of the movement gives it a strange authority, as if she is a yearn-ing statue of herself. Proctor is prevented by his guards from clasping her proffered hand and his face visibly reddens with anger or frustration.

It's strange they can continue to love each other, given their alleged allegiance to Satan. Perhaps marriage is maintained in hell, thinks Sewall. It cannot continue into heaven, because all who go *there* are married to Jesus, and to maintain any earthly tie would be bigamous. But the Devil offers his followers not love but a contract—he always has his pen behind his ear, as Major Appleton claimed. It's a more limited relationship, and might therefore allow his people to maintain *their* relationships with each other after death. Sewall remembers that promise he once made to his own Betty, that he would join her in hell if it should turn out that she isn't one of the elect. Perhaps his wife could come too, and the other children? For a second he has an absurd distracted image of them all resuming their family life for ever more in that dark kingdom. He brushes this fantasy aside—it's as stupid as it is wicked.

There's a pause after Elizabeth Proctor has been escorted out. Mr. Parris clears his throat. 'Before I read out the mittimus relating to John Proctor,' he tells the judges, 'I would like to read another paper which explains its background. I suggest that the documents are filed together.'

Mr. Danforth gives Sewall a quick sideways look. Sewall, pleased to notice this, lowers his brows in order to be fiercely attentive.

Parris's paper begins with detailing a couple of occasions earlier in the month when John Proctor's spectre tormented Abigail Williams. This is obviously intended to demonstrate that there are pre-existing reasons why Proctor *should* have been judicially examined yesterday. Then the document twists round somehow so that it begins to concern the writing of itself.

Parris reads out how the marshall arrived at Mr. Parris's study in the Salem Village manse yesterday evening in order to enquire about the progress of the mittimus regarding John Proctor, but how their conversation was interrupted by Mary Walcott, who was present in order to give evidence of her torments and who suddenly cried out, 'There's Goodman Proctor, he's going to choke me!' and then was immediately choked. (Presumably she was still gasping for air as Parris put the finishing touches to his piece.)

Just as the examinations don't merely assess previous crimes but provide a forum in which new ones occur, so Parris's paper is not just a report of previous hauntings by John Proctor but an account of new ones taking place while it was actually coming into existence. It's as though both yesterday's examination and Mr. Parris's paper have succeeded in parcelling up the witchcraft and delivering it still living to the judges, as an animal in a cage might be presented to a collector, snarling and baring its teeth.

In this respect the examination and the account fulfil the same function, which is perhaps why Mr. Danforth now gives firwall a solemn nod, the sort that's designed to make the recipient nod in turn, which Sewall does.

Parris then reads out John Proctor's mittimus, which takes the same form as those for the women. As he listens Sewall takes note of the temporal words that are part of the required formula: *on 11th of April and divers other times, as well before as after.* . . . Evil has no beginning and no end, just like goodness. Its truth is also tenseless.

The marshall takes John Proctor out to join the two women in the cart, and it soon creaks off towards Boston. They will be benighted long before they arrive, and Sewall wonders where they will stay. The Proctors' inn is conveniently situated for travellers on that road, but its doors are probably closed for now.

CHAPTER 12

D aughter Hannah is to go to stay in the town of Rowley with her mother's cousin William Dummer and his wife, a couple without any children of their own. They decide to break the news to her privately in Sewall's study, and ask Susan to go and fetch her. Timid servant leads in timid daughter. The two girls stand with heads lowered as if waiting to be told off.

'Thank you, Susan,' Sewall says brightly. He and his wife are sitting in chairs on either side of the fire, but the girls have positioned themselves beside his desk, like schoolchildren summoned by the teacher. Susan looks up, bemused, unaware that he is telling her she can go. Young Hannah's hand sneaks over to grasp hers, though whether to give or receive comfort isn't quite clear. Sewall hasn't realised that the two girls have become such friends, but of course Susan is closer to Hannah in temperament than Betty is, being gentle and not tempestuous. 'Susan,' he says softly, hoping not to embarrass her, 'you can leave us now.'

Young Hannah immediately turns towards Susan as if beseeching her to remain. 'But you don't *need* to,' her mother says quickly, seeing this. 'It's nothing bad or secret. We just wanted to tell Hannah that it's time for her to go away for a while. She will live with her Uncle William and Aunt Abigail up in Rowley, so she can get some experience of the world, just like you are doing here, Susan. It's lovely up in Rowley. It's right by Newbury, where Hannah's father comes from.'

Hannah stares at her mother, white-faced with horror.

'You like being with *us*, don't you, Susan?' wife Hannah asks.

'Yes, madam.' Susan's face has gone white in sympathy with her friend's. She and Hannah are still holding hands.

There's a pause, then young Hannah whispers: '*I* like being with us too. That's what I like.' She swallows, and the plunge of her Adam's apple hurts Sewall's heart.

'You will learn all sorts of new things when you're there,' her mother continues. '*You*'ve learned lots of new things since you've been with us, haven't you, Susan?' Susan solemnly nods but at the same time squeezes Hannah's hand harder as if to ask forgiveness for this tiny betrayal.

'But I don't want to learn lots of new things,' Hannah protests. 'I can learn lots of new things if I stay *here*.' She gives a little gasp, as if suddenly becoming aware of having contradicted herself. Then a tear rolls down each of her cheeks.

'Dear child,' Sewall says. 'You're thirteen now. It's time you saw more of the world. You can't stay with us for ever and ever.'

'I *want* to stay with you for ever and ever,' she says. 'I don't want to see more of the world. I don't want to get married. I just want to live here, with you and Betty and Joseph and Mary, and with Sam if he was at home.'

'You don't have to get *married*, dearest,' wife Hannah says. 'Just stay with the Dummers for a while and then come back. That's all you have to do."

'You know I visited Uncle Stephen and Aunt Margaret over in Salem the other day,' Sewall reminds her. 'Well, they have a girl living with them called Betty Parris. She's much younger than you, and she's having a lovely time. She embroidered a cushion with a house on it.'

'She's a witch, that's why she's staying with them. *I'm* not a witch. I've never done any witch magic in my whole life. And

I'm hopeless at sewing. If I wanted to learn sewing properly I could learn it here."

'Betty Parris isn't a witch,' Sewall tells her. They have avoided mentioning her within earshot of the children. It's amazing how stories get around. 'None of those girls are witches. They are afflicted children. They have been *fighting* the Devil, not signing his book.'

'I've never even *seen* the Devil and I never want to. I don't want to sign his book and I don't want to fight him either. I just want to stay THE—WAY—I—AM.' She says this last not loudly but certainly in capital letters, with a pause between each word. Wife Hannah goes over to her daughter and embraces her. Immediately, young Hannah begins to sob loudly. Sewall realises how tall she has become—almost the same height as her mother—so that the raw childlike sounds seem incongruous.

Susan, standing to one side, suddenly looks very alone. She's crying too. It occurs to him that she must find it hard living away from her own family, as she has done for several years. Of course, she has a living to earn while Hannah is only going off in order to be improved (indeed Sewall will pay a small monthly amount to cousin Dummer to cover her keep). There's no way back to her family for Susan, though he can hardly remind his daughter of her own advantage in this respect within the servant girl's hearing.

Eventually Hannah quietens down. She's essentially an obedient child. 'You must not forget your prayers while you're away,' Sewall reminds her.

'No, father.' She is in fact punctilious in her devotions, but seems content to leave complex matters for others (like her sister Betty) to wrestle with. She's never expressed any concern about the question of election. Is that a sign of saintly innocence or spiritual complacency? Certainly in general she is innocent rather than complacent, so Sewall hopes for the best.

'And we won't forget to pray for *you*,' he tells her. This is a mistake because she immediately begins crying once more at the thought of those faraway prayers.

A few days later a letter arrives. It's from Thomas Putnam, father of one of the afflicted children. Or rather it's a copy by Mr. Parris, acting in his capacity of court clerk, of a letter Putnam addressed generally to the judges. Sewall stares at it in bafflement. He has spent many years pondering Revelation but this is prophecy close at hand, in the here and now. 'We, beholding continually the tremendous works of Divine Providence, not only every day but every hour,' declaims Putnam, ' thought it our duty to inform your Honours of what we conceive you have not heard, which is high and dreadful. A wheel within a wheel, which makes our scalps tingle.'

Strangely, Goodman Putnam doesn't go on to explain what it is that the justices have not yet heard, this wheel within a wheel. The letter leaves off abruptly with that tingling of scalps. Next day Sewall is summoned to Dorchester to speak with Mr. Stoughton. He takes the letter along to show him. It's a miserable ride, in pouring rain. 'Ah,' says Stoughton, by way of greeting. He's sitting in his study behind a desk that's empty save for a quill, a sand box, a sheet of paper. The room is cool, no fire lit. Sewall tries to express in his gaze a readiness, if not a need, even a yearning, for some refreshment after his miry journey, but Mr. Stoughton is impervious, not being himself a man prone to yearnings.

'I received a strange letter yesterday,' Sewall says, taking it out of his pocket and placing it on the top of the desk. It is damp and smeary now, compromising its ordered surroundings.

Mr. Stoughton glances down at it and then looks up at Sewall with grey unsurprised eyes. 'I've seen a copy of this already,' he says.

'Do you know what the news is, then? This wheel within a

wheel?' Mr. Stoughton will be privy to wheels within wheels if anyone can be, having wheels within wheels of his own.

'Have you ever seen a man with a performing monkey?' Stoughton asks.

'Yes,' Sewall answers cautiously.

'Well, this nobody, this Putnam, is one of those fathers who thinks his child is a performing monkey. He's just a bankrupt farmer who believes his day in the sun has finally arrived.'

'I see,' says Sewall, somewhat bewildered.

'His child, Ann Putnam, has seen George Burroughs.'

'What? But he's in Maine.'

'He visited her in spectral form, I mean.'

Sewall stares speechlessly at Mr. Stoughton as the implications of this sink in.

'Exactly,' says Stoughton. 'Mr. Burroughs. The minister. That's why we don't need the distraction of Ann Putnam's father tooting his trumpet and banging his drum. The evidence is telling enough without a fanfare.'

Sewall was at Harvard with George Burroughs, though the two of them were never close. Burroughs is a dark-complexioned, stocky, saturnine man, short of stature, who kept himself to himself. Sewall was surprised he ended up in the ministry since he seemed too worldly for that calling, not in the sense of being acquisitive for the world's goods but because he seemed so densely composed of material substance as to leave no nook or cranny for a spirit to flourish. He went to Salem Village as its second minister, following in the steps of Sewall's old friend James Bayley. Like his predecessor and indeed his successors, Burroughs found it hard to manage on the wretched stipend that came with the appointment. His wife died and he had to borrow money to pay for her funeral. He then tried to leave his post without repaying the loan and was imprisoned overnight in the Salem lockup before going back to another ministry in Maine.

Sewall knows all this because Burroughs and his new wife visited Boston for a few days in 1685 and came to dinner, where he recounted the whole sorry story with considerable bitterness. Sewall got the impression that Burroughs lives in a state of bitterness just as a codfish inhabits a state of brine. Hannah didn't take to him either, and thought his wife looked put upon.

'What did he say? Or do?' Sewall asks Stoughton.

'Ann says a man dressed as a minister came to her in the night of April twentieth, the day before her doting father penned his letter. Choked her. Racked her. Told her he had given up endeavouring to bring children to God, and had engaged himself to bring them to the Devil instead. Wanted her to sign the book.' Stoughton recounts all this in a curiously dry tone. 'She didn't recognise him, of course, since she would hardly have been born when he served in Salem Village.'

'How did she know who he was in that case?'

'She asked him and he told her. That's what makes it so compelling. She had no previous knowledge of the man's existence and only discovered who he was during the haunting itself. He boasted to her that he had murdered his first two wives.

'*Two* wives? I knew his first wife had died, and I met the second. I had no idea she had died too.'

'He's now on his third, God preserve her. But that proves the point. You are acquainted with the man and yet you haven't been able to keep count of all his wives up there in Maine. This child knew nothing of him, or of them, yet has the tally.'

A minister. This is the most serious subversion of religion that can be imagined. From the very beginning of the witch infestation, the Devil has been prowling about the Salem Village manse in hopes of suborning the minister and thereby regularising, even *legitimizing*, his observances, if such a term can be used for diabolical practices. Mr. Parris must have resisted successfully, probably because he was deep in prayer at the times in question. Moreover, any possibility of a soft entrance, to use Mr. Mather's term, via his daughter Betty has been abruptly blocked by the intervention of Stephen and Margaret, so the Devil had to cast about for an alternative.

Mr. Stoughton now explains his purpose in summoning Sewall. Once again it's necessary to give an examination more gravitas than Mr. Hathorne and Mr. Corwin can provide alone. At the same time it's important that Mr. Burroughs's hearing, which will take place in the Salem Town meeting house, doesn't become a vulgar spectacle, so it will be held *in camera* and there will only be two extra judges, men who can be relied on to conduct proceedings with discretion and propriety: Mr. Stoughton himself, and Mr. Sewall.

This is a pivotal moment. Religion is being undermined. Perhaps the whole colonial adventure of New England is in the balance. And Mr. Stoughton has entrusted him, Sewall, with the responsibility of making a judgement on matters of such overwhelming importance. The business of the pirates seems securely past. Mr. Stoughton respects his integrity. Mr. Stoughton trusts him as a man of independent mind, one able to stand on his own two feet. Still hungry and thirsty, but exuberant nonetheless, Sewall puts on his still wet coat, mounts his still damp horse, and trots out into the still raining day.

He's almost at the Dorchester town line when doubt suddenly strikes him. Perhaps Mr. Stoughton has once more chosen him for precisely the opposite reason from what he assumed, has chosen him as a colleague because he was *not* independent, and *didn't* stand on his own two feet?

George Burroughs's examination is scheduled for May 9th. Sewall decides to take his daughter Hannah up to Rowley on the seventh, stay the night there, and then make his way to Salem Town next day. He rents a little carriage so Hannah can feel pampered, and Bastian trots along beside them on another horse so that tomorrow he can take the carriage back to Boston while Sewall takes over the horse to ride to Salem.

The Dummers are decent, hardworking people. They lack the capacity for merriment that Stephen and Margaret possess, and in his heart of hearts Sewall would like an admixture of jollity to leaven his daughter's reserved nature. Still, if she won't learn to laugh in Rowley, she might at least discover how to be sensible, even practical.

William Dummer greets them at the front door. He's a short man with a large bulging forehead (even though not given to scholarly pursuits). He is wearing rough farming clothes and is covered in fine golden dust. He explains he has been cleaning the scrag-end of last year's hay from his barn. His wife hasn't come out to greet them because she has a sore throat.

'Ha!' cries Sewall, 'we know a remedy for that. Don't we, my dear?'

'Do we?' asks Hannah.

'Of course we do. Mr. Hobart gave us the recipe when *your* throat was sore.'

'I made Abigail drink a porringer of sage tea this morning,' Dummer explains.

'Sage tea is excellent for easing the soreness. And it can bring on a kindly sweat. But the cure, Mr. Hobart informed me, is best brought about by taking the inside of a swallow's nest, stamping it flat, and wrapping it round the throat.'

Dummer looks taken aback at the radicalness of this solution. 'And did that cure you?' he asks Hannah.

'No,' she replies.

'We couldn't find a swallow's nest conveniently to hand,' Sewall explains.

'I don't think I will be able to either,' Dummer says.

'Hannah can help nurse her back to health. Can't you, Hannah?'

'I wouldn't want to give her a sore throat as soon as she arrives in Rowley,' says Dummer, noting Hannah's recoil at this suggestion.

Sewall rises early the next day but cousin William, keeping farmer's time, is up and out already. And Bastian is seated in the carriage outside the front door, all set to take his leave. Just as he is about to crack the whip Hannah hurries out, her clothes on higgledy-piggledy and her eyes small and blind-looking without their glasses. She clutches the carriage wheel as if to prevent it moving off.

Sewall unpicks her fingers then holds her hand as if his only motive was affection (which in a sense is true). 'Goodbye, Bastian,' she says forlornly.

'Goodbye, miss. I'll come and fetch you back home, when it's time. If the master permits.'

'We'll come together, won't we, Bastian?' Sewall replies heartily. 'To bring my maid home when she's ready.'

'I'm ready now,' Hannah says.

'We will bring her home *sure* enough,' says Bastian.

This assurance is rewarded by a little animal noise from Hannah, a combined sob and sigh. As the carriage departs, she says, 'It's not fair. Bastian's going home and I have to stay here.'

'Shush,' Sewall warns as Abigail Dummer comes out of the door. Her throat is somewhat better, she explains, but Hannah should not give her a kiss in case of infection. Hannah doesn't seem minded to offer a kiss in any case.

Cousin Abigail is short and stocky like her husband. She's wearing an apron over her skirts, and carrying a small bell. 'This can be one of your tasks, Hannah,' she says. 'Ringing this bell every morning.' She hands it to the child, who shakes it so unenthusiastically the clapper fails to move.

'What's it for?' she asks, sounding mulish. It's amazing to see how unhappiness and fear can sour a sweet disposition.

'To call my William in for breakfast. Ring it, Hannah,' she says. '*Ring* it.'

The four of them sit down at table together. Cousin Abigail has prepared yokeheg, an Indian dish made from parched corn ground into a powder and mixed with sugar, then served with milk. Coupled with the smell of soil cousin William has brought in with him, the porridge brings back Sewall's childhood days in nearby Newbury and he feels a pang at the scattering of his own family: first Sam, now Hannah. At the end of the meal he says that he must be off to Salem.

'You have pressing business there, then?' cousin William asks.

'Indeed.'

'This witchcraft foolishness, I suppose.'

The demeaning word makes Sewall indignant for a moment. But he realises it is open to interpretation. William could simply be implying that witchcraft is a foolish activity, which it is, foolish as well as malignant. All sin is foolish, after all. And in any case William's no-nonsense attitude (much like brother Stephen's) is precisely what should make him an effective guardian for Hannah. She will be distanced from the whole crisis in a place where soil and crops and cows leave no room for horror to get in.

He says his thank-yous and takes his leave, giving his daughter a quick kiss on her tear-stained cheek before mounting his horse. She clasps hold of his boot just as she previously grasped the carriage's wheel, but this time Sewall can't reach down far enough to loosen her grip. Instead he jerks his foot backwards in a kind of reverse kick, hating the necessary roughness of the action. Cousin Abigail rushes forward and takes Hannah's arm, clasping it under her elbow in a combination of affection and restraint. Sewall immediately shakes the bridle and trots off, waving one arm as he does so (he isn't secure enough to turn his head for goodbyes).

'No, father, come back! Take me!' his daughter cries. Then, no, no, no!, as she understands he is determined. He persuades the horse to a gallop in order to bring this horrible occasion to an end as quickly as possible, but Hannah's *no-no-nos* continue to resound, like the frantic cawing of a crow.

CHAPTER 13

Only the four judges, Mr. Parris, and the marshall are present in the Salem meeting house. Mr. Stoughton is just about to begin proceedings when Mr. Parris rises to his feet. 'What is it, sir?' Stoughton asks.

'A prayer, before we begin.'

'Ah, yes. Good.'

A prayer is always desirable, of course, but Sewall finds himself regretting the absence of Mr. Noyes. The fact that it is Mr. Parris who delivers it seems to give him authority over the proceedings, and that makes Sewall uneasy. 'Amen, amen,' Stoughton says at the end, brisk as always, 'now let us begin the examination.'

The marshall goes through the left-hand door and reappears with Mr. Burroughs, escorting him to a chair facing the judges. Mr. Parris administers the oath, and then Stoughton tells the accused to be seated. Stoughton turns to Mr. Hathorne and gives him a nod.

'Mr. Burroughs, when did you last partake of the Lord's Supper?' asks Mr. Hathorne.

At the marshall's command, Mr. Burroughs rises to his feet again and stands beside his chair with a hand resting on its back. He has black short hair, jowly cheeks. He wears a black coat and breeches, both of them faded and threadbare—ministerial sobriety (though no falling bands). He stares at Mr. Hathorne for some time without answering. Finally says, 'I can't remember.'

Sewall can't believe his ears. A minister of religion who can't recall when he last received communion! Of course Salem Village church hadn't been admitted to the full covenant when he served there so he wasn't able to administer communion himself, but it seems extraordinary that he hasn't partaken of it elsewhere. Sewall glances over at Mr. Parris, who has stopped scratching with his quill and is staring at Burroughs with a look of triumph. Here is Mr. Burroughs to prove the text of his sermon, a minister who neither ministers nor is ministered to. *Have I not chosen you twelve, and one of you is a Devil?*

'Are your children baptised?' asks Hathorne.

Again there's a pause. Finally he replies: 'No.'

'No?'

'I think the eldest one was.' The man seems remote, hardly to be present in the room at all. Indeed he seems hardly to be present in his own life.

Hathorne performs one of his rapid changes of direction. 'Mr. Burroughs, it has come to our attention that your second wife, before her death, complained that your house in Maine was haunted. Was it?'

Again a pause. 'No.'

'So she was lying?'

He shrugs.

'Are you calling your late wife a liar?'

'She *believed* it was haunted.'

'But it wasn't?'

'No.'

'So why did she think it was?'

Silence. Then: 'I admit there were toads.'

The silence seems to deepen. Then Mr. Stoughton speaks. 'May I remind the court of the account in Sir Matthew Hale's *Trials of Witches*, concerning the case of Amy Duny? A toad was found in the blanket of her victim, one Durrant, and was held in the fire till it made a horrible noise.' Scratch scratch goes Mr. Parris's pen, recording the toads.

'Mr. Burroughs, do you recall a barrel of molasses?'

'No.'

'I have an affidavit here from Captain Wormwood.' Burroughs sighs on hearing the name. Clearly he is no friend of Captain Wormwood. 'He says that on one occasion you inserted your finger in the bunghole of a barrel of molasses and then lifted it from the ground.'

'Which finger?'

Mr. Hathorne peers at the document on the desk in front of him. 'The middle finger,' he says finally.

'I did not.'

'Which finger *did* you insert, then?'

'None of them. What need would I have of a barrel of molasses?'

'I imagine you would have need of a *gun*, up there in Maine with an Indian hiding behind every bush? A good big gun?'

Burroughs shrugs his shoulders, concealing the fact.

'Captain Wormwood says that at another time he saw you insert your finger in the barrel of a gun, your middle finger, a gun with a six-foot barrel, and then lift it from the ground.'

Burroughs holds his hand in front of his face then inspects his middle finger as if to check whether it might have been boasting of how it performed these feats single-fingered while its owner's back was turned. When he raises his head to return Mr. Hathorne's stare he is looking mildly amused. 'I lifted my gun by the trigger guard as many men are able to do.'

'I think it is time to bring in the accusers,' says Stoughton wearily. 'This is just yes-no, tit for tat. It's getting us nowhere.'

The marshall hurries to the right-hand door, opens it, issues instructions. The girls enter in single file, the steward bringing up the rear. The first to bear witness is little Ann Putnam. Her collar is starched white as is the apron over her brown skirts. 'Tell us what you saw in the night-time, Ann,' asks Hathorne.

'I was in bed. It was the middle of the night. Then I saw them. They came into the room.'

'Who were they?'

Ann glances to the right so she does not have to look at the accused. 'Mr. Burroughs's dead wives.' Burroughs lets out a sigh of disgust and turns to his own right so he does not have to look at her.

'Describe them,' Hathorne commands.

She lowers her voice. 'They were in their winding sheets,' she replies. The other girls, standing in a row behind her, gasp and whimper. Mr. Burroughs sighs again, more loudly, as if to express disappointment at the predictableness of this vision.

'Mr. Burroughs,' says Stoughton. He speaks quietly but his voice is loaded like a gun. 'I must ask you to look at the witness.'

Slowly Burroughs turns to face Ann who simultaneously turns to face *him*. At Wells cathedral in Somerset, Sewall saw a clock with manikins who came to life and jousted on the hour and the quarters, and now this choreography brings back the strangeness of that performance. At the precise second Burroughs is facing her squarely, Ann lets out a scream and collapses. Her disappearance exposes the girl behind her to Burroughs' gaze and she collapses in turn, then the next, and so on down the line, one skittle after another, until all the girls lie scattered on the floor.

Mr. Stoughton turns to his fellow judges. 'I think that clarifies the issue,' he tells them. There's a pause while the judges wait for Mr. Parris to complete the mittimus. Hathorne and Corwin talk quietly to each other. Mr. Stoughton has produced a sheet of paper and a quill from a document case and is writing a letter—he's not a man to let time hang heavily.

Suddenly Sewall feels the need to make a point. He glances

down at Mr. Parris, who is sanding the mittimus and giving it a final perusal with a little smile of satisfaction on his face. The document is read out and passed to the marshall. Mr. Burroughs is remanded to Boston prison to await further proceedings. The judges rise to their feet to go their separate ways. Sewall asks for a word with Mr. Stoughton. 'I have a suggestion about the trials,' he says.

'When and if they ever take place,' Stoughton replies grumpily. 'I had hoped the new governor would be here by now. What is it?'

Sewall lowers his voice. 'It occurs to me that perhaps Mr. Parris should not continue to act as clerk. When—and if, as you say—they take place.' Conveniently, Mr. Parris has walked to the opposite side of the building. He now turns, gives a little bow, and leaves by the main door.

'Why not?'

'He is so near the centre of this whole trouble. It began in his manse.'

'You're not——'

'No, no, I'm not. Of course I'm not.' Sewall remembers Stoughton's praise of the appositeness of Mr. Parris's sermon on hypocrisy. He needs to proceed with caution. 'True, Mr. Parris is *near* the centre but he remains to one *side* of the centre, I concede that. But this very proximity gives him—'

'An axe to grind?'

Once again, this is an issue that is clarified in the telling. His doubts have crystallised into a clear sense of a conflict of interest, or at least of a failure of impartiality. 'Mr. Burroughs for example held the very post Mr. Parris now occupies. The situation could easily—'

To his relief Stoughton is there already. 'Have been the reverse?'

Sewall shrugs, not wanting to go too far.

'Perhaps you're right,' says Stoughton. 'It might be better

not to have a minister in that position. We're here to apply the law, not attempt an exorcism. Who would you recommend?'

Sewall is taken aback at Stoughton's willingness to concede the point. He had expected him to want to mull the matter over at the very least. But without thinking he replies: 'My brother, Stephen Sewall.'

Stoughton gives a little start and then smiles at Sewall's promptness, or perhaps at his impertinence. 'Your brother? Why him?'

'He's not a minister. He's a man of affairs. And he disapproves of the whole business of the witchcraft.'

'We all disapprove of it, surely?'

'He disapproves of it as a *topic*. It holds no interest for him.'

'I see. Unlike Mr. Parris he is a *long* way to one side of it.'

'So far to one side that Mr. Parris's little daughter, one of the first girls to be afflicted, was sent to board with him, and has recovered. But he lives in Salem Town, so would be conveniently on hand should the trials take place here. He is well respected. And not just by me.'

Stoughton snaps to a decision. 'In that case I would be grateful if you could sound him out informally, Mr. Sewall. Good day to you.' And suddenly he has gone. He is a man who always has other business elsewhere.

Sewall makes his way to his brother's house, heart thumping. He has shown Mr. Stoughton that he's a man of independent ideas. Then once again it occurs to him that he's proud of the independence of his ideas precisely *because* they have met with Mr. Stoughton's approval. And what kind of independence is it that needs endorsement from the powerful?

Stephen is shocked. He puts down his cup of cider with a thump. Margaret looks nervously at him. It's her turn to worry about family rifts. 'Sam,' Stephen says, 'you know how I feel about the witchcraft. I've no taste for hobgoblins or bugbears.'

'That's the reason I suggested you. We need a man with a cool head to make a record of the proceedings.'

'You want somebody who isn't interested to take an interest,' says Margaret.

Sewall is relieved to get the endorsement of her wit. 'It will need to be a record of what's said and what's seen,' he adds, 'without ought or must or maybe. This witchcraft is a mystical business but the report of the trials must have a hard factual edge for that very reason.'

'I can be cool and hard enough, I suppose,' says Stephen. He taps the edge of his cup and inspects the ripples that flow across the surface of the cider. 'When I'm buying a barrel of fish.' He looks up and smiles at Sewall. 'But how can one tell what's a fact and what's not in this business?'

'The mysticism turns into fact when the Devil reaches from his kingdom into ours. An agitation somewhere else creates an agitation here, and though most of us can't see it we can bear witness to its effects.' Perhaps those afflicted girls, being young and innocent, have an extra sensitivity to the nuances of the wind; they veer towards it like weathercocks, and the rest of us must just observe which way they point. 'It would be your task to make an accurate report of what is witnessed, no more, no less.' He recalls his conversation with Cotton Mather on this topic. 'You won't have to describe the Devil, just the footprints he leaves behind.'

'Hoofprints, surely?' asks Margaret. Again she is trying to give a touch of levity to their conversation, but the image gives Sewall a shiver.

PART 3
THE TRIALS

Our *Sins* are those *Accursed Things*, which by producing of *Breaches* in our *Hedge*, do prove the *Troublers* of our *Land*. Would we have our *Wall* undisturbed? There are then certain *Heads*, I mean *Hearts*, to be thrown over our *Wall* . . .

—COTTON MATHER, *Memorable Passages, relating to New-England* (Boston, 1694)

CHAPTER 14

G overnor Phips's ship, the *Nonsuch*, enters Boston harbour in the late afternoon of 14th May. Her sails are already being lowered and she approaches silently on the glowing gently-rolling water like a vessel in a dream.

Sir William Phips appears on deck as the gangplank is being lowered, resplendent in a blue velvet coat with gold lace, a sword at his hip; beside him the skinny stooping figure of Increase Mather in a plain black coat, his falling bands sparkling bright as they catch the evening sunshine. A long wig descends to his shoulders.

There's a tug at Sewall's elbow, and he turns to see that Bastian has come up beside him. 'Mistress said I'd find you here.'

'What is it, Bastian?'

'Nurse Hurd has come to the house.'

Sewall feels a sudden chill. 'Who—?'

'No, no,' Bastian says. 'Everyone is fine. All the family. It's Goodman Hurd. He's dying, nurse says.'

Goodman Hurd is a tailor, or was. He's about seventy years old, and for the last few years his eyesight has been too poor to allow him to practise his trade. It was sad to see his spectacles grow fatter and his stitches get bigger.

'All right, Bastian, I'll go there. You fetch Mr. Willard in the meantime.' Mr. Willard will be less than delighted to be summoned in this way. He will be preparing tomorrow's sermon, no doubt, and the Hurds are members of the congregation of

Cotton Mather's North Church, not the South. But Mr. Mather will be busy with his father's arrival for the rest of the evening—at this very moment he's rushing up the gangplank to greet him, arms outstretched and his own grey wig cascading on to his shoulders. 'Tell Mr. Willard that my neighbour Hurd needs a final heave toward heaven.'

'A heave toward heaven. Yes sir, Mr. Sewall,' says Bastian, and hurries off through the crowd, Sewall following in his wake.

The front door of the Hurds' little house is open and their goat is standing in the aperture as if on guard. Sewall calls for Nurse Hurd and she replies from upstairs, telling him to come in. Sewall cajoles the goat but she remains obstinately in position, glaring at him with those strange horizontal irises goats have. Finally he tugs at one of her horns and she gradually stumbles forward, bleating at the indignity of it, until he is able to slip past her.

'Come up, Mr. Sewall,' calls Goody Hurd, her voice weak and plaintive. She's waiting for him at the top of the stairs, in a clean grey gown with cap and apron, her plump cheeks shiny with tears.

'I've called for Mr. Willard,' he tells her, 'since Mr. Mather is aboard the governor's boat, greeting his father.'

'You're a kind man, Mr. Sewall,' she says. She releases his hand and opens the door of the bedroom. 'Husband, here is Mr. Sewall to see you.'

There's silence for a moment and then in a fierce voice Goodman Hurd replies, 'Hold your tongue, woman!'

She jumps back as though shot, and stands quite still for a few moments to accommodate the rebuff. Then turns to Sewall, wringing her hands. 'I'm so sorry. He's not himself at present.'

'His voice sounds robust,' Sewall tells her by way of comfort. 'Perhaps it's best if we wait for Mr. Willard.'

They stand awkwardly facing one another on the little

landing in the dim evening light. After a long few minutes
there are noises from below, then Mr. Willard's deep angry
voice, 'Go away, horrible goat! Leave us, madam!'

'That must be Molly,' whispers Nurse Hurd, and gives a
nervous laugh.

Then quieter, calming tones, Bastian, who has a way with
animals. The goat utters an affectionate bleat, and now Mr.
Willard is coming up the stairs. 'I'm sorry to hear of your husband's state, Goodwife,' he says, infusing a little kindness into
his tone (to Sewall's relief).

'Thank you, sir.' She turns to the bedroom door. 'John, Mr.
Willard the minister is here to see you!'

Again a pause; again he calls back, 'Hold your tongue,
woman!'

'Husband! Mr. Willard is here to see you. And Mr. Sewall.'

'Hold your tongue, woman!' Goodman Hurd cries a third
time.

A third time! The words of Jesus come into Sewall's head:
'The cock shall not crow this day, before that thou shalt thrice
deny that thou knowest me.' Thrice John Hurd has rejected
the opportunity to pray and receive spiritual consolation.
Sewall thinks of the goat guarding the Hurds' front door, with
its harsh odour and strange eyes. Many speak of goats as the
Devil's beast, or at least as one of them.

'Let me alone!' cries John Hurd. Maybe that is a fourth
rejection, in which case the analogy with the gospels doesn't
apply. Or maybe it is merely an extension to the third, in which
case it does.

'I wish to pray with you,' counters Mr. Willard.

'My spirits have gone,' comes the reply.

'Instead of complaining about it, you could have used that
same breath to invite us in,' Mr. Willard says in exasperation.

'Oh John!' exclaims Nurse Hurd. Mr. Willard strides past
her and opens the bedroom door.

'This is the last time I shall ask you,' he says. 'You are standing in the very suburbs of eternity. Do you wish us to pray with you or not?'

There is another long pause. 'Yes, for the Lord's sake,' John Hurd replies at last.

On 24th May Governor Phips convenes a Court of Oyer and Terminer, meaning to Hear and Decide. This is a court that doesn't deal with the general run of cases but instead is given a particular task, in this instance to handle the witchcraft charges that have been accumulating over the months. William Stoughton is to preside and a further eight judges have been appointed to its bench, including Jonathan Corwin and John Hathorne, the two men who conducted the examinations in the meeting house of Salem Village, Nathaniel Saltonstall, Wait Still Winthrop, who opposed Sewall over the pirates' reprieves, and Sewall himself. That number should ensure that all relevant questions are raised and obviate the need to have lawyers in court representing the prosecution or defence.

Governor Phips takes his place at the lectern and scans the justices with the hurried impatient eyes of a man of action. 'Before my Court of Oyer and Terminer begins to sit on the witchcraft cases,' he says, 'I proclaim a fast to be held throughout this province of Massachusetts Bay.' He glances down at a paper in front of him to find the wording for the fast, then rattles off the grave instructions as if they are a mere matter of form: 'Its purpose being to seek the Lord that He will rebuke Satan and be a light unto His people in this day of darkness.' He looks up and once more surveys the company with that challenging look of his. 'Amen, gentlemen,' he concludes.

'Amen,' the gentlemen repeat.

Sewall spends the fast day in his study. He prays on his knees for several hours. Gradually the pain of resting his weight on bare boards begins to consume his attention. From now on, two conversations take place at the same time. The first is with God, on the subject of the witchcraft crisis that is overtaking New England. Sewall hopes that the Lord will vouchsafe to dwell with his people and not break up their housekeeping. The other is with Sewall himself, on sundry matters.

One is the pain in his knees. Would the use of a cushion to ease the discomfort be a popish luxury or simply a practical way of prolonging his devotions?

Also he thinks of his dear wife Hannah, who is somehow able to be both good and sensible at the same time, which ought to be possible for all of us, since God has not sown discord and contradiction in the world—those elements have been placed there by His enemy.

The thought of wife Hannah is succeeded by that of *daughter* Hannah, and Sewall wonders how she is faring at Rowley. They have had a number of letters from her, each one tearblotched and complaining. Also one from cousin Abigail, who explains that Hannah is finding country ways and the farming life a little difficult at first, but will settle down in due time. The fast is being observed at Rowley just as it is here, and Sewall is comforted to think that his child, those miles away, may be on her knees this very moment, just as he is. Young Sam, too, up in Mr. Hobart's house in Newton, though his observance is not so assured since he's been known to sneak into the kitchen to restore himself in the middle of a fast.

Sewall can hold out no longer. He shuffles across the room (he daren't unfold his legs just yet to stand up) and takes the cushion from his desk chair. Then he places it in front of his knees, goes on all fours, moves his weight forward on to his arms so he can raise his legs (emitting a huge groan as he does, which he dedicates to the glory of God), places his knees on the cushion and, with a thankful sigh, resumes his praying posture.

At last it's six o'clock. He prays one last prayer, that all the praying that has taken place this day the length and breadth of Massachusetts Bay has edged the province a little toward the light and away from the darkness. Amen, he says, and makes his way downstairs to break his fast.

The family are already assembled in the big hall, waiting for him: wife, little Joseph, baby Mary. On the table are beer, cider, wine, bread, cold meats, biscuits.

'Is Betty still upstairs?' Hannah asks.

'Betty? No.'

'I thought she must be in your study, praying with you.'

'I expect she's in her cupboard.'

'I've looked there. I've looked everywhere. Except for your study. I didn't want to disturb you at prayer. But everywhere else.'

They search the house and garden all over again, calling Betty's name. Sarah and Susan join in too. Sewall remembers the occasion when Sam went missing. Perhaps he's careless of his children?

Just as he's becoming frightened, an old friend appears, John Alden, who has returned from Canada where he has been negotiating the release of hostages being held by the Indians. Alden is one of the original members of the South Church though he misses many meetings because he spends much of his time both as a ship's captain and in the forests of the north, fighting with and against the Indians who live up there. He is a tough, weather-beaten sixty-year-old who smells of the outdoors and has an old battler's pith and shrewdness. He joins the search with a will and he and Sewall walk up and down the road calling out Betty's name, their unconsummated cries dispersing on the evening breeze.

'I must find the constable, and report her missing,' Sewall says finally. 'Why don't you go to the house and wait for me there?'

'No, I'll come with you.'

But before they have taken more than a few paces, there's a clatter of wheels and along comes a carriage travelling at a furious pace, a black man in the driving-seat. As it gets nearer, Sewall sees it's Bastian. Stupidly, he has been so preoccupied that he forgot about his absence, though if he'd been at home Bastian would have been the most diligent of searchers, as he was when Sam went missing. The carriage is one Sewall rented yesterday to take his family out for an airing preparatory to the fast and to his forthcoming preoccupation with the witchcraft trials (they went to the Turk's Head in Dorchester and ate sage cheese, with good beer and cider).

Bastian jerks at the reins and the vehicle comes to a halt. Sewall is about to ask why on earth he is in such a hurry when the carriage door opens and out leaps Betty. He turns joyfully towards her but she immediately bursts into tears, rushes past him and runs towards home. Sewall turns back and looks up at Bastian, who shrugs his shoulders in perplexity at the mysterious ways of the young.

Bastian has been happy to observe the fast, at least in the sense of not having anything to eat. But he was quite unable to spend the whole day in prayer. He can say what he needs to say in a few minutes. The rest will be repetition. He decided to visit a friend called Jane who is a slave belonging to an acquaintance of the Sewalls. Jane had asked if he would come sometime to ease a water-pump which she found difficult to operate when doing the laundry. Since the carriage was still available he rode over in it, intending to return it to the stables just round the corner on his way back.

Finally he repaired the pump and returned to the carriage. When he opened the door he found Betty squashed into a corner, crying her eyes out. She was unwilling or unable to explain what had happened, so he brought her straight back home.

Betty is curled up on her bed, facing the wall. She weeps and says sorry over and over again. Sewall waits as patiently as he is able. It's been a day requiring patience, and despite his concern for his child he can't help thinking longingly about the beer and cider (also the meats and biscuits) waiting downstairs, and about his old friend waiting too. Finally Betty speaks, though her words seem to be constructed out of sobs: 'I wanted to hide.'

'God can find us anywhere.'

'I don't mean God.' Of course she doesn't mean God. The poor child was trying to find somewhere she could observe the fast without any fear of the *Devil*'s advances. 'I went in the carriage because I thought no one would look for me there. And then suddenly it was going along. I was the only one inside it.'

Sewall approaches the bed, puts his hand on his daughter's shoulder. The poor child must have imagined the Devil was driving her off to hell.

'I thought we might be going to the place we hired the carriage from,' Betty continues, 'but we went a long long way instead. Then, when we stopped, I didn't know where we were. After a time I looked out of the window, but it was a strange place. I thought, if I get out here I will be lost, so I stayed where I was. I was there for hours and hours. I think I fell asleep for a while. I was frightened I would never see our house again.'

At last Sewall is able to go downstairs. He briefly explains what's happened. Mr. Alden is amused at Betty's adventure. His own son is long grown and has followed in his father's footsteps (indeed was one of the hostages his father went north to redeem). Then Alden's expression becomes serious again.

'Did your negotiations fail?' Sewall asks him.

'No, not at all. The prisoners were released and I brought them back with me. Elizabeth was delighted to see our John come safely home.'

'And to see you too, I'm sure.'

'Oh, she doesn't worry about me. I'm indestructible, she knows that.' He pauses. 'But there was an unpleasant surprise waiting for me. I've been sent a summons to appear at the witchcraft examinations the day after tomorrow.'

'What? You've been in Canada for these last weeks. How can *you* be accused?'

'If I can go as far as Canada I suppose the Devil can do the same. Or maybe the witches fly there on their sticks. But if they do, I have to say I didn't see them. I hope that my accusers will believe me when I tell them that.'

Sewall thinks for a moment. The trials are due to commence in a week or so. He would much prefer to keep away from the examinations until then—he already feels compromised by his attendance at those two previous sessions. It's not good practice to be present at both ends of a legal process. But John Alden is one of his dearest friends. And it's impossible to imagine him getting involved in witchcraft. Like Sewall's brother Stephen he's too practical, too much a man of action, to countenance such activity. He is a person of the here and now, firmly located in this world. 'I will come with you to the examination,' he says finally. 'Let's see what the accusers have to say.'

John Alden and Sewall enter the Salem Village meeting house by the main doors, along with the rest of the crowds. The girls are already at the front of the dim room (the windows of the shabby building are mostly broken and boarded up). They are crying out and staring round at the people, looking for their tormentor. One of the littlest—Ann Putnam, Sewall realises—slumps forward and is only prevented from falling by a man grabbing hold of her.

'Who's tormenting you?' asks Hathorne.

For a moment Ann seems lost for words. Then the man whispers in her ear and she cries out, 'Alden! Alden! It's Alden who's tormenting me!'

'And where *is* this Alden?' asks Hathorne.

Sewall shakes his head at such a disrespectful manner of speech but the child knows no better and Mr. Hathorne is simply repeating what she said. She raises her arm and points vaguely at the oncoming people. The man behind leans forward again and pushes at her elbow until her pointing is directed squarely at John Alden.

Alden strides with firm purposeful steps to the front of the room and glares at Ann, who shrinks back into the protection of her helper (no doubt her father, the man who wrote that letter about the wheel within a wheel). 'You are playing at juggling tricks,' Alden says. 'You and all the other girls.'

'Please remove your hat, Mr. Alden,' says Hathorne. 'You are in a meeting house now.'

Alden turns to face him. The hat in question is an old leather cap, scratched and battered by all those forays into the northern forests. 'This place is acting as a courtroom for the present,' he replies, 'and as I understand it, all are equal in the eyes of the law. So I think I'll keep it on my head for the time being.'

Hathorne puffs out as if about to rebuke him but thinks better of it, perhaps aware that his future colleague Samuel Sewall is a friend of the accused. 'Mr. Alden, why does this child accuse you?' he asks instead.

'That's a good question, Mr. . . . Examiner,' replies Alden. 'She didn't seem to know *who* to accuse until that man prompted her.'

'Ann,' says Mr. Hathorne, 'have you ever seen Mr. Alden before? In his fleshly form?'

'No, sir.'

'Then how do you know this *is* Mr. Alden?'

'*He* told me.' She points at her father. There is muttering and shuffling throughout the room. Sewall remembers how Mr. Stoughton dismissed Thomas Putnam as an annoying busybody. But of course Mr. Stoughton isn't a father. He,

Sewall, can understand the need to try to guide your suffering daughter to the source of her pain. That's exactly what he would do for Betty, if he was able to.

Mr. Hathorne confers with his colleague, then makes an announcement: 'The examiners would like to discuss this matter *in camera.*'

A baffled silence greets these words. 'In private,' glosses Hathorne.

Everyone is ushered out on to the lane running past the building, accusers included. It's a warm day in late May and after the gloom inside the sun is dazzling. Sewall finds himself in the middle of the crowd while Mr. Alden remains not far from the meeting-house door with a space around him. This gradually clarifies itself into a ring of accusers who begin to sway from side to side, and then to chant *Alden*, *Alden* in time with their movements, then to shout it out. Their movements become exaggerated, turning into a sort of dance.

One of the older ones steps inside the circle. She points at Alden. 'There stands Alden,' she cries out. 'What a bold fellow!' She runs her eyes round the circle. 'He keeps his hat on in front of the judges!'

The others either cheer or jeer at this, Sewall is not sure which. Alden is frozen for a moment. Then he raises his cap, scratches his scalp, replaces it. He shakes his head as if to establish that it's firmly back in position.

'He sells powder and shot to the Indians *and* the French!' Again, those ambiguous cries. 'He lies with Indian squaws!' This time shrieks, mixed with high-pitched laughter. Alden remains apparently impassive. 'He fathers Indian papooses!' Now the girls are squealing and shouting in unmistakeable glee. For a moment they sound like wild Indians themselves.

Sewall recalls Cotton Mather's words about Indians as Apes of God, and the alliance between pagans and witches. Mr. Alden's dealings in the trackless forest have disturbed the girls (and Thomas Putnam too, no doubt). Just as trees twitch and shiver in the wind, so allegiances shift and bend in those dark woods. Your allies one day are united with the French the next. The accusers have heard about Mr. Alden doing business with the Indians (as was his duty, both as a military man and as a father) and assumed the worst. Sewall hopes word of those alleged papooses doesn't get back to Mrs. Alden.

Everyone is summoned back into the meeting house. When they are all in position again the girls cry out that Alden is pinching them. Hathorne tells him to stand upon his chair. The examiners have obviously concluded that the proceedings should continue. Now Hathorne orders the marshall to hold Alden's hands open, so his spirit can pinch no more. Immediately the girls subside. Mr. Alden pulls his hands away in disgust. Still upon the chair, he turns towards the justices. 'Could you explain to me, your honours, why my spirit should come to this village to afflict these children when I never saw one of them in my life before today?'

'Mr. Alden,' interposes Hathorne. 'Please look once again at the afflicted ones.' Mr. Alden sighs. He steps down from the chair with the litheness of a younger man, not needing to grasp hold of its back, then stands and stares at the girls. His eyes are hard and unblinking, his face calm. Immediately, they begin to shriek and after a few moments fall to the floor, gasping in turn at the shock of impact.

Alden takes a deep reflective breath, then pinches his nose a moment as if considering how best to say this. 'Could you explain to me, Mr. Hathorne, why they plummeted to the ground when I looked at them, but now I am looking at *you* and you remain perfectly steady.' He pauses, puts his head on one side, and inspects Mr. Hathorne with some care, as if to confirm his steadiness. 'It makes me wonder how the providence of God can let those children accuse innocent people.'

'Excuse me, your honours.' Mr. Noyes has scrambled to his

feet immediately in front of Sewall. 'With due deference to you as the examiners, if the providence of God is in question, that is my domain.' He looks round at the assembly to ensure they are endorsing his ministerial responsibility. 'I would like to ask the accused why he's had the impertinence to invoke it in his cause.'

'I—,' begins Alden but is straightaway interrupted.

'The providence of God rewards the virtuous and punishes sinners,' Mr. Noyes announces with some force. 'It has nothing whatsoever to do with accusing the innocent.' That seems to clinch matters for the justices, and Alden is remanded to Boston prison.

As he trots home through the hot afternoon, past fields and villages and country people going about their business, Sewall has the uneasy sense that nothing is as it seems, that up is down, white black, that the world all round him, now shimmering in early summer heat, is in fact nothing more than an insubstantial curtain or covering; and whatever lies beyond it is stirring into life, preparing to emerge into the day.

CHAPTER 15

P ies!' shouts the pie-man. Nearby a beer-seller with a barrel on a handcart is calling, 'Beer!' In the distance a ship flies up the coast under curved white sails.

People have come from every walk of life for the opening of the trials, countrymen and women in shawls and smocks, old dames smoking pipes and their gnarled men in fustian frocks or deerskin jerkins, tradesmen in doublets and breeches, wealthier people from Salem and Boston with brass buttons to their waistcoats or virago sleeves to their dresses. As Sewall waits in line with his eight fellow judges he is conscious of the way the bright scarlet of their cloaks of office is slashed across the jostling mass like a wound.

There are some familiar faces. Nicholas Noyes is back at the head of the judicial procession—he has been made chaplain to the Court of Oyer and Terminer. Perhaps it's better that his role should be defined in this way—it might prevent him from trying to sum up the proceedings. Samuel Parris has been relieved of his position as clerk, and brother Stephen is stand-ing in his stead at the end of the file, carrying his portable desk and looking surprisingly clerkly for such a bustling and busy person. In the mêlée is another face Sewall knows well. Thomas Brattle, treasurer of Harvard College.

He and Mr. Brattle were in England at the same time. They saw the sights of London and attended a concert at Covent Garden, the first professional music-making either of them had ever experienced. They sailed back to America on the same ship too. Mr. Brattle began spitting blood in the middle of the Atlantic and Sewall nursed him until, to the surprise of both men, he recovered.

And yet they've never quite achieved the bonds of friendship. Mr. Brattle will inspect you with bland blue gaze and a little smile, then quietly dismember whatever it is you have happened to assert. There are sharp lines graven around his mouth, as though that organ is not just articulate but *articulated*, so as to enforce the greatest possible precision in its utterances.

'Good day to you, Mr. Brattle,' Sewall says.

'Good day to *you*,' Mr. Brattle replies. 'Your honour.'

When the crowds have shuffled in, Mr. Noyes steps forward and intones a prayer, that the Lord might guide the judgement of the jury (who have been installed on benches to the right of the judges), inform the wisdom of the judges, and protect the blessed plantation of New England in its time of greatest danger, that the Devil's attempt to pluck out its Christian heart might be thwarted.

The accused is a middle-aged woman called Bridget Bishop who was remanded at one of the earlier examinations. She has a sharp nose and mouth, small black eyes like currants and, bursting from under her little cap, long straggly hair that's turning from dark brown to grey, giving it an unclean look. She is wearing a grey dress with a white apron and shawl

The court hears there have been rumours about her for a very long time. Ten years ago a little girl called Priscilla developed fits after Bishop had come to her parents' house to demand payment of a debt. As soon as the front door shut behind the unwelcome visitor, Priscilla began screaking (said her father in his country idiom), and Sewall can hear that sound biting into his soul like a saw (little Hull had screaked in *his* fits). The child died two weeks later.

When Bishop was thwarted in a land transaction (she's a businesswoman on a petty and local scale, just like Goody Osborne, now awaiting trial), a sow belonging to the other party went mad and began knocking its head against a fence. Dolls with pins in them have been found up the chimney of a house she formerly owned. She once changed somebody's black piglet into a thing like a monkey. She had an argument with a farmer and then his cart got stuck in a hole that appeared out of nowhere, right in the middle of a meadow that up till then had been flat as a pancake.

Even worse: Bishop's body was examined by a team of nine women with experience in such matters, and a bulge of flesh, otherwise known as a witch's teat, was discovered in a place with no name, the dim and dingy and unfrequented part of the body that lies between the pudendum and the anus. Bishop denied that such a thing was there and accordingly was examined again by the women a few hours later, by which time the teat had disappeared. Compelling demonstration that the Devil was responsible. Who else would be able to remove such evidence once it had been discovered?

But it's the evidence of his own eyes that affects Sewall most. From the moment when Bishop was brought into the court the accusers began to scream, stagger like drunkards, fall over. When she turns her head towards the public in the main body of the hall (perhaps trying to appeal to them), the heads of the afflicted children all turn too, and they cry out in pain at the unwilled movement. When she raises her left hand in a gesture, all the left hands of the afflicted rise up, even though some try to restrain the delinquent limb with their other hand. Every action on the part of Bishop is immediately reflected in the multiple mirrors of those poor children.

A fourteen-year-old called Deliverance Hobbs is called before the jury to testify (she's just a year older than Sewall's daughter Hannah and, cheeks pinked by the occasion, thick spectacles perched on her nose, not unlike her). In a quavering voice Deliverance describes how Bishop, or rather her spectre, came to her and endeavoured to make her sign 'our book'. When she resisted, Bishop took her to a field belonging to Mr. Parris's manse. Here a general meeting of witches had already assembled. They were taking part in a diabolical sacrament of bread and wine, an alternative to the Christian observances conducted in the nearby meeting house. What Deliverance saw, thinks Sewall, remembering his conversation with Judge Stoughton about Mr. Parris's proximity to the witchcraft, was Devilish worship taking place *just to one side* of the communion of saints.

Mr. Stoughton sums up for the benefit of the jury. Bridget Bishop is not on trial for turning a piglet into a monkey or for making a hole in the centre of a meadow. This is merely evidence *suggestive* of witchcraft. What is under consideration are crimes committed by her—in her *capacity* as a witch—against certain children. He raises his head and glares at Bridget Bishop. 'Such crimes took place in full view of the court of examination, and have been repeated today. The children were hurt, tortured, afflicted, pined, consumed, wasted and tormented.'

Mr. Stoughton is about to ask the jury to consider its verdict when his attention is arrested. Mr. Brattle has risen to his feet in the middle of the public seating area. 'Excuse me, your honour,' he says in that quietly spoken, inexorable way of his.

'What is it, Mr. Brattle?'

'I wish to come forward as a witness.'

'The case is concluded. I have just reminded the jury of the charges that they must consider.'

'My testimony relates to the formulation of those charges, your honour.'

'We have already called all the witnesses necessary. The matter has been thoroughly explored.'

'All the evidence has been hostile to the accused. I wish to speak in her defence.'

Silence. Mr. Stoughton stares at Mr. Brattle. Mr. Brattle looks unwaveringly back. Stephen looks up from his desk to see what he should be writing next. Then Judge Saltonstall breaks the deadlock. 'I think, Mr. Stoughton,' he says, 'that we should find out what Mr. Brattle has to say.'

Mr. Stoughton continues to gaze at Mr. Brattle for a few more moments. Very slowly he inclines his head.

Mr. Brattle comes to the front of the room so he can address the jurors directly. 'You heard the charge in the mittimus,' he says. 'That those children across the room were hurt and tormented and so on and so forth. Well, take a good look at them. They seem perfectly all right to me.' The jury all peer over towards the girls, who shift uneasily at this inspection.

'Gentlemen of the jury,' puts in Mr. Stoughton. 'We are not claiming that the children are in torments at present. But think back a few minutes, when the Devil was trying to stop them bearing witness against the accused. It was a different spectacle then.'

'Oh yes,' says Brattle. 'They were squirming on the floor or running about with their arms flapping like chickens chased by a fox.' He looks back towards Mr. Stoughton with his bright blue eyes. 'By a *spectral* fox, I should say. But I was watching them before the proceedings began, when they were as healthy a bunch of children as you could wish to see, hale and lusty to a fault, just as they are now.' He turns back to the jury. 'I ask you to reflect on the words in the mittimus. Pined. Consumed. These are terms that suggest a fading away, a sickness unto death.' He swings back towards the children and points at them. Ann Putnam gives a little gasp then is silent again. 'But these girls are neither pined *nor* consumed. On the contrary, they are fat and happy as pigs in muck.' The vulgar phrase is uttered with as much precision as if it was Latin.

There's another silence except for a little snuffling from some of the girls, shaken at the insult and this attack on their good faith. Bridget Bishop tosses her fading hair, sighs in satisfaction at the unexpected defence. 'Mr. Brattle,' says Stoughton, 'I must object to the offensive language you have just employed.'

'I'm sorry, your honour. That was the first example of cheerful good health that came to mind.' Mr. Brattle looks round at all concerned, jurors, judges, the accusers themselves, to check his point has gone home. Sewall suspects that his reference to happy pigs was intended to undermine those witness statements that referred to porcine distress and transformation. Satisfied he has had an effect, Brattle returns to his seat.

'To clarify this matter, I will make a ruling,' Mr. Stoughton tells the jury. He pauses a moment in thought, pressing the tips of his fingers together. 'You are not to mind whether the bodies of the said afflicted are *really* pined and consumed,' he then says. The jury shuffle uneasily; Sewall does too. It's hard to see what's left of the charges given such a sweeping concession. 'The issue to be considered is whether they suffer such afflictions as naturally *tend* to their being pined and consumed, and wasted, and suchlike. What matters in law, gentlemen, is intention rather than result. Do you understand this point?'

There is a slightly baffled silence, broken by Stephen, who repeats this wording in an interrogatory tone: '*Tend* to their being pined and consumed . . . ?' Mr. Stoughton gives him the nod, and Stephen settles down to scribble this formulation on to his report.

The foreman of the jury, Thomas Fiske, gets to his feet. He is a tall thin man in a neat russet-brown jerkin and breeches, with short grey hair (his own). He runs a greengrocer's in Salem and Sewall has in the past bought grapes and oranges from him as presents for his brother and sister-in-law when on a visit. 'Your honour,' Fiske asks, 'is it like firing a gun, but missing?'

'A more precise example would be to aim a gun, fire it, and

severely wound the target. Who then (I refer to the target) recovers from otherwise certain death because she receives skilled medical aid. Though in this case the aid comes from God, who cures the afflicted when they put their faith in Him.'

'Amen,' says Mr. Noyes from his place in the front row of the public gallery.

'Amen,' repeats the room in general.

The jury finds Bridget Bishop guilty. She has made the children suffer afflictions that *tend* to their being pined and consumed. Stoughton casts his eyes each way along the row of judges to ensure, without it actually being spoken, that they are aware only one sentence is possible. Then he turns to address the convicted woman.

But before he can say anything, Judge Saltonstall intervenes. The General Court has not confirmed that the laws made by the previous governor and legislature remain in full force, he points out. Until that's done, all sentences must be regarded as provisional. By the nature of things, a capital sentence is irrevocable and therefore cannot be passed until this issue is clarified.

Mr. Stoughton, obstructed for the second time in succession, seems to vibrate slightly. The silence goes on and on while Bridget Bishop waits to hear her fate. Her expression is blank. Finally, Mr. Stoughton speaks. 'The *sentence* of death can be passed, since it can remain provisional, being only a sentence. Its *execution* must await the confirmation of the laws passed under the old dispensation. Does that satisfy you, Mr. Saltonstall?'

'It does, Mr. Stoughton,' Saltonstall replies with a little sigh.

Stoughton then turns to Bridget Bishop. 'Goodwife Bishop, it is the sentence of this court that you shall be taken from here to prison, and from there to a place of execution, where you shall be hanged by the neck until you are dead.' Then, more ponderously: 'This sentence to be confirmed in due course.'

At the word 'hanged' a shudder runs down Bishop's form. But the remote expression on her face remains and her little eyes continue to flitter aimlessly. Her body is aware of the horror that awaits while her mind seems impervious to it.

Out in the sunshine again Sewall has one thought—to get to Stephen and Margaret's as fast as he can and enjoy a late dinner (he's going to set off home by ferry tomorrow morning). Stephen has remained in court so that Mr. Stoughton can approve his report of the proceedings, but Sewall and Margaret can refresh themselves with a glass of wine while waiting for him. But he has only taken a few steps when someone grasps his elbow.

'Good day once again. Your honour,' Mr. Brattle says.

'I am not your honour at present, nor anyone else's. I am outside the court walking along the public street. Simply a citizen.'

'In that case, what cheer, old friend?' asks Brattle, making Sewall feel boorish.

They begin walking together along the road. Mr. Brattle is staying the night at the Ship Tavern and intends to catch the same ferry tomorrow as Sewall. Just as they are about to say their farewells, Mr. Brattle looks up at the inn sign. 'I remember how you nursed me back to health when we were on *our* ship,' he says. Sewall clicks his tongue to indicate that he doesn't require any more gratitude in that respect. 'Do you recall that concert we went to in Covent Garden,' Brattle continues, 'not long after we first arrived in London?'

'The next time I hear such music will be in heaven.'

'That wasn't the only entertainment I attended there. In Covent Garden, I mean, not heaven. By no means heaven.'

This emphasis catches Sewall's attention and he feels a sudden twinge of jealousy. Perhaps he should have been more enterprising himself, during his stay in England. 'I went to the theatre,' Mr. Brattle admits bluntly.

'Oh.' Sewall is disappointed it's not something worse. 'Another place. Another time.'

'Indeed it was. I went on a number of occasions, in fact. *Splendida peccata*, I must say. I remember a tragedy by Thomas Otway, *Venice Preserv'd*. And a play by William Wycherley that proved unexpectedly filthy. But very funny. It was called— well, no matter what it was called.'

Sewall takes a deep breath. 'I see.'

'My friend, you *don't* see. You *didn't* see. That's the point of what I am trying to tell you.'

Sewall realises this apparently spontaneous conversation must have been carefully crafted. '*I* didn't see them because plays are—'

'I know what plays are. They are sacrilegious because they appropriate God's prerogative, by inventing men and women. They are immoral because they are constructed of untruths.'

'Mr. Mather the son has called them academies of hell.'

Mr. Brattle's eyes briefly roll upwards, perhaps in annoyance at this forceful phrase, perhaps to remind himself of heaven. 'I know all that,' he continues, 'but I know something else too. I know that the actors, whose profession is to lie for a living, lie so convincingly that while you're watching them you believe every-thing they say is true. If they portray sadness you believe in their sadness. If pain, you believe in their pain. If they die on stage, you think they're dead.' His blue eyes look directly into Sewall's. 'The point I'm making, Mr. Sewall, is that those girls in the court, those so-called afflicted girls, are *lying*. They are acting out fear and pain and distress. Watching them at their tricks is exactly like watching a play in Covent Garden. They are play-acting.'

Sewall takes some breaths to calm himself. He can only argue successfully against Mr. Brattle by imitating *his* calmness. 'And why should they do that, Mr. Brattle?'

'I don't know why. Because they are foolish children. Because children like to play games. Because they want to feel important. They want to have important Mr. Stoughton and his important justices'—important Mr. Sewall included, no doubt—'and important Mr. Noyes and every other important adult hang on their every word and action. But let me tell you, they are simply lying, the whole lot of them. And so are the grown-ups who support them.'

'I may not have seen plays, Mr. Brattle, but I *have* observed children. Indeed, I've had quite a number of my own, some that lived, others that didn't.' Mr. Brattle is not married himself. Sewall doesn't want to adopt a knowing air but there's so much at stake. 'I've had ample opportunity to see for myself the sincerity of children. Far from trying to impress important adults, they've hidden themselves away in dark places where they can confront fear and sorrow all alone.'

'Not those children we saw today. They—'

Sewall reminds himself that this is a moment to be uncompromising. He mustn't succumb to groundless leniency in so serious a matter out of fear of offending one of his peers, as he did in the case of the pirates. There is always a price to be paid for such moral cowardice. In this case a reprieve for Bridget Bishop (even if he could pluck one from his sleeve like some conjuror performing in that back room of Captain Wing's tavern) would give the lie to the afflicted children, and betray their courageous witness so that all their struggles and torments would have been in vain. And he would set free a witch into the plantations of New England, just as he had once set pirates free upon its seas. 'They *were* pined and consumed, despite your argument,' he says with as much quiet definiteness as he can muster.

'It wasn't an argument,' Brattle replies. 'It was simply a statement of what I saw with my own eyes. Or didn't see.'

'But you didn't understand that the torments in question took place in the children's *souls*. Their bodies remain unharmed because it is not their bodies that the Devil is after.'

'Samuel,' says Mr. Brattle, in unexpected (and unwelcome) intimacy, with lowered voice, 'we live a long way from any-where, from everywhere. We inhabit the edge of things. There is a vast tract of wilderness to our west, and a vast tract of ocean to our east. But you and I have travelled.' He takes hold of Sewall's elbow and peers intently into his face. 'We were over the sea in England, where we became acquainted with seats of learning, of science and art, places where great thoughts are thought and great affairs undertaken. Surely while you were over there you didn't leave your wits behind you in this small place?'

Sewall remembers that giant stride of the angel, leaning for-ward from Europe, plunging his foot towards the middle of the ocean and finding a resting-place for it on America's shore. 'Not just my wits, *Mr.* Brattle. I left my heart here too. And my soul. Good day to you.'

CHAPTER 16

A lovely June morning. Sewall is on his way to the Town House where he's going to attend a session of the General Council at which it will finally be voted that the laws passed by the previous legislature should remain in force. As he passes Captain Wing's tavern the door opens and a man with head aflame steps out on to the street.

'Good morning, Major Saltonstall,' Sewall says heartily, though his nostrils twitch as winy fumes dispel the freshness of the day. 'Will you walk with me to the meeting?'

'I'm not going to the meeting.' Saltonstall looks Sewall in the eye and gives that disarming smile of his, shrugging his shoulders ruefully at the same time.

'Why ever not?' Sewall asks, Major Saltonstall being a conscientious and principled man.

'Come in, and let me buy you breakfast,' Saltonstall says, pulling open the Castle Tavern's front door again.

'I've had my breakfast already.' Immediately, the smell of baking pastry and cooking meat wafts out of the aperture and he regrets this testy refusal, brought on by his colleague's unexpected avoidance of his duty.

'Well, I can buy you a drink, in any case.'

They enter the reassuring gloom. When Captain Wing sees who it is he rushes over to greet Sewall enthusiastically, crying, 'Good morning, your honour!' and shaking him vigorously by the hand. Now that the trials have begun people seem to be calling him your honour even when he isn't in court. It's as if his part in these proceedings is the only thing that matters, and his responsibilities as a Council member, merchant, private banker, householder and family man have all been forgotten. 'I got hold of some plump rabbits, yesterday,' Wing continues. 'And have made some excellent pasties with them. Perhaps one each for you two gentlemen?'

'Ah,' Sewall replies.

'And a bottle of wine,' Saltonstall adds.

Luckily the pasties aren't on the scale of the one Sewall took with him on the Salem ferry, but they are golden, fragrant and spherical enough. He decides to make use of his inconsistency. 'Can't I persuade you to change your mind about going to the Council as I have just done in respect of this pie?'

Saltonstall pours himself a glass of wine. His eyes are red-rimmed and tired, perhaps because of the wine he's drunk already, but he's not a young man in any case, more than twelve years Sewall's senior. His bright hair is beginning to turn a little grey, as though depositing ash. 'No, you can't,' he says.

'Surely it's our duty as upholders of the law to ensure there's a law to uphold?'

'Mr. Sewall, the moment we vote to ratify the laws, Mr. Stoughton will sign Bridget Bishop's death warrant. I want no part of it.'

Sewall is startled. True, Saltonstall advocated reprieving those pirates, but now, witches too! 'You saw those tormented children with your own *eyes*.' (Unlike Mr. Brattle, Major Saltonstall has children of his own, now grown.) 'Are you saying they are liars?'

'They testify to what they see and feel. I have to do the same. And I don't see a witch, I just see a frightened woman. You know Mr. Stoughton asked me to join the examination of Mr. Burroughs?' Sewall didn't know, and shakes his head at Mr. Stoughton's lack of frankness. 'I've met Mr. Burroughs several times,' Saltonstall continues.

'So have I. He was in my—'

'He's a vain man and no doubt a bully. If he was being examined for treating his wives unkindly, I would willingly have taken part. But if you ask me to accept the possibility that he killed them by magic, as part of a conspiracy to turn New England into the Devil's kingdom, I'm afraid I just can't swallow it.' He stares down at his pasty and shakes his head.

'Bridget Bishop didn't appear frightened to me, in any case,' Sewall says. He remembers those dark irises of hers, that remote appraising look lacking any hint of female modesty. 'She looked quite calm. I thought she was bold.'

Saltonstall raises his head and fixes Sewall with his sad eyes. 'Numb,' he replies. 'Numb with despair and fear. I've seen it in battle. Numbness overtakes some men, and it's easy to mistake it for courage. For boldness.' He pours himself yet more wine, then holds the bottle over Sewall's glass. Sewall places a hand over the top to say no. He wouldn't mind another drop but doesn't want to encourage his colleague to drink more than he should. To no avail: Saltonstall merely withdraws the bottle and squeezes more into his own glass.

Sewall presents the case he has already made to himself: the verdict was decided by the jury, not the judges; the punishment is prescribed by the law—again, not by the judges. Even as he speaks, this seems a wriggling and evasive kind of argument.

'Yes,' Saltonstall agrees tiredly. 'But if I vote on the ratification, I will be directly responsible for its consequence, the death of the woman Bishop. And since I am not prepared to take responsibility for that, then it would be wrong for me to remain on the bench to hear similar charges against others. So this morning I wrote to Mr. Stoughton, resigning from the Court of Oyer and Terminer.'

Sewall says nothing in response to this astonishing news but simply slides his glass across the table. He needs another drink, come what may. Saltonstall makes to oblige but the bottle is empty. He gives Sewall his sudden charming smile, then turns and signals to Captain Wing for another.

The night before Bridget Bishop is hanged, Sewall lies in bed thinking tumultuous thoughts for many hours (Hannah is spending the night in her own chamber with little Mary, who has the colic, in a cot beside her). That conversation with Saltonstall beats through his brain. The children must testify to what they have seen. I (said Major Saltonstall) must do the same.

But does that mean that the children are seeing what isn't there? And isn't that the same as claiming they are lying, just as Mr. Brattle alleged?

Bishop is a woman awaiting hanging, numb with fear . . . How absurd that Mr. Burroughs killed his wives by magic, that he leads a conspiracy to turn New England into the Devil's kingdom . . .

Sewall wakes with a start, as though he has reached the rope's end himself. He must have been sleeping after all.

Hannah is not beside him in the bed and he gets up to look for her. There she is ahead of him, striding up a hill towards a tree at the top. No, it isn't a tree after all but a gallows, and she is about to be hanged from it. He runs as fast as his heavy body will let him, calling out that there has been a mistake, but arrives at the base of the gallows just as she is turned off. As she falls he perceives it's not a mistake after all, or rather it's his own mistake, since the condemned woman isn't Hannah but Bridget Bishop.

He glimpses Bishop's face just as the rope bites, the expression indescribable, almost unseeable, utter terror, utter pain, utter misery, utter utterness, hardly room on her white countenance for it all, a woman poised for a final moment exactly on the cusp of am and was.

He wakes again, and is in his own bed. Of course, of course, his Hannah is safe in her chamber, with little Mary sleeping close by. He sighs, and collects himself. The room isn't completely dark: morning must be approaching. He needs to piss but since he is alone he can use the chamber pot without awkwardness. He leans over and fumbles under the bed for it, drags it on top of the covers, kneels above it, hoists up the front of his nightshirt and relieves himself. As he bends over to return the pot to its place he realises the back of his nightshirt is warm and wet against his legs and then discovers that the pot is broken, part of the bottom missing, and the Welsh cotton blanket on his bed has been saturated.

He can't think what to do. He feels too mortified to rouse Hannah, and certainly can't confide in Sarah or Susan. He finally tiptoes to the window, opens it and calls down to the outhouse where Bastian has his bed, nightshirt clinging to his calves as he bends forward.

It's odd, shouting in a whisper, but in a moment or two Bastian appears at the door of his small house in a nightshirt of his own, and having looked around for the source of the summons finally raises his face upwards, and then his arm to indicate he has seen.

It doesn't take long for everything to be dealt with. Bastian fetches him a new nightshirt, lights a small fire in the grate, and puts the wet shirt and bedding over the backs of chairs to dry. 'No one will be any the wiser, master,' he says comfortingly.

'Except you,' Sewall replies glumly.

'But I'm no one,' Bastian replies, his chest heaving with almost silent laughter. 'That's proof of it!'

When he has gone, Sewall reflects on the strangeness of the night. He has lost his wife, then followed her to gallows hill, then seen Bridget Bishop executed and remembered his wife again. To cap it all he has wet the bed. Trouble and disgrace can come from any source; the world is composed of little things as well as great ones.

He thinks of Cotton Mather telling him about the way large witchcrafts and hauntings can be born of childish games; by the same token, perhaps, large and important Massachusetts citizens like Mr. Brattle and Major Saltonstall need to understand that the witness of young children is as valid as anyone else's.

CHAPTER 17

'Your adversary, the Devil, is a roaring lion,' Mr. Willard exclaims at Sunday afternoon meeting. 'He has come with power and in great wrath. He ranges everywhere. He takes every opportunity, however small it might appear, however fleeting it might be, to perform mischief on us to the utmost extent of his power.'

When he leaves the meeting house Sewall walks straight into Cotton Mather who is rushing up full of fluster and paperwork, wig awry. 'Ha, Mr. Sewall!' he cries.

'I didn't expect to see you, Mr. Mather. I thought you would be conducting the service at the North Church this afternoon.'

'My father is officiating. I was going to attend Mr. Willard's service, but I was working on this document in my study. To my mortification I lost all sense of time, and set out too late.' A tear forms in the corner of each aghast, protuberant eye. 'I will address the omission later, with prayer and prostration. With gnashing of teeth, Mr. Sewall.'

'I'm sure your work was important in any case.'

'No task, even one to be performed at speed by command of the governor himself, which this is'—patting the heap of papers—'can take precedence over our duty to the Lord. My excuse is that this too was the Lord's business, in its own way, since it concerns the spiritual health of our province.'

Wife Hannah and Betty come up. 'Perhaps you will join us for some dinner, Mr. Mather?' asks Hannah.

'That is so kind, dear lady, but sadly I can't. Time presses.'

He pats his papers. 'But on second thoughts, a glass of wine and a handful of nuts? That will give Mr. Sewall a few moments to pass his eyes over the papers here.' He turns to Sewall. 'I was bringing this for Mr. Willard's approval but it occurs to me it would be helpful to have your opinion first, as a judge of the court.'

The document is titled *The Return of Several Ministers*, though Cotton Mather has written it singlehandedly for the sake of speed, and simply intends to get the approval of other ministers before submitting it to the governor. Mr. Phips has commissioned it because of his concern at Bridget Bishop's execution and the sheer scale of the developing witchcraft, with several hundred people now accused and nearly a hundred in prison awaiting trial (John Alden among them).

They sit in the study, Sewall reading at his desk and Cotton Mather opposite, cracking walnuts with surprising loudness. It's odd how harmless words can seem when they first strike the eye. You perform the mechanical task of determining the sense of what is on the page, and only when you have done that does the meaning sink in. Cotton Mather has attacked the procedure at the preliminary examinations and at the Court of Oyer and Terminer, the noise and chaos that erupts, the tests for possession, above all the phenomenon of spectral evidence because (claims Mather) the Devil can take the form of an innocent person and thereby give the afflicted the *delusion* they are being haunted and tormented by witches.

Sewall sits where he is, taking deep breaths, trying to organise his thoughts. The detonations from Mr. Mather's walnuts continue unabashed. There is noise and chaos in court, thinks Sewall, because crimes are being committed there and then, before the very eyes of jury and justices, and crimes bring suffering, and suffering makes people cry out and fall over, especially when the victims are children. Mr. Mather is a loving father himself; how can he be immune to those cries of pain? And the tests for possession, such as the one where the afflicted touch their tormentors to see if that will return the spectres to their original bodies: how can proof be proved without a test?

And lastly, if the Devil can take the form of innocent people when committing his own crimes, then *all* crimes whatsoever might as well be assigned to him and him alone, and every court, prison and gallows in the whole world can be closed down for lack of custom. In any case, Sewall has previously checked the doctrine that Satan cannot take the shape of innocent persons in his law books. It has been the *primum mobile* of witchcraft cases in England, as asserted by both Glanvil and Baxter.

Aware that Sewall has finished reading, Mather looks hopefully across at him. Within the tendrils of that fulsome wig he looks like the schoolboy he must once have been, awaiting praise for his homework. How can he not understand what he has done? 'You have poured scorn upon the court,' Sewall tells him. He feels suddenly weepy as he says this. 'You have attacked the good faith of the judges.'

Mather blinks in astonishment. 'I beg your pardon?' he replies. 'I was simply suggesting good practice.'

'The moral to be drawn from your *Return* is that the judges have made a terrible mistake in allowing the execution of Bridget Bishop.'

'My dear friend, I would never impugn your integrity. Or that of your fellow judges, all of whom I count as my friends too. Oh dear, oh dear, how to make good? Do you have a pen I can borrow? And some ink?'

Mather begins scratching away furiously. After a few minutes of this he puts down the quill, blows on the page with as much contentment as if cooling a bowl of soup, and passes the document back to Sewall. Then picks up another nut and cracks it sharply by way of writing *finis* to his labour.

Sewall scans the text. Mr. Mather hasn't crossed anything out but simply added a new sentence at the end of his piece. It reads: 'Nevertheless, we cannot but humbly recommend to the government the speedy and vigorous prosecution of those who have rendered themselves obnoxious, according to the laws of God and the statutes of England for the detection of witchcraft.' He looks up in bafflement.

'There,' Mather reassures him, 'this appendix, or one might say, coda, should put the wind in your sails. This is what will stay in the governor's mind.'

Sewall continues to stare. As far as he can see, the appendix (or coda) flatly contradicts everything that has gone before. The trials are a fiasco; the trials must continue; those are the conclusions to be drawn, one then the other. Yet clearly Mr. Mather sees no problem at all with this contradiction. His intellect is so roomy it is able to accommodate both points of view at the same time. As a critic he finds fault with the trials; as a friend to the judges (and sincere hater of witchcraft), he wishes them God speed.

Having concluded the meeting to his own satisfaction, Mather gets to his feet, adjusts his wig, picks up his papers and takes his leave. Sewall accompanies him down the stairs and through the vestibule. Mather pats young Sam on the shoulder as he passes, and to Sewall's gratification his son gives a small bow in response.

Then, as he pulls the front door closed behind the scurrying Cotton Mather, Sewall freezes. Sam? What is Sam doing here? He should be with Mr. Hobart, over in Newton.

For a moment he inspects the wood of the door, as if trying to fool himself into an interest in the convolutions of its grain. Then at last he slowly turns. Sam isn't here. The vestibule is deserted.

Sheer panic. Thoughts scatter, breath comes short, and a kind of nervous irritability overtakes his whole system. What has he seen? A hallucination? Sam was standing in a shaft of afternoon sunshine coming through the window as if painted in light, his form implicit in the molten air, a gold figure in a golden glow. He and young Hannah feel homesick in their respective exiles, while Sewall himself (as well as *wife* Hannah) feels sick even though they remain here at home; sick from the absence of those same children who make their home what it is. Yearning itself can distil necessary treasure from the atmosphere, and Sewall is full of yearning. In the absence of his children, home is a sketchy unfinished place.

No, not a hallucination. *Mather saw Sam too.* He patted him on the shoulder.

You can't *pat* a hallucination. Thirsty men in the desert see imaginary oases but they can't plunge their heads into the shimmering water, nor take a drink.

A ghost? Too dreadful even to think it. And Sewall would know if young Sam were dead. There are some letters that don't need to be sent. When his babies have died something seemed to shift in the way of things, and losing Sam, with all the love that's been invested in him over the years, would be an even greater upheaval. Also, Sam's ghost would have a mournful look, surely, when revisiting its old home, its old haunts. Not politely smile and perform a respectful bow as Mr. Mather came trotting past?

If not a ghost, then a spectre? Worse still. A ghost would mean Sam was no longer in this world. A spectre, that he has doomed himself in the next.

'*There* you are, my dear,' says wife Hannah, coming through the door from the kitchen. 'I've just told Sarah to boil another fowl. You know what an appetite he has.'

'Yes,' replies Sewall in confusion. 'I—what do you mean, another fowl?'

'We were going to have a fowl for our dinner,' Hannah patiently explains, 'and now we are going to have *two* fowls.'

'But Mr. Mather didn't have time to stay for dinner. He ate walnuts instead. Pounds of them. We might just as well have given him a fowl in the first place.' Sewall remembers the incessant concussions of those walnuts and feels bitter about the *Return* all over again. 'A fowl would have been *quieter*, that's for certain.'

'Not Mr. Mather, you goose. Sam, our Sam. Haven't you seen him?'

Something tough and strung in the depths of his body slackens suddenly. 'I thought he was a . . . a vision,' Sewall admits lamely. Hallucination, ghost, spectre, coalesce into that safe word.

Hannah bursts out laughing. 'Our Sam! A fine vision he would make. His breeches are torn and his shirt is dirty. I don't know what Mrs. Hobart was thinking of.'

'But how can he be here? It's the Sabbath!'

'I haven't asked him yet. I think he's rather upset. Be glad to see him, Sam, that's all I ask. *I* am. Very glad. I just wish young Hannah was here with us too.'

Suddenly, over Hannah's shoulder, here is Sam again. He has come into the vestibule from the hall, entering sideways-on (presumably so as to be as inconspicuous as possible). Certainly his head is lowered in shame and he peers at his parents out of the corners of his eyes. 'Sam!' Sewall says sternly.

'Yes, father.'

Sewall crooks his forefinger. 'Come here, my son.' Sam shuffles crabwise up to him. Hannah rests her hand protectively over the back of her son's neck and gives Sewall a warning look. 'How did you get here, Sam?'

'I walked out of Mr. Hobart's house this morning while he was writing his sermon.'

'Did you climb through a window?'

'No, father,' he replies in a small voice. 'I just went through the door. I went out through the door and then walked along the road and then a carter gave me a ride.'

'The carter should not have been travelling on a Sunday. No more should you.'

'I think you are allowed to travel in an emergency, though.'

'And what *was* this emergency?'

'The emergency was, I had to come home.' Tears suddenly run down young Sam's cheeks.

'Was Mr. Hobart treating you cruelly?'

'No, no, not at all,' Sam assures him, wiping his eyes with his sleeve. 'Except that he made me do arithmetic all day long.'

'And so he should have done. That was the arrangement.'

'And God,' Sam continues in a complaining tone. 'I had to study *God* a very great deal.' He broods upon this imposition for a little while. 'God,' he repeats, and nods his head by way of agreeing with the accuracy of his own summary.

There is a pause. Hannah glances meaningfully at Sewall who suddenly opens his arms and embraces his son. 'I am so happy to have you safely here,' he whispers in Sam's ear.

'I am happy to have me here too,' Sam replies, his voice muffled by his father's shoulder. The aroma of boiling fowl wafts in from the kitchen to give a kind of domestic sanctification to the moment.

CHAPTER 18

This is the very tale of America itself, thinks Sewall.

One spring evening almost a quarter of a century previously, John Pressy of Amesbury (across the water from Sewall's own home town of Newbury) just managed to catch the last ferry over the Merrimack River at the shutting in of the light. He then had a walk of about three miles to his own house. He climbed Goodall's Hill and stopped for breath at the top near three stooping trees whose branches clawed down at him, their twisted fingers dark black against the pale black of oncoming night.

He took off his coat, since it was warm now he was away from the river, folded it over his arm and set off down the hill, skirting a field belonging to a neighbour of his called George Martin. He walked on for some time before it occurred to him that he didn't know where he was. There wasn't a proper path in any case, though this was a journey he had made often enough before—but never in the dark. There was no moon and in the dim starlight everything was unfamiliar. Trees and bushes seemed to sidle menacingly close; the grass looked like the pale grey fur of some enormous animal. It was as if nobody had ever been here before, no previous eyes had ever seen it.

John Pressy was bewildered. He wandered for what seemed like a long time until, feeling his steps harder to make, he realised that the land had begun to slope upwards. Finally three stooping trees came into sight: he was back at the top of Goodall's Hill. He waited a while trying to calm himself and to solve the puzzle of how the hill had appeared *ahead* of him when in fact he had walked *away* from it. Then to his joy the moon came out. Once again he set off down the slope, full of confidence this time that in its bright light he would be able to steer himself home.

But once again he became confused. He could see his surroundings sure enough, but they were different from what he would perceive in the daytime, and indeed from what he had (barely) made out in the starlight, the back-to-front light of the moon apparently shifting and rearranging the objects in the valley so that there was no clear route through them. Again he became hopelessly lost, and again he finally found himself once more on top of Goodall's Hill, looking up at the three stooping trees.

He set off a third time. Now, however, because of the knowledge of wrong ways he had accumulated in his previous attempts, he knew where he should go, or at least where he shouldn't, and soon had walked a good half mile on his way. Then he saw a light on his left-hand side, about ten yards off. For a moment he was tempted to walk towards it, but he forbore and continued on his way, leaving it behind him. But he hadn't gone far when the light appeared again, in exactly the same spot in relation to him as previously. Once more he walked past it; once more it appeared. Yet again he left it behind him and proceeded on his way a few more yards; again the light reappeared, this time directly in front of him and blocking his path. He tried to push it out of his way with his walking stick, but in response the light seemed to burst upwards and wave from side to side like a turkey cock spreading its tail.

At this point Pressy began beating it with all his might, delivering at least forty blows with his stick.

Finally he managed to get past. He was just about to move on when his feet were hoisted up from under him, and he found himself lying on his back, sliding down some invisible slope. He only managed to save himself from falling by clutching on to some bushes.

After he'd gone a few more yards he saw Susannah Martin, George Martin's wife, standing a little way to his left exactly as the light had repeatedly done. She said nothing but just stared at him, her head turning so that she could continue to watch him as he went past. He was so upset by this time that when he finally reached his house he carried on right past it and had to turn back. He couldn't call out or even speak until his wife opened the door and addressed him.

Next day the story was all round the neighbourhood that Goodwife Martin had gone back to her house in such a terrible state that her whole body had to be swabbed. Eventually John Pressy was persuaded to tell his story to the local justice, but by then Martin's injuries had healed and nothing could be proved against her. However, she heard about his report, came round to his house and abused him and his wife, telling them they had taken a false oath and would never prosper. In particular that they would never own more than two cows, and even though they might in due course seem to be on the point of obtaining more, they never would.

And sure enough, despite all their best efforts, John Pressy and his wife have never owned more than two cows in all the years that have gone by since then.

Sewall wakes up in his chamber in Stephen and Margaret's house and thinks about John Pressy's testimony. What's odd is that it didn't seem like testimony at all, despite the fact that it had been written down on paper and read out to the court by Sewall's own brother. Instead it was more like an adventure Sewall himself had had. In his mind's eye he can clearly see those three stooping trees with their clutching fingers, feel in his calves that maddening thrice-repeated climb up Goodall's

Hill, view the unexpectedly unfamiliar landscape with familiar eyes, eyes that have become used to that strangeness, remember exactly how it felt to beat at the obstinate, recurring, *substantial*, ball of light, experience in the pit of his stomach the terrible sensation of sliding into a pit that shouldn't be there in the first place.

I remember it even though it didn't happen to me, thinks Sewall, hoisting himself up in bed. How can that be possible? How can he share that pilgrimage of terror with a man he has never even met?

Perhaps John Pressy is Everyman, like the Pilgrim of *Pilgrim's Progress*? Or at least an *American* pilgrim, since his story seems to contain the fearfulness of America as it is now, with townships and settlements that appear so ordered and safe but have the forest hunching its shoulders all around and pagan Indians waiting to attack, with farmland that is tidy and well-tilled but was wilderness just a lifetime ago and recalls that ancestry in any shift of the light or swing of the weather; this current America of 1692 when witches are dressed in sober Puritan clothes, and New Englanders project their dark intentions on to the souls of innocent children.

Sewall gropes for the cup of water beside the bed and takes a drink. He can hear the gentle soughing of the sea and occasional snoring of the shingle, which makes it sound as if the house itself is slumbering peacefully. He slides himself out of bed and tiptoes across the floor to the window, pulls open the curtain and peers out. There, between the houses opposite, the silvery glitter of moonlight on small successive waves looks like the ruffled afterglow of the bestriding angel in Revelation.

While Sewall struggles to slide his bulk back between the sheets, holding his nightshirt against his thighs to prevent it rucking up, an idea occurs to him (he's noticed before that when he's preoccupied with an awkward and engrossing task it somehow frees his mind to have thoughts of its own, like a horse slipping the reins). That name, Goodall's Hill. Goodall could surely be a corruption of Golgotha! And, Sewall realises with sudden excitement, the three stooping trees at its top could stand for the three crosses of Calvary.

Yes, yes, of course. Pressy's three visits to that place, or rather his three descents *from* it, were analogues of the three repudiations of Christ by Peter when the cock crowed (like the dying John Hurd's cries of Hold your tongue! when his wife announced the presence of visitors to comfort his soul). By the same token, the landscape at the bottom of the hill seemed alien because Pressy had alienated himself from his Saviour. His journey through the suddenly strange valley became an errand into the wilderness; and the deceptive light was the blandishment of a witch, leading him a false way toward the pit of hell, into which he almost slipped.

As God, through his prophet Moses, pronounced in Deuteronomy, *To me belongeth vengeance, and recompence; their foot shall slide in* due *time.*

The slide of Pressy's foot was arrested, and he was allowed to clutch at a bush, on account of his struggles against the seduction of the false light. He had beaten back that chimaera, and the black and blue of the beating appeared on Susannah Martin's body, thus demonstrating the hidden link between spectral projection and the witch who provided its source (Sewall has checked the legal precedent for this, in Glanvil, *Sadducismus*, part 2, case of Julian Cox, executed at Taunton in 1663, summing up by Judge Archer). Pressy's adventure happened twenty-four years ago but it prefigures New England's present crisis, as well as reaching back to the eternal and eternally repeated story.

Susannah Martin is one of five accused witches who are being tried over three days by the Court of Oyer and Terminer in Salem. She is a tall lean woman of sixty-seven with a lined face, hook nose and bright probing eyes—a witchy woman, in fact. The afflicted cry out and fall over during her hearing and when she is asked why they are behaving like this, she refers the court (to Sewall's astonishment) to the account of the Witch of Endor in the first book of Samuel, chapter 28. The witch in this passage summoned up a spectre in the shape of the recently deceased Samuel (an innocent person *par excellence*) in order to disconcert Saul with dismal prophesies. In short this ignorant countrywoman makes the very same argument, that the Devil can make spectres in the shape of innocent people, that Cotton Mather made in his *Return*.

Sewall is amazed at Martin's impudence, which can equate Samuel's spectre (even though fabricated) with the apparition of her own unworthy self in order to claim that *it* was fabricated also, as though there could be any comparison between the two.

The other cases are similarly straightforward, with the afflicted suffering such afflictions as tend to their being pined and consumed in full view of the open court, and with copious supporting testimony from other witnesses over the years. It is only Rebecca Nurse who poses a dilemma.

Goody Nurse is the well-to-do and apparently respectable inhabitant of Salem Village who is a covenanted member of Nicholas Noyes's church in Salem Town, and who has regularly attended services in both places. She is small and thin but stands stiffly upright and looks straight ahead, like a diminutive soldier called to attention. A petition in support of her innocence and good character, signed by thirty-nine of her friends and neighbours, is presented to the court. Nevertheless it's notable that when the afflicted girls are in their torments Nurse's face is expressionless.

Mr. Hathorne asks her why she doesn't weep at their suffering.

A long pause. Then in a quiet, rather creaky voice, she replies, 'You do not know my heart.'

There's shocked silence at the arrogance of this remark. It's the court's responsibility to come to a verdict on the content of the accused's heart, so Nurse is in effect accusing it of unfitness to undertake its allotted task. She's denying the validity of the whole legal process. In any case there should be a continuum between heart and utterance, inside and out, appearance and reality. When that is lacking the Devil is able to insert himself into the resulting space and perform his wickedness. Nurse is a member of two congregations yet is prepared to proclaim the secrecy of the self.

The jury retire to consider their verdict. When they are back in place Justice Stoughton asks the foreman, Thomas Fiske, to rise to his feet. 'How do you find the accused?' he asks.

Fiske gives a little cough. 'Not guilty, your honour.'

Stoughton is already passing his gaze along the line of his fellow justices, seeking their tacit endorsement of the death sentence he is about to pass on their behalf. As the verdict strikes home his pale face goes suddenly paler. Over in her makeshift dock, Rebecca Nurse blinks confusedly as she continues to stare straight ahead, obviously not sure what has happened. Slowly Stoughton turns his head towards Fiske, whose spindly form cringes in his glare. 'Please repeat that.'

'Not guilty,' replies Fiske in not much more than a whisper. There's an abrupt outcry from the afflicted girls, shrieks and screams like the wailing of the damned. Strangely, despite the opposition of her interest to theirs, Nurse is crying too, a thin distracted wavering noise, though all the while she continues to stand at attention.

Stoughton raises his arms and the girls quieten. 'I am not satisfied with this verdict,' he informs Fiske.

'Oh?' The foreman is inspecting the floor.

'I will tell you my reason. I don't think you and the other jurors have given sufficient weight to a vital piece of evidence.'

Now Fiske looks up, and manages to acquire a somewhat petulant tone in his voice. 'Which piece is that?'

'It occurred during the testimony of Goodwife Hobbs and her daughter Abigail. They made a series of allegations against the accused. But what was particularly significant was Nurse's reply. As I recall, her exact words were: "What? Are these people giving evidence *against* us now? They used to be *with* us."'

Sewall glances over at Rebecca Nurse. She is still staring straight ahead, apparently oblivious of being quoted. Stoughton continues: 'Since the Hobbs women are also facing charges of witchcraft, the interpretation of Nurse's words is clear enough. She was astonished at being accused by other members of her coven. These witches are not even loyal to their own kind. You may be acquainted with the phrase, *socii criminis*.' Fiske's bewildered look makes it evident that he has no such acquaintanceship. 'Partners in crime,' explains Mr. Stoughton. 'Both Keble in his *Sources* and Glanvil in *Sadducismus* make it clear that guilt by association is a valid argument.'

Fiske puffs out his cheeks. Seeing the greengrocer's confusion Sewall suddenly understands that it's his duty as a justice to make a contribution now. The judges are a team of diverse men, each with his own point of view, and it therefore behooves Sewall to express his. 'It is surely the *jury*'s responsibility to interpret the significance of the defendant's comment,' he says.

Stoughton's face turns slowly towards his, and the eyes in their dark sockets inspect him tiredly. Sewall hears his own heart thudding and wonders if Stoughton can hear it too. Finally, Stoughton speaks. 'You're quite right, Mr. Sewall.' Sewall takes in a deep breath and sighs it out in relief. Meanwhile, Stoughton turns back towards Fiske. 'Mr. Foreman,' he says, 'you have heard Judge Sewall's comment.

Please retire with your fellow jurors and consider your interpretation of the accused's remark.'

Sewall opens his mouth to protest. This is not what he meant at all. The jury have already had the opportunity to interpret. It's improper to ask them to reconsider.

Or is it? Surely all that matters is the truth, and truth, as he has had cause to remind himself on several occasions recently, endures through time or, looked at from another angle, is independent of time altogether. That being the case what does it matter if the jury are engaged in seeking the truth for the second, or the hundredth, time? All that matters is that they should find it.

Or is this a contrived argument to justify his unwillingness to confront Stoughton yet again?

The jury file out once more but return after just a few minutes. 'Well,' asks Stoughton, 'have you reached a verdict?'

'No, sir.' Fiske's tone is one he must normally reserve for informing a valuable customer he's run out of beans or onions. Stoughton closes his mouth with a little plink. A low deep sound begins to proceed from the afflicted girls. 'We wish to ask the accused a question. We will then give our verdict in accordance with her reply.'

'You will then give your verdict, will you? That is very kind of you. Please proceed.'

'Goody Nurse, can you tell us what you meant when you told Goody Hobbs and her daughter that they used to be *with* you?'

Nurse is still staring straight ahead but gradually becomes aware she's being looked at by all the judges and jurymen and allows herself a quick glance at the banks of faces, then flicks back again, overawed by their mute enquiry. There is silence.

'The jury has agreed that if she has no defence to offer, the verdict must be guilty,' says Fiske.

'So be it,' Stoughton replies with satisfaction. The five witches

are sentenced to be hanged on 19 July and Sewall can return to
Boston.

He sits in his study on a lovely sunny morning in early July.
Daughter Hannah has written to him from Rowley, a letter full
of complaints and reproaches.

She doesn't like cousin William's cattle. Gurnippers hover
around them all the time, and bite her too. The cows are very
big and moo at her. When she has to go across the fields to
fetch them her knee hurts. And cousin Abigail said her stitches
were too large. The letter is tear-stained where she wrote how
much she missed him and her mother and Betty and Joseph
and Mary. She didn't mention young Sam because of course
she didn't know he'd returned home.

Sewall puts his thumb gently on the blotches as if he's
resting it on her cheek in order to smudge away her sorrow.
He will have to be careful how to inform her about Sam
because that will certainly increase her sense of injustice. He
wonders whether he ought to bring her home, particularly now
the Susannah Martin case has shown that the witchcraft has
a foothold in the Rowley area. But of course the whole purpose
of her stay with the Dummers is to help her grow up a little,
and her letter, poignant as it is, shows she still has some way
to go in that direction. As for the witchcraft, it is becoming
more and more apparent that if you scratch the surface any-
where in Massachusetts, you will find witchcraft bubbling up
underneath.

What he can do to sweeten the pill is to explain that young
Sam is now taking lessons in Latin with Nathaniel Cheever,
New England's oldest (and most rigorous) schoolmaster.

As he begins to write, in comes Susan. 'Master,' she says,
'here is—,' but, before she can say it, brother Stephen enters in
her wake.

'I'm sorry, Sam. I'm like a bad penny. I know it's only been a couple of days since we were in each other's company but this is urgent business.' Stephen seems to have lost much of his brightness and cheer recently, and Sewall thinks with a pang that that is *his* fault for suggesting his name to Mr. Stoughton.

'Stephen,' he says quietly, resting a hand on his shoulder, 'I'm always happy to be in your company.'

'Not this time, I suspect, brother. I've received a letter in my capacity as clerk of the court from Goody Nurse.' He opens a small satchel that hangs from his shoulder and draws out a paper. 'I made a copy for each of the judges and jurymen and am delivering them in person, since the matter is urgent.' He passes over the copy of the letter and Sewall sits back down at his desk to read it.

To the Honoured Court and Jury

It has been explained to me that I have been found guilty for saying that Goodwife Hobbs and her daughter were of our company. All I meant by this was that they were in prison with me and, as I believed and believe, cannot legally give evidence against their fellow prisoners. And I being hard of hearing and full of grief, no one made clear to me how the court interpreted my words, and so I wasn't able to take the opportunity of explaining what I really meant.

Rebecca Nurse

'Of course,' says Stephen, when Sewall has had time to absorb the letter, 'her argument is invalid, since there is no law that prisoners can't give evidence against each other. As I understand, anyhow.'

'True. But that's not the point.'

'Isn't it?'

'The court took her words to mean that she was a member

of a coven. She denies she meant that. *That*'s the point. The rightness or wrongness of what she *did* mean, or claims she meant, is neither here nor there. Also, the jury convicted her because she failed to answer their question on this issue. Here she gives an explanation for that failure.' Sewall shakes his head at the sheer banality of it. 'She's deaf.'

'Does this mean the court will have to reconvene to consider her case again?' Stephen asks.

'Nurse's letter is an appeal against the court's judgment. The court should not hear an appeal against itself.' Ever since the fiasco of the pirates he has believed this. 'I'll take her letter to the governor.'

'Pisspots,' says Governor Phips. 'The thing is a botch. You sat there on your bench in your red robes like so many'— he hesitates, searching for an appropriate simile, words not coming into his mind as speedily as rage—'so many great red *beetles*, and you didn't take the trouble to discover that the defendant hadn't got a clue what you were *talking* about. God give me strength.' He paces up and down in the hall of his mansion, one hand where the hilt of his sword would be if he was wearing one, as if to make clear he would like to run Sewall through.

'I tried—,' begins Sewall.

'Trying isn't good enough. You needed to *succeed*, God damn your eyes. A woman's life is at stake here. I didn't just *try* to find that treasure on the bottom of the ocean. I *succeeded*. Nothing counts until you're counting the money. Or in this case, *taking* account of whatever God-forsaken muddled drivel the defendant wants to spew out at you.'

'I thought it best if I—'

'I'm going to have to reprieve the deaf old basket. I've no choice in the matter. You'd better let her out of jail. She can fly away home on a stick, for all I care. And for pity's sake, don't put me in this position again. I've only been in my post a couple of months. It does me no good at all to cross swords with the very court I set up when I first got here. It makes me look a damned idiot. Or it makes you justices look damned idiots, which amounts to the same thing.'

This message is repeated four days later when Mr. Stoughton is standing in Sewall's study. 'You have brought our proceedings into disrepute,' he says in a voice bleak beyond fury. 'And in particular you have discredited me.'

Now perhaps the pirates are exorcised, thinks Sewall, since I've managed to fall foul of *two* of my superiors in quick succession.

'Did it completely slip your mind that *I* am the senior judge of the Court of Oyer and Terminer?' continues Stoughton. 'It should have been *my* responsibility to bring the matter of the Nurse letter to the attention of the governor.'

Except that you never would have done it, Sewall thinks.

'Except that I never would have done it,' Stoughton informs him. 'And do you know why?' Sewall shakes his head. 'I will tell you why. Because the court did nothing wrong, that's why. Because there were no grounds for the appeal, that's why. It is not the responsibility of the jury—or of the justices, for that matter—to endorse Goody Nurse's explanation of her meaning, and to run off to the governor with it. It's our job, as a court, to make our own interpretation of her meaning, and that we did punctiliously. When it seemed that the jury had ignored this particular issue they were given the opportunity of considering it. Considering it, I might add, with a specific instruction from me that they should bear in mind what you yourself said, that they should arrive at their own interpretation of Nurse's words.'

'But they asked for further elucidation of Nurse's meaning, and they didn't get it because of her deafness.'

'Deafness is not a defence against a capital charge. Deafness is not an excuse for witchcraft. Don't you understand, Mr. Sewall? If one witch escapes our justice, she will leave a path that others will follow. Our plantation in the wilderness is facing comprehensive destruction. We must counter it with comprehensive defence.'

There's a long pause. 'What do you propose to do?' Sewall asks at last.

'I've already done it. I asked a deputation of Salem gentlemen under the leadership of Mr. Noyes to talk to the governor. Your brother refused to make one of them, incidentally, on the grounds that as an official of the court he had to remain neutral.'

'Mr. Noyes? But he is Goody Nurse's minister! Surely he should remain neutral too. She's a covenanted member of his congregation. Isn't that a conflict of interest?'

'Goody Nurse is no longer a member of Mr. Noyes's congregation. The day after she was found guilty by our court he went to her in prison with some elders of his church and uncommunicated her.'

'That seems . . .' Sewall is at a loss for words. Then he fixes on one. 'Precipitate.' The deliberateness with which he has chosen it makes him think of the word's Latin origin, meaning headfirst or headlong, and he has a sudden mental picture of Goody Nurse falling, falling, from a high and dizzy cliff, falling infinitely and forever, utterly lost, unsaveable.

'It is Goody Nurse who has precipitated the situation,' Stoughton replies, 'to use your own word. As Mr. Noyes said to me, the excommunication was no more than a recognition of what had already happened. Nurse excommunicated her*self* when she made an alliance with the Devil and signed his book. When Mr. Noyes and the other Salem gentlemen fully explained this state of affairs to the governor he withdrew the reprieve.' Stoughton gives Sewall a long restraining look, as you might to a horse that wishes to bolt, reining it back by the power of your gaze. 'She will hang with the others on the nineteenth,' he continues, 'according to the sentence of our court.' He says the last phrase with a certain emphasis, to remind Sewall of his joint ownership of its decision.

Sewall's breathing is coming heavily as if he has been running. Not guilty, then guilty, reprieved, then having the reprieve withdrawn. It is as if the voice of the state has stammered in addressing this elderly woman. He can hardly bear to think of how she has shuttled from danger to safety, from safety to danger, to safety again, then to doom. It's equally terrible to think of the loneliness of excommunication, notwithstanding Stoughton's justification of it, that complete isolation and consequent despair. Sometimes Sewall wakes at night in panic at the thought that he may not be a covenanted member of his own church, because of that wretched episode where he forgot to confess his sins when he stood before the congregation.

But still, she *must* be able to bear it, because the option is open to her to confess and rejoin the faithful. He, Sewall, is a husband, father, church member, justice, merchant, representative, his whole life a series of how-de-dos, handshakes and (where appropriate) kisses. Just as a sculpture is shaped by innumerable carvings and scrapings on the part of the sculptor's tools, so he, Sewall, is formed by the innumerable contacts he has with his surrounding community, his very contours determined by constant intricate pressures from life in society. He pictures diminutive Goody Nurse, standing rigid as one of Joseph's toy soldiers. Recalls her in the dock, remote from the proceedings, with those oblivious ears. Perhaps she has learned to love her silence, to inhabit it snugly like a cocoon?

'That man,' says Stoughton bitterly.

'The Devil?' asks Sewall, surfacing in confusion from these reflections.

'The governor.'

'Oh.'

'I can't imagine what Increase Mather thought he was up to, securing the post for that dolt.'

'Perhaps he thought he would be able to manipulate him.'

'Perhaps he did. But the drawback in choosing a man you can manipulate is that others can do so too. As *you* did.' Stoughton says this with contempt, as though to suggest that if Sewall can make Phips dance to his tune absolutely anyone can. 'And as the Salem gentlemen did after you,' he continues. 'Governor Phips sneers and struts and rages and covers his chest with gold braiding, and yet petitioners can bat him like a shuttlecock from one side of the fence to the other. Anyhow, the court shouldn't be troubled by any more interference from him. He's gone off to fight our enemies in the west of the province.'

'I didn't know there was any trouble there at present.'

'He'll no doubt find some. He'll bumble about until he succeeds in flushing some Indian out of the undergrowth. And while he's doing that, he'll leave the rest of us alone, thank God.'

It hasn't rained for some weeks, and the sun beats down day after day. On 18 July, Sewall decides to go to Salem to see the witches hang the following day. He doesn't normally watch the deaths of those he has sentenced himself, fearing that attendance at the foot of the gallows would be interpreted as gloating or revenge. But in the case of witchcraft there is the possibility of last-minute confession, and it has been decided by the judges that confessors should be spared, at least for the time being, since they can provide testimony in other cases. In Sewall's opinion they should be spared indefinitely, pardoned even. A witch is not guilty of a crime in her own right; rather, she *contains* guilt as a bottle may contain poison. If the poison is poured away, the bottle becomes clean again. A witch can be returned to innocence up till the moment the rope takes hold.

It's too late for the ferry so Sewall sets out on horseback. By mid-afternoon he is passing near the town of Saugus, at about the halfway point on his journey. He is clopping through small fields with stony outcrops and clumps of pine to his right. Every now and then there is a sharp report as a rock splits in the heat. The sky is cloudless and the track dry and cracked, with an occasional flurry of dust kicked up by the sea breeze from Cape Ann. Over the fence to the left a man is harvesting corn, and Sewall suddenly realises there is something strange about him.

He pauses his horse and puts his hand flat to his brow to cut out the glare. The man is some distance away, busily scything.

Sewall realises he's wearing no clothes at all except a pair of boots. He calls him over.

'You lost, sir?' the man asks brusquely when he has approached the fence.

'I might ask you the same.'

'What?' The man screws his eyes to look up at him.

Sewall points down at his body. The man looks down at himself then back up. 'I have to wear them,' he explains. 'The stalks are hard.'

'I meant,' says Sewall, 'the lack of anything *else*, to supplement your boots.'

The man blinks in puzzlement, then inspects his feet again. 'These are just working boots,' he says.

It occurs to Sewall that the man thinks he's complaining that the boots are not well cared for, having taken 'supplement' to mean 'clean' or 'polish'. 'Where are your clothes?'

The man points to a little heap on the stubble some distance away. 'There,' he says. 'Working clothes. Like my boots.' Suddenly he almost snarls. 'Rags! Just rags.'

'But why aren't you wearing them?'

The man raises his arm. Sewall realises he's pointing at the sun. Sewall sighs. 'Clothes are for decency, not just protection from inclement weather,' he tells him. Strangely the man doesn't look particularly *in*decent, or if he does the effect is entirely due to his incongruous boots. What strikes Sewall about his naked form is how ordinary it looks, how *normal*, one might say.

He remembers the allure of Madam Winthrop as she showed him her miry skirts. Perhaps she would also look normal (so to speak) if she wore no clothes at all. He tries to think through this question judiciously but finds himself taking out a handkerchief to mop his forehead (it is oppressively hot). Adam and Eve, having eaten of the Tree of Knowledge, stitched themselves little aprons from fig leaves, and then God sewed them coats of goatskins to wear when expelled from the Garden. He must remind daughter Hannah, unhappy at being taught to sew, that God Himself was willing to ply needle and thread.

Perhaps true indecency is when you can see nakedness *beneath* or *within* clothing, so that the whole sad story of the Fall is as it were compressed into a single image.

'Nobody about,' says the man. He points round at the absence of onlookers, at the presence of insensate fields, trees and rocks.

'*I* am about,' says Sewall.

'You stopped and looked at me a purpose. You could have just rid on.'

'But even before I came along *some*one was looking at you. *God* was looking at you.'

'But God made me naked,' the man says after a pause. 'So why should He care?'

Sewall is impressed by his logic. 'One day, here in America,' he tells him, 'a new dispensation, or should I say, the oldest dispensation of all, will be established and we will be returned to the Garden which was our earliest home. But in the meantime we are a fallen people and have to wear our clothes.' If the man didn't understand 'supplement' he is not likely to comprehend 'dispensation', but in this lonely place Sewall needs polysyllabic buttressing to establish his authority. The thought strikes him that if he was naked too there would be an enforced equality of the body, since social distinctions depend on dress. But those distinctions are as necessary to the sublunary world as big and little cogs are necessary in a clock (he is expecting delivery of a new longcase clock from England)—though of course in *heaven* there will be no need to keep time, no time to keep.

The man pauses for a moment, as if to emphasise that he isn't cowed. Then he shrugs his shoulders, turns and walks slowly towards his pile of clothes, his bearing stiff with resentment, his arse glaring sullenly back at Sewall.

*

The witches are to be hanged from a single frame, a sad coven indeed.

Sewall waits with Nicholas Noyes and other interested gentlemen for the cart to arrive. Around them a hotch-potch of onlookers, relatives come to mourn, accusers and afflicted (a number of the young girls are present, Ann Putnam holding her father's hand) to witness the lifting of their oppression, or at least part of it, and lastly the execution-gawpers, here for entertainment.

The gallows is situated on a low hill not far from the sea, which today is a rich navy-blue with white horses riding the breakers. The sky is much paler than the waters below it, as if the intense heat of the sun has washed away its colour. 'I feel like a lump of fat melting in a pan,' grumbles Noyes. 'I'm sure they should be here by now,' he adds, as though the condemned witches are carelessly late for an appointment. Sewall wonders whether they too resent the delay and wish their suffering over and done with, or whether they cherish these extra minutes, each with the sunshiny world within it.

At last the cart comes swaying up the hill with the five witches sitting awkwardly on its planking. There are five nooses dangling and beside each rests a ladder. The hangman places each witch at the base of her own ladder (puffing his pipe the meanwhile) and when they are in position the marshall reads out the confirmation of their death sentences. Then Sewall seizes his moment to speak. 'As one of the judges of the court that sentenced you,' he says, 'I must remind you that you will not die today if you repudiate Satan. The way to do this is to admit your guilt. If you confess to your witchcraft even at this late hour, you will be returned to prison, and if it is determined that your confession is sincere may even be freed.'

The witches remain in place, saying nothing. Sewall wonders whether Nurse has even heard. She is standing just as she did at her trial, stiffly upright and looking straight ahead. He steps towards her and asks in a loud voice if she has understood. Without turning to face him she replies, 'Sir, I am not a witch. I have nothing to confess. If I should say I was a witch I would be lying to God Himself."

Sewall sighs and steps back to Mr. Noyes. 'Perhaps *you* should speak to her,' he says, 'as her man of God. The twists and turns she has experienced may have confused her. Or made her obdurate.'

'I am *not* her man of God,' asserts Noyes. 'Not now, nor ever was. This Nurse was a hypocrite at the Lord's feast. I excommunicated her as a matter of form but she wasn't one of the saints in the first place. She was a viper in our bosom.' He thumps his own bosom as if to establish the absence of any viper remaining there now. 'I will speak to Goody Good instead. Her name and honorific are two good omens.' He catches Sewall's eye to check this wordplay has struck home, then steps over to Sarah Good, the muttering woman, a forlorn figure in raggedy dress and shawl, even now talking to herself under her breath. 'You must confess,' says Noyes. 'You must seize this final opportunity to redeem your soul and save your life. You're a witch and you know it.'

For a few moments Goody Good continues to mouth her imprecations. Then an amazing thing happens: her voice suddenly rings out across the broad day, loud and true. 'You are a *li*ar!'

Noyes emits a sort of high-pitched whinny. Good continues: 'I am no more a witch than you are a wizard, and if you take away my life, God will give you blood to drink!'

Immediately the crowd begins to murmur, the afflicted with indignation at her impudence but the gawpers (Sewall suspects) to register their approval of this terrible prophecy. Meanwhile Mr. Noyes backs away incongruously on tiptoe. Only when he's level with Sewall does he dare turn round. His paunchy cheeks are white, his eyes bulge, there are drops of sweat on his bald pate.

The marshall has seen (and heard) enough—he waves his hand at the hangman who immediately goes up to Goody Good and signals her to begin to climb her ladder. He seizes one of her ankles to let her know that she has arrived at a suitable rung, then climbs up behind her (still puffing smoke) and ties her hands together behind her back. Then he places the rope around her neck and climbs back down again. Sewall notices how, now that she can't hold on with her hands, Good has flattened her body against the ladder out of blind need to preserve her life for as long as possible. The hangman repeats the process with each of the witches in turn. Several of them are whimpering and groaning in terror and anguish, but Nurse and Good remain silent.

Mr. Noyes begins to recite the Lord's Prayer to a throbbing undercurrent of noise from the crowd, and a few hostile and sacrilegious shouts. The hangman approaches Good's ladder again, gives it a quick twist then drops it to the ground. He does the same to the others.

And there the witches are, dancing at the end of their ropes.

Next day there's a fast in Captain Alden's house, organised by Sewall himself. It's in order to ask God to keep his old friend safe, both spiritually and bodily. Alden himself isn't present of course—he's in jail, awaiting trial—but his wife and newly ransomed son participate in the devotions. These are led by Samuel Willard, who is minister both to Alden and to Sewall himself, but Cotton Mather also attends out of respect to a brave defender of the community as well as to Mr. Alden's late father, *Mayflower* veteran and one of the founders of New England (as Mather announces somewhat floridly at the beginning of the little ceremony).

At the very moment Sewall opens the front door to take his

leave, there's a rumble of thunder. Suddenly the rain is beating down on the Aldens' small front garden and the roadway beyond, sending up a pleasant aroma of refreshed vegetation and heated dust. This break in the weather is a good omen, both for the perturbations of Massachusetts in general and for the fate of John Alden in particular.

Sewall stands on the doorstep a moment inhaling the cooler air. Someone is approaching along the road, a hurrying person, dimmed by rain. As he reaches the Aldens' gate he spies Sewall, waves an arm and turns in. His features clarify as he comes down the path. It's Mr. Brattle. 'Mr. Sewall, good day. This is poor Mr. Alden's house, I believe.'

'We've been holding a fast on his behalf.'

'I see.' Mr. Brattle has squeezed in under the small porch so the two men are almost nose to nose. A silver droplet of rainwater dangles from Brattle's, quivering when he speaks. 'Don't you fear a conflict of loyalties? As one of the judges who will try his case?'

'Prayer is always acceptable, both to man and God. I wish Mr. Alden well, and hope he will be found not guilty of witchcraft. This doesn't preempt the trial in any way.'

'I see. That hasn't always been the case, however.'

'What do you mean?'

'I was present a few weeks ago when—oh, excuse me.' Mr. Brattle has become aware of that jiggling raindrop depending from the tip of his nose. He is a man who likes neatness and order, both in his surroundings and habits of thought. To Sewall's astonishment (and admiration) Brattle raises his thumb and forefinger to his nose and plucks the drop from it, for all the world as if it's a gemstone rather than just sparkling like one. 'When one of the accused, John Proctor, asked Mr. Noyes to pray for him. Mr. Noyes flatly refused because Proctor wouldn't admit to being a witch.'

Sewall recalls how Mr. Noyes also refused to speak to

Goody Nurse at the foot of her ladder yesterday. 'Mr. Noyes wishes to encourage the accused to admit their witchcraft and thereby save themselves, soul and perhaps body also.'

'That's very commendable, I'm sure. But it rests on the assumption that everyone accused is guilty—with the exception, perhaps, of the one prisoner who happens to be a friend of the judges and clergy of this colony, Mr. Alden.'

'And it is as a friend that I prayed for him. Just as, no doubt, Mr. Proctor's friends pray for *him*. Mr. Noyes wasn't present here today because he isn't on intimate terms with Mr. Alden.'

Mr. Brattle smiles a superior little smile with those chiselled lips of his. 'Well, at least he seems to be consistent in withholding his favours.'

'He is consistent in wishing to safeguard our poor province. He's consistent in hammering heretics, as we all should be.'

'I have some news. I don't know whether you've heard it. Relating to the consistency of another gentleman, though consistency of the opposite sort. Mr. Saltonstall, up in Haverhill.'

'What of him?'

'It concerns his judicial responsibilities.'

'He resigned from the Court of Oyer and Terminer some weeks ago, as I'm sure you're aware.'

'Indeed I am. I wrote to congratulate him on his integrity.'

'He could have retained his integrity by sitting on the court. The court *qua* court does not lean one way or another.'

'I wonder if Mr. Stoughton would agree, given his disgraceful intervention in the case of Rebecca Nurse. The friends who prayed for *her* must have lacked sufficient influence.'

'I protested at that point. Major Saltonstall could have done so too, if he'd—'

'Well, anyhow, even though he has resigned from your court he is still the magistrate of his own township.'

'What of it?'

'The witchcraft has reached even that far north. By which I

mean, you must understand, the craze for denouncing so-called witches has progressed to that area. Four poor women were hauled before Mr. Saltonstall's court. But he has refused to hear their cases, which have been transferred back across the river to Andover. No doubt they will be remanded to the Court of Oyer and Terminer in due course, but if they are, Mr. Saltonstall's hands will be clean.'

'It was Pontius Pilate who washed his hands, if I remember,' Sewall replies.

'I'll take my leave,' says Mr. Brattle, 'since it's stopped raining.' He gives a curt little bow and scurries off along the Aldens' garden path.

Indeed, it has stopped raining. In the last few moments the clouds have rifted and the sun is peeping through. And there, over the rooftops, appears a faint rainbow. Sewall sighs with pleasure. He is a lover of rainbows, a collector of them in fact, since he makes a point of recording each sighting. Every time he sees one he thinks of the angel making his enormous stride across the Atlantic to grace America, that angel with a rainbow on his head like a many-coloured crown. Perhaps this present manifestation is to reassure him that the Court of Oyer and Terminer is just and necessary (and pleasing to the Lord) despite Mr. Brattle's snide remarks.

And, more importantly, that it will ultimately rescue Massachusetts from its woes.

He wakes in the middle of the night, heart pounding.

Yesterday Mr. Brattle gave news of four more witches being discovered at Haverhill.

And the day before, Susannah Martin of Amesbury was hanged as a witch (along with the four others).

Both places are adjacent to Rowley, where daughter Hannah is staying. The contagion is sweeping through the area and his child is in danger. He has already ignored the first of these two warnings. At any moment Hannah could be attacked by spectres. At best she will suffer; at worst succumb. She could become a witch herself. And she is only up there in the first place in order to justify a lie. It seems impossible, suddenly, to understand how he can have failed to listen to her cries for help. What can he have been thinking of? Hoping she will learn to sew a cushion while her very soul is endangered?

Dawn comes at last. He slides up the bed, frees himself from the thin sheet and swings his legs over the side.

'It's early, isn't it?' Hannah whispers.

'I have a journey to make.'

'It isn't another trial so soon? I hate you having to attend them. They are so . . . ' She tails off, unable to determine exactly what is so *so* about them. 'I hate them,' she concludes lamely.

'No, it's not another trial. I'm going to cousin William's at Rowley. I think it's time to fetch our Hannah back home. I don't like—'

'Oh Sam! I'm so glad!' She lunges over to his side of the bed and grasps his arm to pull herself up to him. 'You don't know, I've lain awake night after night worrying about her.' She has a pleasantly intimate smell.

'I feel she needs her family around her in this dangerous time.'

'I have felt that all along,' Hannah says without any animus. 'You must have some breakfast before you go. Are you going to hire that little carriage again?'

'I'll leave it to Bastian to do that and follow me there. I want to get to Hannah and tell her the news as soon as I can.'

He arrives early in the afternoon at cousin William's farm, sun beating down upon his shoulders, his horse twitching with fatigue. He calls out but no one comes. He takes the horse round to the barn then knocks vigorously on the front door, putting his ear to its surface to hear the result. The whole place is silent except for the chirping of crickets in the grass and the buzz of bees in a lavender bush by the house of office. No one in the nearby fields even, just some distant cows placidly grazing.

As he rode here he pictured his arrival: Hannah rushing out to greet him, he swinging down from the saddle to take her in his arms (counterbalancing that horrible moment when he had to kick his boot away from her grasping hand as he rode off to Salem).

He tries the door and to his surprise it opens. Perhaps the place is too remote to be in much fear of robbers (and both witches and Indians can effect an entry without the use of keys). He calls again, just in case the door muffled his voice, but still no answer.

It's cool in the kitchen—the oven fire has been let to go out. There's a small barrel of beer on the side. He has had only water on his journey, which became unpleasantly warm in the bottle as the hours went by. He takes down a tankard hanging on a hook and pours himself some. The beer is cool and refreshing but drinking it down makes him feel hungry.

To his surprise the pantry contains only a small portion of cooked chicken and a piece of cake. This is a farm. Where are the smoke-blackened hams, the golden pies, the preserved fruits, the corn cakes and the loaves of bread? He takes the meagre fare to the table, puts it on a trencher and sits down. For some reason he eats without dignity, taking a bite of the chicken, then of the cake, then of the chicken again, instead of finishing the one before starting on the other.

After his meal he sits and waits. He has a Bible in his pocket but can't summon up the energy to read it. Every half an hour or so he rises to his feet, walks to the front door, and looks across the shimmering landscape towards its blue distances, hoping to see the Dummers and Hannah coming back. On one of these occasions he hears a mournful cry. His heart contracts with fear but then it's repeated and he realises it must come from some sort of bird, perhaps a loon calling from a hidden pond. Nevertheless from this moment on he keeps imagining a terrible fate has overtaken the three of them, that they have been carried off, or scalped and murdered, by an Indian raiding party.

The afternoon wears slowly on. The light coming through the kitchen window modulates from white to yellow to pale orange. Sewall sighs to think of his wasted hurry, of that joyful anticipation he experienced while galloping here. A bluebottle whizzes tirelessly about in the room's still air.

And then, a distant sound of hooves, rumbling of wheels, snatch of inaudible conversation, a brief peal of laughter.

Sewall rushes to the front door. The Dummers are still a few hundred yards away, approaching in their cart, William at the reins and Abigail and Hannah beside him. They are all laughing and talking animatedly, and haven't spied him yet. Sewall is amazed to see his daughter looking so cheerful and relaxed. Where is the author of those tear-stained letters?

They pull to a stop on the track by the little gate to the garden, still involved in their merry conversation. Only when cousin William turns to step down from the carriage does he spot Sewall. 'Cousin Sam!' he exclaims. 'What are you doing here? I hope all is well.'

Hannah approaches. She looks up at him with a long face, pink ears, tears forming in her eyes (and magnified by her spectacles). 'Father,' is all she says by way of greeting.

'I'm sorry if I've spoilt the mood—,' begins Sewall.

'Father, is it Mary? Is she dead?'

'Mary? Why should Mary be dead?'

'Because she's the smallest. I thought—'

'Is the news bad, cousin?' William asks.

Because he has arrived unannounced they all think something terrible has happened back at home, just as he imagined that a tragedy must have occurred *here*. But still, the disappointment of not receiving a smile or a kiss from his daughter, let alone the rapturous welcome he expected, makes him grim and taciturn. 'No. No news.'

'I hear five witches were—'

Cousin Abigail finally clambers down from the carriage and joins them. 'I'm so sorry we weren't here,' she says. 'We were dining with our friends, the Harrisons. Have you eaten?'

'I found some chicken and cake in the pantry.'

'Oh gracious! Is that all you've had today? That was just some leftovers from breakfast. We have put all our supplies in the root cellar. It's the coolest place while the weather is so hot. You poor man. I must prepare you something at once. The Harrisons have given us a fine ham.' She rushes into the house and the rest of them start to follow after, but are interrupted by the thud of hooves and clatter of another carriage. They turn and see Bastian trotting towards them, a plume of dust in his wake.

'Bastian!' squeals Hannah in delight. 'It is Bastian come to take me home, as he promised!' Sewall watches as she runs forward to greet their servant. He doesn't begrudge Bastian this welcome but only regrets not having a share of it himself.

CHAPTER 20

Sewall walks through the streets of Boston with young Sam. It's hot as usual and there are few people about, but the ones that pass seem to avert their gaze and speed their steps. He has a sense of people watching from windows, whispering about him just out of sight and earshot. There's been a change of atmosphere since the five witches were hanged a couple of weeks ago. Someone made an unpleasant remark to wife Hannah the other day. He overheard her discussing it with Sarah, though when he asked she refused to repeat it. Also when Sewall took a quick dinner in the Castle Tavern with some fellow councillors, Captain Wing handed him his pie with curious abruptness.

Goody Nurse's supporters presented a petition with thirty-nine names on it. Let us say that perhaps another twenty people or so were sympathetic to her cause but not willing to sign a public document and draw attention to themselves at such a sensitive time, and accordingly round the figure up to sixty. Granted Nurse was a more prominent member of the community than other witches, perhaps one should guess an average at half that number. Then multiply that figure of thirty by six for the witches already executed and do the same again for those persons about to go on trial the day after tomorrow, and add the two together. The total number of supporters of executed witches or of accused witches in immediate danger of their lives amounts to 360. And on top of that there are now over two hundred persons remanded to jail, each of whom will have his or her own retinue. It's hardly surprising that there is unease, disaffection, and downright hostility running through the community.

'My feet hurt,' complains young Sam.

Sewall sighs. 'We haven't walked half a mile yet.'

'The heat makes them blister. They got blistered going to Mr. Cheever's school.' Realising the need for evidence, Sam now begins to limp.

After a few more minutes they arrive at Mr. Perry's bookshop. Sewall pauses and gives his son an expectant look, hoping this will suggest to him that he should tug up his breeches a little, and tug down his waistcoat a similar amount. Sam fails to take the hint however, and he's too old to have his clothes adjusted for him. Sewall sighs: he will have to do as he is. The weather is still hot, and everyone is wilting a little. They enter the gloom of the shop.

Books are everywhere, not just on the shelves but stacked in piles on the floor. The shop is empty at the moment, so Sewall rings a little bell that sits on the table. After a few moments Michael Perry appears at the door of his back room, which he uses as an office and bindery, a sturdy man with a large domed head, as befits his bookish surroundings, and very little hair (but no wig). At the top of his forehead, above the eyebrow of his left eye, there is a hard-looking lump that has always been there. The welcome on his countenance stalls a little when he sees who it is. 'Mr. Sewall. Your honour. What can I do for you?'

'No, no, not "your honour" at the moment. Simply a man, Mr. Perry. And a father. This is my son, Samuel.'

'Good morning, Samuel.'

'Good morning, sir.'

'I was wondering if you had room for a young apprentice to learn the book trade, Mr. Perry.'

'I see,' replies Mr. Perry, somewhat unhappily.

'As you know I was colony publisher for a number of years, and I have hopes that this young fellow may want to get his own fingers inky in turn. Don't I, Sam?'

'Yes, father,' replies Sam, looking as unhappy as Mr. Perry. He contrives to limp again even though he is standing perfectly still, juddering abruptly to one side like a piece of furniture that has lost its foot. He rests a hand upon the table by way of support.

'When we came into the shop,' Sewall continues, 'you were busy in the back room and no one was guarding the premises at all. If my young man were to be employed here there would be no—'

'If this were a grog shop or a bakery I would take your point, Mr. Sewall. But I don't have many ragamuffins creeping in to steal the latest volume of Mr. Increase Mather's sermons.'

'But what about greeting customers as they arrive?' Sewall is aware he is trying to teach Mr. Perry his own business. 'Showing good will.'

Mr. Perry's gaze narrows as he inspects young Sam, clearly trying to associate his slouching form with greeting customers and spreading good will. Then he straightens up, looks at Sewall, and inclines his head as a way of saying 'Follow me'. Sewall steps over to the office with him.

'Mr. Sewall, as you know these are troubled times.' He speaks in a loud whisper. 'Many people are angry and resentful. You are in the middle of the tumult. I am sure you are doing what you think best but . . . It was you yourself who brought up the notion of good will.'

'I am indeed doing what I think best, to defend this poor province of ours,' Sewall whispers back. 'But we are not talking about me. We are talking about my son, Sam. He has no connection with this witchcraft plague, thank God.'

'But he has a connection with *you*. When my customers come in they—'

'Mr. Perry!' comes Sam's voice from the shop.

'What is it?'

'Mr. Mather has come to see you!'

'Mr. *Cotton* Mather,' explains that well-known voice.

Mr. Perry and Sewall exchange a sudden intimate look, as if they have both been the butt of a joke. 'Thank you, Sam,' calls Mr. Perry. 'I'm just coming, Mr. Mather.'

'Ah, Mr. Perry. Mr. Sewall,' says Cotton Mather as they re-enter the shop. 'Have you heard the terrible news? Desolation in Jamaica. A mighty earthquake.'

'Are there many dead?' asks Sam.

'Upwards of one thousand and seven hundred souls.'

'May God have mercy,' Sewall says.

'He doesn't seem to have had mercy so far,' says Mr. Perry rather tartly, perhaps moved to this unwitting blasphemy by the scale of the disaster.

'Also houses and property destroyed. Washed clean away. Ships overwhelmed and sunk too. Can you imagine that quaking sea?' Mr. Mather shakes his head and the wig's curls move as if imitating the rushing of gigantic waves. 'Mr. Perry, I think I can explain why the Lord seems—and the word is well chosen, because it *is* only a seeming—seems to have withheld His mercy in this case. The people of those parts are well-known for their fortune-telling. I shall devote my mid-week sermon to this tragedy. My text will be from Revelation, chapter twelve, verse twelve, "Woe to the Inhabiters of the earth, and of the sea! For the Devil is come down unto you." I will bring it in for printing as soon as it is preached, Mr. Perry. Mr. Sewall, a word with you. May we briefly adjourn to your office, Mr. Perry?'

Once in the sanctum Mr. Mather positions himself strangely close to Sewall, as if about to clasp him in an embrace. 'This is a delicate matter,' he whispers. 'I have received a letter.' He takes a folded paper from his pocket and flips it open with a quick movement of his hand. 'It is addressed to me and four other ministers. I'll let it speak for itself.'

It's from John Proctor, whose trial, along with those of five more accused, begins the day after tomorrow. He is asking the clergymen to intercede with the governor to appoint new Oyer and Terminer judges, on the grounds of prejudice. 'The judges, jury, and people in general have become enraged against us accused because they are afflicted with a delusion from the Devil,' he writes. 'That is the only explanation there can be, since we know in our hearts that we are all innocent people.'

Sewall is shocked at the brazenness of this reversal, whereby demonic possession is transferred from witches to those entrusted with upholding the law and protecting the community. For a moment he has a perverse impulse to resign on the spot and walk away, just as Mr. Saltonstall did. Then perhaps people wouldn't say unpleasant things to his wife, and Mr. Perry would look at Sam with unprejudiced eyes (and Mr. Brattle would no doubt express his admiration for Sewall's stance). Just as physicians are dreaded by association with the very diseases they try to cure, so justices can be implicated in the public mind by the evil they are trying to thwart.

This is the most critical moment yet for the court. Four of the accused who are due to be tried the day after tomorrow are men, an unprecedented number of witches of that sex (every thing about this crisis is unprecedented, as far as the history of Massachusetts Bay is concerned). Moreover, one of those men is himself a minister of religion, George Burroughs.

This particular case presents a two-fold danger. First, there is the problem that the public may find the possibility of a man of such status being guilty (if that is how the case should turn out) hard to accept. Then there is the question of Burroughs's importance as the Devil's recruit (if that should be proved). If, as is claimed, the Devil is endeavouring to establish America as part of his empire, then a clergyman who signs the book must surely be appointed king of that new acquisition.

'I have, of course, discussed this matter with my fellow ministers,' continues Mather in his stentorian whisper. 'We won't be bothering Mr. Phips with this impertinent letter.' He takes it back from Sewall's hand. 'It isn't up to accused persons to choose who will try them for their alleged crimes. If we allowed that to happen, criminals would appear in court before their best friends or their own fathers, and chaos would be the order of the day. We're facing enough chaos as it is.'

'What makes this accusation so unjust,' Sewall tells him, 'is that I did everything I could to ensure that the committal procedure was made as regular as it could possibly be in Mr. Proctor's case, compatible of course with the need to safeguard the public. Indeed, I defied the other members of the court.' He immediately regrets saying this—by defending himself he implies there might in fact be a case to answer about the court's procedure. It's another example of his self-defeating tendency to try to please figures of authority.

'You can rely on my discretion and that of my colleagues. We have agreed no word of this . . . ingratitude should slip out. The last thing we need is any discrediting of the judicial authorities. If justices are slandered, the clerics will be next.' He raises a finger to emphasise the point, then folds Proctor's letter, tucks it laboriously into an inner recess of his waistcoat, nods confidingly and leads the way back into the shop, where Mr. Perry and Sam appear deep in conversation. Mr. Perry looks amused, and Sewall hopes young Sam has been furnishing him with the drollery he can achieve when not preoccupied with bodily and mental ills.

Cotton Mather, as is his way, hurriedly takes his leave and rushes out of the shop as if he's been being held there against his will.

'Your Sam has been congratulating me on not being a fruiterer,' Mr. Perry remarks.

'I beg your pardon?'

'He claims that he is sick and tired of calculating the cost of apples, and would welcome the chance of working out the amount owed for an armful of books.'

Sewall looks at his son in some surprise at this positive news. Sam doesn't quite catch his eye in return, in the way of the young when approval is on offer. He calls to mind his own calculations of a short while ago, using the friends and families of witches and accused witches as the factors for multiplication. Yes, adding up books must be a delightful pastime compared with certain alternatives. It isn't quite as satisfactory as actually *reading* them, and Sewall knows his Sam too well to harbour false hope in that direction, but perhaps some learning will rub off through talking to customers and even by handling the texts, as though one might absorb knowledge through the tips of one's fingers.

CHAPTER 21

George Jacobs is an old bent man in a long brown frock who hobbles along with the aid of two staffs. 'You tax me for a wizard,' he tells the court. 'You may as well tax me for a buzzard.' His voice is phlegmy yet cracked with age, an effect both rough and liquid at the same time.

One of the witnesses is his servant girl, Sarah Churchill. 'He has a servant, see,' Wait Still Winthrop whispers to Sewall. 'Some of these old farmers have more money squirrelled away than you would ever imagine.' Clearly Mr. Winthrop doesn't feel the rapport with farmers that he has with seafaring men.

Sarah Churchill testifies to being terrified at Jacobs's spectre. She doesn't look at her master while she speaks. Jacobs bangs one of his staffs in disgust at this evidence. 'Burn me or hang me,' he announces, 'I will stand in the truth of Christ. I know nothing of it.' Sarah's countenance goes puce with frustration at this denial. As she walks over to join the other accusers, Jacobs mutters 'Bitch witch' at her retreating back.

Sarah is followed by Jacobs's sixteen-year-old granddaughter, Margaret. 'As you know,' Stoughton tells the old man, 'the child was suspected of witchcraft, and at first denied it. But then she turned confessor herself. And she has provided testimony that incriminates both you and Mr. Burroughs. She is now going to be called as a witness against you.'

Margaret has dark hair and eyebrows, which emphasise the chalky paleness of her skin. Her eyes are large and rather tearful and her lips are tremulous. 'Margaret Jacobs,' says Mr.

Hathorne. 'Will you repeat your evidence against your grand-father for the court and people now assembled?'

There's a pause. Then she replies. 'No, sir.'

Another pause before Mr. Hathorne realises what she has said. 'What do you mean, no?'

'I just mean no, sir. Your honour. Or worship.' She looks wildly round the room as if for help.

'Has this wretch threatened you?' Hathorne points at old man Jacobs. 'Has he suborned you?'

Her gaze follows the direction of his arm. 'No, sir,' she says, then points at the accusers. 'It is these who threatened. And suborned. Sir.'

Hathorne follows *her* arm and allows himself a large start of astonishment when he arrives at the destination of its point. 'These? All of them?'

'Mary Walcott, sir, was one.' At this, Mary Walcott lets out a high-pitched shriek and falls to the floor. 'And Ann Putnam another.' Ann Putnam is facing away from Margaret Jacobs but on hearing her own name turns her head to face her, turns it strangely far on her shoulders, like an owl. She neither shrieks nor falls on this occasion but contents herself with giving her accuser a hard appraising stare, a stare that is much older than her years, as if her spirit is becoming seasoned by the constant deluge of suffering that has been beating away at it.

'After I was accused of witchcraft,' Margaret continues, 'these girls came to me and fell down as soon as they saw me. Just as Mary has now.' She looks down at Mary's body on the floor. As if aroused by her gaze, Mary Walcott stirs herself and begins to rise. The other girls help her to her feet. 'They told me that if I didn't confess I would be put in a dungeon, and afterwards hanged. This frightened me so much that I went to the marshall and confessed. Or pretended to. The girls told me that since I was a witch I must be acquainted with other witches. So I accused my grandfather and Mr. Burroughs.'

'You make it sound as if these girls were harming you, when it appears to me, and I am sure to my fellow judges'— Hathorne looks quickly along the line of fellow judges, who bow their heads by way of agreement—'that they were behaving like good friends with your best interests at heart, whether of body or soul.'

There is complete silence in the room, as everyone waits for Margaret Jacobs to reply to this. Finally in a very quiet voice she replies: 'They made me lie. And the night after I had made this confession, I didn't dare to sleep at all for fear that the Devil would carry me away for *telling* such horrible lies. What I said was altogether false against my grandfather and Mr. Burroughs. I did it to save my life and keep my liberty. But the Lord has charged it to my conscience, and filled me with such horror that I can no longer bear it, and I must deny my confession even though I can see nothing but death waiting for me. I'd rather die with a clear conscience than live a lie like that.'

She has said all this standing with her hands clasped in front of her, looking down at the floor. Old man Jacobs watches her intently all the while she speaks and as she finishes raises one hand towards her, waving his staff. The gesture clarifies this whole strange episode in Sewall's mind. The girl is willing to sacrifice not just her life but her very soul for this old man. Sewall remembers the occasion when he told his own daughter Betty he would ask to join her in hell. It is as if the present turn of events in court is designed to demonstrate to him the wickedness of that declaration. Family life can be intense and loving but it must give way before the love of God. Or rather, if one loves one's family aright, there should be no conflict with the love of God.

There's a long pause, then Mr. Stoughton speaks. 'Margaret Jacobs, you will be remanded in custody on a charge of witchcraft, to be examined in court at a later date.'

The girl bows her head and then, while it remains bowed, peers sideways at old man Jacobs. 'I ask your forgiveness, grandfather,' she says, a sob in her voice.

'You have it, you brave girl,' Jacobs replies. 'I shall leave you ten pounds in my will.'

'There you are,' Wait Still Winthrop whispers to Sewall. 'I told you these farmers are well off. It all comes down to money in the end.'

Sewall is not so sure, since the ten pounds will be of little use to Margaret Jacobs when she follows her grandfather to the gallows, as surely she must in due time. As if to confirm this thought, Margaret Jacobs shakes her head and smiles at the old man, as though to say his forgiveness is all she wants.

She is led off and shortly afterwards George Jacobs, having tended to torture, afflict, pine, consume, waste and torment certain of the accusers in full view of the open court, is found guilty of witchcraft.

George Burroughs's trial follows the pattern of his examination, except for two things. One of the afflicted girls, Mercy Lewis, confirms that Mr. Burroughs has been appointed by the Devil to reign over an evil America, should the country be lost to God's word. And that he will have a consort by his side, Martha Carrier, an elderly woman from Andover. She is to be Queen of American Hell, it turns out.

On the face of it Carrier is not the most obvious choice for this most elevated, or rather most ignoble, of positions—she is perhaps twenty years older than Burroughs, a hard-faced country woman. Many of the depositions against her relate to cutting the ears off sows and making cows lose their milk. But she is formidable in her own way.

During the course of the proceedings, one witness falls into a trance and cries out with her eyes rolled up so you can only see the whites, 'I wonder how you managed to murder thirteen persons?' Ann Putnam confirms this charge, claiming Carrier has indeed murdered thirteen people in her home town of Andover.

But Carrier turns to the judges, and takes it upon herself to rebuke them. 'It's a shameful thing you should mind these folks who are out of their wits.'

As she is led off in irons, Nicholas Noyes is so indignant at her arrogance and presumption he cries, 'Rampant hag!' at her clanking, retreating form.

The Proctors have learnt from Rebecca Nurse. They present a petition signed by thirty-one of their friends and neighbours. But this petition is counterbalanced by a swathe of depositions from witnesses who suffered torture from Proctor's spectre and that of his wife—and from other witnesses who are suffering such agonies now while the case unfolds. The two Proctors flutter up to the rafters just as they did at the examination, and Sewall is astonished at how their terrestrial bodies can so indignantly maintain their innocence while their avian projections hop about on the beams and preen themselves in full view of the afflicted girls.

The Proctors too are condemned to death, though Elizabeth Proctor brings a midwife into the court to testify that she is pregnant, so her sentence is suspended until the child is born. Stoughton gives her an icy gaze as he agrees to this delay.

The last case is that of John Willard of Salem Town (no relation to Sewall's pastor). He is a constable who was tasked at the time of the early examinations to bring suspects into court, a good example of the danger of contagion, because after a few weeks he began to defend the very witches he was entrusted to secure.

Mr. Hathorne asks Willard to recite the Lord's Prayer.

Straightaway he is confused, indeed seems to stumble at the

threshold of the prayer before he has even begun to recite it, making strangled sounds much as a fisherman might make preliminary casts before sending his hook to the water. 'Maker of heaven and earth,' he finally settles on. He realises immediately that this is not how the prayer begins, tries again, and misses once more. 'It's a strange thing,' he says, 'I can say it at another time. I must be bewitched just as these girls are. Say they are.' He gives out a high-pitched laugh that chills the marrow, it's so devoid of humour. He tries again, misses. Again, misses. 'Well, this is a strange thing,' he says again, shaking his head. 'I cannot say it.'

There's silence as the court waits. Again he tries, fails. He makes a sort of whimpering noise, sweat beading on his forehead. 'It's these wicked ones,' he says in a cajoling tone, gesturing vaguely round the room to indicate where the wicked ones might be hiding. 'They are overcoming me,' he whispers.

All the prisoners except Elizabeth Proctor are sentenced to be hanged on 19 August.

As the date of the hangings draws near, Sewall lies awake with one thing on his mind, a conundrum, both ludicrous and appalling at the same time. How will the old witch, George Jacobs, who can only walk with the aid of two staffs, mount his ladder in order to be hanged?

The hangman must be used to dealing with the ailing, the infirm, the crippled, above all the faint (not that Jacobs is likely to be one of these). But Sewall can't let it go. With the strange late-night lucidity that descends like a curse when you most want and need to sleep, his mind investigates the problem from all angles.

Perhaps Jacobs will be provided with very long staffs, so that he can continue to grip them even as he climbs up the rungs?

Perhaps the hangman will carry him up the ladder on his

shoulders? (Jacobs is small and thin, as witches usually seem to be, and the hangman is sturdy and strong, as hangmen usually seem to be.)

Perhaps the noose will be lowered so that Jacobs doesn't need to climb the ladder at all, and can be hoisted up rather than pushed down?

All of these are possible solutions but Sewall doesn't know which to fix on, so he tries out one after the other in his head and when he has finished the sequence he starts again. Every now and then he shakes himself vigorously, hoping to shake off the grisly tableaux, hoping to achieve an emptied head, but as soon as he stops the insectile image of George Jacobs enters his mind again, lurching towards the gallows on four legs.

Finally he creeps out of bed to check on Betty (wife Hannah is sleeping in her own room to escape his restlessness during the hot weather). Betty's fears have returned. A few days ago she asked, 'Why does God get angry? He must have been very angry when he killed all those people in Jamaica. Sam told me the earth shook and swallowed up the houses. And the sea shook and swallowed up the ships.'

'Mr. Mather says that the terrible earthquake was probably caused by the Devil,' Sewall told her. 'He had been imprisoned underground but escaped because the people had begun to use evil conjurations.'

Betty pondered this for a moment. 'But the Devil can only do bad things if God lets him,' she then said. This is a point that has been made several times in the trials. The issue of course is not about God *stopping* the Devil, but about the witches allowing him to *start*, just as those doomed Jamaicans did. 'But–why–does–*God*–get–angry?'

'I will tell you why. You know when we go into a shop and buy something that has to be weighed? Some apples, let us say, are put on one side of the scales, and weights on the other, and when the two sides are level we know the amount we are buying. God's anger is like those weights. It exactly equals the offence. If I allowed myself to be angry my anger would be too great or too small. But God's anger is always exact.'

'Sometimes He is very angry indeed.'

'That is because the sin must be very great indeed.'

'My sin is very great indeed. This is how I know I am not one of the elect—I can hear His voice in the night, shouting at me.'

Her breathing sounds regular but as Sewall peers across the dim room from the doorway he can make out the faint gleam of her open eyes. He stands for a while listening intently. If God is speaking to her it will be to her alone, but if His voice is as loud as she says it is, perhaps there will be some sort of after-echo. But he can hear nothing except, very faintly, the tick-tock of his new longcase clock in the hall downstairs. 'Are you all right?' he whispers finally.

She doesn't reply. He is about to turn away but then it occurs to him that she may be too choked up by her terror to speak. 'When I was a young man,' he says quietly, 'I felt great sorrow for my sins, just like you do. I also feared that I wasn't one of the elect.' He is about to explain the cause of this crisis, his unaccountable failure to confess his sins and the subsequent stillbirth of their firstborn son. But he doesn't want to overcomplicate the story, to make it specific to *him* when he needs it to be helpful to *her*. Also, perhaps, he is ashamed of confessing that long-ago failure to confess. 'I was in great torments until one day I read something that brought me some peace. It was such a comfort to me that I learned it off by heart and remember it even now, after all these years. Do you want me to recite it to you?'

It's a short passage written by the great Calvinist divine, John Owen, sometime chaplain to Oliver Cromwell and the man responsible for obtaining the release of John Bunyan from Bedford Prison. But scholarly attribution is not the point here.

'This is what was written,' Sewall tells the prone form of his daughter. '"No man ought, no man can, justly question his own election, doubt it or disbelieve it, until he finds himself in such a condition as to make it impossible that the effects of election can be found in him. If such a condition there be in this world."'

In his mind, the last sentence is italicised, but he no longer remembers whether this was the case in the original or whether he simply underlined it himself when he copied it down. Either way he repeats it to Betty to pass the emphasis on to her: '"If such a condition there be in this world."'

She still says nothing. He wonders if in fact she has fallen asleep. 'What I think it is saying,' he explains, 'is that God is so generous and forgiving, and loves humankind so much, that he has in fact elected *every*body to be his saints.'

He turns and is starting to tiptoe away when Betty speaks at last. 'If we are all elected, then why are the witches witches?'

'Perhaps election is like a birthright. We all receive it but the witches have sold theirs for a mess of pottage. Which in their case is the ability to fly on sticks and send their spectres to torment those who defy them. And suchlike tricks.'

Betty gives a little sigh at this explanation. Perhaps Owen's words will give her some peace, as they did him. But he must not give her vain hopes. He would be a poor parent if he didn't warn her the house might be built on sand. 'The writer doesn't know for sure. Nobody knows for sure. But what he is saying is that we must all live as if we *are* elected. There is no other way to live. Because then we will live good lives to justify our election.'

'I will try,' says Betty.

'My good girl.'

As he takes his leave Sewall wonders if the codicil he has added has undermined the helpfulness of Owen's main thrust, and left Betty subject to doubt and despair once more. That is the difficulty of exploring the paradoxes of election. At the very moment you experience hope you can succumb to fear. God has made their religion an anxious one, for good reason of course. It keeps his people sharp and alert. Hope and fear. Tick and then tock.

CHAPTER 22

Next day young Sam is home early from work. A passer-by came into the shop and berated him for hypocrisy. 'He said I was selling sermons and books of religion,' Sam explains.

'Well, so you were. At least, I hope you were.'

'While my father was hanging good Christian people.' His voice tails off as he repeats this allegation.

Sewall is aware of the way hostility is gathering. Two days ago Susan came back in tears after being sent out to do some shopping. Sarah said she herself would get the provisions for the time being. 'If anyone speaks out of turn to *me*, they're in for a shock,' she announced. 'Let them try to tell me there are no witches. I'll show them a witch.'

'Only proven witches are being hanged,' he tells Sam, 'not good Christian people. Witches, Sam!'

'Yes, father.'

'Witches! The opposite of good Christian people. The enemies of good Christian people.' Sewall takes a deep breath and steadies himself. 'And in any case, that isn't hypocrisy.'

'He said—'

'Hypocrisy is something that takes place inside a single person. When he professes one thing and does another. It can't take place between *two* people. If *I* do one thing and *you* do another, that's simply difference, not hypocrisy.'

Sam nods vigorously as he takes this distinction on board (if indeed he does), obviously keen to nod away any indignation his father might be feeling. But Sewall senses there is something more. 'And?' he asks.

'And what?' Sam looks at him with hot eyes (and cheeks).

'What else did the man say?'

'Nothing.' Sam shakes his head as vigorously as he nodded it a few moments before. Sewall continues to gaze steadily at him. Sure enough his son's evasiveness rapidly disperses. 'He said if anyone was a witch it was you,' he admits at last.

'Did he now?' Though he'd guessed before the boy even spoke, Sewall's heart thumps in his chest and he has to restrain it consciously, like a wilful horse. 'What did Mr. Perry say about that?'

'I didn't tell him. About you being a witch. I just told him about the hypocrisy part.'

Even this abridged accusation would have confirmed the very fears Mr. Perry expressed about employing Sam in the first place. Poor boy, this is not his fault. In fact, it not being his fault was exactly the point Sewall had wanted to get across. 'Was he upset.' Or annoyed.'

'He said I should come home.'

'I see.'

'And re-join the fray tomorrow. That's what he said. The fray.' Sam is obviously a little puzzled by the word.

'Ah ha!' says Sewall. Mr. Perry is a good-hearted man, after all. He might have had reservations about employing Sam, but now feels loyalty towards the lad.

'But perhaps I shouldn't. I don't want to harm his trade.'

'The man who said those foolish things to you was hardly likely to be a customer anyway. If he read books, he would be able to argue more cleverly.'

Sam ponders on this for a moment, like a chess player whose opponent has surprised him with a cunning move. 'Father,' he then says, somewhat tentatively.

'Yes, my son.'

'I don't like to look at Mr. Perry's face.'

'Why ever not?'

'Because he has that barnacle on it.'

'Barnacle? Ah, I think you mean carbuncle.'

'Carbuncle then. He looks as if he is going to grow a horn.'

'You're being silly, my boy,' Sewall replies, alarmed at this flight of fancy, a horn surfacing above that benign bookseller's countenance. Because the Devil is on the loose in Massachusetts, people are imagining him everywhere.

Sam continues unexpectedly, 'Standing behind the counter all day in this hot weather has made my legs swell up.'

'Is that so?' Sewall peers down at the part of his son's legs exposed below his breeches. Sam peers down as well. 'They look fine to me,' Sewall says, straightening up again.

'They must have cooled down by now. But maybe it would be better if I gave them a rest for a while.'

'Legs are for standing on, Sam.'

The following afternoon there's a knock on the door, Mr. Stoughton. Sewall receives him in the hall since his family are still in the garden and they have the room to themselves. He offers him cider to refresh himself with after his journey in the heat, but Stoughton has to be off as soon as he has said what he has to say. 'Mr. Sewall, I will come straight to the point. The next executions are on Thursday. Do you intend to be there?'

Sewall starts, as you do when another person asks a question you've been asking yourself. He has no desire whatsoever to attend the next batch of executions but wonders whether his attendance might be advisable, given that one of those condemned is a clergyman, that most of them are men, that the unrest in the community is becoming more and more audible. He is about to put this case when Stoughton speaks again: 'Don't.'

'I beg your pardon?'

'I would prefer you not to attend.'

Even though this is Sewall's own preference too, he finds himself bridling. 'I think—it may be politic—there is an audible—buzz . . .' He falters.

'Buzz! It's not our business to listen to *buzz*, as you call it. We simply do our duty. But in this instance our duty calls us in a different direction.'

'Oh. And which direction is that?'

'To Watertown.'

Sewall is taken aback at this reply. Watertown is a small community to the west of Boston, the opposite direction from Salem. 'The selectmen of the township are mired in a dispute. They have no meeting house and no minister. But they can't decide who to appoint, and at which end of the town, west or east, they should build.'

The whole point about such matters is that they are the community's own responsibility. Sewall tries to imagine why in this case they should be of concern to Mr. Stoughton and himself. 'They are a divided community, just as Salem Village was,' Stoughton continues. 'We don't want to see those sorts of grievance festering again. Perhaps advice from impartial outsiders might be helpful to them.'

Sewall is shocked as Stoughton's motive dawns on him. Two judges of the Court of Oyer and Terminer are to be seen assisting in the appointment of a clergyman to a troubled community, while thirty miles away, a clergyman from another troubled community is being hanged in accordance with the sentence passed on him by those very judges, along with their colleagues. Stoughton gives him a long unflinching look. 'It was you who introduced the word "politic" into our conversation,' he says.

There are two rival plots of land for the construction of a meeting house at Watertown. One, at the western end, is objected to by the eastern faction on the grounds of its proximity to the woods, which would leave it vulnerable to the onslaughts of Indians. The other is convenient for the dwellings of the easterners, and is therefore objected to by the westerners, in particular those on the outlying farms, on the grounds of the distance they would have to travel.

Despite the deadlock the township is in a great hurry to appoint a minister, only too aware of its need for spiritual protection from the plague of witchcraft all around. While the arguments rage Sewall thinks of the events taking place that day over in Salem Town.

Mr. Stoughton has told him that several other justices are attending the executions, along with a whole bevy of ministers. The hope of course is that one of the condemned will confess, perhaps to be followed by the others, as when a stone in a dam is dislodged and shortly the whole structure collapses. Sewall feels a deep impatience that he is here and not there, almost a jealousy of those who are able to attend. Finally he makes an exasperated suggestion. 'Given that you cannot agree on a place for a meeting house, but need a minister, perhaps you should appoint one first, and ordain him in the open air.'

To his amazement this proposal is greeted with enthusiasm. Mr. Stoughton raises an inquiring eyebrow at him across the congratulations. As they ride away, Sewall explains that he proffered this plan of action in the spirit of Solomon's solution to the problem of the baby, to concentrate the minds of the townsfolk on coming to an agreement (though when he remembers the dilapidated meeting house in Salem Village it occurs to him that open-air religion might not be a bad idea after all).

After Mr. Stoughton has taken off down the Dorchester road, Sewall heads straight for Cotton Mather's house to get news of the executions. Mr. Mather arrives from Salem Town at the very same moment and they talk on horseback at his garden gate, bobbing a little with the restiveness of the animals.

None of the witches confessed before they were turned off their ladders, despite the presence of six clergymen. 'Not even Carrier?' Sewall asks. It's hard to imagine a hard-bitten old country-woman like her forsaking her own best interest, or rather continuing to believe, in the face of the rope, that it is in her best interest to be Mr. Burroughs's consort in hell.

'Not even Carrier.'

Mr. Mather explains he stayed mounted during the executions so that he would not have to look upwards at the faces of the condemned. 'I did not want to crick my neck as if I were the supplicant and those wretches were raised on high.'

This could be Sewall's opportunity to discover how George Jacobs's death was managed but he cannot bring himself to ask the question. In any case Mather is in no mood to chat. He wants to get inside his house and have his supper.

Sewall heads his horse towards home. But as luck would have it, just as he arrives at his own gate Mr. Brattle appears.

'I've just attended a sad spectacle,' he announces. 'I had expected to find you there, in fact, but I gather you and Mr. Stoughton had a more important appointment somewhere else.'

Sewall does what he can to draw the sting from Mr. Brattle's irony. 'Indeed we did. There's nothing more important than assisting in the spiritual well-being of our fellows.' Mr. Brattle says nothing to this but continues to regard Sewall with a cold eye. To think, thinks Sewall, I have listened to *trumpets* with this man in London. 'I've just been speaking to Mr. Mather about it,' Sewall adds.

'Ah yes, Mr. Mather,' says Brattle. 'I hope he told you all that happened. I hope he told you how dignified the condemned were in meeting their fate. I hope he told you how they forgave the jury that found them guilty and the judges that condemned them to death.' He pauses to ensure this last shot has struck home. 'There's one thing I'll wager he *did*n't tell you. The condemned asked if one of the clergymen in attendance, the *six* clergymen in attendance, they asked if one of these six would pray with them before they died, and all of them refused. Your friend Mr. Noyes refused, Mr. Sewall. Your friend Cotton Mather refused. And I have to tell you that seeing these distinguished ministers of our province refuse outright to perform the duties of their office, many in the crowd began to mutter angrily. At that moment I felt the tide begin to turn. I felt the wind swing.'

'Mr. Brattle, the condemned died by a righteous sentence. They had no *cause* to forgive the jury or the judges. And since they didn't confess their sin, the ministers had no cause to pray with them. It would have been hypocrisy—'

'Talking of hypocrisy,' Mr. Brattle butts in, 'I don't suppose Mr. Mather mentioned the episode of the Lord's Prayer either. While on the very ladder facing imminent death, Mr. Burroughs recited the Lord's Prayer without a hesitation or a stumble. While standing beside him on the very next ladder was John Willard, who had been condemned for his *failure* to do that exact same thing. And in front of them there was Mr. Mather, who condemned the Lord's Prayer test in his *Return*, along with all such jiggery-pokery, and yet who still manages to endorse the trials out of loyalty to his friends who conduct them.'

Mr. Brattle shakes his head. 'And another thing Mr. Mather won't have admitted, I'm sure. He remained on his horse the whole time, as if watching innocent people die was just something you might do *en passant*. Or more likely he was all prepared for a swift departure if one of the condemned uttered a not-unjustifiable curse, as happened at the last hangings. Though these people were too serious, and too polite, had too much of a sense of occasion, since it was their last occasion, to indulge in any such vulgarity as a curse. Nevertheless, I expected Mr. Mather to bolt off into the blue at any moment.'

For a second Sewall is tempted to tell his erstwhile friend that he was wrong, at least in respect of Cotton Mather's motive for remaining on his horse, but thinks better of it.

That night Sewall has another unpleasant and turbid dream. In it he recollects that Elizabeth Proctor has now been widowed and he feels a strange, unhealthy empowerment in respect of her because this is (in part) the result of his own signature on her husband's death warrant. She is in fact an attractive woman, and for a moment Sewall understands what it is to succumb to the ruthlessness of an animal that has killed a rival male.

Then her features dissolve into those of Madam Winthrop and he once again witnesses the lifting of those damnified skirts of hers, more comprehensively than in life. And to complete this perverted harem of the imagination, the image of his sister-in-law appears, smiling across the table at him in her sunny parlour in Salem Town, a shimmer of reflected sea-glitter brushing across her face and shoulders as she offers him a portion of fried alewife on a spoon . . .

At last Sewall wakes up. As he lies in his bed (luckily Hannah is fast asleep) he reminds himself who and what he is or at least wants to be. A man trying to do his best in a difficult world, a man who loves his children, and his wife, and his community (most of it, at least). A man who wishes to be decent and kind where possible. How, then, can he have been thinking such wretched thoughts, wishing such wicked wishes?

He remembers John Proctor's charge, that the judges themselves were bewitched. And one of the customers of Mr. Perry's shop told young Sam that his father was a witch.

Sewall feels once again that the world is upside down, this

time literally, so that he has to cling on to his mattress to avoid falling off it. Yesterday a clergyman was hanged. What if he was innocent after all? That would be a work of the Devil— and of his minions. And what sort of man has lubricious dreams of the widow of a man he has hanged, and of the consort of a fellow judge? And of his own brother's wife?

The following afternoon he is at work on some accounts in his study when there's a knock on the door and Susan peeps timidly round it. 'Excuse me, sir, a visitor for you.'

He sighs at the interruption. 'Who is it, Susan?'

'Your brother Mr. Stephen, sir.'

Sewall nearly jumps out of his chair. 'Show him in, my girl, show him in,' he tells her, affecting briskness and animation as a substitute for the cheeriness he should normally feel at his beloved brother's arrival. While Susan is gone he steps round from behind his desk and paces agitatedly up and down the room.

'Hello, Sam,' says Stephen gravely as he comes through the door.

'Ah, Stephen!'

Stephen looks pale, smaller than his usual robust self. 'I had to come,' he says. 'I knew how you'd be feeling.'

'Ah,' Sewall replies. 'Yes.' He nods noncommittally.

'Yes. Because I felt the same. I didn't go, either.'

The hangings! For a second Sewall actually thinks, *Only* the hangings! 'Yes, I had to go to Watertown with Mr. Stoughton.'

'I expect your thoughts were in Salem the whole time.'

'Yes. They were.'

'Mine were too. I mean to say, I was *in* Salem all the time of course but I stayed in my house with Margaret. Safely at home.'

Of course, of course, nods Sewall, with Margaret, of course. 'A comfort,' he says. 'Margaret,' he explains.

'Yes. Hanging a minister.' Stephen shakes his head at the enormity of it. 'A minister hanged, and no confession. No confession from any of them.'

'Stephen, I want to tell you again how sorry I am.'

'Sorry? Whatever for?'

'For involving you in this horrible business.' (Sewall's apology conceals a more substantial one within, relating to his adulterous, even incestuous dream, like a ship declaring cargo to a certain value while smuggling more precious goods down in the darkness of its hold.)

Stephen pats him on the shoulder. 'We're all involved in it in any case, Sam. One way or another. The whole of Massachusetts is involved in it. Except for the governor, who I suppose is sitting in a forest clearing somewhere, keeping his powder dry.' Sewall gives a shrug to acknowledge the governor's avoidance of this crisis. 'But something came to my attention yesterday evening which brought me great comfort,' Stephen continues. 'And I'm sure it will reassure you, too.'

'Oh yes?'

'A young girl called Sarah Wilson has described a meeting of the witches that took place the night before last—the night before the hangings. Mr. Burroughs attended.'

'Mr. Burroughs?'

'In his spectral form, of course. He conducted a sacrament. It was just like the Last Supper.'

'*Simia Dei*,' says Sewall.

'Bless you!' cries Stephen, for a second his old cheerful self once more. 'Was that a sneeze?'

'*Simia Dei*,' repeats Sewall. 'It means Ape of God. It's when the Devil and his minions repeat the actions and observances of Christians.'

'Ah, indeed. Well, the important part of this aping business happened at the end. Mr. Burroughs takes leave of those disciples of his, and says unto them (so to speak), "Stand firm in your faith." In their Satanic faith, of course he means. "Stand firm," he says, and then adds, "and admit nothing."'

'Well, this girl, Sarah Wilson, didn't abide by that instruction for long.'

'Ah, but she's an accuser. She makes it her business to report back on these matters. But the important point, brother, is that those witches who were hanged yesterday had received a commandment just the night before telling them not to confess. So that's why they didn't, even to save their skins.'

The significance finally sinks in. The witches were under a specific order, freshly asserted, not to confess! Sewall was deeply concerned at their failure to do so. He feared that their inexplicable steadfastness might point to innocence after all (his mental perturbation at that possibility might even have been the cause of last night's wretched dream). And now, here is Stephen with reassurance. The lack of confessions may provide *further* proof of the guilt of the witches, not the opposite.

It was so thoughtful of his brother to come posthaste with this news. Being the recipient of such kindness must dispel dark and lowering thoughts. They were merely things of the night, and of no account in the day. 'Stephen,' he says, 'let's have something to drink. And then you must sit down to dinner with us all.' But as he smiles this welcome, Sewall has a sudden fear some fiendish thing might in fact be smiling through the mask of his face.

CHAPTER 23

It's the beginning of September but the heatwave continues. The phenomenon is well-named because large and solid objects like buildings and trees, like Boston Common itself, seem to waver and shimmy in the glare. The witches have brought a taste of hellfire to Massachusetts.

Mr. Stoughton calls a meeting of the judges behind closed doors in the Boston Town House. 'Mr. Alden's escape,' he tells them, 'should concentrate our minds.'

'Mr. Alden?' asks Sewall in astonishment.

'News has come that Mr. Alden made his escape last night,' explains Wait Still Winthrop. 'He and his wife have fled from Boston. It's thought they're making for New York.'

Sewall is conscious of an enormous weight lifting from his shoulders. The prospect of being on the bench while his old friend was on trial for his life has been haunting him ever since he first heard of the accusations.

'And Mrs. Bradbury also made her escape from jail, just a couple of nights ago. Her husband is a shipbuilder, in Salisbury.'

Sewall is a sociable man, living in the heart of the most important town in the province, taking an active part in his community, always interested in the affairs of his fellow citizens, banking their money, supplying their imported goods, sitting in judgement on them when they are accused of crimes. And yet he has noticed before that quite often he seems the last to hear of the latest goings-on.

'In these cases there was a degree of community support,'

Mr. Stoughton continues. 'We all know about Mr. Alden's standing, not to mention his father's. Then at Mrs. Bradbury's examination there was a letter signed by over a hundred of her fellow townspeople from Salisbury—'

'A hundred?' interjects Sewall. That multiplication exercise he contrived while walking with Sam to Mr. Perry's bookshop is out of date.

'As well as one from her minister, who should know better where his duty lies. What I'm talking about is a developing weight of opposition which is helping to undo locks and bribe officials and create a further threat to law and order, which goodness knows is under enough threat already. Just yesterday I received the copy of a deposition by a confessor called George Barker which claims that there are three hundred and seven witches now at work in Massachusetts Bay. This Barker fellow says they specifically cursed us, the judges. They fear, quite rightly, that we are set on undermining their plans for destroying the Christian churches in our province and returning the whole place to the paganism of the Indians. Also for making everyone equal, without any resurrection to hope for or judgement to fear—for making everyone equally *wicked*, in other words. He says that the witches intend that the afflicted and tormented girls should themselves be mistaken for witches, and that the public should start to believe that innocent people are being condemned. Which is precisely what we see is beginning to happen. If we are not careful the wind will veer.'

Sewall ponders on Mr. Stoughton's use of the same metaphor as Mr. Brattle, even though the one fears what the other celebrates. Neither of them is evilly disposed, yet in this current state of affairs they have opposite views as to what is good and what bad—just as the witches intended, according to Goodman Barker's report.

Mr. Stoughton intends to speed up the judicial process in

order to keep abreast of the gathering momentum of witch-craft. A group of trials is already scheduled for 9 September; he wants another to take place just over a week later, on the seventeenth. Then a hanging day to be scheduled for both sessions on 22 September.

Sewall objects: arranging executions in advance pre-empts the outcome of the trials. Stoughton concedes—the hanging day will be *provisionally* scheduled for that date should it be needed. 'This has become a war,' he concludes. 'We must move as firmly, as resolutely, and as speedily as our enemies.'

Outside the Town House the sun beats down as unrelent-ingly as before though now it's mid-afternoon and time for din-ner. Sewall has invited Mr. Winthrop to eat a pie with him at the Castle Tavern. It's by way of secret apology for dreaming of Madam Winthrop in that lecherous fashion the other night.

They have hardly taken a step from the Town House when they bump into Mr. Brattle. 'Well, well,' he says, making a bow, 'two honourable judges at a stroke. And several more over there. A parliament of justices. Or perhaps coven would be more apt?'

'I must object—,' begins Mr. Winthrop. Sewall grasps him by the elbow to remind him of their waiting dinner—there's no point in letting Mr. Brattle provoke them. He's probably been hanging around outside the Town House for that explicit purpose.

'I expect Mr. Stoughton is impatient to hurry matters along,' Mr. Brattle continues. 'I understand the governor is likely to return to Boston in the next few weeks. You need to make your hay while this intolerable sun still shines. Good day to you, gentlemen.'

'Have you heard that news, Mr. Sewall?' asks Mr. Winthrop as soon as Brattle is out of earshot. His obvious alarm makes

Sewall think of young reprobates anticipating the arrival of a parent or a teacher in the room.

'I always seem to be the last to hear about such things.'

'I wonder how Brattle found out.'

'Perhaps he wrote to him. And was written to in return.'

'Goodness. Do you think so? I didn't know the governor could write.' Mr. Winthrop suddenly bursts into laughter, which is infectious, so Sewall laughs too though, as sometimes happens, unhappiness wobbles just beneath his merriment, an unhappiness composed of both indignation and fear as he recalls that contemptuous reference to 'a coven of justices'.

Worse is to come. After Mr. Winthrop has taken his leave at the end of the meal, and Sewall is just brushing crumbs off his cravat, Captain Wing approaches the table, moving sideways as if being blown against his will by a strong wind.

'A word, your honour,' he whispers.

Sewall sighs. He is tired of telling people not to *your honour* him. 'What is it, Captain Wing?'

'I just thought. A word. As a friend. And fellow congregant.'

'Yes?'

'You know how it is, in an inn. Wine. Tongues wag.' He wags his hand like an enormous tongue. Sewall's heart plummets as he realises (almost supernaturally) just what it is the innkeeper is about to say. 'Some people have been saying your honour is . . . ,' continues Wing. 'Just silly gossip. A witch.'

Tit for tat, Sewall thinks, glaring at the table top. Tit for tat, he thinks again, as he rises to his feet and plods to the door. It's because he forbade the magician—what better revenge than to accuse him of being a magician himself, a magician of the worst possible kind?

But once out in hot daylight he reminds himself that Captain Wing is a better man than that. Ever since John Proctor claimed in his letter that the judges were under a delusion from the Devil, that charge has been being whispered abroad. If the witches are innocent, then the judges must be guilty. If the witches aren't witches, then who are?

In the next batch of trials all the defendants are found guilty, and sentenced to hang—except one.

Giles Corey is a barrel-chested farmer of eighty, with deep-set suspicious eyes and a head of thickly growing white hair. Despite his age he looks strong, the way a boulder or a tree is strong. No doubt he has passed his life in close proximity to such things. When he is asked to confirm his name he doesn't reply (just as a tree wouldn't reply). His wife, Martha Corey, has already been sentenced to die on the twenty-second. Mr. Hathorne repeats the question, his voice getting harsher each time, but Corey remains silent. Finally Mr. Stoughton intervenes. 'Just call him Goodman,' he says wearily.

'Goodman,' says Hathorne, 'how do you plead?'

Again Corey is silent, sullenly staring straight ahead. Once more the question is repeated. The public begin to murmur. Stoughton has had enough. 'The justices will consult on this matter,' he suddenly declares, cutting across Hathorne's reiterations, 'and will announce their conclusion in due course. Take him away,' he tells the marshall.

Stephen looks bewilderedly across at Sewall, unsure what, if anything, to write in his transcript of proceedings.

The judges go to Mr. Noyes's parlour for the adjournment. There are several bottles of wine and a platter of small cakes waiting on the table for them.

'It's these farmers,' says Mr. Winthrop, swallowing a cake in one go as if it was an oyster. His eyes bulge a little with the effort of directing speech through this intervening medium. 'They do like to hold on to their money. This Corey thinks that if he pleads and is tried and hanged, the court will confiscate his possessions, especially as his wife will be hanged at the same time. But if instead of being hanged for witchcraft he's hanged for not pleading at all, for whatever you might call it—'

'Perverting the course of justice,' suggests Sewall.

'Perverting the course of justice,' Mr. Winthrop agrees, 'then the money may remain intact.'

'Whatever his motive, Goodman Corey has called our bluff,' says Mr. Stoughton, 'and I need to reflect on our response. I can't think straight here in any case, with that bald-headed vulture hopping about outside the door and listening to every word we say.' He takes a good swig of the vulture's vintage wine. 'I suggest we convene in the Boston Town House in three days' time to decide what to do.'

As they file out through the vestibule, Sewall notices with a pang that Mr. Noyes is indeed hopping, or at least bobbing, as he acknowledges the exiting dignitaries in rapid succession. His large round face looks pale and strained and there's a somewhat anxious and ingratiating smile on his lips.

'Since we last met,' says Mr. Stoughton, opening the meeting at Boston Town House, 'there has been a development relating to another case, and I would like us to start by considering that, before moving on to the matter of Goodman Corey.'

Sewall looks about him uneasily, wondering if this is another escaped prisoner that everyone knows about but him. However the development consists of a letter from one of the condemned, Mary Easty, who like Goody Cloyse is a sister of Rebecca Nurse. 'She addressed it to all the judges,' explains Stoughton, 'so I have had it copied to enable each of you to read it for yourself.'

Mary Easty explains how she was imprisoned, then released, then imprisoned again owing to the wiles and subtlety of her accusers. She knows she is innocent, and therefore concludes that many others of the accused must be innocent too. I petition not for my own life, she says, but for those others. The judges are on the wrong track, and making terrible mistakes. She suggests they interrogate the accusers separately from each other, and also bring to trial some of the confessors—this, she predicts, will soon bring an end to their strategy of saving themselves by apportioning blame to others.

She concludes on a strangely serene note of forgiveness, as if she has been appointed by some higher power to be judge of the judges themselves: 'I don't question that your honours are doing your best to detect witchcraft and witches,' she explains, 'and that you would not be guilty of shedding innocent blood for all the world.' Sewall finds his eyes blurring as he reaches this generous conclusion, so different from Proctor's harsh accusation.

'Good to have her vote of confidence,' says Stoughton drily, when everyone has looked up from their reading. 'Now, the reason why I wanted you to look at Easty's letter before we move on to consider the wretched matter of Giles Corey is this. Our court is under attack. People are questioning not merely our decisions, but our basic procedures and the legitimacy of the court itself. This state of affairs is hardly surprising since our plantation as a *whole* is under attack.

'But when you are under attack you have to be strategic. To use a word of my good friend Mr. Sewall, you need to be *politic*.'

Sewall is startled to hear his name enter Mr. Stoughton's monologue in this fashion. He looks around the table, almost wanting to shake his head and deny saying it, though of course he *did* say it, even though it now seems foisted upon him. It's Mr. Stoughton who is being politic.

'And one of the most politic and strategic of manoeuvres,' Mr. Stoughton continues, 'is to give a little on one front while remaining firm on another. Goodman Corey refuses to cooperate with the court; he refuses, we may infer, to *recognise* it.

This is absolutely unacceptable, and I use the word "absolutely" with its full force. We must go to any lengths, any lengths at all, to make an example of him and ensure that others aren't tempted to the same defiance. But to demonstrate that we are willing to listen to *legitimate* concerns we will at the same time take Mary Easty's advice and prosecute some of the confessors at next week's trials. Since she is not asking in order to save her own neck we can do this without the appearance of weakness.'

Sewall is appalled. The last thing he wants is for the confessors to face trial. By the very act of confessing, as far as he is concerned, they have cleansed themselves of demonic possession. 'I must protest—,' he begins.

'I thought you might,' says Mr. Stoughton, with a small smile. 'If they should be found guilty, which is highly likely since they have already confessed, they will not hang with the others on the twenty-second. Rather we will store them away (under sentence of death) for future use, like so many root vegetables in a root cellar. We can't afford to lose the information they give us about their fellow witches.'

This is such a travesty of his real concern that Sewall finds himself literally speechless. While he is in that state Stoughton explains the sanction he has found to apply in Giles Corey's case. It is an old English punishment called *peine forte et dure*, never repealed and fully applicable in America, though not till now invoked. The condemned man is buried under a great heap of rocks until he can breathe no longer. 'It's designed to ensure the malefactor feels the full weight of the law,' Stoughton concludes.

A cautious laugh goes round the table, his hearers not being entirely sure whether his words are meant for a witticism or not. Sewall however stares mutely straight ahead just as Giles Corey did in the court.

Stoughton goes on to explain that to mitigate the draconian

nature of this punishment, Mr. Corey will have until 19 September to consider his position, and during that period can be reasoned with by friends and sympathisers, and indeed by the judges themselves. Even when the punishment has begun, he can still stop its continuance by agreeing to speak. There would then be a trial specially convened for him, and if found guilty he can be hanged in a civilised manner with his wife and the others on 22 September.

The trials of 17 September proceed in the usual way. All the accused are found guilty. This includes five confessors, who are remanded indefinitely for sentencing while the others are condemned, making a total of nine in all from the two September sessions to be hanged on 22 September, eight women and a man.

As well as Giles Corey, who is to be pressed to death on 19 September.

Like the other judges Sewall makes several visits to Corey in the Salem lock-up where he is being held pending execution, pleading with him to speak and recognise the court, but to no avail. Corey just looks straight in front of him as if he is all alone in the little stone room. The horror of being pressed to death, as opposed to the comparatively speedy process of being hanged, is explained to him (though none of the judges, of course, has witnessed a judicial pressing so they have to improvise the medical details). Corey remains impervious.

The morning of the nineteenth dawns hot and fair, as every other morning has for weeks. Sewall can eat no breakfast—he wonders whether, over in the lock-up, Corey is having anything, or whether in view of what is to happen he'll consider it wiser to abstain. Margaret comes up, rests a hand on his shoulder, and looks him in the eyes. 'Is there nothing that can be done, brother Sam?' she asks.

'We've tried everything we can, but he's obdurate. We'll try again this morning, of course, just in case.'

'That's the thing about these old farmers,' says Stephen. 'They can be so pig-headed.'

Stephen is trying to reinstate a sense of normal life, Sewall understands, as if being pig-headed about the prospect of *peine forte et dure* is much the same as being stubborn about when to plant your seeds or harvest your crops.

'I didn't mean about changing Giles Corey's mind,' says Margaret, 'but rather the court's.' She stands in front of him, a warm and attractive woman, her dark eyes brim-full of sympathy, yet Sewall feels a flush of anger at her very kindness. Perhaps this is resentment at the way she tempted him in his dream, though that was hardly her fault. It may simply be that her sympathy reminds him she has the comfort of home and family on this bright September day while he has to confront the darkness of the witchcraft.

'The court has to stand firm,' he tells her. 'If it falters, it will be destroyed, and so will our city on a hill.' He thinks yet again of the pirates, and of his weakness in that matter. Perhaps that was the very moment when the door was opened to allow this overwhelming evil to enter Massachusetts, the moment when the judicial system failed in its responsibility to be *absolute*, to use Mr. Stoughton's word. 'I'm sorry, Margaret, we can't give way. There is too much at stake, there is everything at stake.'

Margaret takes her hand from his shoulder, makes it into a fist and punches it into her other one. 'You *can't* budge, and he won't,' she says. 'It's—I don't know what it is. It's a horrible collision.'

'But we are the stronger party,' says Sewall. 'It's he who'll be crushed.' He stops abruptly, aware of the unlucky literalness of the verb he has chosen. He thinks of all those petitions by friends of the defendants, of the intercessions by ministers of the accused, of the increasingly angry complaints of the people at large, and wonders how true it is in any case.

A heap of rocks has been made on the grassy area in front of the gallows. They have been carefully selected so that each one is quite heavy but not so large that it can't readily be picked up and put in place by the hangman or his assistant. They are also fairly flat in shape so that they can be piled without rolling off.

Sewall has conceived a dislike of the hangman, a man called Sturgis. His is not, of course, a lovable trade in any case, but this particular specimen is a squat, strong individual (not unlike Corey himself in figure) with long muscular arms (his hands reach almost to his knees), and he is very brusque in his treatment of the condemned. He always has a pipe in his mouth and bustles about his business in a cloud of smoke as if he, like the master of his recent, current and pending clients, has made his entrance on to this stage through an aperture in hell.

It's about nine-thirty when Sewall arrives. Mr. Stoughton and several other judges are here already, as are Mr. Noyes and Cotton Mather. There is also a large crowd, kept at a distance from the execution area by temporary paling fences which are patrolled by a surprising number of constables. Like the last time he was here, Sewall notices a lack of the jollity normally associated with executions. There are no pie-men or beer-sellers despite the fact that this event is likely to last some time, and some of the people seem to be bad-mouthing the judges, though they cunningly pitch their voices below the level of audibility.

'I didn't expect you to come,' he tells Mr. Mather. He can't imagine anyone attending today who isn't duty-bound to do so.

Cotton Mather's face has lost its rosy colour and peers out

whitely from beneath his wig. 'This execution is a new thing in our country,' says Mather. 'I needed to be here.' Sewall is unnerved by this reasoning—Mr. Mather has come because of the scientific importance of the occasion, as you might for the dissection of an unusual frog.

Mr. Stoughton steps over to them. 'I'm glad you're here,' he tells Cotton Mather. 'The governor will arrive back in Boston shortly. He has sent me word that he is perplexed to hear of all the witchcraft hangings that have taken place, and of the ones that are arranged, and wishes to have an account of the proceedings from an impartial observer. I think the ideal person for the task would be you, Mr. Mather, after your work on *The Return*, which proved a helpful document in the end.' Sewall wonders how loaded that last word is, since Mr. Mather's essay *criticised* the trials until the postscript, which he wrote in response to Sewall's complaint.

Mr. Mather gives a deep bow, obviously delighted with this task.

'The governor also expresses his extreme displeasure at the sentence we have passed on Giles Corey,' adds Stoughton grimly.

'Does this mean a reprieve?' Sewall asks, unable to keep hope from his voice even though he accepts the necessity of the sentence and has limited faith in the governor's judgement.

'No, indeed. The law must carry through its course, though painful and long.' Stoughton gives Mather and Sewall a significant look to check that they've registered this reference to the old French term for the punishment.

Mr. Noyes, who has been hovering about on the fringes of the conversation, now intervenes. 'I think I can suggest a reason for the governor's concern,' he says. 'There are rumours of witchcraft concerning his lady. Informal accusations of course. I am told that that is the main reason why he has returned from his business in the forests, whatever that was. His *déjeuner sur l'herbe.'* He gives a pleased look at the felicity of this sarcasm, couched in today's language of choice.

'Be that as it may,' says Stoughton. He turns rather obviously, so that his back is to Mr. Noyes, and continues in a lowered voice to ensure that neither Mr. Noyes nor the spectators can make out what he's saying: 'Giles Corey should be on his way here now. The execution will begin at ten o'clock. I have told Sturgis to arrange matters so that it is all over by noon. I think that will be long enough.'

The remaining judges arrive, and soon the cart trundles up the hill with Corey sitting on the back of it, still strangely imperturbable. When they arrive, Sturgis drags him off and pushes him over to stand beside the rocks. At this a half suppressed moan is emitted by the onlookers. Once again Mr. Stoughton asks Corey if he will plead, speaking loudly this time to ensure that the crowd understand the condemned man is being offered every chance. Once again Corey says nothing but remains looking straight ahead.

Mr. Stoughton then gives the nod to Mr. Sturgis, who indicates to the condemned man that he should lie down. But Corey's hands are pinioned in front of him and he is unable to do so unaided, though he bends his knees a few times. It's horrible to see his efforts to cooperate with the appalling thing that is about to be done to him, this man who has not cooperated in any other respect. Sewall avoided the sight of George Jacobs coping on his crutches with the gallows (except in his nightmares) but now has to watch this old man struggle instead.

Suddenly Sturgis kicks Corey's legs from under him. Immediately there are angry shouts from the crowd. Mr. Stoughton shakes his head at Sturgis to make it clear this roughness is uncalled for. Sturgis just puffs out smoke in reply.

Luckily—luckily?—Corey's eyes have opened: he has not lost consciousness. Mr. Stoughton walks slowly up to him, and then ponderously and deliberately kneels, almost as if he is asking forgiveness. Again in a loud voice (so loud and so near his ear that Corey flinches, the loudness being once again for the benefit of the people) the request for him to plead; with the same result.

Mr. Stoughton rises to his feet, gives a sigh, shakes his head again, then makes a signal to Sturgis, who uses a rope to bind Corey's legs together. He gathers up the first of the rocks and places it carefully on Corey's midriff so that it will act as a sort of keystone for the ensuing structure. Soon there is a row of rocks the length of his trunk, with Corey's head poking out of the end of the mound. His face has become very red and his breathing is laboured.

Stoughton indicates to Sturgis that he should pause in his work. He then approaches Corey, kneels once more, and asks if he will plead.

At eleven, a start is made on putting a second row of rocks in place.

There is now a continuous deep growling from the crowd, like the noise an angry dog makes in the back of its throat except that it comes from all quarters, the dog being a general dog.

When these stones are all in position, Sewall notices that Corey's face has gone from red to blue, and his breathing is now shallow and rapid. Every now and again his eyes seem to roll up into his head and it is with a seeming effort of will that he brings them back down again. They are perhaps the last part of himself over which he can assert some sort of control.

There's another wait. Then towards noon Mr. Stoughton approaches the condemned man for a final time. Once again he kneels and asks him the question, though this time it's not clear whether Corey could reply even if he wished to. Then he straightens up and nods to Sturgis to continue piling up the rocks.

Sewall daren't turn away—it would seem like a shirking of his judicial responsibility, with the hostile crowd looking on. By the same token he daren't even close his eyes, but he manages somehow to withdraw from his own gaze, as if his eyes are a pair of windows that his inner self has chosen not to look through. He is aware though of the third row of rocks being completed, of Sturgis looking up at Mr. Stoughton, of Mr. Stoughton giving a nod, of a fourth row being commenced.

Then he hears a low detonation, faint but deep, followed by another. The sounds are like the remote crumps of a cannon fired in some faraway fort. He realises with horror that he is hearing Corey's ribs collapse, and there's another noise too, that of himself whimpering, which he aborts at once with a brisk clearing of his throat.

A sudden tiny movement snags his attention and now he is looking out of his eyes once more, seeing in fact with a sudden clarity as if he has put on a pair of spectacles. Corey's own eyes stare fixedly upwards, and his tongue has sprouted from his mouth like a toadstool. As Sewall watches, the marshall steps over, raises his staff, places the tip delicately on the end of Corey's tongue and pushes it neatly back into his mouth again.

Mr. Mather steps over to Sewall. His face is ashen but his eyes are bright with excitement. 'Consider,' he says, 'the French for tongue is *langue*, which also means language, that is to say, a form of speech. Giles Corey is being executed for remaining silent. But now it's as if his body has agreed to obey the court even while his mind stays obstinate. In short, he's ceased to hold his tongue.'

The symbolic symmetry of this obviously pleases him immensely, gives him the sense that a task has been completed. But in fact Sewall can't see that anything has been achieved. Corey has defied the court despite his tongue's waywardness; the court has in turn been as implacable as the condemned man.

Sewall wonders at the strength of a Devil's contract that can bind a man to silence in the face of such appalling suffering.

Now Mr. Stoughton addresses the crowd. 'All signs of life are extinct. The execution is completed. The body will remain in position for another hour, and then will be released for burial.'

Sewall waits fearfully for the crowd's reaction to this bald assertion, but none comes. They seem too sick at heart to respond and gradually start turning away and trudging off.

Mr. Noyes comes over with strange jerky movements as if suffering from St Vitus' dance. 'Well, well,' he says. 'Well!' His eyes are feverish. 'I must say, the court is vindicated. It has vindicated itself. People will think twice before trying to defy it again. I must hurry home and tell Anne all that has happened.'

Just as Sewall is leaving the execution ground he is confronted by a man he faintly recognises. 'We are well rid of that creature,' says the man. 'He tormented my daughter Ann on innumerable occasions.'

In his confusion Sewall thinks for a moment that the man is referring to Mr. Noyes's housekeeper, but then realises that he's the father of the most tormented of all the accusers, Ann Putnam (according to Stephen the little girl has been the victim of over seventy witches to date). He opens his mouth to reply but no words come out and to his horror he finds himself weeping, tears blinding his eyes and streaming down his face. All he can think of is the pain, the terrible pain, *peine forte et dure*, pain lasting so long, and so endured!

CHAPTER 24

It is boiled bacon and cabbage, and he eats and eats, not tasting the food. Afterwards, a tart Margaret has made with preserved raspberries from earlier in the summer, and cream. When at last he has finished Sewall sits where he is, not daring to speak.

Margaret glances at Stephen, who looks back at her. His honest troubled face then turns towards Sewall, who doesn't catch his eye but continues to look slightly downwards at his empty plate. 'Brother,' says Stephen, 'you must remember it was Mr. Stoughton who chose this punishment, as senior justice of the court. It was not your doing. I doubt you had even heard of it before he dug it out of some old law book.'

Sewall thinks: yes, but I promised myself I would defy Mr. Stoughton, or any other man in authority, if I thought he turned from the right way. After the pirates, that was my resolution. But all I have done is protest about little things, tweaked a decision here, made a small objection there. When it came to crushing a man to death I did nothing to stop it. He would like to tell Stephen this. But if he opens his mouth to speak, his words will be swept away on his breaking tears like drowning voyagers in the middle of the ocean.

'Also, Giles Corey was given ample opportunity to plead to the court. You tried with him over and again, and so did others. It was his choice to remain silent, and suffer the consequences.'

Sewall thinks: if Giles Corey had chosen to plead he would have pleaded not guilty, and then he would have been found guilty, like all the others.

It could be that this is because the evidence is true, and its repetitive nature simply reflects the repeated attacks of the witches to gain purchase in New England. That is what Sewall has always believed. But the fact remains that not one of those condemned has so far confessed to avoid execution, despite the fact that no actual confessor has yet been executed. They have gone to their deaths firm in their assertions of innocence. And Corey has gone to the most terrible death of all without even spelling innocence *out*, as if the word would simply be wasted on the sceptical ears of the judges. He died a mute martyr and left his crushed body to plead for him. If you plead not guilty and then are found guilty you have been contradicted. If you don't plead no one can answer you.

And if he is innocent what does that make Sewall, and the other judges?

From far away there is a knocking and Sewall wants to say I hear death knocking for me, the Devil has come to my door, but he daren't open his mouth, not for fear of tears this time but of vomit, for fear that what will fly out will be vomit.

Stephen comes into the room, though Sewall is unaware he'd left it. 'This is a strange thing,' he says. 'There was no one there. And then I found this letter had been slipped underneath the door. Sam, it's addressed to you.' He holds the letter over the table top, then withdraws it. It's one of those moments when Sewall can read what is in his brother's mind as if it were in his own. The thought has occurred to Stephen that the letter might contain abuse relating to Corey's execution. 'Shall I open it for you, brother?'

Sewall holds out his hand and Stephen gingerly passes it over. It's simply a piece of folded paper, without a seal, addressed to Justice Sewall. The letter is from Thomas Putnam. In it he explains that his daughter Ann was visited by a ghost in a winding-sheet just last night. The spectre told her that he was a farmworker called Jacob Goodale. Nearly twenty years previously Giles Corey had murdered him in an argument over wages. Then he had made a pact with the Devil, who had promised that he would never hang. Strangely during Corey's appearances in court no one remembered that this had happened.

Sewall hands the letter over to Stephen who reads it out to Margaret, then springs to his feet. 'As it happens I have the Salem court records in my study,' he says. 'I borrowed them so that I could make my account of the Oyer and Terminer proceedings conform. I will check to see if there is any record of a case involving the murder of this Jacob Goodale.'

Sewall also rises to his feet, and follows Stephen into the study. It takes the latter about twenty minutes to find the reference. One day, eighteen years ago, Corey beat Jacob Goodale over a hundred times with a stick. The poor man died a few days later, having refused to swear a complaint against his master. As a result of this silence Corey was merely charged with abuse, and fined. Because the case itself (as opposed to the actual assault) was a minor one, it wasn't referred to in the witchcraft hearings. And perhaps the neighbours of the violent old farmer were too intimidated to bring this old story to anyone's attention.

Thomas Putnam said in his letter: 'God so hardened his heart that he wouldn't listen to the advice of the court and so die an easy death.' Perhaps. Another explanation might be that Corey's own sense of guilt stopped him pleading; that is to say, because his victim hadn't sworn against *him*, Corey refused to swear in turn.

These thoughts swirl around in Sewall's mind after Stephen has read out the relevant entry in the court report. 'Beating is a kind of pressing, isn't it, a sharp and sudden kind?' Sewall asks him.

Stephen frowns at the odd question. 'Perhaps,' he says in a humouring voice, unsure of Sewall's drift.

His drift is that in these circumstances *peine forte et dure* wasn't an arbitrary and cruel punishment, but one that turned out to be surprisingly appropriate for the case, though the judges themselves didn't even know it; that behind the judicial deliberations it is possible after all to discover God's guiding hand.

He steps round the desk and hugs his brother. Margaret, hearing affirmative noises, comes into the room, and Sewall hugs her in turn (in a chaste and brotherly fashion). He feels, despite those pounds of boiled bacon, despite that mountain of cabbage, despite successive wedges of raspberry tart, strangely light.

Next day he's off to see his pastor, Mr. Willard, hoping to discuss his discovery about the Corey case with him. The minister answers the door himself, peering round it cautiously. He motions with his head for Sewall to come in. It's comical to see his grave furtiveness.

Safely in his study, he explains: 'There has been some talk.'

'Talk?'

'People have been talking about me.'

'What can people have to say about *you*?' asks Sewall, realising straightaway that this hardly sounds polite.

Mr. Willard looks about his study as if to make absolutely sure nobody is spying on them. 'They've been saying I'm a witch.'

Sewall looks at him in astonishment.

'Also Mrs. Willard,' the minister continues.

'*Mrs.* Willard?' That is even more absurd. Mrs. Willard is a quiet, somewhat mousey woman, very much in the thrall of her husband. Wife Hannah laughs a little at her tendency to preface every statement with Mr. Willard thinks that, or says this. 'Who has been saying such things?'

Willard gives a bitter little laugh. 'Everyone. No one. You know how it is. Do you remember how in that remote time before this terrible heatwave began we used to sometimes say,

"There's rain in the air"? When you couldn't see it and you couldn't exactly feel it but there it was, as though hiding round some corner of the breeze?' Persecution and fear seems to have brought out a poetical side to Mr. Willard. 'That's how it is with these whispers.'

'I'm amazed,' Sewall says. He nearly adds: since the witches already *have* their minister, Mr. Burroughs, but thinks better of it.

'And as you know,' continues Willard, 'one of my congregation, my good friend John Alden, has had to flee for his life."

'My good friend, also,' says Sewall. 'As are you too, of course.'

Mr. Willard nods in appreciation of this compliment. 'That's exactly why I seemed cautious when I saw you at my front door. I was alarmed someone would see us and think I was suborning you in some way, seeking your protection from a charge of witchcraft. Mr. Sewall, I think this witch business has gone on long enough. It's running out of control.'

Sewall came here to share his sense of relief in the matter of Giles Corey, and now here is Mr. Willard sounding just like Mr. Brattle! Yet only a few weeks ago he gave that militant sermon in which he described the Devil roaming about New England like a roaring lion. 'That's out of my hands,' Sewall tells him grumpily. 'I'm simply a member of a properly constituted court to try the witchcraft cases that are sent to it. The governor will be here soon. He will decide on the future.'

'I shall be speaking to him about it,' says Mr. Willard grimly. 'I understand his lady is being harassed in the same way.'

Somehow it doesn't seem the moment to announce the court's vindication in the case of Giles Corey. Instead, Sewall says (as if he has been intending to all along), 'We shall go for a picnic to Hogg Island. Tomorrow, while this weather lasts.' (He doesn't say, before the next hangings take place the day after.) 'You must come, and Mrs. Willard, and all the young

Willards. My Sam will be so pleased to have Josiah there. That will take your minds off these anxieties.' (*Our* minds, he secretly thinks.) 'It will be'— a happy phrase comes into his head, made available by some recent conversation or other—'a *déjeuner sur l'herbe.*'

They clear Mercy's Point and sail past the great hump of Noddle's Island on their right. As they approach Hogg Island itself, the cadaverous form of Sewall's tenant, Jeremiah Belcher, is visible on the wharf, obviously having spied the approaching vessel from the window of his house. He helps them to moor. 'We are going to have a picnic,' Sewall tells him. 'You must join us. And Mrs. Belcher, of course. And the . . . ,' Sewall cannot recall the name of their child, or indeed its sex, ' . . . and your little Belcher.'

Sewall leads the party to a grassy knoll he has spied out before with picnics in mind. There is a flat piece of land near its summit which has every convenience, a gnarled old tree for shade, some smooth rocks and boulders for the men and young people to sit on (Sewall has brought along joint stools for the ladies), soft turf for any cavorting that has to be done, and a view of the sunlit sea (actually there is a view of the sea from all points on Hogg Island, it being a small island), with Noddle's Island raising its great noddle out of the waves and beyond it the Boston wharves and the rest of the everyday world half a mile away over the sparkling waters.

The smaller children soon begin to play at hide-and-seek, including the young Belcher who seems to be, for all Sewall can find out, perfectly anonymous. Their high-pitched cries (not good strategy in this game) mingle with the screams of the gulls. The older boys fling a ball to, or rather at, each other with great ferocity and make bellowing noises with their newly deep voices. The older girls sprawl prettily on the grass in the far corner of the little meadow, as far away from the rest as they can be without rolling down to the beach below, and are straightaway engaged in shocked conversation. Wife Hannah, Mrs. Willard and Mrs. Belcher sit on their stools in the shade of the tree, quietly talking over the sewing each has brought with her. Baby Mary is strapped into a little chair beside them, a miniature lady in her own right, from time to time pointing at the objects of the world with her chubby finger. And finally, Mr. Belcher, Mr. Willard and Sewall share a boulder.

'I think it is time for some bread and butter with honey,' says Sewall, 'to tide us over until dinner.'

'Shall I call for your little maid?' Mr. Willard asks.

'No, no,' Sewall tells him. 'She's deep in gossip with the rest. I'll get it myself.'

Wife Hannah joins him when she sees him rummaging in the picnic basket. Young Hannah comes over too, clearly pleased to have an excuse to escape from the flights of the other girls. Susan looks up and points to herself in enquiry but Sewall shakes his head: let her be waited on for once. Betty, the youngest of the sprawling group, is too absorbed in its affairs to even notice.

They have bowls of curds and cream with their bread and honey, then afterwards all resume their activities with renewed zest. Sewall has used a spare stool as a shelf to put some flasks of wine on, along with a bottle of fruit spirits prepared by wife Hannah herself last year by immersing pears from their own tree in aqua vita (kill-Devil, Sarah called it while stowing it in the basket, perhaps understanding that this picnic is intended to dispel witchcraft for the moment). There's also a small cask of beer by the picnic basket. Sewall asks his companions on the boulder if they would like a drink, but just as he approaches the stool a ball whizzes over his shoulder and knocks the bottle of spirits to the ground where it unluckily hits a stone and smashes to pieces.

Sewall turns in surprise and there is Sam (Sam, of course!)

standing shamefaced. Then he looks over at Hannah (they are her spirits after all) but she merely smiles and shrugs her shoulders philosophically. Sewall takes the hint: it's not a day for blame. Instead he improves the moment by announcing to the whole party that this accident is a lively emblem of our fragility and mortality, though his voice breaks unexpectedly when he says those last three words. One of the girls (Elizabeth Willard, he suspects) giggles at the suddenness of his allegory. Normally he would find that disrespectful but on this occasion it seems to relieve an awkwardness in the atmosphere.

When drinks have been poured for all who want them, Sewall and wife Hannah set to discovering the treasures of their basket, aided by young Hannah. There is very good roast lamb, a whole turkey, several fowls, a loaf of pumpkin and Indian corn, and a monstrous apple pie.

A convenient rock, which they christen table rock, does for the setting out, then Mr. Willard says a prayer. After that Sewall leads the whole party in singing Psalm 121 (in the Bay Book version, translated into rhyming verse as an aid to singing):

The Lord thy keeper is, the Lord on thy right hand the shade (Sewall, following the example of little Mary, points to the shade of the tree, which unfortunately is on his left hand).

The sun by day (Sewall points at the sun), *nor moon by night* (luckily the moon is visible even though it is not night, so Sewall points at it), *shall thee by stroke invade.*

Then he runs his pointing hand over the little company: *The Lord will keep thee from all ill: thy soul he keeps alway . . .*

As he sings this verse he becomes aware of tears trickling down his cheeks once more, just as they had after the execution of Giles Corey, though whether they are tears of hope on this occasion, or of sorrow, or even of fear, he can't tell. Luckily the people around him seem unaware, just as they are unaware of other thoughts and feelings he has experienced recently.

PART 4
JUDGEMENTS

When a man has ventured upon the Doing of any thing, that is not according to the Known Rules of *Piety*, and of *Charity*, it may be said of him, as in *Ecclesiastes, He* ~~breaketh an Hedge, and a Serpent shall Bite him. 'Tis by~~ breaking the *Hedge* of Gods Commandments, that we lay our selves open, for *Serpents*, to come in, and Crawl and Coyl about us, and for many *Troubles* to fasten their direful Stings upon us.

—COTTON MATHER, *Memorable Passages, relating to New-England* (Boston, 1694)

CHAPTER 25

Hanging day. Sewall can't attend even if he wishes to (he doesn't): a meeting has been arranged at his house. Mr. Stoughton is there, also Cotton Mather. Stephen is on his way over from Salem with his records of some of the trials, which he will pass over to Mr. Mather to use in the book he must write for the governor. The weather is changing. Today dawned grey and lowering, cooler than for many weeks.

While they wait for Stephen they discuss the implications of the governor's imminent return. Mr. Stoughton feels it poses a threat to the rule of law itself. He is very unhappy that the executive might interfere with the deliberations of the judiciary and even attempt to overturn its decisions. 'It will mean that the witches have accomplished their mission,' he claims. 'Not only will they be able to perform their conjurings unhindered, but they will have broken down the edifice of governance in the colony only months after it was re-established as a province.'

'We will have moved from order to anarchy, unless the governor approves the procedure of the courts,' agrees Cotton Mather and sighs. 'Though from another point of view the development can be tracked back over many years.' His voice takes on a firm hortatory ring, as if he has suddenly recalled his sermonising manner. 'When our forefathers settled here they drove away the heathen in order to establish a colony on the vegetable principle.'

'Vegetable?' asks Mr. Stoughton irritably. 'What vegetable do you mean? A carrot? A dish of beans?'

'It was a vine.'

'Oh, I see,' replies Mr. Stoughton sarcastically. 'A vine.'

'It was deeply rooted,' Mr. Mather insists. 'Or so it seemed. It soon covered the whole of New England. God made a covenant with our fathers, the planters, and fertilised it with the blood of his Son. But over the years since then we have neglected our husbandry. We have lost our vegetable unity. And now the witches are trying to grub the withered vine out of the ground. They are intent on replacing the blessing of grace, freely given, with transactions signed by two parties, each giving and taking according to crafty calculation. We have become a country of trade rather than charity.'

'That is all very well,' says Mr. Stoughton. 'Sadly the governor is not a vegetable himself, nor indeed any sort of metaphor, but a man of flesh and blood. We will have to manage him as best we can.'

'From the earliest days of settlement, things had to be bought and sold, imported and exported,' Sewall points out. 'Ships had to come and go across the ocean to *sustain* our vine. It was always—'

'But not hearts,' says Mr. Mather. 'No one in those early years was buying or selling their *heart*. Or their soul.'

Sewall longs to say, 'You may not have bought and sold your heart but you did buy the hair upon your head.' Instead he holds his tongue. Witches are dying today. The battle for New England continues. At this rather tense moment there's a knock on the front door. 'Ah,' he says, relieved. 'Here's Stephen with the trial records.' But when the hall door opens, it's not Stephen who Susan shows in but Mr. Brattle.

'Good morning, gentlemen.'

'You're wet,' Sewall says. He remembers how Mr. Brattle appeared at the Aldens' front door on the day of the fast for

John Alden's safety. That was in fact the last time it rained in Boston. He recalls the droplet that clung to the tip of Mr. Brattle's nose, and the surprisingly neat way he disposed of it.

Mr. Brattle gives the company a sharp, birdlike look. 'It's just as well you gentlemen are not attending the hangings. You might have caught a cold.'

'Perhaps you should state your business,' says Mr. Stoughton.

'Mr. Willard told me you were to hold a meeting to discuss how to present your case to the governor. I have come to say I am writing to him myself, to explain why the trials have been based upon false premises and have therefore reached erroneous and unjust conclusions. I shall recommend the closure of your court.'

'For what reason, may I ask?'

'You claim to be eradicating sorcery,' says Mr. Brattle. 'In fact you have been *practising* it, with your touch tests and similar nonsense.' (Mr. Mather looks hot and uneasy.) 'The wisest words in this whole sorry affair were uttered by that poor old woman, Rebecca Nurse, when she said, "You do not know my heart." Sometimes people weep with joy; sometimes they can't shed a tear even when overcome by great sadness. And sometimes nonsensical young girls will say they see things that they do not see. Or perhaps the Devil invades *their* impressionable young minds and makes them see what isn't there. Or they just faint because they faint. I read of a man in the city of Groning who would faint at the sight of a swine's head.

'The court has consistently judged people by their surface. But we can't expect to bring souls out into the light of day like so many fish being hooked out of the sea. People are forever mysterious. I'm even a mystery to myself.'

'You're a mystery to all of us,' says Mr. Stoughton.

A sense of unease overtakes the company when Mr. Brattle has made his departure. Perhaps Stephen has been held up by the conditions. Finally Mr. Stoughton has to take his leave. He had hoped to go through the transcripts with Sewall and Mr. Mather and advise on which cases would most effectively illustrate the procedures of the court. As he departs he reminds them of what is at stake, which is more or less everything.

The rain is still pounding at the windows, and Bastian comes in with a basket of logs to make up a fire for them. Still, the atmosphere is less oppressive now that Mr. Stoughton has gone. Mr. Mather takes out his notebook and begins to make jottings for the introduction of his projected work. Sewall pours them both some wine.

Stephen doesn't arrive until almost six, drenched, exhausted, his eyes hectic. Hannah takes him off to find some spare clothes and he comes back into the room looking lost in his brother's garments, still shivering and blue-lipped. He left Salem later than he intended, having decided on the spur of the moment to witness the hangings. 'I had not been to any so far, and as clerk to the court I felt it was my duty to attend at least one batch, particularly as . . . ' He tails off.

'And?' asks Mather. 'Did anything significant happen?'

'No,' says Stephen, shaking his head. 'Nothing significant. Just ordinary hangings. There were no confessions.'

'Was Mr. Noyes present?'

'Indeed he was. When they were all—when they were all dangling there, he strode along below them and—' Stephen stops to gather himself. 'Pardon me, gentlemen, I think I must have caught a chill in the rain. He strode along below them and said, "What a sad thing to see eight firebrands of hell hanging here!"'

'"Firebrands of hell": a robust description,' says Mather. 'Clearly Mr. Noyes hasn't been discomfited by the curse that hag of a witch spat at him—what was her name?'

'Goody Good,' Sewall reminds him.

'Ah, yes, Good. Goody Good. No wonder it slipped my mind for a moment.'

Over these last months Sewall has taken comfort from the fact that Mr. Noyes has not been harmed by the muttering woman's curse. His continuing health seemed to suggest that Good's claim of innocence was a lie, and that therefore her execution was justified. But now the thought strikes him that the curse might have failed simply because she *wasn't* a witch.

'The executed people didn't look much like firebrands of hell to me,' Stephen says, as if continuing his brother's thought. 'A wind came up, a rain wind, and they all began to sway together. One of them hadn't died completely and seemed to fidget for a while. Then the downpour began and they were saturated. I could smell the wetness of their clothes. There was lightning flickering along the far edge of the sea.'

'And the dismal rolling of thunder, no doubt,' suggests Mather.

'And some thunder, yes.'

'God's anger at seeing those wicked witches take their place in hell.'

'Brother,' says Stephen, 'I'm not feeling well.' His teeth have begun to chatter though the fire is now burning brightly.

Mr. Mather gathers up the records Stephen has brought him, stuffs them under his coat to protect them from the weather, and takes his leave. He will decide on the exemplary cases himself. Soon afterwards Sewall and Hannah usher Stephen up to bed. They haven't long done so when there's a knock on the door.

'It will be Mr. Mather,' Sewall tells his wife. 'He must have forgotten something.'

In fact it's Mr. Stoughton. He is wet to a most extraordinary degree, water cascading from every orifice and fold in his clothing. 'The tide washed over the causeway,' Stoughton explains, 'and dragged me half off my horse. The water was swollen with the downpour and a wave washed away my hat. I nearly drowned.'

Once again, Hannah rushes off to fetch towels and spare clothing. Sewall finds it strange to see Stoughton kitted out just as Stephen was—as if the house is filling up with smaller (or at least thinner) simulacra of himself. She drapes the two guests' sopping garments over a clothes horse and puts it in front of the fire for the night, then retires to bed. Sewall warms his guest with a glass of brandy (and takes one himself for company's sake), and the two men play a game of checkers before saying a prayer together and retiring (Mr. Stoughton will share Stephen's room).

When Sewall enters his own chamber, Hannah is still awake. 'Poor brother Stephen,' she whispers. 'I hope he will feel better in the morning.'

'Poor Mr. Stoughton,' Sewall says in turn, putting his candle on the table by the bed. 'He was all but washed away.' Suddenly he pauses. Mr. Stoughton is the chief judge of the witch trials—could his adventure foretell the washing away of the Court of Oyer and Terminer?

'He was dreadfully wet,' says Hannah. 'Very very wet indeed. He was like a drowned rat.' Suddenly she begins to laugh. Into Sewall's mind comes the picture of Mr. Stoughton's low-crowned hat, upside down in the water and revolving like a small coracle just as Sam's friend Sam Gaskill's had when the boys went on their fishing expedition, and now he is laughing too at the indignities that have overtaken that important man (including of course being humbled at checkers).

He gets into bed, still laughing, and then an odd thing happens. Amusement turns into passion, and the passion immediately transmogrifies itself into ugly lust.

There is no trace of husbandly affection in it—while he caresses Hannah his mind is teeming with evil images, as it did once before. This time he is being visited by the two most attractive witches. The freshly widowed Elizabeth Proctor returns and is accompanied by young Margaret Jacobs, the girl who withdrew her confession in order to save her grandfather, and Sewall rejoices in his own status and power as judge over these women; leers at them. Other images mingle with these: whores he has seen on the wharves, the doxies that hang around the entrances of London's theatres (perhaps Mr. Brattle has sampled these, in his play-going days, making full use, as Sewall failed to do, of the fact that he was for a time inhabiting a different place, where being New Englandy was not demanded of him). Sewall pictures pimpled and dirty women, draggled women, women with nothing to lose and just one thing to offer. Mixed up with them, those respectable ladies who have been degraded in his previous wicked thoughts. Madam Winthrop showing her legs, showing *every-thing*, in exchange for his signature on the pirates' reprieves; lovely buxom Margaret, wife of his own brother Stephen who even now is lying ill in the bedroom along the landing.

All these female bodies swirl and twist like fleshy flames, beckoning with their hands, flaunting their breasts, pushing their hips at him, looming and fading in the smoky atmosphere of his mind even as his body engages with Hannah's. And then the imperative of desire takes him beyond these fantasies, beyond everything and everyone except desire itself, and he finds himself vanishing into the enormousness of his own need, leaving only a home-made bonnet floating on its surface to mark where he once was.

When it is over he lies face-down on the bed, too ashamed to look at Hannah. He feels like a sea-monster washed up on the beach, some disgusting creature intended to live its life out of sight, in the darkness of deep waters. How can he have become such a thing? Is it possible to be evil without even real-ising that you are, without ever making a choice? Perhaps he has been a witch all along but has simply not been aware of it. He has lived his life as Judge Sewall, respectable member of the community, brother of his dear brother Stephen, doting father of his children, lover, husband, friend of wife Hannah, while all along, while his own back was turned, so to speak, he has been practising wickedness, the dark arts.

After a while he pushes himself up into a sitting position. Hannah is now asleep. The candle is still glowing dimly and he picks up the Bible from beside it and opens it at random. He finds himself reading from the beginning of the first epistle of John. *If we say that we have fellowship with him, and walk in darkness, we lie, and do not the truth: but if we walk in the light as he is in the light, we have fellowship one with another, and the blood of Jesus Christ cleanseth us from all sin.*

He puts the book back and lies down again. The rain drums faintly on the roof; Hannah is breathing softly beside him. He thinks of the words he has just read: 'if we walk in the light as he is in the light, we have fellowship one with another.' And when that is achieved, Christ will cleanse us from all sin.

Then he sleeps.

CHAPTER 26

It's a dull October day with a chill in the air. Bastian is about to begin splitting logs for the winter pile when Sewall interrupts—he wants to do it himself, get warm with the exercise, become tired. Bastian hands over the axe and Sewall raises it. He stares down at the log, trying to look at it so intently his eyes will make a path for the descending axe to follow. Then he gathers his shoulders together for the swing.

At exactly the last possible second, Bastian speaks: 'Master.'

Sewall gives out a whimper of baffled exertion and lowers the axe. 'What is it, Bastian?'

'I wish you to marry me.'

Sewall stares at him for a moment, perplexed. 'Marry you?'

'Yes, master. Marry me to Jane.'

'Ah, to Jane! That is good news indeed.' Sewall puts the axe down and shakes his servant's hand. 'I wish you both joy of it.'

'Thank you, master. Will you? Since you're a justice, you have the authority.'

'Of course I will! It will be a pleasure. It will be a privilege. Ah, but one thing. Jane is a slave. What does her mistress say?'

There's a pause. 'We haven't asked her yet,' Bastian says finally.

'I see. Do you want me to speak to her?'

'Oh please, master. You are so good to me.'

'No, Bastian,' says Sewall, squeezing his arm, 'it is quite the other way around.'

Bastian shakes his head and to Sewall's relief (since he doesn't want a witness to his log-splitting) backs away to find some other work to do. Sewall raises the axe once more. At the exact moment he commits himself to his swing, another voice. 'Father,' says young Sam. With a mighty effort Sewall arrests his swing and carefully rests the axe against the log block. Sam is standing with his head bowed.

'What are you doing here, my boy?'

'Mr. Perry sent me home.'

'And why did he do that? Don't people want to buy books any more?'

Sewall knows for a fact that the opposite is the case. Mr. Perry explained to him that sales have increased since the governor returned and promptly suspended the trials, as if the people were trying to find guidance as to the best course of action. There is no shortage of books to advise them on their quest. Indeed several have appeared in the last few weeks. Cotton Mather for one has already published his defence of the trials, with the arresting title of *Wonders of the Invisible World*. He dealt with five cases and this time endorsed the procedure of the court in each one.

His father, however, has written what amounts to a counterblast, called *Cases of Conscience Concerning Evil Spirits*. The Devil, Increase Mather explains, has great skill in optics and can cause things to appear far differently from what they actually are. Indeed, he remarks, a journal published in Leipzig, the *Acta Eruditorum*, tells the story of a Frenchman who learned from a demon to use Borax water to produce glittering optical effects and even to create the shapes of innocent people afflicting others. The suggestion is clearly that the accusers, jury and judges were all deluded.

Even more disturbingly, Mr. Willard has ventured into print with a dialogue, *Between S and B*, in which S and B argue over the merits of the witchcraft trials, with B taking the sceptic's part, and S the supporter's one. Sewall guesses that S stands for himself, with B representing Mr. Brattle. B crushes S's arguments about the witches' guilt by asserting 'None knows another's heart'—a poor reward for providing Mr. Willard, along with Mrs. Willard and all the little Willards, with that golden September day on Hogg Island.

Sam understands that his father's question is ironic, indeed sarcastic, and doesn't reply at first.

'Well?'

'No.'

'No, which? No, they aren't buying? Or no, they—'

'No, father, they *are* still buying. It's very busy.'

'If it's so busy perhaps you can tell me why you've come home early.' He glares. 'I would have thought—'

'I've been rushing around so much, serving all the customers. My feet are sore.'

'A little while ago you were complaining that your legs were swollen with the heat. And before *that*, as I remember, your feet were blistered.' Oddly, the listing of these absurd infirmities snaps Sewall out of his bad mood.

'The floor gets harder in cold weather. The flagstones make my feet ache so much I can hardly walk.'

'I see.' He smiles at his son. 'Well, since you're home now, you might as well rest those weary feet of yours so that they will be ready for the cold flagstones tomorrow.'

'Yes, father,' says Sam joyfully, and scuttles into the house.

A crack like a musket shot, then a clatter as each half of the split log hits the ground. After a few minutes with no further interruptions Sewall's body surrenders to the rhythm of his task, collecting a new log, placing it on the block, raising the axe, sighting the path, bringing it down, fetching another and repeating the sequence. But while his body becomes absorbed in the work, his mind teems with difficult and uneasy thoughts.

Stephen groaned and winced as Sewall took him back by

carriage to Salem the morning after he had brought the trial transcripts for Mr. Mather to quarry. He had insisted on returning home despite a high temperature and painful joints. Since then the fever and weakness have steadily increased. Sewall visited just the other day and Stephen was in a poor way indeed. When he became aware of Sewall's presence he slowly turned his head and fixed him with unnaturally bright eyes. 'I wish—,' he whispered.

'Yes?'

'I wish I may live.' The nakedness of his fear brought Sewall to the verge of weeping and for a moment he didn't dare try to reply. Instead he wiped his hand gently over his brother's forehead. 'I wish I may live,' Stephen said again.

'I'm sure that—'

'So I may serve God better than I have done.'

'You did what you were called upon to do,' Sewall told him. 'As did I,' he adds a little tentatively.

Tomorrow Mr. Stoughton will once more ask the governor and Council whether the Court of Oyer and Terminer should sit again in a week's time, when the governor's suspension will have expired. Stoughton, with that iron will of his, is determined to continue. Consistency is all-important, in matters of law as well as matters of religion, he told the Council at its last meeting. 'Oh yes,' said Mr. Brattle, meeting Sewall on the street, 'for the sake of those who have already died, the only fair procedure will be to execute *every*one. Then nobody can complain about being singled out.'

Whatever the outcome, Sewall senses that the crisis is over. He has felt this since the night he made his disgraceful and unuxorious assault upon Hannah's person (though afterwards she peacefully slept as though nothing untoward had happened), and then comforted himself by reading from John's first epistle: 'if we walk in the light as he is in the light, we have fellowship one with another.' The congregation of the saints has been terribly divided and now is becoming reconciled once more.

Swing, bang, clatter. Bastian has sidled back and is picking up the split logs and piling them in a lean-to against the side wall. Sewall loves his Bible, his accounts, his legal books, his toing and froing in the affairs of city and province, but for the time being he thinks how delicious it would be to do nothing *but* doing, without any pause for thought.

Then: a shriek, scratched on the grey October air like the call of a bird. And another. It's Betty, and her scream contains that terrible unrefusable demand of a child: *you must help me.*

Now, another cry, voice deeper, that barking awkward almost-manly timbre of his boy Sam. And even in these lower notes, the same demand: *you must help me.*

Sewall has dropped his axe and is running towards the house, but hearing Sam's voice underlining Betty's he turns and picks it up again. Bastian scurries towards him from the lean-to with a split log as weapon in each hand. As the two men near the back door, Betty bursts out of it like a cannonball and flies straight past them, on down the garden.

Now more screams are adding to the medley, high-pitched sobs from Susan, angry shouts from Sarah, woebegone cries from young Hannah, wavering uncertain moans from Joseph, lusty baby-bawling from little Mary.

Sewall rushes through the kitchen gripping the shaft of his axe with both hands, Bastian, less encumbered (and more fleet of foot) just ahead of him. Bastian crashes through the door into the hall which swings back and cracks Sewall's forehead and several of the fingers that grasp his axe, but he follows valiantly, deferring the pain in that strange way you can when pressing business is in hand.

First thing he sees: wife Hannah. She is leaning against the wall and *laughing*, her fist against her mouth. Scattered around the room are the others, faces pink, eyes wide, mouths like Os, each one (even little Mary in her chair) transfixed by—of all things—a bear! It must have let itself in through the front door and now stands on its hind legs in the middle of the room.

The bear is brown and furry with a long snout, yet there is something wrong with it (quite apart from its presence in a house). Sewall's eyes track down from head to foot—yes, that's what's wrong, it does indeed have *feet* rather than a bear's enormous paws, and those feet are shod in shoes.

Bastian is standing in front of the strange beast, his hands, or at least his logs, on his hips, and suddenly he too bursts into laughter. Sarah strides past him, right up to the creature, raises her arm and grasps its nose, giving it a sharp indignant tug. The bear's snout is nothing more than a fold of material, and with Sarah's tug the whole pelt comes off, revealing itself to be an old brown rug beneath which stands an elderly woman in wrinkled skirt and apron, a cap lopsidedly on her head. She raises both arms in front of her, fingers bent like claws, and gives a small growl, then shakes with silent merriment. It's Goodwife Duerden. She lives alone in a little shack not far off and is addled in her wits. Indeed there have been rumours of witchcraft.

Bastian turns, shaking his head at the performance. 'I will go and fetch Miss Betty from down the garden,' he informs Sewall.

'I'll go,' says Sam. He looks hot with shame at his recent terror and obviously wants to redeem himself by comforting his sister.

Sewall casts his eyes around the others. Young Hannah's lips are still trembling and she is looking reproachfully at her tormentor. Little Joseph is marching around the room, perhaps trying to imitate a bear, or at least a cub, himself. Baby Mary has noticed she is the only one still distressed and is undecided whether to continue to be, or to recover. Wife Hannah has got over her amusement and is looking at Goodwife Duerden with an expression of sympathy and concern. Susan has her hand over her mouth as if to stifle laughter or shock. Sarah is glaring. 'What on earth did you think you were up to?' she demands.

The goodwife gives her a cunning look, her shoulders hunched and a finger over her lips as if insisting on the need for secrecy. 'I wanted to say boo to the children,' she replies.

Mr. Stoughton rises to his feet. 'Your Excellency,' he says, 'fellow councillors.' His gaze passes over the council chamber. Sewall flinches when it strikes him, conscious of the bandage round his head where he was struck by the swinging door during that alarm of the bear. 'On three occasions in the last month I have stood before you and asked that the suspension of the Court of Oyer and Terminer be lifted so as to enable it to resume its duty. That duty is to try the cases of sundry citizens of our province who have been accused of witchcraft, a heinous crime and one that threatens the very existence of this Christian plantation of ours.' Again his look passes over the whole assembly. 'This is the last time I will ask you,' he says finally.

There's more shuffling, a shifting of backsides on benches, a rustle of papers. Stoughton remains standing, his head still methodically scanning the members of Council, pausing occasionally when he manages to catch the eye of one. The power of his gaze slowly eradicates the small defensive noises of the members; these die away to be replaced by total silence. It's as if no one is even breathing. Initially Sewall interprets this as preliminary to a response but then understands that none will be forthcoming. Or rather, that the silence is itself the response.

This realisation strikes Stoughton at the same moment. He emits a long contemptuous sigh, turns on his heel, strides out.

Excited chatter breaks out all over the chamber, some

members rising to their feet and stretching as if they have been seated for hours instead of just a few minutes. Sewall himself feels a huge sense of relief. Ever since the night when poor Stephen came over from Salem to deliver the papers for Cotton Mather, he's felt that the trials had run their course and come to an inevitable termination. Now the silence of the council chamber confirms that indeed they have.

The incessant rain tails off for a moment and the sun peeps out. Sewall peers hopefully through his study window. Sure enough, after a few minutes a rainbow shimmers into existence, forming an arc from ocean to land. 'Laus Deo,' he whispers.

A little later, there's a knock on his door. In comes Susan and gives a bob. 'Someone to see you, master.'

It's Mr. Brattle, who sweeps in, takes off his wet coat (he has received yet another wetting on his way here) and places it on the back of a chair, upon which he promptly seats himself.

'I have just seen a rainbow,' Sewall tells him, pointing towards the window.

'Ah!'

'I took it as a sign.' No doubt Mr. Brattle will attribute his interpretation of it to yet more mysticism and superstition.

'Well, I do come with news, though of a worldly sort rather than a heavenly one.'

'I see.'

'The governor has announced his nominations for the Superior Court of Massachusetts. Apparently he wishes the Council to ratify the names tomorrow.'

A panel of five judges is to be appointed to this new Superior Court, one of whom will be chief justice of Massachusetts. Sewall has taken this proposal as a rebuff to the cancelled Court of Oyer and Terminer since it points to a wish to give a professional status to the justices who will be entrusted with the province's most serious cases. The implication is that the witchcraft judges were inadequate to their task. This suspicion is confirmed by Mr. Brattle's obvious glee at his imminent announcement (he seems to have had the ear of the governor ever since sending him his letter). Sewall looks dolefully across his desk at him. 'Oh well,' he says, 'I have many other affairs to see to.'

'A finger in lots of pies,' agrees Mr. Brattle. He is a lean man himself so his reference is perhaps a sly dig. Sewall feels a sudden ridiculous urge to defend the consumption of pies. So many discussions and meetings take place over a good meal; so much business can be transacted; so many friendships cemented. Dinner is at the heart of family life, just as the Lord's Supper is at the heart of congregational worship. Indeed, eating is a kind of discourse, spoken not in English or Latin or Algonquian but in the language of meat and fish and cheese, vegetables and fruit, bread and pastry.

But Mr. Brattle will think him foolish if he takes his comment so literally. 'So who *are* the nominees for the Superior Court?' he finally asks.

Mr. Brattle gives him a look of sharp-eyed amusement. 'Well, John Richards for one.'

'Mr. Richards? But he served with me in the Court of Oyer and Terminer!'

'Also Mr. Winthrop.'

'And he did too!' Sewall stares at Mr. Brattle in astonishment. For a moment he wonders if this is some sort of trick to discomfit or confuse him. But no, sceptic he may be but Mr. Brattle wouldn't stoop to lying. Sewall can't stop a feeling of jealousy, that these colleagues of his have been forgiven, so to speak, for their participation in a court of which the governor disapproved, while he himself has been sidelined. Perhaps it's the price you pay for trying to maintain a certain independence of mind. 'And who is to be the chief justice?' he asks.

'Mr. Stoughton is to be given that honour.'

Now Sewall is speechless. The implacable Stoughton. Mr.
Stoughton, who demanded that Council support him, and
was rebuffed. Mr. Stoughton, who turned his back on fellow
members (and on the governor himself!) and strode from the
hall.

'You look as if you have seen a ghost,' Mr. Brattle says in
that pungent ironical way of his, giving a little laugh. 'Oh, I
nearly forgot. *You* have been nominated to the bench as well.
Congratulations, old friend.' He gets to his feet, steps over to
the desk and shakes Sewall's hand.

'But I thought—you dis, you dis—'

'I did, I do. I disapproved, I distrusted, I disliked. I hated
those witch trials while they were in progress. But I know an
honest man when I see one. And law and honesty don't always
go together.'

'I'm lost for words,' Sewall says. He feels oddly tearful at
this unexpected turn of events and in particular at the sudden
kindness of Mr. Brattle, who for months now he has seen as an
enemy. Those words from John's first epistle come into his
head once again: fellowship one with another. 'But how—I
mean, the governor was so angry with our court.'

'And he has swept that court away. And I can't say I'm
sorry. But he is a politic man. He has changed the judicial system as a result of the trials but he has also appointed certain of
the men associated with them. Change and continuance, that's
how he thinks. He wants to keep opponents happy, like myself,
and supporters, like yourself. And this I think he has successfully done. The fifth member of the Superior Court is to be Mr.
Danforth, who of course became an opponent of the trials. Just
to provide a little grit in the oyster.'

In fact Sewall had been most perplexed on discovering that
Mr. Danforth (rather like Mr. Willard) had turned against the
trials in the course of the summer, having seemed so implaca-
bly against witchcraft during the examination of the Proctors,

and so familiar with the legal precedents for the trials. But already that worry seems irrelevant in this new fellowship that has been established. 'Mr. Brattle,' he says, 'we will be eating shortly. It would be a great pleasure to have you dine with us.'

After dinner Sewall shows Mr. Brattle to the door. When he opens it, there on the step, just about to knock, is brother Stephen.

'My rainbow!' Sewall cries.

'Rainbow?' asks Stephen. His face is very thin—indeed, his whole body is emaciated from his illness, and of course just like the last time he came here, he is soaking wet.

'Stephen, Stephen,' Sewall says. He and Mr. Brattle both back themselves into the vestibule to allow Stephen to come in out of the rain. Then Sewall shakes his head in disapproval. 'Stephen,' he says again, 'what do you think you're doing coming all the way from Salem in this weather?'

'I knew how worried you were, brother. I told myself that as soon as I was able to leave my bed I would come and reassure you.' Sewall understands what he is saying of course—that he doesn't blame his brother for nominating him as clerk of the court and thereby (perhaps) bringing about this long illness in the first place.

'I am pleased to see you're up and about,' Mr. Brattle tells him. 'I believe you've been ill in bed for weeks.'

'Where are we now?' asks Stephen. 'Mid-November. Yes, nearly two months. But here I am, back in the land of the living.'

'So are we all,' says Mr. Brattle. 'Let's hope we can remain here.'

Sewall arrives early at Council the next day. Indeed only one member is present when he walks into the hall, Nathaniel Saltonstall. He's sitting on a bench near the back of the room apparently talking to himself.

Sewall steps up to pass the time of day with him.

'Very merry,' Mr. Saltonstall says by way of greeting.

'Oh, yes?'

'Very merry. Merry river.'

'River? What river?'

'What river?' Saltonstall demands, clearly annoyed. '*Merry* river. Merrimack River.'

'Of course,' Sewall replies. The Merrimack was the river of his childhood days, and Mr. Saltonstall lives near its northern bank.

'Frozen over,' Saltonstall claims. 'Right over.'

That can't be possible so early in the winter, and in any case Mr. Saltonstall has been in Boston for the last few days while Council has been in session. It did freeze in the coldest part of last winter however—perhaps he's remembering that. Other councillors are now filing into the chamber, glancing over at Saltonstall and sitting down as far away from him as possible.

'You could slide on it!' Saltonstall exclaims triumphantly. His face falls. 'Then it broke.'

'It thawed.'

'It broke!'

'The ice broke up.'

Mr. Saltonstall grasps Sewall's shoulder and gives it a fierce shake, as if to shake the explanation out of him. 'You broke it!'

'And how did I do that?'

'You spoke to Mr. Phips. Mister Pip. Governor Pip.'

'The governor? What do you imagine I said?'

'Told him not to nominate me as a judge in the Superior Court.'

'And why would I do such a thing?'

'Because I resigned from the Court of Oyer and Terminer even though you advised me not to. You are angry with me because I don't believe in witches.'

'Mr. Saltonstall, I was taken aback at your stance. I was

alarmed. But I wasn't angry. Any more than you were angry with me when I opposed the reprieving of the pirates.'

'Then why did you tell Pip to bar me from Superior Court?'

'I can assure you I did no such thing. I haven't spoken to Governor Phips on any topic whatsoever, least of all to influence his appointments to the Superior Court. That would have been completely inappropriate. He appointed Mr. Danforth to the court and he, I understand, came to disapprove of the trials just as you did.' For a moment Sewall debates repeating Mr. Brattle's explanation, but he thinks better of it and contents himself with whispering, 'It's just the way of the world, my friend.'

Not only has Nathaniel Saltonstall not been appointed to the Superior Court, but he has been the subject of malicious rumours. Apparently people have been accusing *him* of witch craft, presumably on the basis that his denial of witches might have been self-interested. It seems impossible for a judge to avoid the taint. If he punishes witches it is because he is a witch himself. If he refuses to, it is for the same reason. The inexorability of this paradox actually affords Sewall some relief, and he feels a sudden warmth towards Mr. Saltonstall, who has other problems to contend with too. There is talk of him losing the command of his regiment of militia. Hardly surprising, then, that he's taken refuge in drink, though that of course has damaged his reputation even more.

For the next couple of weeks Saltonstall makes no appearance in Council, so Sewall decides to write him a letter.

Sir, Not seeing you in the Assembly, I am writing to wish you well and to offer you my sympathy in respect of the accusation that some people have been afflicted by a spectre in your shape. I fully believe in your innocence.

I would also like to say I was saddened you had drunk to

excess when I met you a fortnight ago. You explained you were very merry, and then went on to talk about the breaking up of the ice on the Merrimack River—that's the occasion I'm referring to.

Please, break it off. I'm not talking about the ice now, but the drinking. As for the governor turning you down for the judge's position, I had nothing to do with that decision, and I don't know of anyone who did. And I was as surprised as you are to hear talk that command of your regiment might be given to somebody else.

Please don't give your enemies any ammunition. I want you to understand that I'm writing this out of friendship, not prejudice. And from a sense of my duty to you. Accept it in good part from someone who desires your everlasting welfare.

Samuel Sewall.

He leaves the letter on his desk to wait until he has an opportunity to send it to Haverhill and goes off to attend a Council meeting. When he arrives he is surprised to see that Mr. Saltonstall has turned up at last. He smells a little of drink but doesn't seem to be intoxicated. 'I've written you a letter,' Sewall tells him. 'I was going to post it.'

'Oh yes? What does it say?'

'Perhaps it would be better if you read it for yourself.'

'You've whetted my appetite,' Saltonstall gives him a charming smile. 'You can't leave me dangling. I shan't be returning to Haverhill for a day or two.'

'I'll send it along to your lodgings later.'

That afternoon, after dinner, Sewall thinks about what he should do. He could rewrite the letter, omitting the reference to drinking and confining himself to denying Mr. Saltonstall's suspicions and to sympathising with him in his plight. But that would be dishonest, as well as a betrayal of the obligations of friendship. He will ask Bastian to deliver the letter as it is. No, he thinks again, I can't hide behind my servant. I will deliver the letter myself.

He still has hopes that Mr. Saltonstall will simply take it and wish him goodnight, but he invites him into his lodgings and asks him to have a seat while he reads. It's hard to sit calmly while your companion is discovering how drunk he was.

When Saltonstall has finished he continues to sit in silence, obviously reflecting on what Sewall has told him. Finally he raises his head. 'Thank you, Mr. Sewall.'

'My letter was written in a spirit of fellowship,' Sewall assures him, aware of his face turning red.

'I read it in that spirit. I would only ask you one more thing. Please remember me in your prayers.'

'If you will remember me in yours,' says Sewall, and on that note he pats Mr. Saltonstall on the shoulder and takes his leave.

PART 5
THE GAP IN THE HEDGE

It is Written,

In EZEK. XXll. 30.—

I sought for a MAN among them, that should make up the HEDGE, and stand in the GAP, before me, for the Land, that I should not Destroy it . . .

The Rest of what is *Written* in the Verse, I will not Now Read unto you, as Wishing and Hoping, that it may *Never* be *fulfilled in our Eyes!*

—COTTON MATHER, *Memorable Passages, relating to New-England* (Boston, 1694)

CHAPTER 27

Nearly four years have passed since the enforced closure of the Court of Oyer and Terminer. All the accused witches awaiting examination, all those awaiting trial, all those awaiting execution, have long since been released. Mr. Alden has returned (to be welcomed by his friend Sewall), as has Mrs. Bradbury and many others who escaped from prison or chose to flee the accusations of the afflicted. The crisis started as a children's game and like a children's game it has run its course and now the players have gone home to bed (except of course for the ones who died).

It's a summer's night and Sewall is asleep (wife Hannah lies in her own chamber in the last stages of pregnancy). He begins to dream of each of his children in turn. Firstly, young Sam. He is eighteen and serving customers in Mr. Checkley's shop where he now works (after finishing at Mr. Perry's on the grounds of assorted ailments afflicting him there). The shop is bursting at the seams with pots and pans, gardening implements and woodworking tools, cups and plates, tankards and cutlery, carpets and bolts of cloth (some of which have been imported by Sewall and sold on to Mr. Checkley at wholesale prices).

In his dream Sewall is a customer and asks Sam for a certain item (the dream doesn't specify which). Sam scuttles off to fetch it and Sewall waits for him as patiently as possible by the shop's table. Waits and waits, shakes his head, drums his fingers, reflects that Sam is slow, so *slow*, always has been. Finally he begins to search for him all over the shop, behind the piles of odds and ends, under the very table at which he has been standing, through a door that leads to the back office and store, but Sam is nowhere, nowhere at all, and the loss of his child, which would be terrible enough in life, is even more horrible in the dream world where nothing can be understood or explained.

Next young Hannah. Sewall is galloping towards the Dummers' farm (she is thirteen in this dream, as she was in life when staying at the Dummers', not seventeen and nearly as tall as her father, as she is now). No one greets him on the threshold, no child rushes out to embrace him. Sewall lets himself in but the house remains silent save for the creaking he makes by treading heavily on the boards, and Hannah is gone, gone irrevocably, gone forever.

The cupboard in the vestibule is black dark. Sewall is kneeling on the floor, praying, and Betty is sobbing quietly over her sins just an arm's length away. Then her sobs peter out. The silence deepens. He finds a candle and looks all about him, but though the space is too small to hide in, Betty is nowhere to be seen.

He daren't dream any longer and watch his remaining children disappear, schoolboy Joseph who cons his lessons so much more effectively than his big brother Sam ever did, and who has left the calculation of apples far behind already, little Mary, less intense than Betty and less timid than Hannah, already happier and more at ease with herself than either, baby Sarah, born last year and the very embodiment of friendliness, with a way of wagging her arms and legs at you in greeting like an overturned beetle (though subject to fits from time to time).

When he wakes, morning light has entered the chamber. He puts his head round the door of wife Hannah's room but she is peacefully asleep, and baby Sarah likewise in her adjacent cot. Then he washes his face, puts on his clothes, and goes down to join his other children for breakfast.

The Bible passage for today is from the fifth chapter of the Acts of the Apostles and it's Betty's turn to read it. She reaches the first part of verse four: *But Peter said, Ananias, why hath Satan filled thine heart to lie to the Holy Ghost*—and then her voice stumbles and stops and she can go no further. As so often she rises to her feet in order to make off to her cupboard, but on this occasion Sewall reaches out to grasp her elbow and stop her flight. It isn't good to retreat into darkness and secrecy all the time. Though this is valid reasoning he is well aware of what underlies it: the fear that when he follows his daughter into that dark constricted place he might not be able to find her inside it. 'Dear Betty,' he asks as he tugs her (as affectionately as possible) back down on to her chair, 'can you tell us why that verse upset you?'

She gasps and hiccups for a little while. 'It's about lying to the Holy Spirit. I believe *I* lie to the Holy Spirit too. I might fall down dead at any moment just like Ananias and Sapphira did.' Suddenly she breaks into a torrent of weeping.

'Sam!' Sewall says. 'I think we need our minister. Go and ask Mr. Willard to come.' Sam rises to his feet. 'And Sam. When you have spoken to him, you should proceed directly to Mr. Checkley's shop. You are late for work already.'

'But shouldn't I bring Mr. Willard back with me?'

'No, Sam. Mr. Willard can find his own way to our house. He's been here enough times.'

When Mr. Willard arrives, he asks if he can go with Betty to a private place. Sewall mentions her cupboard but explains it is windowless and dark. 'We are all in the dark, old friend,' Mr. Willard replies somewhat sententiously, and requests a candle. (Sewall has never felt confident of their friendship since reading that dialogue between S and B.)

When the two emerge some time later, Betty is quiet again, but it's impossible to tell whether her sorrows have been dispelled. 'She finds it difficult to explain her troubles,' Mr. Willard tells Sewall in confidence. 'She says she's confused. This whole province is in a sad state of confusion. I believe we are still in the grip of that witchcraft tragedy.'

'But that was four years ago. And in any case, Betty—'

'Four years is a mere blink in the eyes of the Lord. And of course Betty is concerned in it. We are all concerned in it. In fact I am going to petition the governor for a fast day so our province can ask forgiveness for the injustices that occurred.'

Ask forgiveness for injustices committed by a certain *S*, thinks Sewall bitterly.

The acting governor has resisted confronting the events that happened before his appointment. Mr. Phips might have adopted a different stance, but Mr. Phips is no more. Within a year of the cancellation of the Court of Oyer and Terminer he began to succumb to strange fits of rage, assaulted Mr. Brenton, Collector of the Port of Boston, and furiously caned Captain Short of the frigate *Nonsuch* (the very ship that brought him to New England to take up his office) in an argument over Admiralty jurisdiction. It's as though the turbulent passions that afflicted the province the preceding year and which he so assiduously distanced himself from at the time, caught up with him at last and drove him into a frenzy. He was summoned to England to explain himself, where he promptly died (of apoplexy, Sewall assumes) and for the time being his place has been taken by William Stoughton, of all people.

'Before I go,' Mr. Willard says, 'I will say a prayer with the family.'

'Madam Sewall is still in her bed,' Sewall tells him. 'She is near her term.'

'Of course. Give her my good wishes when you speak to her. Her condition will give me my theme for the prayer.'

When the children (all except Sam) are assembled round the table, Mr. Willard says his prayer. 'The Lord bring light and comfort out of this dark cloud that hangs over our dear sister, Elizabeth Sewall. Grant that Christ Himself is being formed within this sweet child, and that the issue of the pangs she now experiences will be the birth of the Lord in her spirit.'

Betty looks tense and pale but perhaps somewhat vindicated at hearing this prayer. Hannah regards her admiringly, no doubt impressed at the scope of her perturbations and the grandeur of their possible outcome. *Amen*, say all the children, *Amen*, says Sewall, strangely comforted by the appositeness of Mr. Willard's words.

Later that morning Sewall decides to take a walk. He might go to his warehouse on the wharf and run through his books. But his real motive is to call in at Checkley's shop and see how Sam is getting on.

As he walks across the Common he is approached by Mr. Melyen, leather-dealer and part-time constable, a stocky man with stubbly cheeks and rheumy eyes but usually affable enough in casual conversation, though this one begins strangely.

'Do you see that?' Mr. Melyen asks. He twists his head by way of pointing. 'Do you see it?' he repeats, stepping rather closer to Sewall than is usual (or indeed quite polite). His rheumy eyes look up at him indignantly.

Sewall screws his eyes up against the glare of the sun and tries to see what Mr. Melyen wants him to. There are people going about their business; there are shops and houses, horses and carts; that's all he can make out. 'What is it?' he finally asks.

'It's big enough, damn your eyes!' Mr. Melyen replies. He takes a deep furious breath. 'How *can* you stand there and tell me you can't see it?'

'I didn't tell you I couldn't see it,' Sewall replies in as mild a tone as possible, hoping to calm his companion down. Again he peers across the Common. 'I simply don't know what it is I'm looking for.'

'It's the biggest thing in the whole town! How can you deny you see it?'

Once more Sewall looks, with his hand held above his brow to shadow his eyes. There are no giants among the people scurrying to and fro, no sign of an elephant or giraffe unexpectedly shipped here from Africa (in any case Sewall keeps himself up to date with Boston's imports). 'No,' he admits at last, shaking his head.

'Your honour,' Mr. Melyen says with obvious contempt (reminding Sewall of Mr. Brattle's use of the honorific in the darkest days of the trials), 'your honour, how can you *not* see Beacon Hill?'

Beacon Hill is the steepest slope in Boston, rising up on the far side of the Common. 'For heaven's sake, I didn't know you meant Beacon Hill!'

'I told you it was the biggest thing in Boston.'

'You might as well have said the sky, or the ocean, or the globe itself.'

'You will admit there is nothing bigger in the whole town? Even Mount Whoredom is not so large.'

'Well, yes. But you are simply making reference to geography.'

'I need you to say,' Mr. Melyen says the words slowly and ominously, 'that Beacon Hill is the biggest object in the whole of Boston.'

'All right, I agree,' says Sewall, smiling as if this has been an amicable discussion after all. 'Beacon Hill *is* the biggest thing in Boston.'

'Well then.' Mr. Melyen pauses. 'If I should see a man hoist Beacon Hill on his back, then walk for a while over the Common where we are now, still carrying it, and then return and set it down where it was in the first place, do you know what I would say, Mr. Sewall, your honour?'

'No, what would you say?'

'Nothing, that's what I would say. Nothing at all. Mr. Sewall, I would see this man carrying his mighty burden, and I would make nothing of it at all.' With a final glare from those watery eyes of his, Mr. Melyen stumps off.

Sewall watches his receding form in bewilderment. What on earth could he have been driving at? Has the man gone completely mad?

He continues on his way for a few moments, then stops dead as the explanation dawns. Mr. Melyen was referring to George Burroughs, the minister-witch, and those feats of strength of which he was accused by Captain Wormwood: putting a finger into the bunghole of a barrel of molasses and then raising the whole thing, or lifting up a six-foot long musket, again by means of a mere finger inserted in the barrel. What Mr. Melyen was saying is that he would regard any feat of strength, no matter how prodigious, as ultimately explicable in the ordinary way of things, without resort to supernatural solutions.

That's why he was so angry—because it was the judges themselves who had fallen under the spell of the supernatural, not the accused. Mr. Melyen is repeating that old charge: that Sewall himself, and his fellow judges were the true witches.

It is as if the Court of Oyer and Terminer was sitting only yesterday, feelings are so raw. As the province of Massachusetts Bay becomes more and more embattled (the failure of this latest harvest has led to a scarcity of bread; Indian and French attacks are on the rise) a feeling is developing through the community that the trials need some kind of expiation.

He walks on to Mr. Checkley's shop, sidles up to the window and peers in. There in the dim interior stands Mr. Checkley himself, serving a customer. Sewall screws up his eyes (just as he had when trying to spot the largest thing in Boston) but he can't see Sam. Perhaps he's been sent out the back to fetch something the customer has asked for. The customer leaves. Now Mr. Checkley is standing all by himself in his shop.

Fear rises. Daughter Betty is tormented by verses from the Bible. Here is one to torment Sewall himself, from the book of Daniel, chapter 4, verse 5. As the words resound in his head he feels himself grow cold despite the heat of the day.

I saw a dream which made me afraid, and the thoughts upon my bed and the visions of my head troubled me.

Sam isn't in the shop.

Sewall continues to look in the window. Perhaps it is not just Massachusetts in general that is being punished, but he, Samuel Sewall, in person, for his part in what happened. It takes him some moments of blank staring before he becomes aware that Mr. Checkley is signalling him to come in.

'He hasn't been in the store all morning,' Mr. Checkley explains. He's a tall, broad-shouldered man with a large midriff. No wig but long, thinning hair, turning grey, teeth somewhat long and thinning too and also grey, but kind eyes.

'What can have happened to him?'

'The problem, Mr. Sewall, is that he's not suited to the trade. He moons about the shop and is obviously bored and unhappy. I imagine that he's mooning about the streets this morning instead.'

'I see.'

'His heart isn't in it, I'm afraid. I think he needs to look for something else. He doesn't want to *be* here. That's why he isn't here now.'

'He was very upset this morning. His sister—'

'But it's not just this morning. It's every morning. And afternoon. He *never* wants to be here.'

'I see.

'Mr. Sewall, I like the lad. It isn't everyone who is cut out for this business.' He turns to look around at his large, almost haphazard stock.

'I suppose not,' Sewall agrees. 'You have to be interested in . . . ' He can't think what would describe an interest in Mr. Checkley's supply of general goods. 'In the variousness of things,' he concludes.

'Exactly!' Mr. Checkley is pleased with the phrase and repeats it: 'The variousness of things. Mr. Sewall, it's a matter of finding out where young Sam will be happy.'

Indeed it is, agrees Sewall, as he makes his way back home. The whereabouts of happiness is a fraught matter, and not just for poor Sam. None of his older children seem to have located it yet, and perhaps the smaller ones are cheerful simply because of their innocence. It's a long time since Sewall himself felt any spark of happiness. The last he can remember was when he heard of his appointment to the Superior Court, was reconciled with Mr. Brattle, and greeted his brother Stephen on his recovery from that terrible illness, all in the same afternoon. For a moment it had seemed as though the witchcraft tragedy was already being dispelled, but the years since then have shown the hollowness of that hope.

A figure is running towards him across the Common—it's Bastian, approaching fast. 'Master!' he pants out. 'I've been looking for you everywhere! You weren't at the warehouse.'

'What is it, Bastian?' Sewall's heart contracts. *Who* is it? would have been a more appropriate question, but he couldn't quite ask it. Not Sam, please Lord, nor Betty, nor Hannah, not those children he lost in last night's dream! Some chilling words of Cotton Mather's come into his head: *Sudden death brings night before sunset.*

'It's madam, sir. She's in labour.'

'What, already?'

'Well on the way, according to Sarah.'

'You must hurry to Goody Weeden's, the midwife.'

'I already have. She's with madam now. I fetched Nurse Hurd too.'

'Ah, good, good.' It's been taken care of, for the moment. He sighs with relief. 'I will be sorry to lose you, Bastian.' Several years ago Sewall wed Bastian to his Jane, the first black couple to be married in Boston. But she is still a slave to Madam Thayer, and the couple live there together, with Bastian walking the two miles to the Sewalls' house every morning. The agreement is that when Jane has a baby, Bastian will work mainly for Madam Thayer as compensation until Jane's period of servitude expires in a couple of years' time— and Jane has now become pregnant.

'And me, sir,' Bastian agrees.

The house has that upside-down feeling it always does at times of birth, with much scurrying around and conversation *up*stairs, and peace and quiet below, where Sewall finds himself sitting for a few minutes, then pacing for the same amount of time, then standing, as if trying to establish which of these actions and inactions provides the most effective strategy for coping with anxiety (all are equally *in*effective, as he already knows).

Joseph and Mary are at school; Hannah and Betty have taken baby Sarah off to the Torreys' house in order to eat strawberries in their garden (saving some, Sewall hopes, for their mother). He wonders if he should go off in search of Sam, but fears missing the crisis. He should read a sermon or consult the Bible, but is unable to concentrate his mind. Even his silent prayers have a way of petering out, his brain being too distracted to pursue them to the conclusion. So he sits, paces, stands, in regular sequence; he listens to the ticking of his long-case clock.

The hands of which are almost at three in the afternoon when finally Susan gives a little tap on the hall door and enters.

He looks up at her (he is in seated mode); she looks down at him. Her eyes seem to grow larger. For a second he is puzzled by this; then understands they're filling with tears.

He is up and running before he has time to think, as if he only has to travel fast enough and he'll be able to prevent whatever catastrophe has in fact already taken place. Up the stairs, along the landing—and there is the door to Hannah's chamber shut fast against him.

For a moment he glares in fury at its wooden impertinence. Though this is his own house he can't enter the room without permission. Then the substantial form of Goody Weeden is standing there, a smear of blood on her apron. 'Madam Sewall?' he gasps out.

Goody Weeden steps to one side to allow him in. 'She's sleeping,' she warns.

Sewall stands beside the bed, looking down at his wife's white face. He suspects she is sleeping deliberately, so to speak, as a way of deferring the sadness and weeping that lie ahead, her own grief as well as that of her husband and their living children. A family is an instrument for sharing life's sorrows, but by its very nature it also multiplies them. He bends over and kisses her brow, strokes her hair.

Widow Hurd has stepped over to his side. 'Was the child a boy?' he whispers. She nods another solemn nod. As always when a baby is lost a great guilt sweeps over him. If he had been more attentive, more alert, above all if he had concentrated more on spiritual matters rather than on the dailiness of daily life, this child might have lived. He didn't even pray properly while Hannah was in labour.

Perhaps his dream of the loss of his children was a true prophecy after all, and this baby has been taken away from him as punishment because he has as yet failed to undertake sufficient penance for the witch trials.

The child conceived through his evil lust on the day of that meeting to defend the Court of Oyer and Terminer (that day on which the last batch of witches was hanged, and brother Stephen, having seen those hangings, was drenched to the skin, so beginning his long illness, and Justice Stoughton was washed off his horse and drenched to his skin and beyond), that poor little misconceived infant (who though guiltless himself was the offspring of a guilty father) inevitably died. But baby Sarah was born subsequent to that bereavement, and she still lives, so Sewall was able to comfort himself with the thought that the tragedy was behind him. However she is subject to fits and perhaps this disability was a warning of the approaching wrath of God, like distant thunder.

And now the storm has struck.

'Please show me my son,' he asks Goody Weeden.

Without saying a word she turns and leads him out of the bedroom to his own study. The baby is in the cradle that was made ready for him, covered by a little sheet. Sewall lifts it. The little boy is lying stretched out, unencumbered by clothing. He looks perfect in every way except for not being alive.

Sewall gets down on his knees beside the cot and begins to pray for forgiveness for the sins and the lack of attentiveness that let this child die. He is there for an hour. At the end of that time he replaces the sheet, leaves the room and tiptoes down the stairs. To his surprise, waiting for him in the hall is young Sam.

'I'm so sorry, father,' Sam says at once.

'It's not your fault, my son.'

'Isn't it?' Sam looks astounded.

'It is my responsibility, as the parent.'

Sam looks mightily relieved for a moment, and then his face clouds over.

'No, father, that can't be true. I have to take the blame. It's just that—everything is different. There's not one thing the same as another.'

'That's why we must always be vigilant,' Sewall tells him. 'Each thing and each person in this world is itself, and not another. That's why we have to make space for each one. And the only way for a father to do that is to examine himself, and pray, and do all he can to remove the sin that poisons the ground and chokes the air and stifles the life out of the new little one before he even lives. Alas—'

'And every one has a different price, and yet none of them are marked.'

Sewall looks at his son in bewilderment. 'How so?' he asks.

'Well, I asked Mr. Checkley, and he says that in the case of books you can write the price on the flyleaf, but with *things* it would be necessary to attach a tag to each one and that would be more labour than it's worth. But, father, I could never learn them all.'

'Sam, your little brother is dead.'

Sam is horror-struck. His mouth sags open and his eyes fill with tears. 'Joseph?' he asks finally.

'No, no, not Joseph. The new boy that your mother was carrying in her womb.'

Sam stays exactly as he is for a few moments. 'I thought you meant Joseph,' he says finally in a small and shaky voice. 'I thought he had died because I didn't go to work today. Because I choked his ground. And poisoned his air.'

Later that afternoon Mr. Willard arrives. Hannah is still sleeping. Goodwife Weeden has gone, leaving Nurse Hurd in attendance. Betty and young Hannah have come home, and are weeping together in their bedroom while Sarah attends to little Sarah. Sam is helping Bastian with some chore in the garden, assisted by young Joseph. 'Mr. Willard,' says Sewall. 'Thank you for coming.'

Mr. Willard looks nonplussed for a moment. 'I came to ask for your opinion—'

'Didn't Bastian come round to tell you of the death of our little boy?'

Mr. Willard's confusion deepens. 'Oh, yes,' he says finally. 'He was stillborn, I understand.' Sewall nods, not trusting himself to reply to this somewhat businesslike phrasing. 'Please accept my condolences. And pass them on to Madam Sewall when she's ready to receive them. Mrs. Willard and I hope she will be up and about very soon.'

'I thought you had come to pray with us.'

Mr. Willard has dark, furry eyebrows, most susceptible to cocking. He cocks one of them now. 'Of course I'm always willing to pray with you,' he says finally. 'But what I *came* for was to ask your opinion on the cause of this terrible harvest.'

Under the pressure of his emotions, Sewall feels himself beginning to lose his temper. 'Mr. Willard, I lost my new son today.'

'Ah,' says Willard. 'Let me explain. Perhaps this will be of comfort to you. Your son did not live (as I understand it). Therefore you haven't lost him. Indeed, you didn't *have* a new son at all.'

It's Sewall's turn to succumb to astonishment. He thinks of that little pink body lying in its cot upstairs. 'Whose son is he, if not mine?' he asks. As he speaks, he realises how arrogant and possessive he must sound. 'And Hannah's,' he adds. Then thinks a little more. 'And God's, of course.'

'Dear friend, the little corpse belongs to none of you, not even God. He cannot be part of the human family because he was never alive.'

'He is not just part of the human family, he is part of *this* family. With his brothers and sisters. The day after tomorrow we shall inter him in the family tomb where his grandparents lie, and other dead babies and children. I was going to ask you to accompany us there.' Funerals are not sacraments, any more than weddings are, but relatives and friends usually attend an interment.

'He cannot be buried in the family vault.'

'Why ever not?'

'Because those within are awaiting the resurrection,' Willard says with a sort of laboured and impatient patience. 'The stillborn one can't await the resurrection because it was never alive in the first place.'

I am the resurrection and the life, Jesus said. Well, life is exactly what his dead son requires. (And it is *he*, not *it*: the child may never have had the chance to live a boy's life, but there he is in his cot in the upstairs study, all complete, waiting his time to *be* a boy.) 'Whether you come or not, we will inter the child in our family tomb,' he assures Mr. Willard.

'Dear friend—'

'No friend of mine, if you reject one of my own!'

'Mr. Sewall, you're overwrought. Tomorrow you will see this in a different light. But in the meantime I must speak to you as your minister. The body must not be consigned to a tomb with people in it. There must be no confusion on the Day of Judgement between the dead and those who haven't lived or received baptism.'

Sewall remembers Cotton Mather explaining that God gave us all different faces, unlike chickens who have to share the same one, so that He could tell us apart on Judgement Day. Even his dead baby has a face of his own, though unused.

'You must accept my word on this matter,' Mr. Willard continues. 'On my way here, I went to Goody Weeden's, to confirm the stillbirth. Then as I entered your garden I saw Bastian and your Sam at work, along with young Joseph, so I asked them to dig a grave in some convenient spot in your garden. I suggest we place the body in it at once.'

Sewall stares at him open-mouthed. The thought that Sam—well-meaning, hopeless Sam—and innocent little Joseph have been cajoled into putting their own brother into the anonymous dirt hurts him more than any of the other distressing things that Mr. Willard has said. He feels utterly betrayed.

'Come, Samuel,' says Willard (he has never used Sewall's given name before). 'Let's do it now, and get it over with.'

'No. *No!*'

'If you wish, you can consult Mr. Cotton Mather on the theological—'

'No,' says Sewall, 'Not today. Not while his mother is still sleeping.'

Willard opens his mouth to argue yet again. Sewall understands exactly what he is going to say. Madam Sewall is *not* the mother because there is nobody to be the mother *of*. Before he can do so, Sewall continues. 'In any case I want to ask Bastian to make a coffin.'

'A coffin?'

'A coffin. Surely you wouldn't want wild animals to dig him up again?' Sewall asks with a bitterness he has never felt in his life before.

The baby is buried in the garden two days later, enclosed in a tiny coffin constructed by Bastian. Only the family (including Bastian, Sarah and Susan) are in attendance. Boy or not a boy, human being or not a human being, the baby is wept for. And Sewall prays that though he has been denied life temporal he will be granted life eternal.

CHAPTER 28

It is mid-December, 1696. The failed harvest has been followed by an early winter and snow is already piled deep except in the busiest streets. Frozen boats groan at the wharves. New England is clothed in forest but the prematurely cold weather has drastically reduced the cutting and transporting of logs so the price is high, as it is for bread and flour following the failure of the crops last summer. The only abundant harvest is that of dead people from cold and malnutrition, in particular (as usual) the old and the young.

For weeks Mr. Willard has been importuning Sewall to propose a bill to Council nominating a fast day in expiation of the errors and injustices committed during the witchcraft crisis and in hopes that God will once more look kindly on the doings of his poor New Englanders. Sewall resisted for a time. He is still angry with his minister over the matter of the garden burial of his stillborn child. But finally reason prevails. He fears his son may have died because of his own guilt in the matter of the witch trials; Mr. Willard wishes the community to expiate that same guilt; therefore it is quite illogical to oppose Mr. Willard.

Moreover he suspects that one of the reasons for his hesitation is a fear of Acting Governor Stoughton's reaction to the suggestion of a fast. But fear of authority, or at least the desire to placate those in power, is the very failing he has been trying to combat for years. So Sewall finally proposes to Council that a fast bill is needed. He already has a form of words in mind and is prepared to promise Mr. Stoughton a draft for Council's approval by tomorrow morning.

Acting Governor Stoughton looks around the council chamber with that grey hard gaze of his, his mouth a tad ajar as if in readiness to give vent to the opposing argument. But what he sees is a group of men who are deeply disturbed by the hardships that have overtaken their community and willing to clutch at any straw (this is how Sewall construes Mr. Stoughton's contemptuous expression) in hopes of alleviating them. Mr. Stoughton's mouth closes while his response is revised. Then opens again. 'Mr. Sewall.'

'Yes, your honour.'

'It seems to me that Mr. Cotton Mather would be the most appropriate person to draft such a bill. He has a thorough understanding of the Salem trials and has written learned commentaries on them. Since you have introduced the subject to Council perhaps you could deliver this request to him.'

'Yes, your honour,' Sewall says weakly. He sits down again. The shock of this unexpected twist makes him feel almost tearful. The fact that in every confrontation he has with Mr. Stoughton the latter always gets the upper hand only adds to his woe.

Cotton Mather is delighted to receive the commission, and paces up and down in his study while he digests the task. Sewall has caught him wigless at his desk, scratching away with his quill on a sermon for Thursday lecture. 'It's a challenge, Mr. Sewall,' he says. 'What is needed is, how to describe it?, a diplomatic form of words.'

'Diplomatic? Surely it needs to be heartfelt rather than diplomatic?'

'Ah ha! That's a common mistake, I'm afraid, old friend. People construe the word as meaning evasive or even mendacious. But diplomacy is far from obfuscation. Indeed it's a kind of precision. It weaves in and out of the complexities of a situation,' (he weaves a hand in and out of these hypothetical complexities) 'making a judicious claim here and an appropriate admission there' (plucking a claim and an admission in turn like imaginary apples from a tree).

A snow-encrusted Cotton Mather, now bewigged, knocks on Sewall's front door first thing next morning with his fastday proposal. Sewall doesn't have time to appraise it before setting out himself to read it to Council.

Cotton Mather has produced a long list of reasons why the province is facing its present adversity: backsliding from the faith, loss of family discipline, discouragement of the guardians of the law, failure to bring piracy under control (reading this one makes Sewall blench), vanity in dress (this one should make Mr. Mather himself blench), selling strong liquor to the Indians, uncleanness, failure to thank God in times of good harvest (times that now, alas, seem remote), and so on. In the middle of this melancholy itemization is a fleeting reference to the hardship meted out to innocent persons as a result of certain errors. The Salem witchcraft trials are to be buried beneath a great weight of assorted wrong-doing.

Mr. Stoughton is delighted with the document and eager to pass a proposal for a day of fasting on such general grounds. Sewall, though, is deeply disappointed. This is just the sort of thing he feared. As far as he is concerned, the proposal represents diplomacy in exactly the bad sense that Cotton Mather repudiated. Yet again he prepares himself to make a case against authority (both Mr. Stoughton's and Cotton Mather's).

To his surprise it turns out not to be necessary. Member after member stands up to complain that Massachusetts is not as riddled with faults as Mr. Mather's ingenious stocktaking suggests, that the issue is solely the matter of the witchcraft aberration. Sewall offers to revise the proposal's wording. His suggestion is greeted with such enthusiasm that even Mr.

Stoughton, staring over the excited chamber with those dark-rimmed eyes of his, cannot gainsay it.

That evening Sewall goes into his study and reflects.

First he kneels on the floor and prays for guidance. Then he sits down at his desk and thinks back on the events of that summer four years before.

If there were no witches at work in this land, then what there was was a *fear* of witches, a fear that must have been implanted by Satan himself. And Satan was able to do so because the colony had lost confidence in its original endeavour. It had cleared a space for itself in a heathen land and planted a Christian community there. Then a lifetime had gone by. The founding fathers began to pass away, and their plantation had to find a way of maintaining itself, not simply as the spiritual enterprise of a holy generation but as a land like other lands, persisting through history.

Doubts inevitably crept in. People began to assume that the colony would be choked by the wilderness it had kept at bay, that the heathen forces that lay beyond its bounds would slip into it and reclaim their territory. The Indians were *Simia Dei*; their allies in Satan's army, the witches, also parodied and mocked Christian sacraments from their vantage point in the very heart of the community. That was the fear.

Which, it turns out, was entirely unfounded. For one thing, the witches were not witches at all. Cotton Mather was quite right to criticise spectre evidence in his *Return*, as Sewall realised some time ago. One day he had suddenly recalled Mr. Putnam's claim that the spectre of Jacob Goodale, the farmworker murdered many years ago by Giles Corey, had appeared to his daughter Ann to inform her of the condemned man's wickedness. Goodale was a spectre and at the same time innocent (certainly in the sense of not being a witch), yet the whole basis of the trials was that it was impossible for anyone other than a witch to be a spectre! The child also claimed to have been visited by the spectres of George Burroughs's dead wives—two more spectres who were manifestly not witches.

The whole edifice of the trials had been built on false foundations. Those suffering children were not being afflicted by their fellow villagers. They were playing games, or hallucinating, or being manipulated by their parents—or the Devil. Perhaps all of those things.

And far from being *Simia Dei*, the Indians are actually the key to the fulfilment of the colony's Christian destiny, as Sewall has always believed; they are the lost tribes of Israel, and their conversion will usher in the millennium.

Sewall puts pen to paper and drafts his Fast Day proposal.

God has shown his anger by cutting short the harvest, and following a bad summer by a severe winter. A fast day will be appointed for 14 January 1697 so that whatever mistakes were fallen into during the recent tragedy that was brought upon by Satan and his instruments would be subject to God's awful judgement; that He will humble us and pardon the errors of all those who desire to love His name and will visit atonement on this land. Also that God will bring the American heathen into the Christian fellowship, and cause them to hear His voice, so reviving that joyful proverb in the world: one flock, one shepherd.

Next day in Council there's an uneasy silence after Sewall has read out his proposal.

'This paper seems more concerned with Indians than with witchcraft,' Mr. Winthrop eventually complains.

Nathaniel Saltonstall rises to his feet. He gives Sewall that characteristic warm smile of his. 'I think, Mr. Winthrop,' he says, maintaining his gaze towards Sewall, 'the reason is that in our province we have Indians aplenty but no witchcraft at all.'

Saltonstall knows of what he speaks. He denied the existence of witches even in the middle of the frenzy but has encountered his share of Indians. Only last year his town of Haverhill was attacked by a band of eighty but under his leadership drove them away, a feat that earned him promotion to Colonel of the North Essex Regiment. It seems a long time since he suffered that fear of losing his commission.

'It is precisely because we have an abundance of Indians that I am cautious about this talk of fellowship,' says Mr. Stoughton.

Sewall's heart sinks. The word 'fellowship' seems to him the key for exorcising the long shadow of the witchcraft injustice and walking once again in the light.

In the end the last sentence of the proposal is truncated, joy is eradicated, and hearing the word becomes obedience to it, so that it reads: *Also that God will bring the American heathen into the Christian fellowship, and cause them to obey His voice.*

But the word 'fellowship' has survived, despite Mr. Stoughton's immediate objection to it, and it is a word that can bring other good things in its wake.

Susan opens the front door when he finally reaches home. 'Look, I'm a snowman,' he tells her.

'Nurse Cowell is here, master.'

'Nurse Cowell?'

'Nurse Hurd is here too. She is attending Madam Sewall. Madam has got her sickness again.' Hannah is prone to terrible prostrating headaches from time to time, coupled with stomach upsets.

'So who is—?'

'Nurse Cowell is with baby Sarah.' Susan suddenly breaks into tears. 'She has her fits again,' she gets out at last.

Nurse Cowell is a plump matronly figure. She puts a finger against her lips as Sewall bursts into the room. 'Quiet, please,' she whispers fiercely. 'Sarah is sleeping.'

Sewall stops in his tracks. The snowy lid on his bonnet is thawing already and water trickles down his neck. His little daughter is pale as snow herself as she lies on her bed. Her closed eyelids have a faint blue sheen as if the eyes beneath are peering through them. Her tiny lips are almost white. As he looks down at her a shudder runs through her whole body. He turns to look enquiringly at Nurse Cowell.

'I gave her some milk and marigold jam but she vomited it up,' she tells him. 'The fits are still upon her, but much reduced while she sleeps. Leave her in peace.'

Sewall goes to his wife's chamber. She is also asleep or at least lying peacefully in her bed. Goody Hurd is by the dresser mixing medicine for her, dictating the measurements to herself out loud so as not to make a mistake. She has become an old lady now, Sewall realises. He undoes the bow beneath his chin, removes his bonnet and places it to dry in the hearth of the little fire. He does the same with his cloak, then takes up the poker and stirs the logs. At this sound Goody Hurd turns to face him with her hand over her heart.

I'm sorry,' he mouths to her across the room, then makes his way over to Hannah's bedside and sits down on a chair. She mutters a greeting from far away. He takes her hand which is lying on top of the coverlet. The room is cosy after his arduous journey through the cold, and very soon he has fallen into a doze.

From which he is rudely awakened by tuggings at his sleeve, little Susan pulling at him the way a child pulls at a grown-up to persuade him to go in a wanted direction. Across the room Nurse Hurd turns from her potions and looks aghast.

'I am so, so sorry, sir,' says Nurse Cowell as they enter the child's room. 'I would have called you if I'd known. I thought she was all right for the time being. Just sleeping.' Her face is white with shock and sorrow and fear.

Sewall pats her shoulder. 'My child has dreamed her way to heaven,' he tells her.

'I must not have been paying her enough attention.'

'You mustn't blame yourself. The neglect is mine, not yours. I am her father.'

That evening Sewall and the children sit mournfully around the fire in the hall. Wife Hannah remains upstairs in her bed (after the news of Sarah's death was broken to her, Nurse Hurd administered a sleeping potion). The children have all cried plentifully and are now mainly confining themselves to the occasional wavering sigh or sob.

'I think we should have a reading from the Bible,' Sewall tells them after a while. 'It is always a comfort in times of sorrow.' He nearly asks Betty to do it since she is still the best reader of them all, but he fears that she will be overcome by grief which, at the present moment, will be more than he can bear, so instead he invites Sam to read chapter twelve of Matthew's gospel.

Sam begins in a monotonous voice: *At that time Jesus went on the Sabbath day through the corn; and his disciples were an hungred, and began to pluck the ears of corn, and to eat . . .*

But when he gets to the seventh verse, an extraordinary thing happens.

Sam, at eighteen, has a husky retreating voice for much of the time (except when larking with his friend Josiah) but now it seems to have become strangely forceful and commanding (like Goody Good's did, when she addressed Mr. Noyes from the foot of the gallows), so that the words of the seventh verse of Matthew 12 echo and re-echo in Sewall's head: *But if ye had known what this meaneth, I will have mercy, and not sacrifice, ye would not have condemned the guiltless.*

Sam continues to read but Sewall can no longer follow. His mind is wholly concerned with this one verse which, he realises, directly relates to the Salem tragedy. *Ye would not have condemned the guiltless.*

He remembers what he said to comfort Nurse Cowell: the

neglect is mine, not yours, I am her father. Only now its true significance strikes him.

Yesterday he objected to Cotton Mather's fast day proposal on the grounds that it buried the witchcraft injustices in a heap of other lapses, sins and errors, some big and some small. Then just this morning he himself put forward a proposal in which his own responsibility for those outrages was buried in a generalised confession on the part of the community as a whole. That too was an evasion.

Sewall was a judge at that court. He condemned the guiltless. He failed to show mercy. In the years since the ending of the trials he has comforted himself with a collective view of the whole tragedy, concentrating on the notion of fellowship, a fellowship that disappeared when the community divided against itself, then formed again.

But that was simply a convenient way of getting lost in the crowd. He has to recognise that it is not just society as a whole that has to atone, but he himself also. He imagined spectres on a roof beam and was fooled by supernatural trickery and fraud even while condemning magicians' tricks. He was the father of that miscarriage of justice in Salem just as he was the father of little Sarah. And to remind him of that connection, God has taken away his daughter as He took away his little stillborn son in the summer. These children were indeed the victims of Sewall's neglect, his neglect of the sins he committed in 1692.

Suddenly the lost boy claims his father's attention in his own right. There he is at this moment, out in that dark night, buried in the garden under a heap of soil and a drift of snow, all alone.

Next morning Sewall speaks to Bastian. 'I have a hard task for you,' he tells him.

'Yes, sir.'

'I want you to dig up my little son.'

'Your son?'

'My little son who is buried in the garden.'

'The stillborn one?'

For a moment Sewall is tempted to ask Bastian how many sons does he think are buried in the garden, but holds his tongue. The man is remembering Mr. Willard's assertion that the infant wasn't a son at all, wasn't anything. 'The stillborn one,' he agrees instead.

'But, master—'

'I know it's a difficult task, the snow being so deep. It won't be easy to find the correct spot. And underneath the snow the ground will be hard.' The thought of his boy in that hard ground suddenly catches in his throat. 'But tomorrow we place little Sarah in the family vault, and I wish to put her brother in there with her, so they can be together and with all the rest.'

Bastian gives him a long sympathetic look with those large brown eyes of his, then nods his head. 'I will do it, sir,' he says quietly. 'I know where he is.'

Mr. Willard strides into Sewall's study. 'May I ask what you think you are doing?' he demands.

'I am sitting in my study, thinking—'

'Don't pretend ignorance to me, Mr. Sewall. I have just come across Bastian digging in the garden.'

'Sitting in my study, thinking about the interment of my two children tomorrow morning,' Sewall continues mildly. 'I have prayed for them and shortly I will pray again. Perhaps you will pray with me, Mr. Willard? As my minister. And my friend.'

'I don't know how often I must tell you this. The stillborn one was never baptized. He cannot be placed alongside members of the family.'

'Mr. Willard, it is *my* family.'

'I am using the word family in the larger congregational

sense.' Mr. Willard stands over Sewall and says in a loud voice, poking him in the chest with his finger after each word: 'The–family–of–the–elect.' Then he steps back, takes out a handkerchief and blows his large nose (somewhat blue from the cold) with a parsonical trumpeting. 'The stillborn is not part of the Christian family because he never drew breath,' he continues with great stress and emphasis, folding the handkerchief and tucking it into his sleeve meanwhile. 'He wasn't *baptized*. If you insist on trying to include him, you will only succeed in *ex*cluding yourself.'

Once more Sewall recalls the promise he made to Betty, that if she should go to hell, he would join her there. It applies to his son also, to all his children.

'Mr. Willard!' says a loud voice from the doorway, making both men start. It's the housekeeper, Sarah, standing there in cap and apron, her large and floury arms sternly folded across her bosom. 'I could hear the rumpus you was making right down in the kitchen. I shouldn't have to remind you that my poor little namesake died yesterday.' (Sarah was extraordinarily proud to share her given name with the little girl, and— Sewall suspected—assumed the child had been named in her honour rather than after Abraham's wife.) 'This is a house in mourning and I can't have you upsetting the master like this, minister or no minister.'

Mr. Willard gives Sarah a long look. She gives him a long look back. Surely, Sewall thinks, *this* is what a family is: wife Hannah, his children (living and dead, the old dead and the new, including that stillborn boy), servant Bastian who is even now digging on his behalf in the freezing garden, Sarah standing over in the doorway and boldly defying the minister, Susan going red-eyed about her business downstairs, brother Stephen on his way from Salem for the funeral, sister Margaret, their children, and so on and so forth. Family. Fellowship. Walking in the light.

Mr. Willard breaks off his exchange of looks with Sarah, and turns back towards Sewall. 'I will leave you now,' he says. Sarah gives a harrumph of satisfaction and stumps off down the stairs. 'But think on these matters. If you defy your minister, and step outside your congregation, where will you be?'

An hour later, in comes Cotton Mather, just as Mr. Willard did before him, striding forward in a rage. 'I have been waiting, Mr. Sewall,' he says when he is in front of the desk, 'for a visit from you.'

'I am afraid I have not been in a state to make social calls. My—'

'Social calls! I'm not talking about social calls. I am a minister of religion, Mr. Sewall, and I deserve an explanation. I deserve an apology.'

'Mr. Mather, yesterday my daughter Sarah died and—'

'I have heard that news and I'm sorry about it. But we mustn't let bereavement conflict with matters of religion. I lost a son one morning, and gave a sermon that very afternoon. Our duty to God overrides personal considerations.'

At this moment there's a knock at the study door, and Bastian pokes his head round. He's about to speak but then sees Cotton Mather standing there and pauses.

'Yes, Bastian?' Sewall asks him.

'Sir, I just wanted to say—I have done that thing you asked.'

'Thank you, Bastian. That is good of you. I will see you in a minute.'

'Yes, master.' The door closes.

'I'm not sure what I have to apologise for, Mr. Mather,' Sewall continues in a firm voice.

Cotton Mather turns back from looking at the interruption. 'Instead of respecting my authority as a minister you treated me worse than a . . . than a *negro*. You brushed aside my fast day proposal and took the opportunity to substitute one of your own.'

'Mr. Mather, it was felt—' Sewall immediately realises that this form of words constitutes the very error that characterises his own fast day proposal, by concealing his individual responsibility in that of the community as a whole. '*I* felt that your proposal did not sufficiently address the issue of the witchcraft.'

'If there is hunger you do not offer an apple but a full meal, Mr. Sewall. Our fast day *hungers* for a comprehensive synopsis of our sins. Are you acquainted with Nathaniel Wardell?'

'The chairmaker?' asks Sewall, perplexed at this sudden turn.

'The same.'

'Yes. He repaired—'

'He is a member of my congregation. Yesterday he discovered that some evil-minded persons had stolen the house of office from his garden. Carried the whole thing away. He stood and stared at the place where it was, he told me, unable to believe his eyes. He has offered a ten pounds reward for its return.'

'Mr. Mather, I don't see—'

'Our province has become a place where even a necessary house is no longer a safe refuge. The list of our backslidings has to be comprehensive.'

'Our fast day must be devoted to the witchcraft tragedy. Above all to the personal failings that turned it into a catastrophe.'

'You are completely unrepentant then?'

'On the contrary, Mr. Mather, I am completely *repentant*, as far as a man can be.'

Sarah's coffin is placed by her grandmother's. The stillborn's is carefully positioned on top of his brother John's, who was the first of the Sewall children to die, nearly twenty years previously. John was the original casualty of Sewall's sins of omission and commission. Hannah had been pregnant with him when Sewall failed to confess his sins on the occasion of joining the South Church, and he has always suspected the death of the baby resulted from that strange carelessness. The two tiny coffins are parentheses marking the spiritual negligence of his adult life.

Back at home a note from Mr. Willard is waiting for him. It expresses condolences in relation to the committal of Sarah, but no mention is made of the stillborn. He goes on to say that it would be better if the Sewall family didn't attend the forthcoming New Year's Day service since they had (for the time being) stepped aside from the family of God.

Sewall sits at his desk staring at the letter through a blur of tears. What comes into his mind immediately is the memory of Rebecca Nurse standing below her noose and the words that Mr. Noyes spoke to him on that occasion: 'I am not her minister of God. Not now, nor ever was.' Sewall was blind to the injustice that was being committed on that day and on those other days in the summer of 1692; he was blinded by his own sins, just as now he is blinded by his tears.

He feels a soft hand on his shoulder. It is Betty.

'Father,' she says. He cannot speak for the moment but presses his hand against hers instead. 'Father,' she repeats. 'Our little brother is safe now.'

Sewall knows this to be true. The child is no longer buried in the garden like a squirrel's nuts or a dog's bone. He can await the resurrection in his proper place, surrounded by his kin, intact in that little coffin. In respect of him Mr. Willard is mistaken. But nevertheless he is undoubtedly correct in saying that Sewall has stepped outside the family of God. Or perhaps it is more accurate to say that he has never stepped *into* that family, that he stumbled at the very lintel of the door and in his subsequent endless fall has brought woe and destruction on to so many who have not deserved it. 'Yes, he is safe,' he tells his daughter. He shakes his head sadly. 'But I am not.'

There is a long pause. Then, 'Father,' she says again.

'Yes, my child.' He looks round at her. She is gazing down

at him, her face full of warmth and sympathy. She will be fifteen in two days' time, exactly on the cusp between child and woman. Whereas he tried to ease his way into salvation without a proper inspection of his own soul, she has struggled with her sins for the whole of her life. No one could be more rigorous in encountering the problems and paradoxes of election than she has been. She represents the spiritual heart of the whole household; she is the flower of the family.

'Once, father, when I was in despair, you told me something that has given me great comfort in all the days since. Some important minister said it, I can't remember who. But I remember the words, a lot of them, anyway. *No one should question his election until he finds himself in such a bad state that it's impossible he has been elected.* Something like that. Then the next bit which is the bit I love most: *If such a condition there be in this world.*'

She repeats these last words almost under her breath this time, and Sewall realises how important they are to her, how often she must have repeated them to herself over the years. And suddenly he understands their meaning. The greatest sin of all is to be without hope, because that is a denial of God. And that must be the whole meaning and significance of the act of confession: an assertion of hope. Even of *negative* confession. The condemned at Salem *didn't* confess precisely because of their hopes of salvation and a life ever after.

Because, in other words, they had nothing to confess, at least in relation to the charges against them. But he has.

CHAPTER 29

'Brother, you erupted! It was a Mount Etna eruption. Two Mount Etna eruptions!'

Stephen is gleeful at Sewall's confrontations with ministers of God. For a moment Sewall sees himself through his brother's eyes: the way he takes life hard, the way he worries through his problems, the way in which his ruminations can finally reach a crisis. But he knows this is a distorted picture—or rather he knows that it is a true picture from the point of view of Stephen but not one he can endorse for himself.

Life *is* hard. People died. Of course, Stephen is aware of that. That's why he's here—he is going to pass the fast day with his brother. After he made himself witness the final batch of hangings at Salem he was so ill he nearly died. But that in itself points up the difference. He was ill, he suffered, he recovered, he resumed his normal life. In the meantime, Sewall himself has become more and more beleaguered and lost. He has climbed Goodall's Hill time after time, encountered the three crooked trees, looked down upon a landscape that has become strangely alien, descended and tried to make out his way, only to find himself ascending once more and beginning all over again.

Sewall pours his brother a glass of wine, and one for himself. It's after dinner on 13 January, and the fast won't begin until six o'clock this evening. Snow is fluttering against the study window, but there's a good fire. 'Sam,' continues Stephen.

'Yes?" asks Sewall, thinking Stephen is addressing him by name.

'*Your* Sam.'

'Ah, *Sam*. Yes, yes, indeed.' Sewall sighs. '*My* Sam.'

'How long is it since he left Mr. Checkley's?' asks Stephen.

'That was in the summer.'

They sit in silence for a moment, both staring at the window as if tallying the months since then in flakes of snow.

'And how has he passed his time since?'

It's a good question. Helping Bastian (hindering him more likely), running errands for his parents, distracting Josiah Willard (who is at Harvard) from his studies, rattling about the house, getting himself unexpectedly *liked* by all and sundry.

'He hasn't settled to anything yet.'

'I thought not. My suggestion is that after the fast day I take him back to Salem to stay with us. Salem is a small town. There's work to do wherever you look. I can secure him an apprenticeship or some useful occupation without any difficulty. And being in a new place might give him a fresh outlook.'

Stephen's suggestion overcomes Sewall like a benison, a gift, an act of grace. It seems to complete some long unfinished business. First he tried to send Betty to that household, then he nearly delivered young Hannah there by accident. Now at last his Sam will go. To Salem, the place where so much came to an end. Perhaps his son will make a new beginning there.

Mr. Willard is standing by the door of the South Church, greeting the members of the congregation as they arrive, which they do in surprising numbers given such snowy conditions, the thick flakes blotting much of the external world from view, though obstinate robins continue to utter their notes. It's gratifying to know so many are prepared to brave the weather on this fast day, though Sewall's heart nearly fails him as he thinks of how full the meeting house will be.

Since being excluded from the New Year's Day service the

Sewalls have done their praying and sermon reading at home. Now Sewall and his brother lead the way up to the meeting house door, wife Hannah, the children and Susan following behind. Mr. Willard is standing underneath the little porch and when he sees who is approaching his face falls, but brother Stephen strides straight up and shakes him heartily by the hand.

'Good day to you, Mr. Sewall, and welcome,' says Mr. Willard in a somewhat croaky voice (perhaps brought on by the dismal weather, though Stephen's handshake itself can sometimes take the breath away).

'And to you, Mr. Willard. May I introduce my brother, Mr. *Samuel* Sewall. And here behind are Madam Sewall and the young people.'

Mr. Willard's drawn face reddens. 'Good day to you,' he mutters.

Sewall gives a little bow. 'Mr. Willard, I have something for you.' He takes a paper from his pocket and passes it over. 'It's a confession.'

'Is that so?'

'I ask that during the course of the service you will read it out to the congregation. If you give me a signal beforehand, perhaps a little nod, or alternatively a pointed finger, I will rise from my pew and stand below you while you do so.'

Mr. Willard has been running his eyes over the paper while listening to this. Sewall sees him give a little jerk as he understands what it's about. He raises his head and says, 'Are you sure?'

'Oh yes. I'm sure.'

The moment comes. Mr. Willard catches his eye and Sewall rises to his feet and steps across to the front of the meeting house.

He has recently bought a set of scales from Caleb Ray, chief scale-maker of New England, who has a workplace in the alley near Governor's Dock. They are for measuring his own weight, the first to be used for that purpose (so far as he knows) in Massachusetts Bay. His current total, established only this morning, is two hundred and thirty pounds, and at this moment he wishes it were rather less. A plump man standing in penitence cuts the wrong sort of figure. A scrawny, even haggard, outline would be more appropriate for an occasion of this sort.

He consoles himself with the thought that this is *not* an allegory. This is Samuel Sewall, all of him, standing beneath the pulpit and exposing his ample self to the gaze of the congregation, some of them distinguished members of Boston society, justices, councillors, merchants, military men. John Alden is here, back in his old pew, and—just to point up the strangeness of that distorted summer—nearby is Wait Still Winthrop who (like Sewall himself) would have sat in judgement on Mr. Alden if the latter hadn't had the resourcefulness to escape from prison and flee the province. Madam Winthrop is in the women's pew next to Madam Sewall and only two ladies distant from Mrs. Alden, who went into temporary exile with her husband.

Other members of the congregation are more menial, artisans and servants (like Susan, for example, though Sarah isn't present owing to the badness of her legs, the sad state of which has been exacerbated, Sewall suspects, by her anger at the way Mr. Willard raised his voice at her master). Every element of the community is represented, in fact, tavern-keepers like Captain Wing and nurses like Goody Weeden, young people and old, men, women and children; almost all of them are Sewall's own long-standing friends or family or acquaintances.

Because Sewall has stood, several others stand also, but Mr. Willard quells each one with a peremptory glare from under those beetling eyebrows of his, sending their bottoms pewward again. Then he speaks. 'Brothers and sisters, this fast day is in recognition of the injustice and tragedy of the Salem trials of 1692, and in hopes that Almighty God will forgive us for our guilt therein. In respect of this solemn occasion I am going to read to you a paper which has been handed to me by our brother, Samuel Sewall, who is now standing before you all.'

He opens out the paper, takes a pair of spectacles from his pocket, puts them on, and begins to read. His voice is clear and unhurried, slightly quieter than might be expected so as to force the congregation (experienced minister that he is) to listen attentively.

Samuel Sewall—

– Sewall bows slightly, as if being introduced to the congregation—

– *Samuel Sewall, sensible of the reiterated strokes of God upon himself and family; and being sensible that as to the guilt contracted, upon the opening of the late commission of Oyer and Terminer at Salem (to which the order for this day relates) he is, upon many accounts, more concerned than any he knows of, desires to take the blame and shame of it, asking pardon of men . . .*

Mr. Willard pauses at this point, mid-sentence (it is all one sentence), to draw breath, or perhaps create an emphasis. Certainly there is a stunned silence and then a collective sigh as the import of what Sewall has written sinks in.

Sewall feels stunned himself, stunned at his own emotions. He had expected to feel remorse, perhaps of an elevated, noble kind. Instead, as Mr. Willard read the words 'more concerned than any he knows of', he experienced a sudden surge of resentment. Was he *really* more concerned than anyone else?

Certainly there were others who were equally implicated. But Sewall is making an assertion of proprietorial rights over the whole Salem enormity. Has he singled himself out in an act of sinful vainglory, a wish to be (or rather, to have been) more wicked than anyone else?

Mr. Willard's voice drones on. Afterwards, there is silence in the meeting house, silence of a tense, pent sort. Sewall feels he has to do something, but is not sure what. Finally he turns and bows once more to Mr. Willard. This is a different bow from the one of introduction, more a sort of thank-you for reading out his apology. Mr. Willard removes his spectacles with a certain flourish and gives a little bow back. This interaction seems to Sewall to be smug and contrived.

Still an atmosphere of expectation persists. He has turned back to face the people but is bereft of what to say or do. Eventually he turns to the left and bows to that section of the congregation. Next to the front, then the right, so all in attendance have shortly been bowed to. It occurs to him that this is exactly what actors do on stage, at the completion of a performance. He has never seen this himself but has a sense of the inevitability of the gesture, as if that immediate moment when your words have been received must draw it out of you. It's a hypocritical action, as you would expect of the theatre, since it pretends humility while claiming credit. The assembled people begin to mutter and shuffle excitedly and he quite distinctly hears Mr. Winthrop's voice gabbling away in an indignant tone.

Mr. Willard resumes: 'Let us each pray that the Lord will put his finger into our soul's lock, so that our bowels turn and our heart swings open. We will now sing the twenty-third psalm. Mr. Sewall, perhaps you will set the tune.' He looks warmly at Sewall while he makes this request. Even as Sewall obliges—and despite his relief that the apology has been completed, and despite his habitual pleasure in setting the tune—

he has another dark thought. Mr. Willard is so overjoyed at this massive reinforcement of his own fast day initiative that he has clearly forgotten all about the business of the stillborn! Yet if Sewall had let himself be swayed by the minister's earlier disapproval, his little boy's soul would still have been lost and wandering, looking for a home.

At last, the service comes to an end. Now he should experience a deep sense of peace. However remiss he was when he first took the covenant here, the comprehensiveness and seriousness of this confession must surely have made up for it. This is his place, his church, his people. Long-dead Goodman Walker, who has no doubt been sleeping in some lavender-scented nook of paradise just as he did for so much of the time during his long stay on earth, must surely bestir himself now to welcome Sewall as a fully-fledged member of the South Church of Boston. But all Sewall can feel is the coldness that has entered his bones during the course of the service.

Despite the snow, people are neighbouring just outside the door of the meeting house. One after the other comes up to shake his hand. Mr. Willard does so with particular vigour. 'That was remarkable,' he says warmly. Flakes have already settled on his thick black eyebrows, giving each one the appearance of a gable arching above its designated eye. 'A remarkable act of penitence. And humility. I think it sets the seal on this fast day. I believe we have reached the turning point of the whole crisis. And that can largely be credited to your brave act.'

He is clearly giving word to a general sense of relief that at last the unfinished business of four years previously has been definitively dealt with. But Sewall thinks of young Margaret Jacobs renouncing her own confession and facing the certainty of death as a result (though as it happened the trials were abandoned before her case came up); of Rebecca Nurse, refusing at the very foot of the gallows to lie to save herself; of George

Burroughs reciting the Lord's Prayer with the noose around his neck; of Giles Corey accepting the appalling death that was visited upon him. Those were the brave acts, not this one.

Sewall can make out Wait Still and Madam Winthrop on the fringes of the crowd of well-wishers. Despite the depth of snow, Mr. Winthrop is hopping about in a way that resembles a small child with urgent need of the house of office. Madam meanwhile is waiting without any of her usual animation— indeed appears strangely slumped and despondent. As on that memorable occasion of the pirates, her skirts have been damnified by melting snow. This sight reminds Sewall of how cold he is, so he takes his bonnet out of his pocket and positions it carefully on his head.

While he is still tying the strings under his chin, Mr. Winthrop approaches, shaking with rage. 'That's a fine *thing* you have done,' he says, his voice rising on 'thing'. 'You've tarred all your fellow judges with the same brush.'

'I confessed on behalf of myself alone,' Sewall tells him—a little sullenly as he reflects on the fact that most of the congregation are pleased because his apology relieves them of the responsibility of making one themselves.

'Rubbish! You might just as well have hanged us in a row like we hanged those witches! You confessed on my behalf when I didn't have anything *to* confess,' he continues in a more muted and more sorrowful tone. 'I did my duty to the best of my ability. We all did. Including you, though you seem to have forgotten it.' Now he thrusts his head at Sewall and lowers his voice still further into a whisper. Sewall is aware once more of the sourish edge to his breath. 'Madam Winthrop is not at all happy. She guards my reputation. Guards it jealously.'

Both men look in unison at Madam Winthrop as if they are allies rather than at daggers drawn. Madam Winthrop looks unsmilingly back. Sewall almost blushes to think that in the past he has had inappropriate—no, today is confession day—

lewd and adulterous thoughts about her. Then Mr. Winthrop turns back to Sewall. 'And when Mr. Stoughton hears of this, well, you can imagine how *he*'ll react.'

Stephen has plodded up to join them. He bows to Mr. Winthrop. 'Mr. Stoughton, eh?' he asks.

'He will be enraged,' Mr. Winthrop assures him.

Stephen turns to face Sewall and shakes his head. 'Brother, brother,' he says. 'You are a Mount Etna indeed.'

Now Hannah and the children have approached. The latter stand in a little row, peering wide-eyed at their father through the descending flakes as if not quite sure who he has become. Wife Hannah steps close, however, reaches up to his face and under the flap of his bonnet, and gives his left ear a little tug.

It's a few weeks later. Sewall has just been to Thursday Lecture at the South Church. Each time he attends a service he hopes that once inside the meeting house he will *truly* be within it, like a tortoise in its shell. Instead he continues to feel as though he is perched ambiguously half in, half out, like those creatures that haven't ascertained whether they live on land or in the water.

He has invited two friends to dine with him—not at the Castle Tavern since Captain Wing has also been attending the service and, Sewall reasons, cannot therefore have been attending to his pies, but at a rival establishment, the Blue Anchor, run by Mr. Monk.

As it happens this is a mistake, since George Monk (with many apologies respecting snow, ice, the buffeting of strong winds and the like) produces very meagre fare indeed, just some roast beef and a mince pie to share between the three of them, and bare-legged punch to drink.

Worse is to come. Several Council members are seated at the next table (eating a rather more substantial meal—Mr. Monk explains that they ordered theirs in advance). One of them, Elisha Cooke, leans across and asks Sewall if he will be there tomorrow.

'Where?'

'Why, at Mr. Stoughton's of course. In Dorchester.'

'I know where Mr. Stoughton lives.'

'Well, he has invited us there for dinner. The whole Council, as far as I can make out.'

'Not me.'

'There must be some mistake.' Mr. Cooke waves his arm vaguely. 'The snow,' he explains.

Sewall stares down at the few crumbs of mince pie remaining on his plate. 'Yes,' he agrees gloomily, 'perhaps it's the snow.'

'I'm sure it will arrive today. Or even tomorrow.'

Wait Still Winthrop is seated at the far side of Elisha Cooke's table, and now suddenly speaks. 'And if it does not, you should go there anyhow,' he informs Sewall in almost a growl. 'You *are* a member of Council after all.'

For a moment Sewall has the unworthy thought that Mr. Winthrop is trying to lure him into a position of even greater awkwardness than he feels already. But no. Mr. Winthrop is feeling indignant on his behalf as a fellow member of Council, just as he felt indignant *at* him in his capacity as a fellow judge.

Next day, from noon onwards, Sewall sits in his hall just below his longcase clock, listlessly looking through Calvin on the Psalms while listening to the chimes for the quarters and the hours. Finally the clock strikes three. All hope has now irrevocably gone. No messenger can possibly arrive with a delayed invitation. Even if one did, Sewall would not be able to get to Dorchester until long after the meal was over and would no doubt arrive just as his colleagues were taking their leave.

But he knows in his heart of hearts that no messenger was ever sent. He has not been invited along with his colleagues. It is even possible that Mr. Stoughton arranged this whole event merely in order *not* to invite him to it.

Ever since the episode of the pirates, Sewall has endeavoured to try to follow his own conscience, even if that led to conflict with authority (above all to conflict with Mr. Stoughton). On a number of occasions he has failed in this resolve and on others has felt uneasy or compromised. Now, at last, he has unequivocally succeeded. In his imagination he pictured this moment as one of triumph and vindication: a stalwart, self-confident, heroic Sewall, utterly committed to the defence of the integrity of his spirit, resolutely defying the rest of the world. But now it's finally arrived it doesn't feel in the least like that. Instead he pictures a despised and repudiated Sewall, forever cast out of the favour of the most important man in the whole province and therefore out of the favour *of* the province, doomed to scuttle about forlornly in the lonely places of America.

He had expected his confession to enable him to enter the very heart of his community. But as darkness closes in outside his windows (a darkness strangely whitened by the flakes that have begun falling yet again), he has the bitter thought that this ostracism is after all the inevitable and appropriate outcome.

CHAPTER 30

Three months have passed and it's a stormy spring night. For some reason Sewall experiences a sudden, urgent need to visit his childhood home again. He feels a kind of panic about it, and has to pace around his study for an hour before he's calm enough (or tired enough) to go to bed.

'Hannah,' he says next day at breakfast.

'*Yes*, dearest,' wife Hannah replies emphatically, as if to say she is all ears.

He immediately feels a pang. It isn't her he's addressing. He loves her dearly but she's part of his grown-up life, not his childhood.

'No, no, my love, I meant *daughter* Hannah.'

'Oh,' says wife Hannah, cocking her head a little in surprise.

Daughter Hannah is addressing a rye drop-cake (brought by Sarah hot from the oven), brow furrowed. When she has taken a tiny bite, with a click of her teeth like a rabbit severing a blade of grass, she raises her head and only then does she seem to notice the little interchange that has just taken place. 'Me?' she asks, blushing.

'Yes, my dear, you. I am intending to make a little journey up to Newbury in a few days' time, and I wondered if you would like to come with me? Perhaps we can rest overnight with our Dummer cousins with whom you stayed a few years ago.'

Of course she was no more part of Sewall's Newbury childhood than wife Hannah was, but she passed a little of her own childhood not far away, so perhaps the visit will have something of the same significance for her. 'Oh father,' she says. 'I would love to come so much.' She casts a quick enquiring glance at her mother, who leans over and strokes her arm to reassure her that she is pleased too.

The weather shifts just in time, so Sewall and his daughter arrive at the Dummers' place on a sunshiny day in early April. Their hosts must have seen or heard their carriage approach because they are standing by the gate. They are not demonstrative people and their two small forms look like dumpy statues placed there to guard the entrance to the farmhouse.

Sewall hands his daughter down from the carriage and she walks over to them. For a moment none of the three says a word, and Sewall wonders if this visit might be a mistake. After all, Hannah wrote tearful letters about how oppressive she found it here and how much she resented being required to fetch cows and stitch her cushion under the stern supervision of her mentors. Still, he thinks as he watches the silent triangle, she has nothing to fear from them now. She is eighteen years old, not thirteen as she was then, and at least half a foot taller than each of them.

And then suddenly, as if a command has been given, the three of them *dive* (so to speak) towards each other and embrace. Hannah sinks her head on to the shoulders of the two Dummers, who both have an arm extending over her back while clasping each other at the same time. All three are sobbing joyfully. Sewall stands at a little distance, feeling unexpectedly excluded as if, in the absence of Bastian (now a father and working for Mrs. Thayer at present), he's merely the carriage driver who has enabled this happy reunion to take place. He remembers a similar feeling five years before when, after waiting all afternoon, he came out to see the Dummers and Hannah returning from a visit in the full flush of happy conversation and without any apparent need of him.

Finally cousin Abigail extracts herself from the embrace and steps over to him. She peers up at his face and he bends down to touch his cheek against her tear-stained one. 'You must remember, dear cousin Sam,' she whispers, 'that Hannah has been eighteen years a daughter to you, but she was three months a daughter to us, and in the absence of another, that little is all we have.' She smiles at him, which has the effect of making her round face rounder still

Now cousin William steps over. 'I was just explaining to your girl that today was the first time our cows have been let out of the barn. They'll be skittish, not being used to the new ordering of their day. So I asked her if she would like to come with me after dinner and help fetch them.' He turns towards Hannah who is standing by the gatepost arm in arm with Abigail. 'As I recall, Hannah, you always loved to bring the cows in when you were here before, didn't you?'

'Oh yes,' Hannah breathily replies, 'I always loved to do that.'

It's another beautiful spring day. Sewall and his daughter left the Dummers immediately after breakfast and are now close to the township of Newbury, approaching the top of Old Town Hills. The road has dwindled away and they alight from the carriage to take the last stretch to the little summit on foot.

Sewall suddenly notices that Hannah is limping slightly. 'Have you hurt your leg, my dear?' he asks her.

'No, father. It's just my old knee.'

Sewall ponders on this. Yes, he can remember her complaining about her knee when she was younger but he thought nothing of it at the time, assuming she was suffering from the bumps and bruises of childhood, or imagining things like her brother Sam. He hasn't noticed anything untoward since those days, perhaps because Hannah isn't a very active person. But of course that might be precisely *because* of the problem with her knee. 'Does it cause you much pain?' he asks.

'No, father. It's nothing.' She repeats what she said before: 'Just my old knee.'

He decides not to press her further. It will only worry her. He will ask wife Hannah about it on their return—she will be aware of it. But his girl's limping has made him self-conscious about his own gait and the way that he has to shift his weight from one hip to the other as he takes each step forward. For the first time he realises that a sort of waddle has intruded itself into the way he walks.

So here they are, father and daughter, limping and waddling their way to the viewpoint on the top of the hill.

It's as if he is looking at the years of his childhood in this place all at once. Far off on the horizon is the sea, gleaming like the scales of the very fish that swim beneath its surface. Then the sand dunes of Plum Island, acting as a breakwater for the estuary of the Merrimack River. And on the river's banks, a mile or so inland, are huddled the little wooden houses of his home town of Newbury, and a little closer the sinuous stretch of the River Parker as it winds towards confluence with its bigger brother.

'What can you see, Hannah?' He turns to his daughter and her spectacles flash briefly as she surveys the landscape that stretches out before her.

'I can see a pond, over there,' she says. Sure enough a pond lies just to one side of Newbury like a small disc of polished silver in this brilliant light.

'That's Crane Pond,' Sewall tells her. 'I used to fish in it as a boy.'

'Did you, father? What did you catch?'

'Oh, this and that. Perch mostly. And sometimes a big pike would come up and gobble the bait.'

'And a herd of cows,' she says. 'A lot more than cousin William has.' The cows are grazing in a field that lies at the base of the next rise of the ground, known as Turkey Hill. Hannah sighs. 'I love cows,' she says dreamily.

Sewall recalls her complaints about the way the cows mooed at her and for a moment this pleasant experience is threatened by a pang of resentment. But no, she didn't mislead him then, and she isn't telling untruths now. As the past makes its pilgrimage to the future it must transform itself or there would be no heaven to look forward to.

Back home Sewall begins to write a little book. He wants to explain to his fellow colonists why they have all been so harried (himself included) by fears they betrayed and destroyed the great enterprise of America; why they all succumbed to such an acute fear of failure they allowed themselves to fall into the witchcraft delusion. It's because they believed that their forefathers, in coming to these shores on the *Mayflower* and the *Arbella*, were setting up God's Kingdom in its final form. But nothing is immune from history save God himself.

So he begins: *Not to begin to be, and so not to be limited by the concernments of Time and Place, is the prerogative of God alone.*

Most countries have existed for time out of mind, so are reconciled to being historical, but Massachusetts Bay has come upon the scene so recently it's not comfortable in making the step from present to future, and creaks and groans as it shifts its bulk, like a laden galleon bellying through difficult waters. When it began it was the creation of its founders, but now it is more than a lifetime old its people belong to *it*, and have to accept that diminished status.

The first settlers were not escaping from history (any more than he, Sewall, can escape his own past). They were simply renewing it. And after every setback and injustice it must be renewed again and again. We have to live in time; though time's ultimate destination is eternity.

Five years ago Sewall delivered twenty sentences on people who had done no wrong. His apology was a different sentence from those, one that sentenced the past. Now he writes a different one again, addressing the future. The previous sentences were uttered inside meeting-house walls but this one must step out of doors, into America itself:

As long as *Plum-Island* shall faithfully keep the commanded Post; Nothwithstanding all the hectoring Words, and hard Blows of the proud and boisterous Ocean; As long as any Salmon, or Sturgeon shall swim in the streams of *Merrimack*; or any Perch, or Pickeril, in *Crane Pond*; As long as any Cattel shall be fed with the Grass growing in the Medows, which do humbly bow down themselves before Turkie-Hill; As long as any Sheep shall walk upon *Old Town Hills*, and shall from thence pleasantly look down upon the River *Parker*, and the fruitfull Marishes lying beneath; As long as any free and harmless Doves shall find a White Oak, or other Tree within the Township, to perch, or feed, or build a careless Nest upon; and shall voluntarily present themselves to perform the office of Gleaners after Barley-Harvest; As long as Nature shall not grow Old and dote; but shall constantly remember to give the rows of Indian Corn their education, by Pairs: So long shall Christians be born there; and being first made meet, shall from thence be Translated, to be made partakers of the Inheritance of the Saints in Light.

—SAMUEL SEWALL, *Phaenomena quaedam Apocalyptica ad aspectum novi orbis configurata: Some Few Lines Towards a Description of the New Heaven as It Makes to Those Who Stand upon the New Earth* (Boston, 1697)

ACKNOWLEDGEMENTS

Samuel Sewall's *Diary*, edited by M. Halsey Thomas in two volumes (1973), gives more insight than any other work into the day-by-day experiences of a colonial New Englander, though Sewall devotes little space to the Salem trials. A list of other primary and secondary sources can be found in my biography, *Judge Sewall's Apology* (2005), where I also acknowledge the individuals and institutions who provided assistance with research for that nonfictional encounter with the man and his times.

The writing of the present novel was aided by a Hodson-Brown Fellowship, which provided access to the John Carter Brown Library's collection of early American material for two months during the fall of 2013, and gave my wife Jo and me the use of a wonderful colonial house in Chestertown, Maryland, for a further two months in the summer of 2014. During that time I was able to work on the novel in my office at the Starr Center for the Study of the American Experience at Washington College, situated in the Custom House on the banks of the Chester River. I would like to express my gratitude to Neil Safier and his colleagues at the JCB Library, and to Adam Goodheart and all at the Starr Center for their support; also to Ellen and Frank Hurst, our neighbours in Chestertown, for their friendship and hospitality (which included visiting membership of the local bocce league).

Thanks also to Tracy Brain, Julia Green, Tessa Hadley, Richard Kerridge, and Boyd and Elizabeth Schlenther, all of whom read an early draft of this novel and offered encouragement and suggestions. I had expert advice and help from my son Will and daughter Helen, while Jo has been involved all along, as always. Lastly I'm grateful to those concerned in bringing the novel to publication: Caroline Dawnay and Sophie Scard of United Agents in London, Alice Whitwham of the Zoe Pagnamenta Agency in New York, and my Europa editors on both sides of the Atlantic, Kent Carroll and Daniela Petracco.